Onset

Shannon Hunt

For Ben, my favorite

Prologue

March 1883

Every time she woke, Alice prayed they would not be there.

More and more often now, she opened her eyes to find her bedroom full of faceless strangers. They weren't always the same characters, but all of them had a complete disregard for Alice's possessions. A young woman plucked the embroidered roses from her quilt, and a gardener tore rows in the fabric with his hoe, filling them with handfuls of soil and seed. A ginger cat left tufts of pale fur in its path as it rubbed against draperies and engraved chair legs with its claws. Only a slight man in a ratty fur- and sealskin coat kept his hands to himself, but his stillness unnerved Alice most of all.

Mostly she tried to ignore them until fatigue overtook her once again. She felt as if she had swallowed metal shavings; they caught in her throat every time she tried to speak, and Alice had to weigh the effectiveness of the complaint against her own discomfort. But she couldn't stay silent when an urchin of uncertain sex tried to slip her silver hairbrush into the pocket of its filthy apron. Or when the gardener caught her arm with his rake, leaving red streaks on her skin. At the sound of Alice's cry, Mother or Mrs. Connors would rush in and hold her hand or press a cool cloth to her brow or tip a bit of broth down her throat. Their presence seemed to discourage further aggravations, but only temporarily.

Her caretakers never acknowledged anyone else in the room, so Alice wondered if the people she saw were simply hallucinations. They were certainly not the spirits that her mother claimed to see in her séances, not filmy figures or glowing hands freed from their bodies. These people appeared to Alice in daylight, when she could confirm that they were more than coatracks and chairs draped in clothes that projected frightening shadows. Their garments looked to be of ordinary fabric and their hands were pinkish and opaque. Only their blurry faces suggested they were something other than human; Alice could never quite make out their features.

She knew she was in bed because she was sick—the sweating and shivering and pain confirmed it—but she did not know with what or for how long. Little bits of a former life flitted through her head like butterflies. She remembered reciting Robert Browning in front of a classroom, rolling hoops down a hill, drinking tea and eating strawberry tarts. But whenever she tried to catch a pleasant memory, so as to study its details, it eluded her grasp.

And what was to say her fever wasn't fabricating those memories? The other day, Alice had been convinced that her skin had become transparent and her bones were trying to find their way out. She lay motionless for what seemed like hours, terrified to look under the blankets and see through herself, certain that even a twitch would spur an ankle bone or a rib to escape into the bedclothes. Later she would chide herself for believing something so ridiculous—but that wouldn't make her any less gullible the next time, when she was drowning in seaweed or growing gills.

These visions might have troubled her more had she the strength to stay awake and ponder them. As it was, when Alice grew agitated, Mrs. Connors fed her spoonfuls of a sweet medicine that eventually lured her back to sleep.

Now the room came into focus slowly as she blinked the film from her eyes. Since her last awakening, the gardener had decided the wooden floor needed raking. The cat was gnawing on the tassel of a pillow it had already disemboweled. Neither was taking much notice of Alice.

Her gaze shifted to the far right corner, where a shadow was moving of its own accord, no breeze or changing light to explain it. As it came towards the bed, Alice saw that it was not a shadow at all, but a woman, garbed and veiled entirely in dull black crêpe.

A mourner. What could she want from Alice? The lilies on the drapes around her bed? A curl for her mourning brooch? Alice had plenty to spare; when Mrs. Connors brushed her hair for her, half of it seemed to come away in the bristles.

Alice took her eyes off the woman to frown at the gardener's making what sounded like dreadful grooves in the polished planks. She dared not scold him; last time he had come after her with his hoe, cracking her on the kneecaps and leaving them stiff and swollen. When Alice looked back at the mourner, several others in black had joined her.

In the next moment the pungent smell of crêpe overwhelmed her nostrils, and an inky blur obscured her vision.

Her cry for help came out as nothing but a scratchy hiss. Alice's arms and legs were slow to defend her; her joints screamed with the effort of bending. When she could not kick her legs free of the bedclothes, she struck out with her hands, trying to push away the black gowns and suits.

But her hands found nothing but air.

It was becoming more difficult to breathe. This couldn't be a simple hallucination. Alice tried to convince herself that she was dreaming, but the inability to breathe continued, as real as anything.

Then the black curtain parted slightly, and in the doorway Alice caught a flash of graying hair. Mrs. Connors had come! and Alice would be safe. Even if the housekeeper couldn't see the widow, surely she could see her charge's distress.

But Mrs. Connors came no further, only stood there with a look of sorrow on her face. Darkness obscured Alice's vision again, and she felt as if the crêpe were bleeding its horrible dye into her eyes, her mouth, her nose.

In desperation, she reared backward, her head struck the headboard, and the blackness broke into a rainbow of colors.

Get up.

Her mind commanded her body to act, but Alice made herself count a few breaths, a few heartbeats, before letting herself believe she was still alive.

Cautiously, she opened her eyes. As usual, all traces of their presence were gone. She picked at an embroidered pink rose on the bedcover where her hand lay; it had somehow grown back despite the gatherer and the gardener. The floor shone unwounded, gleaming from a fresh polish. Her bedclothes were tidy, as if someone had tucked them in around her. Even the reek of crêpe hadn't lingered.

But the pain remained as proof of what had happened. There was an ache in her throat beyond the usual burn, and swallowing was near impossible.

She could not just lie here and wait for the widow to return. She would make herself rise, and find her mother, or father, or Mrs. Connors, and tell them…

Mrs. Connors, who had stood by while Alice was strangling. She had been keeper of the Boydens' house in Cambridge for over twenty-five years, preceding even Alice's mother. Why did she offer no help to the girl upon whom she had doted like a daughter?

Her thoughts' uneven edges and strange tangents scraped against each other and made her brain throb with the heat of their friction. How nice it would be to burrow once more beneath the blankets and let herself slip into sleep!

But no, she was no longer safe here in her bed. She had to find help before the crowd reconvened. At the thought of the attack, Alice felt her pulse fluttering beside her stomach, as if her heart were a baby bird fallen out of the nest.

She braced herself and eased out of bed, using the bedpost and the nightstand to steady herself. She wobbled violently upon her first few unsupported steps, and thought how she could crawl instead. But no, she had to walk, she must walk. Crawling would make her nothing but prey. Slowly, slowly, grabbing onto anything near, she managed to inch her way through the door and into the hallway.

The hall was quiet and empty. Alice leaned into the wall and let it take on her weight, clinging to the chair rail. She prayed that someone was on the second floor, that she would not have to attempt the stairs. As she rested against the wall and slowed her breathing, she heard sounds emanating from the room at the end of the hall, her mother's séance room. A few shuffle-steps closer, and she could make out the high-pitched voice of Mrs. Key, as controlled by her spirit guide.

Alice had been instructed from an early age never to interrupt her mother's séances. Some women hosted sewing circles; Caroline Carr Boyden held dark circles, and had for as long as her daughter could remember. But this was an emergency; surely her mother would forgive the disturbance. If she could make it there.

It was all Alice could do to keep herself upright. She counted the loops in the chair rail pattern to distract herself from the ache in her legs. When that ceased to be diversion enough she began to recite poetry silently, surprised that she could still pull some from her fevered brain.

But do not let us quarrel any more,
No, my Lucrezia; bear with me for once;
Sit down and all should happen as you wish.
You turn your face, but does it bring your heart?

But what was the fifth line?

While her memory snagged on Browning, Alice's hand found the handle of the door. She wiped a bit of drool from her chin with the cuff of her nightgown and put her ear to the wood. The voice of the medium—or rather, that of her possessing spirit—had gone silent. Knocking would be of no use, as the sitters would only believe the sound to be a spirit rapping messages to them. Alice depressed the latch and opened the door slowly.

For a moment, the dim gaslight illuminated eight pale heads suspended over the round table, all of which turned to look at Alice as the faint outlines of their dark clothing emerged. Only Mrs. Key remained stationary, her eyes rolled back in her head so that only the whites were visible. The medium began to moan and twitch.

"Alice, oh, Alice!"

Alice's mother jumped up from her seat and hurried to her daughter. The stares of the men and women around the table made Alice look down at herself and remember she was wearing nothing but a nightdress. She felt her feverish cheeks grow warmer still; even in her haste and weakness, perhaps she should have thought to don a dressing-gown...

But instead of whisking her out the door in search of appropriate clothes, Mrs. Boyden enveloped Alice in a fierce embrace and stroked her thinning hair. Alice let go of the doorframe and slumped into her mother's sturdy arms.

"My dear, dear girl!" Mrs. Boyden's voice broke, and she put her forehead to Alice's shoulder.

"It is a miracle to have you with us again!"

Alice felt her shoulder grow damp. And suddenly she stopped wondering why the other women were crying as well, why the gentlemen had not averted their eyes. Her mind cleared as if someone had blown the dust away.

They thought she was dead. The séance was for her.

Chapter 1

June 27, 1883

"Alice, be careful!"

"Don't worry, Mother, I'm fine." Alice managed to regain her balance and climb up into the coach beside her mother, but the near-fall had bled beads of sweat from her neck. Some of the cheap red paint from the doorframe had rubbed off on her hand; she wiped it on the seat and squeezed the cushion for a little stability.

"That's all I need, for you to fall and hit your head," said Mrs. Boyden. "I asked your father to help you up—where is he?"

"Most likely he's making sure our things make it to Onset." Alice peered out of the carriage and saw her father supervising the men dragging trunks from the baggage car to the stagecoach, stammering unheeded warnings to take care with those holding his laboratory equipment. When one of them moved to take his microscope box, Mr. Boyden snatched it up and clutched it to his chest. The man gave him an odd look but left it alone.

Alice sat down again, but she had moved too quickly, and her world spun for a moment. She steadied her breath before she spoke. "I think he's coming."

A tremble emanating from the coach roof suggested that Nora, their maid-of-all-work, had climbed up beside the driver. A minute later Alice and her mother watched as a pair of hands bearing the microscope box pushed its cargo across the bench opposite them. It caught on a button in the cushion and tipped onto the floor with a *thunk*. Mr. Boyden scrambled in after.

"Could neither of you catch that?"

Mrs. Boyden made a slight move, but only to tuck a blanket around Alice's legs. "I am glad that you care more about the state of your instruments than you do about the well-being of your daughter."

"She told me she would be all right on her own." Mr. Boyden donned his spectacles, upon which he depended for the details of the world, and assessed the damage inside the box.

"Please, Mother, it is plenty warm enough—I don't need this." Alice pushed the quilt to the side. "It makes me feel as if I were going to a sanitarium." Having a blanket on her lap reminded Alice of the wheeled wicker chair that she had been grateful to shed—her legs, undependable for a few months, were now strong enough to be her sole form of transport. Certainly there were ailing people in Onset who benefited from the briny water and air unpolluted by mill soot, but Onset focused on the eternity of the soul, not the mortality of the body. It was not a place full of fragile, shawl-wearing people who spoke in coughs and wheezes and gestured with tremulous blue-veined hands.

The Boydens had been members of the Onset Bay Grove Association for five years now. Alice's mother was fascinated by those who could make contact with the spirit world, and she wished to be in their company as much as possible—despite, or perhaps because of, her own lack of mediumistic powers. Before Onset, Mrs. Boyden had left her family in Cambridge during the summers and in order to travel from spiritualist camp to spiritualist camp. Sometimes Alice had wished she could be one of those children who attracted rapping spirits, thinking her mother might stay for the summer and study her instead.

But while summers deepened Mrs. Boyden's devotion to the cause, Julys and Augusts were when Alice had her blind acceptance chipped away by her skeptic father. The professor thought that any graduate student he employed would steal his results and claim them as his own, and so he had employed his young daughter as a personal assistant. Between his influence and that of the scientific tomes from his office that comprised her summer reading, Alice abandoned the desire for furniture to fly around in her presence and for knocks to resound from the walls in a spectral staccato.

Mrs. Boyden had only convinced her rational husband to invest in this new establishment by extolling the virtues of waterside living and promising that he could spend the whole summer studying water insects instead of spirits. Once Mr. Boyden had also extracted a promise that neither he nor Alice would be required to go to séances, he capitulated.

"At least keep the blanket between yourself and the coach wall—use it as a pillow," said Mrs. Boyden, tugging at the covering in question. "You know how bumpy the ride—"

The coach lurched forward with a jolt that seemed to make Alice's brain vibrate in her skull. She took a deep breath and closed her eyes, praying the trip wouldn't cause one of her sick headaches, a late echo of the scarlet and rheumatic fevers that had kept her in bed for months. As soon as a string of pain-free days convinced Alice of her sudden and complete recovery, a powerful megrim would counter her optimism.

Even if the affliction didn't repeat itself for another week, the memory of it might keep Alice on edge for days after.

"Why did I agree to take the later train?" Mrs. Boyden fussed. "We'll have hardly any time to get settled before the clambake."

The clambake. Alice's stomach lurched at the thought of it—not because she disliked any of the food provided, but because it would be her first large-scale social event since she had fallen ill.

"I can't see how it would have been possible to take the earlier train," said Mr. Boyden. "We were nearly late for this train as it was. You hadn't even locked your trunks by the time the cab arrived."

Mrs. Boyden glared at her husband. "Well, since you can't be bothered to pack a wardrobe for yourself, I had to do it for you. *Really.* Were it not for me you'd be wearing glass slides and book pages."

"Oh, and Alice," said Mr. Boyden, pointedly ignoring his wife, "since you'll be occupied with the festivities tonight, perhaps we should take this opportunity to review the schedule I've developed for you."

Alice groaned inwardly. The fever had kept her from completing high school, and her father was determined to have her catch up in preparation for college courses. She knew that not all women had such academic opportunities thrust at them, and that college was not even a possibility for many. But she resented that her father put her educational future on a spoon and forced it down her throat—and had done so since she was small. While her peers learned to read, Alice was memorizing the Latin names of plants and insects.

But she did not love science as did her father, who would sleep in his lab if given the chance. Nor did literature, history, or arithmetic inspire the same level of passion. Alice had long waited for an academic subject to introduce itself as hers, but they had all been standoffish.

"I will ask you to present a brief summary—150 words or so—of your morning reading every afternoon at lunch. At the end of the week, 500 words addressing the common themes you find within your reading."

Alice blinked at her father. "But it's the summertime."

"Ignorance knows no season."

"All the other people my age will be out enjoying themselves."

"All the other people your age have earned the reward of summer break after a spring of hard work in school. You who cannot claim that labor do not need a vacation from it."

The explanation did not satisfy Alice. Growing up near a college campus had led her to doubt her father's impression of most students' work-to-carousing ratio.

"Would you have propped her upright and tied her to a schoolroom chair, that she might have continued her studies uninterrupted?" Mrs. Boyden glared at her husband. "She needed rest, not intellectual exercise. I'd like to see you try to study through such a headache."

"And the lack of exercise has made her brain weak, so we must strengthen it. It is not a punishment. It is the way to return her to the track of her academic life." Mr. Boyden turned to Alice. "Think of what will happen to you if you sit for the Annex exams this fall, and do not pass them. What will you do with your time?"

Her father wanted only the best education for his daughter, but he considered coeducation unfair and looked upon the new women's colleges with doubt as to their true academic merit. So when Harvard announced that it would be setting up a separate school for ladies—soon nicknamed the Harvard Annex—Mr. Boyden determined that his daughter would go there. As a Harvard professor and graduate with a family tree full of alumni, he did not believe that any other institution could provide superior instruction.

"Not all of these women will have the benefit of a Harvard professor as tutor," Mr. Boyden continued. "You ought to think about that before you reject your summer course of studies."

Alice wondered about these other women, fellow students; would they have similar backgrounds, similar interests? Similar intelligence? She did not quite know how to gauge her own anymore. After the fever, sometimes her spoken thoughts would come on a delay or not at all, sentences snagged somewhere in production. She never let on how basic words could elude her, barely visible but almost entirely illegible through the cobwebs. Often she hadn't the time to pick them apart, as the other members of the conversation waited for an answer—but she was terrified that some of those words would be completely lost to her the next time that she reached for them.

"I'll peruse it tomorrow morning," she said. "I don't think I can read in the coach without becoming ill."

"Very well," Mr. Boyden said. "But I'd not put it off any longer than that." He withdrew into the bench and his book, an elbow resting protectively on the microscope box.

Mrs. Boyden sniffed. "I do hope that the schedule can be adjusted, should Alice prove popular with the gentlemen this summer."

"Caroline, we have discussed this many times. I want Alice to finish school before she even considers marriage, and she has not."

"Yet you wish to throw her straight into college after a social drought," said Mrs. Boyden, wagging her finger. "Why, this summer might be her only chance to catch someone's fancy before she is hidden behind a stack of books!"

When it came to her daughter, Alice thought, Caroline Boyden seemed to have a set of priorities that contradicted decisions she had made in her own life. Caroline Carr had received a fine private education but was never given the opportunity to pursue learning beyond high school. Instead she directed her intelligence into various causes—woman suffrage, temperance—and married much later than was seemly, at a positively ancient forty. Now that Alice had the opportunity to attend college, she wondered if her mother was jealous—jealous enough to redirect her daughter into a domesticity she herself never considered as a young woman of nineteen.

Her parents were now citing conversations about Alice's future from years ago. "It was when she was fourteen," said Mrs. Boyden, in reference to who knew what. "No, don't shake your head at *me,* I *know* she was fourteen because it was our first summer in Onset..."

Deciding it best to ignore her parents' discussion—weighing in on her own future would only invite criticism—Alice picked up the promotional booklet Onset issued every spring. It seemed a product of the generous dues that members paid—clean, crisp printing, tight stitches along the spine. Frequent handling had already blunted the corners of her mother's copy, and interest had dog-eared every third page. She flipped past the description of Onset Bay Grove for newcomers, the train schedules, and the camp rules, to the Calendar of Events, Tentative. The clambake this evening would be exclusively for members of the association, though a picnic the next day would be open to all daytrippers as well. Various bands would play music during meals and social hours.

"...what she wears." Her mother's voice reentered her conscious thought. "I'll not have her looking like *you,* like a pauper who can't afford a new vest. She'll be interacting with her fellow students throughout her time there, perhaps even students from Harvard proper..."

"I have urged you before to think of it this way: the fewer articles of clothing I purchase, the more you can afford to buy," replied Mr. Boyden.

The advertisements amused Alice the most, in part because they seemed deliberately arranged—the mundane always alongside the fantastic. An advertisement for a Fine Restaurant faced one for Mrs. Bella Smith, Clairvoyant. Horace Worth promised Levitations, Apparitions, and Spirit-Rapping while G. W. Bell made it known that he was an Excellent Plumber, especially familiar with Summer Cottages.

She turned from a bayberry soap advertisement to woodcut cameos of the featured guests. Most looked like Alice's mother: probably quite pretty in their youth, now round-faced with bosoms like bulwarks. But it was the picture of a young man on the second page that captured Alice's eye.

He was clearly the youngest of the bunch, and one of the few of his sex depicted. His hair waved dark and heavy down the sides of his head, clipped around the ears. A striped cravat seemed to prop up his angular chin, and rather than looking straight ahead his eyes were turned away and up, as if he were engaged with a higher plane. *Thomas Chester Holloway* curled around the bottom of the picture in the same luxurious fashion as the subject's mustache.

"Don't we have a brilliant lineup for the summer?" Mrs. Boyden snatched the booklet from Alice's hands as if she had been waiting to see it for a long time. "I'm very glad Charles Sullivan is returning. I thoroughly enjoyed him last year. Oh! And Maud Drake. Always a revelation."

"I didn't recognize Mr. Holloway's name," said Alice—casually, she hoped. "Do you know much about him?"

"Thomas Chester Holloway." Mrs. Boyden savored each name. "Such a fine young medium. From New York *City.* The other camps in the area haven't discovered him yet, although they are sure to poach him for next year. This summer, therefore, we secured him for the entire season. And Mrs. Thatcher said she's arranged for us a private supper and séance—the séance being optional for you and your father, of course. But I suspect this one will be very impressive if you care to stay."

"I think I'd like that. The dinner at least," Alice hedged, unsure if any mustache was worth being trapped in the dark with the emotionally oversensitive. "We shall see about the séance. I know that last year I said I would try one, but after this spring..."

"Of course," said Mrs. Boyden. She patted her daughter's shoulder, and Alice had a sudden vision of herself in a nightgown, making the trek down the hall to the séance room. Even though she now knew that the séance had actually been for Mrs. Connors, who had died the day before, Alice could not help feeling that death was a precipice in a fog, and that she would never again be safe from falling over the edge.

Over her mother's shoulder, Alice studied Mr. Holloway's face again. She did not know if his closed-lipped mouth hid bad teeth, or if his calm gaze belied a foul temper. But Alice thought that this might be someone she wouldn't mind calling on her.

"Of course, there will be a young man at the table that I'm sure will be pleased to dine with you..."

Alice looked up in confusion at her mother. Had she said something out loud about Mr. Holloway?

"...Letitia implied as much in her last letter. Arthur won't be here for the clambake, as he is rowing against Harvard today, but she promised he would be present at dinner."

Alice suddenly felt seasick. "I thought he was to be in Maine with one of his college friends."

"Well, apparently he has changed his plans—perhaps realizing he would miss the company here." Mrs. Boyden raised her eyebrows. The son of Mrs. Boyden's spiritualist friend Letitia Thatcher, Arthur was several years older than Alice and an eager member of the Yale crew team. The mothers had a not-so-secret hope that romance would blossom between their children. But while Alice had considered Arthur a chum when they were younger, university life had turned him pompous and boring. She started to say something to this effect, but the carriage crunched to a halt, and her teeth snapped shut on her tongue.

"Onset!" barked the carriage driver.

Chapter 2

The Boydens waited outside the cottage while Nora opened all of the windows to begin the airing-out process. Once she had emerged, looking dusty and dazed from stale air, Mr. Boyden went immediately to his study at the back of the cottage, presumably to inspect the state of nets and jars left behind over the winter. Alice wrinkled her nose as she stepped inside; the cottage smelled as she expected a just-opened tomb to smell, of darkness and mold. Nora began to pull the dustcloths from the furniture. Suddenly she shrieked.

"Goodness, Nora, what's wrong?" Mrs. Boyden hurried in from outside.

"Sp-spider!" Nora stammered. She raised her boot to squash the intruder.

"Don't kill it!" yelled Mr. Boyden from the study. He rushed in with a dusty bell jar and a piece of pasteboard. As an entomologist, he knew that women's shrieks more often than not meant something interesting for him to study, and he came prepared.

"I've told you, Nora, we don't crush things in this household. Especially arachnids." Alice and her mother looked away, as if they might be occasional violators of the rule.

"Sir, you're going to kill it anyway."

"Yes, well, I need an intact exoskeleton if it's going to be of any use at all. Now, where is it?"

Nora whimpered and pointed towards the corner of the room, then mumbled something about going to fetch the trunks, moving with a speed most unlike her. Mr. Boyden rolled his eyes and went to his hands and knees.

"George, that's your best traveling suit!"

"I'll be changing for dinner, Caroline," he replied, his voice slightly muffled on account of his head being under the curtain. "Aha! There you are." He emerged with the spider under glass, the pasteboard slipped beneath. "You have the distinction of being this season's first specimen," he told it, and turned to his wife. "This is why I asked that you include 'must not have a fear of insects' in the advertisement for a maid," he said in a low voice.

"But she alerts you to specimens in the area," said Mrs. Boyden. "Besides, I would never put something like that in the paper. People will think our house is full of vermin."

"It is full of vermin. They are just usually in jars." Mr. Boyden carried his prize down to his study. When the door had shut, Alice let out a snort of laughter. Her mother frowned at her.

"If it were *your* husband who was prone to such antics, I doubt you would find them so amusing. Hurry and tidy yourself—we don't have much time."

Alice didn't really blame Nora's fright. It was the maid's first time opening a cottage, and Alice doubted that Mrs. Boyden had prepared her for the amount of crawling creatures she could face—dead or alive—when cleaning a place closed and left to nature from September to July. Even Alice, who was generally comfortable with the insects her father revered, disliked evidence of mice in her drawers or cobwebs that had linked the dustcloths in her absence. She would walk around with her eyes slightly squinted until the floor was swept and crevices cleared of tiny carcasses.

During the summer, Alice always found it difficult to believe that she was once cold enough to require a woolen hat, a scarf, gloves. She had left these accessories behind during a night of Christmas caroling and had come home to the scoldings of the housekeeper. Alice remembered falling asleep and dreaming of wassail so hot it scalded her throat.

That night had been the last time she had seen Mrs. Connors alive; fever blurred the rest of Alice's December and January, her February and March. The doctor later confessed to Mrs. Boyden that Mrs. Connors had known about the cancer in her breast for some time, but that she had refused an operation. Two days later, Mrs. Boyden held a séance to ask Mrs. Connors why—and Alice shocked everyone in attendance by walking into the room and speaking after being bedridden and incoherent since Christmas…

"Miss?" Nora entered with the face and tone of voice reserved for one who might soon be in trouble, and Alice looked at her suspiciously.

"I can't seem to find your dress, miss."

"Nora." Alice sighed. "It is right at the top of the trunk."

"I mean to say that I don't see your trunk of dresses at all."

Alice threw on her duster and went to see for herself—but all the trunks were open and unpromising, and rifling through each yielded no dress, no matching blue petticoats or stockings or neckerchief. She marched down the hall to her father's study and knocked.

"Father! Are you sure you collected all of our luggage at the station?"

The door creaked open after a few beats and Mr. Boyden peeked out. Alice recognized the confused look on his face, one that suggested he had already dipped into his books and would take a few moments to regain the power of human interaction.

"Why, yes, I suppose so..."

"Are you *certain*?"

Mr. Boyden grew flustered. "Well, there is always the chance one could have been left behind. We had a great many trunks this year; if only you and your mother could pack fewer dresses..." He trailed off as Alice stared at his pile of books and equipment.

"I packed *one* trunk of dresses, Father, one, and it's not here. If you think it was left at the station, I will send Nora back for it," said Alice.

"No, there's no time," said Mrs. Boyden, hurrying in. "We need to be there in half an hour, and Nora won't even be to Agawam by then."

Alice looked around in frustration. The thought of appearing in her sweat-dampened and dusty traveling dress mortified her. Did no one understand her need to look presentable tonight?

"I can iron your dress and freshen it up with some lavender water," said Nora, probably hoping for an activity that would keep her from a jarring round-trip on the coach.

"Oh good, that's good," said Mrs. Boyden, clapping her hands. "See, dear, you'll be all right for this evening. We'll have them sent for tomorrow."

I just want to look my best! Alice wanted to wail. But soon Nora was pressing the dress, Mrs. Boyden was back at her toilet, and Alice stood alone, clutching her duster to herself. She had quietly dreamed of making a grand return to Onset, a phoenix from the ashes. The new blue-and-white dress had been her armor; her old dress only reminded everyone that nothing of consequence had happened in her life since last summer.

The association had pitched an enormous tent in a clearing close to the beach, its flaps tied up as people arrived and mingled, then let down for the insect-filled evenings. The parade of long tables sat thousands, and although tonight's affair would be more intimate, casual visitors from New Bedford and Nantucket would fill the tent to capacity and thensome in the weeks to come. Faint music could be heard from an offshore boat—people who had come in for the afternoon and brought their own band. Onset's evening entertainment readied themselves outside the tent; they depressed valves, tightened drums, and twittered through mouthpieces to warm up their lips.

Alice saw the steam of the rock oven first, then heard its hiss and the occasional pop of a rockweed bladder. She liked to be early for clambakes, if only to observe the artful construction of a bed of stones, stuck with branches and jagged slabs of driftwood, then set ablaze. It was strangely thrilling to see something burn outside the brick confines of a fireplace.

"Alice! Come say hello to Mrs. Thatcher!" Mrs. Boyden pulled her daughter inside the tent.

For the first time in her life, Alice wished she were a potato; they lay closest to the hot rocks, well hidden beneath the layers of weed and clams and corn, and she envied their cover.

She had only half turned toward the women when Mrs. Thatcher's hands cupped her face, so that Mrs. Thatcher actually steered her towards them. She braced her ears, for Mrs. Thatcher only spoke in exclamations at a piercingly high pitch.

"My dear girl, how good to see you up and about again! I hardly think your mother needed to tell you how concerned we were for you! How are you feeling!"

"I'm quite well, thank you." Alice had already told herself she would not be one of those people who shared their ailments with others, even if she had to fi b. She hoped her glances around for a way to escape were not obvious; but Mrs. Thatcher was studying Alice's dress with a frown.

"Let's the four of us ladies plan a shopping trip into Wareham soon! But don't let me keep you from the young people! Why, Isabelle is right over there—Isabelle! Come say hello to Alice!" Mrs. Thatcher waved frantically at her daughter, as if she were worried that Alice would escape. Alice squirmed inwardly; the mere sight of Isabelle Thatcher and her honey-colored hair made her feel several times smaller. Isabelle rushed over, an exaggerated smile molded to her face. As she drew closer, Alice noticed that Isabelle was wearing a dress in the same cerulean blue as her missing frock.

Isabelle Thatcher was the unofficial social queen of Onset and, Alice assumed, high-ranking in West Hartford and at her Farmington boarding school as well. Alice always considered her to have all the components of beauty, just not assembled quite correctly: the warm blonde hair attached by a hairline that reached too high, a small, straight nose disproportionate with the size of her eyes and mouth, and an inclination to roundness that had to be brutally tamed with stays. But everyone called Isabelle "a great beauty," and the boys certainly agreed, and the girls would never say otherwise.

"Darling Alice!" Isabelle kissed her on the cheek. "How wonderful to see you on your own two feet."

"Yes, I'm much improved this past month," said Alice, supposing that her mother had embellished her daughter's ailments in letters. Perhaps Isabelle had looked forward to pushing Alice around in a wicker chair. *What a friend is Isabelle!* people would say. *How kind of her to help poor Alice.*

"And I imagine you're wanting to see Arthur!" said Mrs. Thatcher. "I'm sorry to disappoint, but he won't be here until tomorrow—his team is rowing against Harvard!"

"I'm wearing blue in honor of the race," said Isabelle. "If I were there watching, I'd be simply covered in blue ribbons."

"Well, I hope he emerges victorious," said Alice, although her father would have cringed to hear an endorsement of Yale come from her lips, however false. Even her mother—whom Alice noted had abandoned her and gone off in search of new ears to commandeer—wore crimson Harvard ribbons when the team was in town.

The brief comfort she took from not being caught in the enemy's color quickly vanished as she watched Isabelle's gaze flicker up and down her dress. "Oh, that was one of my favorite dresses that you wore last year. I see you don't have to worry about reducing this summer. I couldn't fit into last year's gowns if you used a shoehorn on me."

Alice looked down at the faded fabric of her skirt against Isabelle's bright one. "My new dresses were forgotten somewhere along the journey today. We've sent for them."

"Oh, that's a shame!" Mrs. Thatcher let out an exaggerated gasp that seemed part sigh-of-relief at the realization that Alice had a good reason for looking shabby.

"I hope they'll arrive in time for dinner the day after tomorrow," said Isabelle, a bit too brightly. You are coming to our cottage to dine, aren't you? We shall have Thomas Chester Holloway as our special guest. He is staying with us a few days as his tent is prepared." Without giving Alice time to stammer her surprise that the meal would be so soon, Isabelle continued. "My father has been Mr. Holloway's escort for the day. He is a *most* amiable gentleman. We had a lovely discussion over luncheon about New York City. I go there as often as I can. Have you been?"

Alice shook her head. For a family in a solid financial position, the Boydens did relatively little traveling, and her father once told her that New York was a filthy and overgrown shade of Boston. "I hear it's lively," she said to Isabelle.

Isabelle laughed at Alice's generalization. "At the very least."

Surely no one would object to her seating herself early, Alice thought; it had been a long day for many of the travelers, and while the tables were still bereft of food, people were pulling out chairs to sit and talk with their friends, taking care not to disturb the napkin-and-plate setup in case it did not prove to be their seat for the evening. So when Mrs. Thatcher redirected her urgent points of conversation to her daughter, Alice tried to sneak away—and nearly ran into the ample midsection of Mr. Thatcher. He reminded Alice very much of a walrus, with his bristly mustache and baggy eyes. Every summer, when Alice saw him for the first time in ten months, she was always vaguely surprised that he hadn't yet sprouted tusks.

"Why, what lovely ladies we've found here!" he barked. "Will you have some punch?" He had two cups in each hand, his pudgy fingers looped through delicate handles. Isabelle and Mrs. Thatcher accepted the cups held out to them with identical giggles.

"Hello, Mr. Thatcher," said Alice, her attention still focused on the asylum of the platform, though the structure itself was largely obscured by Mr. Thatcher's girth. She put up her hand to deflect the punch. "No, thank you." Alice avoided alcoholic drinks in the vicinity of her temperance-minded mother, who had once snatched some holiday cheer out of Alice's hand at a party. Her father did keep a bottle of spirits in his desk, but moved it frequently to avoid detection; sometimes Alice was the one to deliver it to its new hiding place.

But Mr. Thatcher was speaking again already; his mind was always one step beyond the other person's response.

"Alice, I'd like you to meet our distinguished guest, Mr. Thomas Chester Holloway. This is Miss Alice Boyden."

Mr. Holloway stepped out from behind Mr. Thatcher, a slim, dark antithesis of his host, and bowed as best he could with a punch in each hand. He offered one to Alice.

"Miss Boyden. How do you do?"

A beat went by before Alice realized that she was gaping at Mr. Holloway, and that he was awaiting a greeting from her.

"How do you do," she managed. Unwilling to again excuse herself from the punch, Alice accepted it and smiled at the giver. She was thankful that the punch cup had no saucer; it surely would have rattled in its resting place.

"Alice, Mr. Holloway is a medium from New York City." Mr. Thatcher stepped in, taking Alice's hesitation for lack of recognition.

"Ah, yes—I read your biography in the program. How are you finding Onset, Mr. Holloway?" Too late she realized that everyone must ask him that as a matter of courtesy, and why had she not come up with something more creative?

"Well, it has only been a day now..."

Of course. Alice felt foolish.

"...but already I feel as if I shall have a most enjoyable summer."

Alice smiled. "I am glad of that."

Mr. Holloway smiled back, but no one else spoke for a few moments. Mr. Thatcher's mouth was occupied with draining one cup of punch, then sipping at the next; the small cups nearly disappeared in a wave of bristles. Alice panicked, unsure if she could keep her eyes on Thomas in expectation of further conversation, or look away shyly and blush in a show of delicacy. Instead she studied her cup, and took a sip. The strength of it briefly made her eyes cross, but it was followed by a sort of internal glow that she found very pleasant, and so she sipped again.

"Lovely punch," Alice murmured into her cup.

"An ideal refreshment on such a fine—but warm—day," said Mr. Holloway. "Tell me, did you just come in?"

Alice took another sip. "Yes, from Cambridge."

"I hear it is lovely there, though I've never been."

Alice positively beamed at his admission, which made her feel less ashamed of her lack of travel. "It is lovely. Onset is a refreshing break from the city, but I always miss Cambridge by the end of August."

"I'd imagine you don't have the opportunity to see your friend often, though."

For a moment Alice had no idea to whom Thomas was referring, but he nodded his head to Alice's right. She glanced over to see Isabelle in the remains of a glare. In a blink Isabelle brightened her face into a smile, but she had clearly seen something she did not care for. *She's not my friend in the least,* Alice wanted to say. But Isabelle had linked her arm through Alice's.

"We both keep quite busy during the year, but look forward to the summers when we can be reunited," Isabelle chirped. Alice managed a weak nod of agreement, and took another sip.

Mr. Thatcher stepped in, now waving his second empty cup. "You'll beg my pardon, ladies, but I must convince this crowd to make an orderly line before they descend upon the clam pits and begin digging out dinner for themselves. And I still I have many people who wish to meet Mr. Holloway." He tapped the arm of his guest.

"It will be a wonder if I retain any names at all," said Mr. Holloway, a look of mock helplessness on his face. "It was very good to meet you, Miss Boyden. I shall hope to see you later this evening."

"Yes, I shall look forward to it." Later this evening? Did that imply that he wanted to dance with her? Once Mr. Holloway turned away, Alice tipped the cup again, but only a drop remained at the bottom.

"Are you dry? Shall we refill?" Isabelle held out her hand for Alice's cup.

Alice shook her head, and the chairs in her view rippled. She closed her eyes. "I think I'm going to take a seat. The day has been tiring."

Isabelle clucked. "Nonsense. Punch is just the remedy for that. We will have you ready to dance." Alice watched Isabelle disappear into the crowd with her cup and wondered if it would come back full of poison. She joined the food line, keeping her head down so that she could collect her meal quickly and not be recognized. From her position, she could just see the piled plates of gray shells and ears of corn, their green sheaths crisped to yellow. The homey smell of sweet potatoes made her mouth water.

"Why, Alice Boyden!"

Alice turned to her left to see Miss Davis, who came to Onset every summer with her elderly mother. She was not much in the mood for conversation, but the spinster was a genial soul.

"Hello, Miss Davis. How are you faring?"

"Oh, it is the usual. Nothing much changes for us year after year, although every summer Mother seems to have a new ailment. But you must have all sorts of thrilling things happening in your life."

"Well, I may attend college in the fall."

Miss Davis clapped her hands together, as if that was the best news she had heard today.

"I wish you the best of luck. You always were a bright girl."

Alice smiled back at her as they encountered the food table, thinking that once they began filling their plates, the conversation would be over. But Miss Davis continued, this time with a slightly lower voice.

"It's an awkward time of the summer, isn't it?"

Alice concentrated on transferring an ear of corn to her plate. "I'm not sure that I understand."

"Well, getting to know everyone again after ten months' absence. I find that conversations always snag during the first few days."

Miss Davis did not seem to be having difficulty now, but Alice knew what she meant. In June, she usually had trouble thinking of things to say to people she had known for years—let alone newcomers. Let alone handsome newcomers.

"Oh, I don't know," said Alice. "You get by somehow."

"Yes," said Miss Davis after a pause, seeming embarrassed. "Well, I suppose you have a great library of topics in your head, from all your reading." There were bigger bookworms in Onset than Alice, but her appearance as a precocious fourteen-year-old that first summer still formed the basis for her reputation.

"Would everyone be so kind as to take their seats?" Mr. Thatcher's voice boomed throughout the tent. While the chatter hardly decreased, people began to make their way to chosen tables and chairs. Alice nodded politely to Miss Davis.

"Lovely to see you again."

"And you, Miss Boyden!"

Alice walked away as quickly as possible, exhaling in relief until she realized that Miss Davis had called her "Miss." *It means nothing*, Alice tried to tell herself. These people were intimate companions for two months out of the year, near-strangers for the other ten, and so it would make sense for someone like Miss Davis to switch between "Alice" and "Miss Boyden."

But it conjured up a mental picture: ten years later, Alice at the same clambake, her mother and father the only ones using her Christian name, everyone else having adopted the proper title to reflect the fact that she would probably never switch to "Mrs." Spending her mornings working for her father, afternoons playing card games with Miss Davis, subject to the whisperings and giggles of the younger set at dinner, who would look upon her as a curiosity…

Alice scolded herself for the thought. Was her mother not far beyond the "old-maid" boundary when she married? But, then, she thought as she considered her mother squawking away at their table, she had no desire for that sort of marriage.

As she took her place beside her parents and across from Mrs. Thatcher and Isabelle, Mr. Thatcher ascended to the podium. Though he contained his stout midsection with pants and coat, his jowls wobbled disproportionally as a result. They quivered whenever he was excited or distraught, and they quaked now as he waited for the crowd to settle.

"Your attention, please, ladies and gentlemen!" The crowd shifted into a respectful silence, save for the peppering of unfinished conversations determined to continue. Those quieted as well once the participants realized how audible their clucking had become.

"Welcome to those of you who have just completed the long trip down—or up, as the case was for us from Connecticut; we don't want to forget our Rhode Island and Cape Cod members either—and we hope that the sustenance provided here refreshes your body, as we hope the community of Onset Bay refreshes your souls."

A "hear, hear," rippled through the assembled, and gentlemen pounded their canes out of habit, though the sand-clogged grass muffled the motions into a series of dull thunks.

"We have a tremendous list of speakers scheduled this season, coming from Boston and beyond. As has become custom, the estimable Mr. Charles Sullivan has joined us for this first week in July." Mr. Thatcher gestured to Mr. Sullivan, seated at a table amongst others that

Alice recognized as speakers, and he stood and bowed, with the feigned reluctance and smile of one who thrives on public introductions but pretends to be embarrassed by them. "The Misses Campbell will visit us in the beginning of August, as will Mrs. Drake," Mr. Thatcher continued. "And, with us all summer"—he drew the "all" out like a drumroll—"will be Thomas Chester Holloway, a young medium from New York City."

The podium had obscured Mr. Holloway's presence at the table, but Alice saw him rise and acknowledge the spirited applause of the crowd with a wave, then stepped away from the table and over to Mr. Thatcher, who relinquished the podium. Even for Alice, sitting right near him, his first few words were lost in the clapping, and he had to repeat them several times.

"Mr. Thatcher kindly allowed me to say a few words of greeting. I know that you have more friends to reconnect with and more clams to shuck..."

Laughter fueled by punch rippled through the audience, as tablemates turned to each other and waved nibbled ears of corn or clam bellies on forks.

"...I for one have not even started on my plate here. But the delay in dining has been worth the opportunity to meet with many of you. I just wanted to say that it's a pleasure to be a part of this vibrant community for a summer—a community that takes its spirits seriously but still emphasizes the enjoyment of life for those who have not yet crossed into the other world. I look forward to getting to know you all as neighbors and friends."

He turned his head toward Alice's table and smiled.

Was he looking directly at her? Alice's heart certainly thought so; it executed a celebratory flip in her chest—but the glance could have been for Isabelle. Before she could make the determination, he had stepped back to his obstructed spot at the dinner table.

Alice let her mother, Mrs. Thatcher, and Isabelle fight for dominance in the dinner conversation, and plotted her escape: could she excuse herself for a walk along the beach before dessert? When her mother and Mrs. Thatcher announced their intention to do the same thing, however, Alice was forced to devise another plan. She stared at the empty clamshells on her plate as if they held the answer in their grooves.

"May I presume that your parents have vacated these seats, and that there is room for an interloper?"

Mr. Holloway had appeared at their table, plate in hand, and was looking from Alice to Isabelle expectantly. Isabelle let out a tinkling laugh.

"You are no interloper. You are our honored guest. Please, sit with us." Her hand swept gracefully in front of her as if she were inviting Mr. Holloway to take his seat in front of fine china and crystal goblets.

"Now, perhaps you ladies, who are used to this sort of feast, can clarify something for me." Mr. Holloway pointed to the empty shell of one of the few clams he had consumed. Why do I see purple in this clamshell?"

"Those are quahogs," said Alice. "Only those who make their habitat in New England have purple in their shells. Being in New York, you'd probably only have seen white shells. When I was younger, I used to collect the purple shells left over from the clambakes and pretend I was an Indian princess."

The punch had loosened her tongue and allowed one too many sentences to tumble out. Mr. Holloway looked at her in confusion. Isabelle smirked. Alice hurried to explain. "The shells were used as currency among Indian tribes here, and the purple ones were particularly valuable. And on occasion the clams make elegant purple pearls."

Isabelle brightened at this. "I have a purple pearl necklace!" Knowing the rarity of purple pearls, Alice doubted this; but now to say that she had one in a pin at home seemed inadequate.

"Alice is a great reader. She knows everything," Isabelle continued, oozing modesty. "And, this fall, she will be one of the first women to attend Harvard..."

"It's not quite Harvard; it's classes for women taught by Harvard professors," Alice clarified. "And I haven't yet taken the entrance exams."

Isabelle paid no attention to Alice. "Me, I'd like to take a few courses before I turn my attention to homemaking. But I suspect Alice has loftier aspirations than marriage. She will be making great discoveries as a lady scholar while the rest of us lead our ordinary lives with husbands and children."

The blazing of her cheeks made Alice think that some horrible-looking heat rash had erupted on her face. "I have not yet made any such decisions about my future."

But Isabelle was not finished. "Well, I suppose there is an interested candidate. My brother will be attending Harvard Law in the fall, so perhaps he and Alice can begin that courtship our parents have always desired for them. Wouldn't they make a brainy pair!"

She wanted to tell Mr. Holloway that Isabelle was gravely mistaken, that she had no interest in Arthur at all—but Alice simply turned her attention back to the debris on her plate. The mess of inedibles—empty shells, bare corn cobs—turned her stomach, as did the realization that vile Arthur would soon be living close by.

"I'm sorry—I suddenly don't feel well. Would you be so kind as to excuse me?" Alice finally forced herself to look up at Mr. Holloway, who looked perplexed but gave her a kind smile.

"Of course."

"I hope you enjoy the quahogs," she managed to say before the lump in her throat seized her power of speech. Before she was even out of earshot, as she hurried down the few stairs, Alice heard Isabelle say:

"Poor thing. She's only just recovering after a long illness, and trying her best to participate, but I suspect the dancing would be too much for her."

Or was that Alice talking to herself?

At dusk, the clouds sat heavy and purple over Buzzards Bay, much changed from the white candy puffs of the daytime. The red sky behind them, however, promised fair weather for the next day. Once on the road of crushed clamshells, Alice gulped a mouthful of the cooling evening air. As her shoes gathered white dust and the hubbub from the dinner tables receded, however, she began to curse herself for her cowardice. She had left an ideal opportunity in which to talk to Mr. Holloway, Isabelle or no. He had seemed interested in what she had to say. But rather than brushing off Isabelle's attempt to derail his interest and deftly changing the subject, Alice had let Isabelle have him. They'd likely dance together tonight, beginning a campwide rumor about their courtship, and what an ideal pair they were. And Alice would simply be alone for the summer, as she probably would be for the rest of her life.

Never before had Alice feared spinsterhood like this; in truth she had rather relished the possibility. In her mind, unmarried women were deliciously threatening: they had escaped the home of their parents and reimprisonment in the home of a husband. What did they fill their days with, without a husband and children to care for? Liberal causes, certainly; left-wing hysteria; toxic amounts of book-learning. Beautiful and/or pleasant Misses were particularly intriguing: why did they not marry, if unhindered by appearance? Were they shrews who pleased no man or harlots who pleased many, and would they try to steal someone else's husband if given the chance? For Alice, *spinster* conjured up the image of a woman established in her Beacon Hill home, the brick walls and wrought-iron gates sworn to protect her independence, wealth, and secrets.

But the garrulous Miss Davis was not a resident of Beacon Hill. Her mother had not obligingly expired when her father had, and so both of them lived on the savings of their patriarch—savings that Alice suspected were less than adequate. Far from being independent, Miss Davis was obligated to keep her mother company until one of them gave up and died. And if Miss Davis were the survivor, most likely one of her brothers would take over the house and make her a part of his household, rather than allowing her to live there alone. Although Alice had no male siblings to worry about and her parents were already in their sixties, they enjoyed fairly robust health. Barring an epidemic or accident, they could last another two decades.

Alice's eyes were drawn to light seeping out from the back of the cottage, which puzzled her; her mother had told Nora she could be dismissed once the trunks were unpacked and the cottage cleaned. Then Alice realized she had not seen her father since the beginning of dinner. She tried to let herself in quietly, but the rusty hinges mounted a protest. The door to Mr. Boyden's study creaked open in answer. A frown formed over the rims of his spectacles.

"Alice, what's wrong? Why aren't you at the dance?"

Looking at her father's face and seeing it uncharacteristically tinged with concern, Alice had the urge to tell him about Isabelle's cruelties, her interest in Mr. Holloway, her trepidation about the Annex, her fear of being an old maid. Instead she rubbed her stomach.

"Too many clams, Father."

"Ah! See, I was going to use that excuse when your mother confronts me tonight about leaving early. Now I have to think of a new one."

"I think it's a common enough complaint at the first clambake of the summer."

Mr. Boyden waved a finger at his daughter. "You're right, you're right. I raised a clever girl." He began to close the door, then paused. "I believe there is some bicarbonate of soda in the kitchen if your malady keeps you awake."

"Thank you, Father."

Through the open windows, Alice could hear the band begin to play, suggesting that the dancing was about to begin. She wondered if she couldn't simply slip back into the crowd gathering for the dance and pretend as if nothing happened.

But Alice realized that something *had* happened. She had taken to her sickbed a schoolgirl and had awakened to find herself on the other side of childhood, facing the rest of her life.

Chapter 3

When the sun woke her before breakfast time, Alice liked to wrap up in a blanket and tiptoe down to the edge of the water, barefoot of course, and walk in up to mid-shin. She got a delicious thrill out of thinking that at any time, one of their neighbors could wander out of his or her cottage and see a sliver of the Boyden girl's bare legs, peeking below her nightgown and above the rippling surface. Once the rest of the household was stirring, Alice would take a cup of tea, butter-on-bread, and maybe a piece of fruit. She could not think of a more perfect meal than such a breakfast in Onset.

Unfortunately, this morning the Boydens were to meet the Thatchers for a hotel buffet. Alice disliked communal breakfasts; she thought the day's first meal should be the most private of all. But her mother insisted that breakfast offered a better opportunity for social interaction than did lunches; given the busy lineup of lectures and séances and the difficulty of making the dead stick to a schedule, lunches at Onset were often impromptu affairs.

None of the Thatchers were early risers by nature, and it took them several minutes of grumbling at each other before they could shift to a cheerier demeanor. Once the transition had been made, Alice smiled and nodded in response to their obligatory inquiries about her health. They had missed her last night. Was she feeling better?

Alice blamed her absence on a headache, taking care not to look at Isabelle. She set to work on a shriveled sausage with her fork and knife. By closing her eyes and not breathing through her nose, perhaps she could imagine it as ham. The bread, however, would be impossible to transmogrify; try as she might, Alice could not replace the burned-crisp toast with a feather-light bun.

"Attention Elis!"

Alice looked up and saw a man still in traveling clothes, brandishing a newspaper. Mr. Thatcher stopped speaking immediately and turned his attention to the newcomer, his face expectant.

The man removed his hat and held it to his chest with exaggerated sorrow. "I regret to inform you of your team's crushing defeat at the oars of the Harvard Crimson. I have brought an article from the *New York Times*, entitled—" he paused to retrieve a pair of spectacles from his pocket—'The Day After the Race: Explaining Why the Yale Crew Was So Badly Beaten.'"

A whoop went up from several of the men gathered for breakfast, while others grumbled or sat in quiet shock. In a surprising show of emotion, Mr. Boyden chuckled and slapped Mr. Thatcher on the back, who gave him a startled look. Mrs. Thatcher held her hand to her mouth, looking as if she had recently been informed of a death in the family.

The messenger continued to read from the article: "'The Harvard men were noticeably smaller, but the nine men in the boat formed a beautiful piece of mechanism, quick and powerful in its movement, unvarying in time, lithe, graceful, poetic.' Isn't that a lovely description? Now, as for what they have to say about Yale..."

"Well, well, I think that's enough of that," said Mr. Thatcher, his jowls flushed red. "And I hope no one will make light of it in front of my son when he arrives. He's likely to be crushed." The Harvard alumni quieted somewhat, but still wore smirks on their faces; Mr. Thatcher had never made allowances for them or their sons upon a Crimson defeat.

"Poor Arthur!" said Mrs. Thatcher. "He had so been looking forward to bringing us news of victory."

"I am not so sad that I left my ribbons at home," said Isabelle, looking away.

"I am surprised to hear you so fickle, Isabelle," her father scolded.

"Arthur bragged that their team was older and bigger, and that theirs was a guaranteed victory. They have four seniors!"

"I certainly hope you're not speaking in this manner when your brother arrives," said Mrs. Thatcher. "I'm sure his classmates are critical enough; he needs his family to be supportive."

"Well, he should have pulled harder," muttered Mr. Thatcher.

"John! Not you, too."

Alice scanned the room for Mr. Holloway. She was at once disappointed by his absence and grateful to have a little more time to rebuild her self-confidence. A poke of her eggs released a milky fluid, and she put her fork down, her appetite gone. She would have to supplement the meal with something at home.

After some jam and toast, Alice sat down at her desk to review the schedule her father had prepared for her. Along with the expected healthy dose of sciences, he had prescribed history, mathematics, and a surprising amount of literature. Alice was sure her examinations would not require her to read Milton's complete poetical works, but here they were, in her trunk.

Her father had long pushed her to tackle the least enjoyable task first when it came to schoolwork, so with a sigh she gathered up her notebook and pen and separated Milton from his fellows. Perhaps reading on the veranda would make the assignment somewhat less loathsome. She settled in the rocking chair and allowed herself a few minutes to savor the morning landscape. A spunky breeze had made the bay somewhat choppy, and gulls squawked greetings at each other in between sudden dives for fish.

Alice had devoted half an hour to Milton when she became aware of a familiar pressure in her right temple. At the same time, her vision began to fail her: the lines of poetry ceased to flow straight across the page, words dripped from their proper spots, and letters turned red and green. At first she thought it just the motion from the rocker, or her boredom manifested, but the words continued to blur, and a fuzzy greenish spot blocked some altogether, like she was looking through a fishbowl thick with mud and algae.

In spite of previous experience, Alice hoped that if she could simply put herself to bed and relax, she could repel the headache. Slowly, she made her way to her room and drew the heavy curtains. A high-pitched ringing dominated her senses. She loosened her stays with a crooked finger and pulled off her boots. It was too warm for a counterpane; she lay on top of the bedclothes.

The first wave of pain crashed upon her sooner than expected; Alice had not prepared for it properly, and it bowled her over as if she were an inexperienced bather in the sea. She grabbed for the ropes that would lead her back to shore, but her hands splashed and found nothing. A brief surfacing allowed some air into her lungs and a call for help.

"Nora? Nora, I'll need some lemon sugar in water."

Her head immediately punished her for this outburst, with a clang of heavy steeple bells. The thump and click of Nora's shod feet added to the din.

"The headaches again, miss?"

"Yes. And please, would you remove your shoes?"

"Certainly, miss." After what sounded like a slight struggle in the doorway, the maid's retreat was muffled.

Her body parts seemed to come and go. One moment she was deeply aware of her arms clasping the pillow; the next her feet itched to be released of their stockings; then a lock of her hair prickled her cheek, but she couldn't employ her hands to brush it away. She tried lifting her head slightly, but the pain promptly nailed her down again.

Sleep would be so blissful now, but she could not move beyond a painful daze.

First it sounded as if someone were knocking on her skull, not the door. Most of the firecrackers threatening to explode inside her head had fizzled out, but the burning memory of them remained, directing twinges through her brain like the conductor of a symphony.

"Miss, are you feeling better?"

Alice had to admire the complexity of the rhythm—just when she thought she had grasped it and could properly brace herself for the next beat, it surprised her in a crescendo of sparks. Annoyed to have been interrupted in her concentration, Alice said, "Not well enough to get up, clearly. Why are you bothering me?"

"It was at your father's request, miss," replied a more quavering version of the voice on the other side of the door. "He heard you tapping your feet and wondered if you wouldn't be ready to dress for dinner."

Alice stuck out her tongue and half-heartedly moistened her lips so that they wouldn't crack with the strain of responding. "Don't be silly. I've been lying here since you left me. Tell Father it must have been a squirrel in the walls."

"Squirrels don't wear heeled boots," another voice boomed through the keyhole. If only she had something to plug up the hole, like pine pitch, maybe the noise would stop and she could go back to decomposing the painful orchestral performance in her head.

Alice lay there silently until two sets of footsteps had retreated from the door. Her own feet felt strangely weighted. Puzzled, she peered down the bed. Her feet wriggled inside her boots, neatly buttoned.

But she remembered removing them before taking to bed. Had she been sleepwalking? It seemed unlikely; she'd been but half-asleep most of the time, and hardly inclined to move if moving meant pain.

Alice reached to the bedside table, feeling around for the now-warm glass of sugar water. What she found instead was a pile of loose paper, jagged-edged, and a pencil broken in two, the lead core jutting from a circle of splinters.

Examining a handful of the papers proved they had been torn from her own notebook, but the handwriting—alternately ornate and jagged—was not her cultivated cursive. The first page was covered in loops and peaks that began to form letters but then lost motivation partway, collapsing into tangles. And yet, the second time Alice scanned it, she discovered two words in the rubble:

hello hello

Alice held the paper close to her face, her diligence rewarded by the conductor, who flicked the back of her eyeball with his baton and sent a small patch of sight back into murkiness. Instinctively, she tried to blink away the obstruction, but the spot refused to budge. Her good eye persevered, and on the second line of the next page saw:

here

which appeared twice more on the paper, though the others could also be *her* or *there*. She picked up the third page.

PLEASE

The capital letters seemed to leap into her face. She brushed her fingers over them; the force with which they were written had engraved them into the page. A tiny hole lingered at the end of the E.

Her sleepy mind fumbled for an explanation. Its best theory was that some child had come into the room when she was unconscious, vandalized her notebook with the few words it knew how to write, and hurriedly left the debris on her table when she stirred. The urchin who was so fond of her hairbrush and jewelry back in Cambridge came to mind, though Alice doubted its literacy. Or was Nora playing a cruel trick, perhaps angry at having to retrieve the dresses?

Alice picked up the functional half of the pencil; it fit into a pink groove on her middle right finger, as if she had been gripping it tightly.

Sleepwalking—or sleepwriting. She did not think she had ever done something like this before—at least not without the influence of opiates. During the early part of her convalescence, the doctor had prescribed laudanum for the pain, which sometimes made her feel as if she were floating around the room. Nora must have slipped some laudanum in the lemon water, trying to help, forgetting Mrs. Boyden's moratorium on opiates for common use. But could laudanum alter one's handwriting?

The more Alice looked at the pages, the more they frightened her.

No need to sort this out now, while you are weak, she told herself. The pencil stub she shut away in the drawer of the bedside table to prevent future scribbling; then, feeling that that was too close, she buried it in her desk drawer beneath some notes. Her underthings, stiff with sweat, made her feel grimy; she stripped them off and donned a nightgown. All of her movement signaled to the orchestra that the intermission was over, and they began to tune their instruments. Alice hurriedly gulped some lemon water and lay down again, powerless to stop the dissonance.

The sound of crunching leaves baffled Alice; she stood on a trail muffled in pine needles, and the oak trees were interspersed with foliage still rich in chlorophyll. But the sound continued, growing louder in her left ear, though the landscape remained constant in all directions. Repeated mental commands to her feet yielded no movement, and she could do nothing but await whatever was coming for her.

Waking slowly, heart still pounding, Alice took a few moments to realize that the rustling sound remained in her ear. She fumbled for the cause, and realized that her pillow was covered in paper.

Her eyes opened and adjusted to the darkness. She had no sense of the hour, only that night had fallen; the house was silent save for the clock keeping brisk time in the parlor, and faint trickles of moonlight eked from the cracks between curtains. Her body had the slight syrupy feeling of one no longer in pain but exhausted from the fight. On one hand, she was curious to examine the papers tucked under her cheek; on the other, unsure if she wanted to read them at this time of night. Seeing that unfamiliar scrawl in the relative comfort of afternoon allowed her to postpone explanation, but she was wary of how her imagination would work in the small hours.

As a child, Alice had dreaded waking in the middle of the night, her cloudy mind vulnerable to paranoia. Oftentimes the early morning convinced her that she could smell smoke as a fire lapped its way up the stairs to the bedrooms. Or that a drooling wolf was outside her window, awaiting a delectable meal of little girl. Adulthood had reined in her imagination somewhat, but the fever had revived such nightmares with a cruel amount of detail. Then, every antagonist her brain could invent roamed freely around the room, sometimes daring to show themselves in broad daylight, in the presence of Mrs. Connors, the doctor, her parents.

Her hand went to her breast. *It's all right, heart,* she wanted to tell it. But when she lifted her hand, it came away sticky. She looked down. As her eyes adjusted, she observed a dark stain across her chest.

She tried to scream, but as if she were in a dream, no sound came out. Gingerly, she felt around for a wound, wanting to find the source of the blood and yet scared to. No flesh or fabric seemed torn, and although a dull ache in her head persisted, she felt no sharp pain anywhere that would suggest physical injury. This must be a dream, then, she told herself.

Her shod feet settled on the floor with a clunk that startled her. At her next step, something crunched under her sole. *A bone, a bone,* her morbid mind declared before she had a chance to investigate. She picked up the object and dropped it immediately; it too was sticky. The weapon. She fumbled for a candle and brought it down to the floor. As her eyes adjusted, the pieces of a shattered pen became clear. Alice held her damp hand to the light; it was blue.

Ink. Not blood, just ink.

There was only a little water in the pitcher by the washbasin. She poured it over her stained hand and scrubbed it vigorously with bayberry soap. Some color did come off in the soap lather, and her fingers had been spared for the most part, but the palm of her hand remained quite dark. Her nightgown was likely ruined; she used it to dry her hands and wipe off what had soaked through to her chest.

Clothed in a fresh nightgown, she cautiously picked up one of the pages. The strange handwriting from before had returned, now accompanied by lines in her own hand. It was as if she had walked into a conversation between mutes, or spliced a letter and its reply.

In the mortal world I was known as Mary—this was in the loopy writing.

Do you have a different name now? —this in Alice's hand.

Sometimes. Sometimes people in the spirit world do not wish to remember their mortal selves, their former lives, and so they take a new one.

What is your name now?

It does not much matter.

Have you tried to contact me before?

A series of loops, as if for confirmation. The words continued on the next line.

No one wore black for me.

I am sorry for that, Mary. But why are you contacting me?

You are acquainted with my aunt.

Who is your aunt?

Letitia Thatcher née Smith.

Thatcher? But why not contact a medium while she sits with your aunt, who is always at séances?

More loops. And then:

But you are *a medium.*

The transcript ended there. An involuntary shiver shook Alice. For a moment she thought, *maybe?*

No. No. Alice tore the paper to bits and threw them in her trunk, along with her notebook and any pens and pencils she could find. She locked it and held the key in her hand, wondering where she could put it. Under the mattress? In the clothes-press? Alice decided to try the bottom of the pitcher; if her somnambulant self even remembered where it was, there was a good chance she could knock it over with fumbling hands, and the noise would wake her.

Part of her did not want to return to sleep, fearful the writing might reoccur; yet she was more afraid of what her waking mind might deduce during the long hours before daylight. Alice climbed into bed and tried to calm herself with peaceful thoughts of Onset: the bay breeze that waved the grass on the bluffs, the smell of salt and sand, the warmth of the noon sun on a cool day. She pictured herself gathering beach plums to make jam or pretty shells to press into the soil of the cottage garden. Her heart continued to pound for several minutes, but gradually its pace returned to normal. *You have been dreaming,* Alice told herself. *There is nothing wrong. You are dreaming.*

And she almost believed it.

Chapter 4

Her sleep must finally have been sound, for Alice awoke to a crick in her neck. Now her throat and mouth begged for the moisture it had lost, and she fumbled for the glass of water from the day before. It took her a few gulps before she realized that there were no pieces of paper on her bedside table, or her desk.

Perhaps it was indeed all a dream, she thought, her brain awakened by the sugary sediment at the bottom of the glass. Her memories of wakefulness, though, were accurate: the trunk key waiting at the bottom of the pitcher; bluish water standing stagnant in the basin; the discarded nightgown heaped at the legs of the washstand like soiled snow.

The pain was mostly gone, but she still felt woozy. What time was it? Alice found the summer's long days disorienting; the light seeping through the curtains could mean seven or noon. She threw on her dressing gown and tiptoed out to the parlor to check the clock there. Nine-fifteen. Alice sighed with relief at missing the hotel buffet. Her luck continuing, she found a pot of water on the stove, still warm, and some dry but edible biscuits from yesterday.

Soon Alice had resettled herself on the porch with a cup of tea and a book of poetry. She liked poetry at breakfast—the lines short enough for a sleepy mind to absorb, the deeper meanings apparent after fortification by food and a warm beverage. When a shadow moved over her reading, her hand moved to flick it away as it would an insect. But the dark shape remained, and Alice was forced to squint up at the obstruction of sunlight.

"Are you feeling better?"

"A bit." Alice eyed her mother warily. Her tone of voice suggested that she was about to present an activity.

"Well, if you think you are well enough for an outing, I am going to a séance later this morning. It will be a small one, only me, Mrs. Thatcher, and a few other women."

Alice sighed, rueful that in her moment of weakness over the woodcut of Mr. Holloway, she had agreed to try a sitting this summer. "I don't think so, Mother. I think a walk this afternoon would be preferable for my constitution. I have had enough of being in dark rooms." She continued to stare at her book, hoping the answer was firm enough, but still her mother's shadow lingered on the painted boards of the porch.

"Is there something else?"

Mrs. Boyden pursed her lips together as if she were trying to keep something inside her mouth, but it escaped. "Why haven't you told me that you are in touch with Mrs. Thatcher's niece?" she bubbled over. "Why, I didn't even know that you had been experimenting with automatic writing."

The memory of the night before, which Alice had pushed further and further back in her mind, surged forward and set her heart to pounding. But how could her mother know? Alice kept her eyes trained on her book. "I don't know what you could be talking about," she told her mother, trying to infuse her voice with the right combination of incredulity and assurance.

"I came into your room earlier this morning—I had heard you walking about, and wanted to see if you were feeling better, but when I opened the door I found you fast asleep. Truly, I wasn't looking through your things—some pages were scattered on your blotter, and I glanced at them and saw Letitia's name."

Mrs. Boyden's plump hand held out several pieces of paper covered in loops and occasional words. Alice sucked in an audible breath as she studied the whole, unwrinkled pages she remembered tearing apart last night.

"I cannot believe you would take something from my desk. And now, without consulting me, you've come to this silly conclusion." Alice made to tear the papers into pieces—they would be smaller pieces, this time—but her mother snatched them back.

"No! Don't you see that this spirit needs help? Don't you think Mrs. Thatcher deserves to hear from her niece? As a spirit-writer, you have a responsibility— "

"I am not a *spirit-writer*. I am not a medium of any sort. I wrote some gibberish in my sleep, that's all," said Alice, her frustration rising along with her mother's excitement.

"Question-and-answer gibberish? Half of those lines are written in handwriting that does not even resemble yours."

Ignoring her mother, Alice yanked the papers away again and briskly made eighths of the pages, stuffing the scraps into the pocket of her dress. Mrs. Boyden let out a little cry, as if she had been wounded.

"What a selfish girl you are. Don't you want to help this poor woman?"

"Enough!" cried Alice. "I've tried to explain, and yet you believe what you want to believe. I was sleepwalking; the writing is nonsense. I beg you to consider what you're saying—it makes no sense that the dead would speak to *me*."

"We know so little about death as it is," said Mrs. Boyden, taking her daughter's hand between hers and petting it. "How can we know why the dead do what they do?"

Alice looked at her mother in disgust. Clearly she had entered a state that reason could not penetrate. She wriggled out of her mother's grip.

"It is not *my* fault that the spirits have other plans for you!"

In reply, Alice stomped up the stairs and slammed her bedroom door.

Her pleasure reading spoiled, Alice sought to complete some of her schoolwork instead, yet her bizarre night ultimately made a rest the most attractive option. But no sooner had she closed her eyes than a rap sounded on her door.

"Miss?" said Nora.

Alice put on her strongest scowl before opening the door, but Nora seemed unaffected. "Your mother's brought a guest for lunch, and they are waiting on your presence." She frowned as she looked Alice up and down. "She won't be pleased with the state of you."

A guest. Alice remembered who was set to arrive today, and her chest filled with disappointment. "I'm afraid I can't entertain this afternoon. I'm feeling poorly."

Nora glanced around and lowered her voice. "I was told to bring you out even if you were unconscious."

Alice sighed, resigned. Her dishevelment would serve as armor, she told herself—some protection against Arthur's amorous intent. She entered the cottage just in time to hear her mother say: "She so wanted to come this morning but was still feeling the effects of the headache, poor thing, and didn't want to chance a relapse."

That's fine; paint me a sickly creature and perhaps he will not pursue me, Alice thought, until she entered the parlor and saw the back of not a short blond student but a tall, dark-haired man. Her nervousness changed course, and she frantically swiped at her hair, hoping that she did not look too frightening.

Mrs. Boyden took notice of her daughter and raised her eyebrows, confirming Alice's fear. "Ah, at last my daughter is able to join us."

"Hello, Mr. Holloway. I would have been more prompt for lunch if my mother had informed me that we were expecting a guest." Alice did not look to see her mother's reaction to this comment, but she imagined her puffing up like an angry hen.

"Hello, Miss Boyden." She allowed her eyes to shift upward, and as she had feared, the sight of his smile paralyzed her. "I hope you are feeling well enough to receive me."

"Yes, of course." Alice recovered and managed to respond in a timely manner. "I was just catching up on my studies."

"Mmmm, yes," said Mrs. Boyden, with a suspicious look at her daughter's tousled hair. "Nora! We're seated."

Alice had not noted the absence of her father until now, when she saw his chair vacant. "Where's Father?"

Mrs. Boyden raised her eyebrows. "Playing horseshoes, the last I saw. I assume he'll take lunch at the hotel."

"Social this summer, isn't he," murmured Alice. To Thomas, she said: "My father tends to spend the entire summer in his lab or out in the field."

"The field?"

"Outside—looking for specimens. He's an entomologist."

"Ah."

Alice could tell by the response—she knew the tone of voice—that he was unfamiliar with the term.

"He studies insects. He's a professor at Harvard."

Mr. Holloway paused in the process of unfolding his napkin and glanced around, as if worried that some winged thing was waiting in a corner to attack.

"He keeps them all in his lab, in cages," Alice hastened to say. "Or pinned to boards." Oh, why had she even mentioned her father's profession? It inevitably put people on edge, gave them the impression that something must be crawling on them.

Mr. Holloway chuckled as he lay his napkin across his lap. "That is good to hear. I'm afraid I have somewhat of an aversion to spiders."

"It is most unseemly to let one's test subjects run free," muttered Mrs. Boyden. Mr. Holloway looked perplexed.

"Mother is thinking of Professor Henderson, who is a zoologist," Alice quickly explained. "He has a monkey, as well as several other unusual pets, who are given free reign of the house and have escaped more than once."

"Can you imagine, a monkey making its way through Harvard Square?" said Mrs. Boyden. "It is a blessing that Mrs. Phelps with her heart condition was not out that day."

Alice hoped they were not making Cambridge sound ridiculous. It was full of eccentrics—but then, Alice reminded herself, so was Onset. And the Harvard faculty, for all their quirks, were still grounded in scientific study; devotees here were anything but grounded.

"I have seen some dogs here, but no monkeys," said Mr. Holloway. Mrs. Boyden had seated him at Alice's usual place, so that he would have a view of the bay. And like Alice, his eyes were continually drawn to the view of the water.

"Your cottage certainly is at a lovely spot. Have you been here long?"

"This is our fourth year at the cottage. The year before that, while it was being constructed, we stayed in a tent." Alice suddenly found herself jealous of the picturesque scenery, knowing it would distract him from her.

"I must say, while a tent is ideal for a summer séance, I am glad not to have to spend nights in one. "

"Not terribly pleasant when it rains. Even when one is camped on a platform. And while it should be more comfortable to keep the flap open on hot nights, the insects swarm, which is undesirable even for my father."

Mrs. Boyden cleared her throat quite loudly then, and Alice stared at her, wondering what she could find inappropriate about such a statement. She had been the worst complainer of all before the construction of the cottage, inevitably leading to an expensive stay in a crowded hotel. Alice wondered how her mother had survived all those years of camp meetings where "camp" was an entirely appropriate term.

"Ah, Miss Boyden," said Mr. Holloway, putting down his salad fork. "Your mother said you had something important to discuss with me." When Alice stared at him in confusion, he shifted in his chair and cleared his throat. "The automatic writing."

A fiery anger flashed red behind Alice's eyes. She glared at her mother, who looked triumphant.

"*No*, Mother." She turned to Mr. Holloway. "I have produced no spirit writings, Mr. Holloway—you see, I have these headaches, and am often semi-conscious for a time, and yesterday I woke to find some non-sensical scribbles on paper near my bed. Mother wants to think that they have some meaning. I am sorry for you to come out here for no reason."

"The spirit identified Letitia Thatcher as kin," said Mrs. Boyden.

"There was no spirit to speak of." Alice continued to address Mr. Holloway, as her mother was not responding to sense.

"I can see you are unsettled by these revelations," Mr. Holloway said gently, "and I do not blame your reluctance to believe that they have a supernatural origin." Alice noticed he did not look to her mother to see her reaction. "But would you oblige me with an experiment? I would like to put you into a trance, and see if you will deliver more words from Mary. Perhaps we can discover who she is trying to reach, and can help her make contact with that person. Perhaps nothing will come of my test, and such negative results will reinforce your own theory."

Alice looked at Mr. Holloway's kind face, and her mother's eager one. Should she humor them? When Mr. Holloway found that she could not reproduce the phenomenon, then perhaps that would settle the matter once and for all, and she could move on with her summer...

"If nothing comes of it, I wish nothing more to be said of it—"

"Oh, but Alice," blurted Mrs. Boyden, "even the most experienced mediums sometimes have unproductive days. One fallow sitting does not prove anything."

"I respect Alice's wish," said Mr. Holloway. Forcing the matter will only antagonize her further, and unwillingness could produce faulty results, anyway."

Mrs. Boyden made a face not unlike that of a five-year-old denied a treat. The gesture prompted Alice to say, "And I wish my mother to leave."

"Why?" cried Mrs. Boyden. "I won't make a peep—I'll only watch. And wouldn't you feel more comfortable with me here in the room?"

Alice shook her head. At the present time, she felt far more comfortable with a near stranger than she did with her mother.

"I do think it will help Alice's concentration, to remove the concern about your reaction," Mr. Holloway said. He paused, looking uncomfortable. "And if you are concerned about propriety..."

"Oh, no, it's not that," said Mrs. Boyden, getting up with some reluctance. "It's only that I myself have wished for the gift of spirit communication for so long, and to see my daughter channeling spirits—well, it is almost as satisfying as seeing mediumistic powers of my own emerge."

Alice had suspected that her mother's envy was a driving force behind this intervention, but she was surprised by the ready admission.

"We have not proven anything yet, Mrs. Boyden," said Mr. Holloway. "I'll let Alice have the benefit of the doubt for now. Sometimes oddities are just that—oddities. We must keep our minds open in order to let the true miracles in."

Mrs. Boyden gave a reluctant nod and looked at Alice rather wistfully as she led them to the parlor, then left the room.

As Mr. Holloway closed the door, Alice felt a flutter of panic—she wanted to be alone with Mr. Holloway, yes, but what would she say? She had no idea what to say. He would think her impossibly awkward...

"Now. I hope that her absence will help calm and focus you, Miss Boyden."

"Oh, it *will.*" Alice spoke so emphatically—so grateful for both his actions and the opportunity to reply to something—that Mr. Holloway chuckled.

"Thank you very much for humoring me. If it puts you at further ease, you might think of me as a doctor, for I believe I can help you."

Alice thought back to what she had read about Mr. Holloway in the summer program. "I did not know you were a spirit-healer as well."

Mr. Holloway laughed and shook his head. "I'm not, Miss Boyden. But I will offer a hypothesis concerning your headaches. Your mother explained that you were very ill this spring—"

"I wish she hadn't," said Alice. "I am not an invalid. I don't wish for people to treat me like one. But she insists upon exaggerating—"

"So you were not close to death?"

Alice's mind went back to the day she walked in on Mrs. Connors's séance, thinking it her own. The memory made her shiver. She said nothing.

"Sometimes people who have been severely ill unwittingly form a connection with the spirit world," Mr. Holloway continued. "It is as if spirits believe you more sympathetic, since you were once almost in their position. I think you have made that sort of connection. Now, they are trying to produce coherent communications, and the strain on you, who have never actively practiced as a medium, is overwhelming. Without a spirit guide to manage their many requests, the pressure is causing you actual physical pain."

Alice nodded slowly. His ideas were like bricks without mortar: they stacked neatly and looked sturdy, but could be toppled with a simple push. They were not wise additions to her wall, but she couldn't help but consider them with curiosity, unattached as they were to reason or scientific fact. "My mother, as you might have divined, has been an active part of the movement for a while now," Alice said. "But—" and suddenly she grew embarrassed of what she was about to say—"I don't really believe in any of it. I think at best, it is telepathy; at worst, it is chicanery."

She looked at him then, wondering if he would be insulted by this slur against his world, ask her to leave, try and convince her otherwise through a series of metaphysical arguments. Instead, he simply said, "Many people feel that way."

Alice was surprised by his lack of reaction—other spiritualists would not hear of skepticism within their community, and she had seen the sweetest ladies turn into hissing serpents when faced with naysayers or scientific theory. But Mr. Holloway sat there calmly, his broad hands folded.

"For this incident, you can offer no rational explanation. And that terrifies you."

"I can offer a rational explanation," Alice protested. "Somnambulance."

"Do you often suffer from that affliction?"

"I am not sure. I would not remember if I did." Mr Holloway looked somewhat sheepish, and Alice hung her head. She had not meant to be sarcastic.

"Well," Mr. Holloway continued, "if this is not sleepwalking but spirits trying to communicate, and if you fight them and refuse to listen, they will only cause you more pain. If you share what they have to say, they will be relieved of their burdens and so will you."

Alice tried another tack. "If the spirits only come when I have a headache, what am I to do? Hold séances from a couch? And I cannot predict when one will strike."

"My opinion is that an induced trance, such as the one I am about to put you in, will replicate the same sort of mental state in which you find yourself during a headache—but without the pain. Here, have a seat at the desk." Mr. Holloway indicated the rolltop in the corner of the parlor. "I'm afraid I don't have my slates with me, but perhaps we'll have the best chance of replication if you use paper and pen as before."

Alice's mind hesitated, but her body followed Mr. Holloway's direction, sitting at the desk and pulling a sheet of paper from the drawer, taking the pen from its inkwell home.

"Now. May I place my hands on your shoulders?"

She nodded, suddenly shyer. He indeed spoke like a doctor, cushioning invasion with a calming tone. His fingers pressed down against the tense muscles in her shoulders. "Relax," he said. "Take a deep breath and close your eyes."

Alice let her lids fall loosely yet completely, so that the fringe of her lashes brushed the hollows beneath her eyes. She focused upon the kaleidoscopic colors that bloomed in the darkness.

"Now, imagine as if you are wrapped in gauze," said Mr. Holloway, his voice even and soothing. "It has separated you from the ordinary world. You are in a liminal space, and the sound of my voice is the only living one that can penetrate the fabric. But spirits are free to speak to you in this space; it is a place where they are comfortable, where you welcome them, where you are willing to hear whatever they have to say..."

A violent shudder suddenly snapped her eyes open and made Alice gasp for breath. She heard the pen clatter on the floor. Mr. Holloway bent to pick it up. When he resurfaced, he was smiling at her, and Alice could ask for no better balm for the shock of waking.

"That was marvelous, Miss Boyden," he said. "What a talented medium you are, to have such success on your first induced trance."

Alice looked down at the desk. Indeed, the paper that had lain pristine before her just a moment ago was two-thirds filled with writing.

"I wrote down the questions I asked of you, so we have a complete record here." Mr. Holloway handed her a sheet of paper. Alice read the first questions, then the answers.

Where are you buried, Mary?

Ground. No stone.

Are you in a graveyard? A backyard?

Field.

As it had been the first time, the answers were of limited eloquence. But Mr. Holloway had been patient.

In what town did you live, Mary?

Warren, Ohio.

Then the writing grew messier, the loops bolder, more urgent, as if the author could not contain herself.

Look under the tallest tree in the field at the back of the house. The Sawyer house. I want to be buried in the family plot in Connecticut. I want to be beside my father.

Did your husband kill you, Mary?

No.

A series of loops. Then:

But he did not let me live. How do I know he will not come for me in the spirit world, when he passes? I am relatively new here. I do not know all the rules. I do know that spirits can marry other spirits, but I am not sure whether or not marriages made in the mortal world are binding in the next.

From my contact with spirits in the past, earthly marriages continue if you want them to. But there is no law binding you to an unworthy spouse.

That is a relief.

What would you like to say to your aunt?

The spirit world is pleasant, from what I have seen so far. I am here with my father now, who died when I was only six. I am sorry not to have contacted Aunt Letty before. When you are not a believer in the spirit world, as I in life was not, it does not occur to you that your interactions with those in the mortal world need not end. And not all spirits here wish to correspond with those still living, even if they had happy lives. Some simply enjoy the opportunity to start over, to try again. But when I found Father, he reminded me that Aunt Letty was a spiritualist, and might accept a message from me.

And we will deliver it.

Thank you.

"These loops indicate where you lost the connection with her for a time," said Mr. Holloway, pointing. "But overall, the connection remained very strong. An induced trance gives you more control from the outset. You'll receive clearer, more complete messages in a shorter amount of time." He sat back in his chair. "I wished to give you the benefit of the doubt, Miss Boyden, but these certainly seem like spirit messages to me."

Alice suddenly wanted to cry. "How do you know for certain?"

"Well, one can never be certain about such matters, but in my humble opinion, I think these communications are genuine."

"Well, if they are, why can Mary not seek the assistance of one of the many mediums here? Or even someone who wants to be a medium, like my mother?"

"We do not understand the intricacies of death, the separation of soul and body, the forces that divide this world from the next. How can we know why they pick whom they pick to be their voice and hands on earth?"

Alice bit her lip.

"But as I said before, I think spirits—at least Mary—find your soul to be an understanding one. Even if your mind has not yet reached that level of enlightenment." Mr. Holloway interlaced his fingers beneath his chin, and Alice took in the intricate creases of his knuckles, and the fine dark hairs that covered them. They were hands that looked ten years older than the rest of their owner. "I think in time you'll desire to deliver these communications yourself, but I can understand that you may not be able to accept your powers right now. So I am here to offer my services. I can put you into a trance like I just did, mimicking the state of half-sleep you were probably in when you put pen to paper here. It is a signal to spirits that you are open to their contact, and they will be encouraged to use your hand as theirs. Rather than waiting for their requests to reach a point of crisis—and cause you physical pain—we can skim off these messages as they come. I will then present the writings to my spirit guide, Dr. Anderson, for his consideration."

Alice tried not to grimace at this; he had seemed reasonable before mentioning his "spirit guide." At least this "Dr. Anderson" did not sound like an Indian spirit guide; they were all the rage at Onset. Alice had never known an Indian herself, but she doubted that the buckskinned apparitions and rough, halting English of various mediums calling themselves Little Fawn and Brave Wolf were very much like the real thing.

"He will not only help deliver the messages to their intended recipient, if that recipient is at Onset, but will try to contact the spirit again for additional information. With this responsibility lifted off your shoulders, we shall see if your headaches subside. My guess is that they will—with regular trance sessions, that is."

A realization suddenly broke through Alice's prepared objections. If she went along with Mr. Holloway's plan, she would have to visit him on a regular basis. In private.

"And you will not tell anyone from where the messages come?"

Mr. Holloway shook his head. "I swear to you, I will keep silent. However—" he thought for a moment. "Perhaps Dr. Anderson can ask Mary to come forward at the séance after dinner tomorrow night. Perhaps she will say something that will convince you she's not simply a hallucination."

Alice ducked her head. "My father and I usually excuse ourselves after dinner. I've never attended a séance before." She was surprised to feel a little ashamed to admit that fact.

"Never been to a séance? Well, then, you must come to mine. Don't you feel ungrounded in your skepticism of something you have never experienced?"

"It was an agreement between my mother and my father that I not participate in séances until I was nineteen," Alice was quick to explain. "When the time came, I could make my own decision."

"And you've not had the opportunity to attend one since? With your mother as enthusiastic as she is?"

"My birthday is in November, and I was occupied with school," Alice said defensively. "I came down with scarlet fever not a month later."

"Oh, that's right." Alice saw the timeline click together in his head. "I am sorry."

"Please don't pity me." Alice stared directly into Mr. Holloway's eyes. Normally her gaze nervously flitted back and forth between him and the floor, the wall, her hands. As a result, she had dismissed his eyes as brown, simply because they were dark; but close up she realized they were a deep blue-gray, the color of the Atlantic in winter. She fell in.

"Miss Boyden, I only pity you for your lack of faith," he said, looking back calmly, yet with a strange intensity. "But I hope that I can earn your trust. Please do come tomorrow. If your spirit writings are validated, then perhaps you'll consider my suggestion."

Any self-righteous protest that Alice had left dissolved in his gaze. She took a deep breath. "All right. I will."

Chapter 5

Arriving at six sharp, the Boydens were met by the Thatchers' longtime maid, Prudence, whom Alice thought looked every bit like her name. She couldn't be older than thirty, and yet her general temperament had already soured. Her small mouth lent to a disapproving look even when she wasn't pursing her lips, and her slanted brows gave her a perpetual frown. Alice reasoned that she wouldn't smile, either, if she had to work for such a family.

Mrs. Thatcher followed close behind Prudence for contrast, bubbling a welcome. "So glad you could join us! But I am afraid I bear bad news! Arthur has decided to summer in Maine again this year! I know that you must have been eager to see him, Alice!"

"Too embarrassed by his performance, I suppose." Mr. Boyden attempted a murmur, but his hardness of hearing meant that his comment was amplified instead. Mrs. Thatcher gave him a dark stare.

The news of Arthur's absence was like a breeze in the room; Alice had been readying herself for an evening of dull conversation and parental speculation. Her mood lifted further when she saw Mr. Holloway already seated in the parlor. He rose to greet the newcomers, shaking Mr. Boyden's hand, bowing to Mrs. Boyden.

"And Miss Boyden."

He bowed and kissed the knuckles of her kid-gloved hand, then fixed her with a pair of eyes that had turned algae green since yesterday—owing, surely, to a different light and attire, but she had not noticed their capacity for brightness and color in the different light of her family's cottage. She could barely shift her gaze to drop a curtsy and bow her head in turn. When she looked up again, Mr. Holloway was studying her. Then he smiled, as if making some deduction.

"Why, a mermaid!"

Alice stared at him in confusion, then felt her scalp prickle as she thought of what she was wearing. Foamy blue and green petticoats and ribbons, a shell comb that her mother had found at one of the Onset shops—she must look as if she were wearing a costume. She heard a familiar little snicker, and realized that in her captivation with Mr. Holloway she had not noticed the presence of Isabelle. Her cheeks flared—but, then, Mr. Holloway still held her hand. She felt the warmth of his fingers seeping through her kid gloves.

"How preferable you are to the peacocks in New York, Miss Boyden. One is induced to sneeze in a room full of fashionably plumed women there, but your ornament provokes no such affliction."

He finally let go of her hand. Alice could only nod her head again and blush some more, though she noticed in a sideward glance that Isabelle had quietly plucked a white feather from her coiffure and tossed it into the corner. Isabelle wore pongee as well, but hers was a pale yellow, trimmed with more feathers. The whole ensemble had the unfortunate effect of making her look like a giant baby chick, overfed and groomed for Easter.

There was a lull in the conversation then, and one could clearly hear Mrs. Thatcher fussing at the servants in the kitchen. Mr. Thatcher burst in a little too loudly with, "Well! A drink for you, George?" He wore a white suit that seemed to make his florid face glow from within.

Under his wife's insistent gaze, Mr. Boyden held up his hand. "No, no thank you, John. A soda water would be fine for me." Alice noted the slight wistfulness in his voice, and she wondered if his roving bottle had been forgotten in Cambridge.

"Really, Letitia, you should see about the Temperance Union League in New Haven," Alice heard her mother say in a stage whisper, fixing a cold glare on Mr. Thatcher as he poured something for himself. "The arguments for abolishing the consumption of alcohol together are so *sound.*" This was an intervention Mrs. Boyden attempted at the beginning of every summer, and one which Mrs. Thatcher always deflected with muted exclamations.

"I don't think that moderate consumption in a proper home does any harm! It's the immigrants that get the drink in them and beat their wives and lose their jobs! Perhaps that cheap stuff they drink could be taxed more heavily, and then they wouldn't be able to afford it!"

Alice closed her ears to what was sure to be a sanctimonious comment by her mother about fair treatment of the working classes. Mrs. Boyden met regularly with other upper- and middle-class women to discuss the rights and welfare of workers, but Alice doubted her mother would actually keep company with a working-class woman herself.

A yellow cloud appeared in her peripheral vision.

"Perhaps one of our first events for the younger set should be a lecture on fashion by Miss Alice Boyden," said Isabelle.

"My mother found it today in Onset—the comb, I mean—and the credit belongs to her," said Alice, unable to think of a cleverer answer than simple fact. She told herself she should not care what Isabelle thought. Mr. Holloway had approved.

Mercifully, Prudence announced that the soup was ready, and they all followed the smell. Some sort of fish stew or chowder, Alice guessed, and she wondered why they would serve something so thick and hot now. It felt too close in the house already.

At one end of the table, Mr. Holloway discussed mesmerism with the two mothers, something Mrs. Boyden was always interested in and that Mrs. Thatcher professed to practice. Isabelle wasn't quite bothering to pretend interest in her mother's contributions, but her face lit up with fascination whenever Mr. Holloway spoke. Mr. Thatcher interjected during the rare instances when his mouth was not full.

On her right, Alice's father seemed to be entertaining a battle with his stew; the spoon clunked ominously against the side of the bowl and punctuated the conversation of others. Mr. Boyden was never a good guest at dinner parties. To his credit, he had no functional purpose at most events, was merely an escort for his wife. He could not discuss the details of spiritualism without smirking; he knew little of culture—what plays were running in Boston, etc.—and he was likely the only member of the party who would be excited if a fly were to land in his stew. Indeed, with all the clattering, Alice wondered if he was trying to recover the body of a six-legged drowning victim.

"Mr. Boyden, forgive me. I've not yet asked about your work at Harvard." Mr. Holloway had shifted his attention across the table.

Did Alice see her father's face flush? Perhaps it was only the warmth of the day, but people here were rarely interested in whatever crawling or flying thing had the misfortune of being under his microscope that month. He set his spoon down on the tablecloth, which immediately darkened as the stew seeped through to the wood beneath.

"Well, I—you see, there's been a sort of movement lately to clear the name of members of *Odonata*—"

"Knitting-needles and other lacy-winged insects," Alice explained.

Mr. Boyden blinked at his daughter, as if he had forgotten that she was also present. "Yes, indeed. Dragonflies and damselflies, you might hear them called. Perfectly harmless, but you can't imagine how many people think the creatures are out to sting them."

In fact, Alice recalled how some sunbathers in Onset had been doubly startled the previous summer—once by the unexpected visit of a dragonfly, then again when Mr. Boyden emerged from the rushes with a net.

"They subsist on gnats and other pests, so people should welcome their presence." Mr. Boyden's voice grew defensive, but he seemed to catch himself, after realizing the tone was unnecessary. "I'm examining their stomachs to determine how varied their diet can be."

Mr. Holloway nodded, with a convincing look of interest attached to his face. "And have you made any new discoveries?"

"Not so far, but this is only the first week, after all. I'm also interested to observe how they are affected, if at all, by the influx of people in July. For instance, is there a different proportion of gnats in their bellies then?"

"I shall look forward to hearing the results," said Mr. Holloway. "Do you intend to publish them?" He paused to take a large spoonful from his bowl. Alice was amazed by Mr. Holloway's endurance for discussion about insect digestion during dinner; she herself was feeling a little queasy, although she was used to the inappropriate timing of her father's descriptions of work. Sometimes it was necessary to ignore him altogether during mealtimes, especially if he had spent hours before that meal at his microscope.

"Eventually. If Harvard would give me fewer graduate students to babysit I'd publish far more often."

Alice heard Mr. Thatcher clear his throat. "Have you heard that Arthur shall be attending Harvard Law in the fall?"

Her father's head turned so quickly from Mr. Holloway to Mr. Thatcher that Alice thought he might have injured his neck. "I have not! Why, that's marvelous! Is he burning his blue togs, then?"

Mr. Thatcher chuckled. "He wrote that he's already had one of his rowing shirts painted red by the team. They dared him to wear it on race day."

At the mention of the race, everyone at the table went silent. Mrs. Thatcher was looking at her husband with trepidation, as if he might suddenly explode in anger or tears. But Mr. Thatcher was perfectly calm.

"Who knows. Perhaps it would have helped his boat!"

Mr. Boyden let out a hearty guffaw, which was soon joined by more tentative chuckles from around the table. "Yes, he should use his colors wisely—and by that, I mean he should always wear crimson."

Alice observed this display of chumminess and wondered if Mr. Thatcher had freshened her father's glass with something besides soda water.

"And what about you, Mr. Holloway?" said Mr. Boyden. "Are you a Crimson or a Blue man?"

Mr. Holloway swallowed his mouthful before answering. Alice would never have guessed that she would find a man's throat attractive, but it was certainly a fine feature of his. "Blue—but Michigan blue. So I hope I might be allowed to stand on neutral ground."

"Michigan, yes. One of my colleagues, Professor Morris, received his doctoral degree there." Alice was thankful her father did not mention his general dislike of Morris, whom he had more than once referred to as a country bumpkin. "What did you study?"

"Oh, I only claim the colors as my own because I grew up in the state. I received my education in the séance parlors of New York City."

"Ah." Mr. Boyden's tone was notably without enthusiasm.

Seemingly unfazed, Mr. Holloway looked at Mr. Boyden, then briefly at Alice. "I hear your daughter will be having her own academic adventure this fall."

"Yes, well, we shall see how she fares on her studies this summer. She's already behind, and the examinations in September are unforgiving."

This was the first time that Alice had heard her father question her acceptance to the Annex, and his casual remark—made in front of other people, no less—humiliated her.

"Father, it's only our first week here," she said, a few beats delayed.

"Yes, why not let her enjoy these beautiful days?" said Mr. Holloway. "There will be some rainy ones perfect for studying, I am sure."

Mr. Boyden fixed him with a stern gaze. "I'm not sure that you understand the difficulty of these examinations, Mr. Holloway. They are the same as those given to young men entering Harvard as undergraduates. As my daughter was unable to finish secondary school, we must not only have her catch up to her peers, but she must spend time studying for each particular examination as well."

"Father! No one wants to hear about my academic rigors." Alice twisted and twisted her napkin in her lap. She looked down and saw that her hands had turned red and white with the strain.

"Yes, well, if some people doubt the amount of preparation needed to enter Harvard—"

"I did not mean to sound as if I were doubting the difficulty of admittance," Mr. Holloway said quickly. "It's only that I saw a great number of young ladies Alice's age on the beach today, and I hoped that she would be able to enjoy it as well. Perhaps once her studies are done for the day."

Alice could picture them: their hair tucked beneath smart little hats, laughing and absorbing the warmth of the sand while trying to keep every pale limb covered to prevent freckling.

"Those young ladies have no ambition," said Mr. Boyden. He huffed as if Thomas were a graduate student who had seen fit to question him. "They are different than my Alice."

"Not very, I hope, Father," Alice said.

"If you think that, then have you absorbed any of my council over the years?" At her father's glare, Alice felt herself deflate a little, and sank down in her chair.

"I do hope you all will enjoy the salad!" said Mrs. Thatcher, waving the servant girl over to clear bowls. "We ordered it at a café in France last year, and it is ever so suitable for warm days such as this!"

Alice had never before been so grateful for Mrs. Thatcher's skills of interruption.

Sometimes she thought she felt Mr. Holloway's gaze on her, but whenever she looked up, he was concentrating on the latest squawking from one of the other women. Alice longed to say something to regain Mr. Holloway's attention—gibberish, anything—but the memory of her father's expression stopped her.

Her father was right. Those girls on the beach were different. Some of them might go to college, certainly; their parents could afford it, and they were likely clever if not bookish. But for them it would only be a stepping stone to the shore they had had in sight since their childhood: marriage.

Once the diners had scraped up the last bit of trifle with their dessert spoons, and Mr. Boyden had again refused a sherry, Mr. Thatcher raised his empty cordial glass.

"Now, for the entertainment of the evening," he said. "I cordially"—he laughed at his own joke, though no one else did—"invite you upstairs for a séance led by Mr. Holloway."

"Well, then, it's time for me to take my leave," said Mr. Boyden, rising from his chair. "Alice?" He held out his hand to help her stand as well. Alice accepted but dropped it once she was on her feet.

"No," she said. "I think I'll stay tonight."

Mr. Boyden opened his mouth as if to argue with her, but then closed it and shrugged. "Suit yourself. Thank you for the lovely dinner, Mrs. Thatcher. Mr. Thatcher, Miss Thatcher." He acknowledged each in turn. "No need; I'll let myself out," he said as Mrs. Thatcher approached to see him out the door.

Alice glared at his retreating figure, focusing on the upper half of the chest, where his cruel heart would be beating within his ribs. As soon as the door closed, Mrs. Boyden let out a little squeal.

"Alice! I'm so glad you're willing to try this. Your father can speak ill of spiritualism all he wants, but the fact remains that he has never experienced a séance in his life, and he should not make such judgments without that experience."

Alice recoiled inwardly at her mother's evangelism, but she reminded herself that she was not here for her mother. She was here as the invited guest of Mr. Holloway.

"Miss Boyden?"

Mr. Holloway was holding his arm out. When she took it, Alice felt a jolt as if from static electricity. Thankfully, her arm did not recoil, but completed the link. His arm felt soft and solid at the same time, and she had to resist the urge to rest her head upon his shoulder. "Your first séance! This is a momentous occasion. You must sit by me in the circle."

Alice felt everyone's eyes upon her. Did they suspect she was somehow involved in this evening's entertainment? Had her mother already bragged to everyone of her daughter's skill?

"I'd be honored," she told him.

Chapter 6

The Thatchers led their guests to the cottage's attic, the air becoming thicker with each floor. Mr. Holloway and Mr. Thatcher had to duck as they filed into the small room; the sharply pitched eaves offered a number of painful obstacles for the very tall. The women enjoyed better mobility, and Mrs. Thatcher hurried to the small triangular windows opposite the staircase and unlatched them, pushing the panes outward with a small poof of dust, the filaments visible in the light from the waning sunset.

"Isabelle, I thought I asked you to air out the attic this afternoon," said Mrs. Thatcher through her teeth.

"I was making the centerpieces," said Isabelle. "I told Prudence to do it."

Mrs. Thatcher sighed, but turned to Mr. Holloway with a sweet smile. "You'll have to excuse the stuffiness. Our custom is to visit other members' tents and cottages when we first arrive; we've hardly been here but to sleep."

"Well, Dr. Anderson is rather fond of warm temperatures, owing to the years he spent in the Australian bush," said Mr. Holloway. "This might prompt a retelling of one of his adventures, I warn you. But I daresay he and his fellow spirits have a tendency to make things chilly no matter the season."

"Oh, but of *course,*" said Mrs. Thatcher, whose emphasis suggested some embarrassment at her comment, which smacked of inexperience. Even Alice knew that the presence of spirits were supposed to influence the temperature of the séance room. She watched Mrs. Thatcher tack a piece of black gauze over the window to filter the fading light.

"And we hope to be perfectly freezing in good time," said Mr. Thatcher, trying his best to remain jolly despite the sweat beading on his brow. He took a few moments to extract his handkerchief from his pocket and draw it across his face. When he put it away, the happy upturn of his mouth remained. Alice wondered if he had to be purposefully glum when company was not present, if only to give the muscles in his face a rest.

Mr. Holloway gestured at the table, and everyone, after some glances at whom they were near and whom they would like to be near, positioned themselves behind a chair. Alice had already claimed her spot to the left of Mr. Holloway; Mrs. Thatcher took the seat to his right as part of her prerogative as hostess. Isabelle stood between her father and Alice's mother, looking as if she would much prefer sitting next to the guest of honor.

"Excellent, excellent." With Mr. Holloway's approval, everyone sat. The contrast between the pout on Isabelle's face and the innate cheeriness of her yellow ensemble made Alice want to laugh. She forced herself to keep her eyes on the table, where five shallow furrows cut through the polished wood in front of her. Alice stared at the marks, trying to figure out what could have made them, when she realized that the tracks could have begun with five curled fingers and five nails scraping. She tried to swallow her agitation, but it stuck somewhere in her throat.

"Mr. Thatcher, the gas, if you please." Mr. Holloway nodded to his host, who turned the key so clumsily with his fat fingers that Alice thought he'd put out the lamp entirely—but finally a small but steady lick of a flame glowed, illuminating the table but nothing beyond it. Mr. Holloway closed his eyes. "Let us see what Dr. Anderson has for us tonight."

This is not real. This is not real, Alice repeated to herself as everyone settled themselves and her mother and Mr. Holloway took her hands. The grip on her left was a little too tight and she wriggled her fingers to make those enclosing them release a bit. For a few minutes silence prevailed, punctured only by the murmurs of passerby below the open window.

Then a spasm suddenly made Thomas's head snap up and his hands jerk, sending the movement through Alice and Mrs. Thatcher, enough to startle the other sitters at the table. Then the medium coughed deliberately, as if clearing his throat.

"Good evening, ladies and gentlemen," said the moderately pitched, strangely accented voice emanating from Mr. Holloway's throat. "For those of you who do not know me, my name is Dr. Anderson; I was once a physician in Australia and elsewhere, and now I am honored to serve as a guide to the spirit world for Mr. Holloway. But you do not need to know much about me, for most of the time I am merely Charon, ferrying the dead across the Styx so that they might speak to you." He went quiet again, and Alice found herself holding her breath.

"Ah, yes. Here I have a spirit named Mary who wishes to speak to her cousin. She would very much like to use her own voice, to explain, but is feeling weak today..."

Already? thought Alice. *Shouldn't he summon an unknown spirit first, to better convince me?* There was silence for a moment, and then Mrs. Thatcher squeaked. "Mary! Is it my cousin, Mary Sawyer?"

Another pause. "Yes."

Mrs. Thatcher pressed her hands to her mouth. "Her family's not heard from her in a year—but we thought it was her husband's influence..."

"She did write letters, but now she realizes that her husband must never have posted them. Her illness came on suddenly and she hadn't time to write her family. She does not know what it was that killed her. Her husband buried her in Ohio without a funeral and without telling her poor mother and sisters."

"That scoundrel!" cried Mrs. Thatcher. "Isaac Sawyer didn't like her family, wanted to take her far away from us, and we thought he had convinced her to be rid of us entirely!" She put a handkerchief to her eyes, sparkling with tears in the faint lamplight. "Oh, and to think that all this time I was upset with her for not returning letters! Why has she not contacted her Aunt Letty before?"

Mr. Holloway paused again, and his expression saddened. "She says she's not the strongest spirit, and that she has tried to contact you often, but other spirits are more insistent, and throw themselves at the medium in an effort to be heard first. By the time Mary has a chance to speak, the medium is usually worn out and the séance ends. This time she resolved to be a little more bold, and she caught my attention. Oh, wait—she will try to speak now—"

"Aunt Letty?"

Alice went suddenly cold. It was like being in Cambridge in February with no woolens on; the chill cut straight through to her bones. She thought she could see her breath. Part of her continued to deny that any of this was real—her illness had created the character, hysteria now brought her to life and changed the atmosphere of the room. But the voice that came out of Mr. Holloway's mouth conjured a picture for her: a woman in homespun with hair the sandy color of Mrs. Thatcher's, her skin tanned and cracked by the sun and wind that bullied the flat prairies. It certainly did not sound like a man trying to imitate the higher pitch of a lady's voice.

"Mary? Oh, Mary, you must tell me where you are buried so that I can bring you home!" cried Mrs. Thatcher.

"Behind our house in Warren, Ohio. Isaac never mixed with the townspeople much but they'll know where he lives all the same. I want to be buried next to Father. I do not want to be where *he* is."

"Of course, of course!" Mrs. Thatcher was weeping steadily now, so much that her handkerchief was soaked through and Mr. Thatcher had to retrieve his. Watching her, Alice felt a pang of guilt for wanting to hide the messages.

"Mary apologizes, but she doesn't have the strength to say much more." Dr. Anderson's accent again. "She's sorry to leave you but will try to speak again soon. In the meantime, she hopes you enjoy these gifts."

Mr. Holloway's mouth clapped shut, and a number of objects flopped onto the table, causing everyone to start. Alice could not see them clearly, but the scent was unmistakable. Roses! Reaching out to take one, she was immediately scolded by a thorn. She put the affected finger briefly to her mouth to suck on it.

"Thank you, Mary!" Mrs. Thatcher held the rose closer to the light, where it brightened to a warm pink, and her face crumpled again.

"Pink roses! She wanted pink roses at her wedding, but they were so dear at the shop—this was December—so she carried ones of white silk from my parlor!" Mrs. Thatcher pressed the handkerchief to her face so that only her damp eyes were showing. "Oh, Mary, I'll plant a pink rosebush on your grave, I promise you that!"

But the medium was still silent, staring straight ahead.

"Dr. Anderson, are you still there?" asked Mr. Thatcher.

A few moments passed, and the voice of Dr. Anderson was heard again, tired now. "Please, no more tonight. It takes a great deal of strength to listen to someone with such a faint voice as Mary."

Mr. Holloway's head fell to his chest. His loose locks tumbled over his forehead.

Everyone immediately turned to offer handkerchiefs and soothing words to Mrs. Thatcher, save for Alice. She stared at Mr. Holloway, who had not moved.

"I remember cousin Mary," Isabelle said with a practiced tremble in her voice that suggested an eagerness for attention. "She was so kind. She used to give me sweets whenever we visited."

Alice felt as if she were doing something incredibly private, watching Mr. Holloway unconscious, but she could not take her eyes away. The voices of Dr. Anderson and Mary had not provided any information beyond what she had written down, but Mrs. Thatcher confirmed it all as accurate. And then there were the roses. She imagined that if they had been hidden in the rafters, they would be warm and wilted. But these were crisp in shape, slightly damp and cool as if they had been picked during an early summer rainshower. She stroked the soft petals and briefly allowed herself to imagine the border between the spirit world and the living world as a gray raincloud through which these flowers had passed.

And suddenly her picture of Mary and her own memory fit together in her head—the hands, young and old at the same time, that had stolen the roses from her bedspread in her fever dreams. Pink roses.

The wheels in her mind began to whirr again, attempting to produce a reasonable explanation. Did this mean that the people from her fever dream could all be spirits, spirits who also wanted to tell her something?

But her thought process stopped abruptly when Mr. Holloway's head rose up and his eyes fluttered open, coming into contact with hers. A brief dazed look gave way to a smile, and Alice smiled back before she was even conscious of the movement of her mouth.

Chapter 7

Just before seven the next morning, Alice arrived at Mr. Holloway's tent, so identified by a wooden sign staked out front. With the profusion of inns and hotels that now graced Onset, guest mediums had no need to sleep in such rough quarters. But they still received visitors in one of the sturdy platform tents that had served as shelter for the original members. Wrinkling her nose at the chemical smell of the heavy tent fabric, Alice lifted the flap and ducked inside.

"Mr. Holloway?" Used to the bright morning light outside, Alice's eyes could make out nothing more than a gas lamp, which seemed to be floating in the middle of the tent. A few more squints showed the outline of a table, a chair, and a figure.

"Miss Boyden. I'm glad you came." Mr. Holloway rose from his spot at the table and gave a little bow, then pulled out the opposing chair for Alice. "I thought we might begin, not with your trance, but with mine," he said as she took a seat.

Alice nodded, although she did not understand. She had a habit of nodding automatically, afraid to admit confusion or ignorance about some topic—a trait passed on by her father, who had never been incorrect or ignorant about anything in his life.

"I presumed that while the séance left some unanswered questions, you still doubt your abilities—and mine."

"Well..." she paused, unsure of what to say. She hadn't firmly settled on doubt or belief, but allowed herself to float somewhere in the middle. Her fingers pinched tiny bits of skirt fabric that briefly made her lap into a mountain range, little peaks of blue everywhere.

"You needn't be embarrassed, Miss Boyden." Mr. Holloway closed the tent flap and settled himself in his chair. "In time I think you will accept the task that has been presented to you, and will trust others who have the same ability. But I want you to come to that acceptance by yourself." He laid his hands upon the table, palms up. "Will you take my hands?"

Alice had worn her white kid gloves; she hesitated for a moment before unbuttoning them and offering her bare hands to the medium. It was all she could do not to gasp when he wrapped his fingers around to enclose hers; the impact of his touch was even greater than when she held his hand in the attic, where he had to share his intensity with everyone else.

"I thought you might have some questions—especially questions for which only a spirit would have an answer. I am very familiar with the spirits, but they do not necessarily confide in me the particulars of their situation."

"I do," said Alice. She had been about to nod again, but she had realized that she had not said a word since her initial greeting, and should probably confirm she still had the power of speech. She did not mention that "Dr. Anderson" made her uncomfortable, and that she was here to visit with Mr. Holloway. She felt his pulse through his palms.

"Excellent." Mr. Holloway smiled. He sat up straight, eyes closed, taking deep breaths, and Alice began to grow a little sleepy in the quiet and the heat of the tent. She found herself studying Mr. Holloway's features to keep herself awake. His lips were full, almost feminine, and deeply shadowed in the lamplight. The dim glow carved out his chin, cheek- and browbones as if he were made of marble. Suddenly his eyes jerked open and met hers. She jumped in response.

"Good morning, Miss Mermaid."

Alice fought to keep herself from laughing at the sudden appearance of the accented baritone. "Good morning, Dr. Anderson," she murmured, breaking eye contact with Mr. Holloway. Perhaps it would be easier to stay serious if she did not look directly at him.

"I cannot detect the presence of your spirit guide. Tell me, am I acquainted with him or her?"

After a slight pause, Alice said, "I have no spirit guide." She thought to leave it at that, but honesty elbowed its way into her mouth. "I'm not a medium, Dr. Anderson. I've had some strange spells, but my mother's interest in the spirit world is why we are here at Onset. I am here for the clambakes." She realized how flip she sounded, and rushed to apologize. "I'm sorry, I don't mean to be disrespectful..."

But Dr. Anderson was chuckling, a husky rumble unlike Mr. Holloway's moderately pitched laugh. "Miss Boyden, I do not begrudge you your clambakes. It is important that camps such as these invigorate the body as well as the soul. But I find it hard to believe that you are not a medium yourself, for there are spirits all around you."

A chill prickled Alice's skin. She thought she could feel them now, hovering, reaching out with their ephemeral fingers.

She raised her head again, and Mr. Holloway/Dr. Anderson was looking at her with a smile fixed on his face. "My dear Miss Boyden, the spirits know you can help them, but they are disappointed when their messages do not reach their intended recipient. You must not be afraid of this wonderful gift, which gives you the ability to provide people with the final wishes of their departed loved ones. You'd not deprive them of this comfort, would you?"

Alice shook her head, feeling remorseful.

"I understand that you are a recovering skeptic. It's often the most skeptical who are simply bursting with psychical power. But by denying the existence of a spirit world they are doing themselves, not to mention the world, a great disservice. Because they refuse to accept something so intrinsic to their being, they go through life as an incomplete person—someone who has lost their way. They may get by, but their souls are starving. They have consciously refused to accept their destiny, and therefore denied themselves an opportunity for true fulfillment."

The life of a medium still did not seem a fulfilling one to Alice, but she kept quiet, and remembered Mr. Holloway's suggestion to ask questions of Dr. Anderson that his medium might not be able to answer.

"And is my resistance to these communications what causes my headaches? Mr. Holloway thinks so."

The medium cocked his head, as if listening to a response. "The spirits say they are sorry to cause you pain, but they see so many false prophets, so many who think the séance a mere amusement. You've put up a resistance to believing in the existence of life after death, and who could blame you, with scientists attempting to disprove the concept and corrupt mediums giving them fuel for their high-minded journal articles. The spirits hoped, by making you so vulnerable, that they could get you to listen. They say they have tried to reach out to you before, but have not had a method with which to communicate. They blur your vision to attract attention, but you always retreat and close them off. The notebook provided their first reasonable opportunity, and they thank you for being open to them at last."

Alice thought of all the times her vision had been hijacked by inkblots before the pain of a migraine set in. Now she tried to think of the spots as coming from the exterior, from individual spirits. It was enough to make her head hurt again. "And if I listen to them, will my pain cease?"

"I cannot make that assumption for all of your headaches, but yes, the ones caused by spirits will vanish." The medium tipped his head back, even though his eyes remained closed. "You have the sort of gift we do not often see. Your powers are unrefined, yes. You will need to work with my medium, break down that disbelief. Even the greatest mediums sometimes question their powers, but they do not resist them. Think of it as an enlightenment, this other world opened to you. Why use legs to swim in the ocean when you have a tail at your disposal?

"I'm afraid I must retire now, in order to reserve my strength for the long day ahead of me. But I will leave you with a gift. A garland for the mermaid!"

Alice gasped as something cold and wet fell around her neck. Unable to see it clearly in the dim light, she put her hand to her shoulder and felt a slimy strand, then a slippery bulb. Seaweed. She had never actually touched it before, had only watched it smoke on the beach in a clam-pit or lifted it idly with a walking-stick. Her high neckline absorbed most of the water that still clung to the plant, but at length she felt the drops traveling down her back and pooling at the top of her corset.

Mr. Holloway's body started and his eyes jerked open. "What—oh, my goodness." He stared at Alice's neck ornament. "Oh, Miss Boyden, I'm so sorry. Dr. Anderson can be quite a prankster, though I've told him he must be more polite to ladies. I'm surprised you didn't faint at this cold mess; the shock of it should be enough to take anyone's breath away—there."

His hand accidentally brushed her cheek as he pulled the garland away, making Alice shiver more than the seaweed had.

"Have you taken a chill? No wonder—your collar is soaked through." Even his fingers touching the fabric at her neck prompted another shiver. Alice smiled at him.

"No, really, I'll be all right. It's warm today; I daresay it will prove refreshing," she said.

Mr. Holloway shook his head. "Dr. Anderson usually presents people with scarves and flowers. Here he's given seashells, but never seaweed. I'm worried that a hermit crab will be next. And I'm afraid you won't want to come back after this."

"Dr. Anderson said I would need your guidance," Alice said softly. She watched Mr. Holloway's expression change from one of concern to one of relief.

"I am glad he has such confidence in me that he thinks I might guide someone myself." Mr. Holloway put his hands together as if in prayer and flexed his little and ring fingers. The straight fingers he pressed against his lips as he regarded Alice.

"If Dr. Anderson did not repulse you too much with his prank, I think we should try writing on a slate today. I want to see how adaptable your spirits are."

My spirits, thought Alice. She imagined ghosts floating around in the darkness of the spirit world—for she could only think of the spirit world as darkest night and nothing else—pinned with paper tags on them reading "Alice." Perhaps pins were unnecessary—perhaps anything pressed upon the spirits caught in their mysterious essence.

Mr. Holloway drew a slate from a basket near the table. He opened it to reveal two clean surfaces, not yet clouded by chalk dust. He laid it in front of her, then moved to stand behind her. "Now, as yesterday, I am going to put my hands on your shoulders. Breathe deeply. Close your eyes."

Alice obeyed and tried to settle her mind. She convinced her heart that Thomas's touch was a calming, soothing thing, nothing to accelerate the pulse. The door to unconsciousness was easier to open than she would ever have thought. Still, she entered slowly, easing along and then letting gravity take her down the rest of the way. But suddenly she had the feeling of falling into her chair, and her eyes snapped open on impact. They found Mr. Holloway staring at her.

He looked away so quickly—had she embarrassed herself while in a trance? Had she failed completely? She looked down at the slate.

MY DEAR THUMB BLESS YOU! WHAT A FINE GIRL YOU HAVE HERE. HAIR THE COLOR OF AUNT ETHEL'S. REMEMBER THE SUMMER VISIT WE PAID HER? SUCH FUN. YOU STILL HAVE A STONE FOR SKIPPING, IF I AM NOT MISTAKEN.

Puzzled, she slid the slate over to Mr. Holloway for inspection. But he held up his hand.

"I've already read what's written there, while you were waking. Tell me, Miss Boyden, do you know anything of my family history?"

"No. How could I?' Alice suddenly had the feeling of someone who had not done her homework. Then she realized she was not supposed to know—that this was only a test.

Mr. Holloway brushed his hands against his trouser legs and cleared his throat. "My mother, who was somewhat of a clairvoyant herself, died when I was eight."

"My condolences to you." Alice cast her eyes downward.

"But why should I need your condolences? My mother's spirit is with me always, and here is proof." He tapped the slate with his finger. "My mother used to call me Tom Thumb, or Thumb for short—since, of course, I was always small in her earthly life. We paid her sister Ethel a visit a few months before she died. Her hair was the color of coffee—dark with hints of gold and red, like yours."

Unconsciously, Alice's hand went up to her coiffure. She had never thought of her hair as anything but brown, but Mr. Holloway made it sound almost attractive.

"I skipped stones on the lake by Aunt Ethel." Mr. Holloway reached into the pocket of his waistcoat and pulled out a smooth, flat stone. "I carry this as a sort of talisman, a reminder that my mother is with me as much as this rock is."

He pressed the stone into Alice's palm, and she closed her hand around it, feeling the warmth Mr. Holloway's body had already transferred to it. Her mind struggled to explain the coincidence while her fingers delighted in the object they held.

"You seem to have a gift for receiving messages from those spirits who cannot make themselves heard through other mediums. Mary took strength from your presence last night and made herself known to Dr. Anderson. My mother is rarely heard from. So for you to receive a message from her on one of your first attempts—why, it's marvelous. Absolutely marvelous. And she apparently thinks well of you too."

Alice realized that her smile must be comically wide, and she struggled to keep it under control. Had he simply written the message himself while she was entranced? It did not matter, because his agency would carry an even stronger indication that he wanted to see her again.

Whatever was happening here, Mr. Holloway was pleased with her. And she could be satisfied with that.

They made arrangements for more sessions, all at seven in the morning to avoid interruption. Sometimes it took several mornings to produce an entire message, when a spirit either wrote solely in short spurts or had much to say. Mr. Holloway said that Dr. Anderson tried to make such spirits understand that they would also have the opportunity to speak through his medium, but they still wrote what and how much they wanted to.

Although Mr. Holloway was the main motivation for her visits to the tent, Alice began to enjoy analyzing the messages that she produced. A number of spirits were willing to state their name and with whom they would like to be in contact, making Alice's task simple. She had only to provide Mr. Holloway with a physical description of the proper recipient. More often, however, there were pieces missing; sometimes none of the pieces she had quite fit together, and she had to wonder if they belonged to different puzzles entirely.

To keep her father from suspecting anything, she spent her afternoons buried in scholarship. While reading the pages that many had read before lacked the novelty of spirit messages, it gave her a chance to reset her mind and leave behind the surreality of Mr. Holloway's tent. Some days, however, she could never really regain focus, and it showed in her failure to answer many of the questions her father asked her at dinnertime. She felt oddly wistful for the mindless secretarial work of past summers when she came out of her trance one morning to find Mr. Holloway scratching in a notebook.

"Do you always write in shorthand?"

Mr. Holloway looked up in surprise. "Do you know shorthand? Or can you only recognize it?"

"I can write in and read shorthand." Alice drew herself up in her chair. "I've taken dictation from my father since I was twelve." She recalled the girls in her stenography course that seemed so old then, their hair pinned up and waists pinned in by corsets. Alice had still worn skirts that did not quite reach to her ankles and a big bow in her long, loose hair, expertly tied by Mrs. Connors in the morning. At the time she had relished the glares and exasperated sighs of her classmates, thinking them only jealous of her intelligence and precociousness. Later she realized that the others were there because they needed jobs, some the sole or primary support of their families, and that they were likely annoyed by the optional nature of Alice's attendance.

"I've made a few small changes to the Pitman method that better suit my style of writing, the way I hold my pen," said Mr. Holloway, showing Alice the positioning of his fingers and thumb.

"Why, you write like I do—with your fingers all squashed together." Alice held her pencil to demonstrate.

"Then perhaps you should adopt my revisions." He ran his finger along the open page of his notebook and settled on a symbol. "This, for instance, is an open u sound. For me it just makes more sense to tilt the pen like so..."

Alice scanned the page and laughed. "These aren't just small changes—you've invented your own method."

"Well, nothing that someone as bright as you can't pick up. I shall make a chart for you. I promise that your hand will ache less."

"I'm afraid I haven't been doing much shorthand lately, only the old-fashioned sort of writing." Alice idly filled in one corner of the slate with her pencil, careful to avoid smudging the spirit messages. "My father has relieved me from secretarial duties in order that I might spend time on my own study."

"And how is that progressing?"

Alice sighed. "Not as well as he might have hoped."

"I hope this is not too much of a distraction for you." Mr. Holloway frowned. "I do not wish to interfere with your plans for college. But I would imagine it is easier to study without the headaches."

"Oh, certainly." And Alice realized two weeks had passed since her last attack.

Alice found herself longing to engage Mr. Holloway in less superficial talk—for most of the time she spent with him, her voice was not her own. Before she went into a trance, they spoke only of the weather or the events planned for the week; the time after they spent culling useful information from the scrawls on the slate. But one morning, when her trance was brief and unproductive, Alice seized the opportunity to shift the focus of the conversation.

"I was wondering if you would tell me how you came to spiritualism?" She quickly attempted to bolster the request with reasoning. "I'm curious to know if it was at a later age, or if you were born with the talent. This is all part of trying to make sense of it myself."

"Oh, I don't know if you want to hear the gloomy details of my life 'til now." Mr. Holloway picked at his jacket front and let a piece of lint flutter to the floor.

"Please?"

Mr. Holloway glanced at his pocket-watch. "It is lunchtime now. Do you mind being a bit late?"

"Not at all."

"Then let us begin in Michigan." Mr. Holloway cleared his throat and crossed his legs, folded his hands and cupped his kneecap, pulling it back towards himself.

> I was born in Detroit. My father had come west from New York to establish a better business that he could support in his home state. My mother, of Canadian birth, was a schoolteacher. One day my father was taking a stroll in the park, minding his own business, when he heard someone behind him say, "I've been looking for you."
>
> He glanced backward, and standing there was a woman he'd never seen before. He wanted to correct her, but she was too beautiful—he couldn't simply say, "I'm sorry, you must have the wrong person."
>
> But he couldn't think of what else to say to keep her there—my father was rather shy—so he simply smiled at her. Luckily, she continued to hold the lead in the conversation. "My name is Marie Chester. What's yours?"
>
> So perhaps she wasn't mistaking him for someone else—surely she would have known the name of the person she was seeking. My father suddenly felt a little uneasy about this woman, who had fixed her bright, earnest eyes on his face and would not break eye contact—whenever he looked away and back again, her gaze stayed in line with his.
>
> She certainly was dressed respectably, and so despite her boldness my father decided she must not be a lady of ill repute. He introduced himself as Allen Holloway. She laughed at this and he began to think she must be mad.
>
> "You probably think I'm mad—and I would not blame you," she told him. "But you see, last night I peeled an apple in one piece and threw the peel out the window and it formed the letter A. And

then I dreamed of a man I'd never seen before—that's you—and I thought that he must be my future husband, with whom I was yet to become acquainted. Lo and behold, the next day…"

She trailed off at this point, as if realizing for the first time that my father had said but two words. "You aren't already married, are you?"

My father shook his head, in disbelief at his fortune. He thought he would never find a wife, as he had no way with words around women, and pretty ones especially were hard to come by in this still quite spread-out state. If this woman thought they were meant to be married, he thought that was a fine idea.

"So, you see, Miss Boyden, my mother sometimes dreamed of things that were going to happen, although she never referred to herself as a medium." Mr. Holloway had been looking up during his story, towards the apex of the tent, but now he addressed Alice directly. "We all thought these occasional premonitions were just a normal motherly occurrence—we being my older sister Maggie and me."

"Did your mother know of your powers before she died, then?" asked Alice.

"In truth, I am not sure I had any powers at that age," said Mr. Holloway. "If I had, then surely I would have foreseen the death of my mother. But it took me quite by surprise."

We moved to a small town outside of Detroit while I was very small; we enjoyed a broad plot of land and genial neighbors. My mother had a generally cheerful disposition, and so the afternoon I came in from play and found her crying into her apron, I knew something had to be wrong.

She held me close and gave me several firm kisses on the forehead. "Oh, my dear boy, my dear dear boy," was all she could say.

I let her squeeze me and cry on me much longer than most boys of eight could tolerate, but finally I had to ask what was the matter. Mother smiled at me, although I could see her eyes were still sad.

"Our next two months together are going to be wonderful," she said, and went back to making bread, humming as she kneaded, as if nothing out of the ordinary had happened. And I promptly forgot about her tears, for the time being.

And the next two months *were* wonderful—it seemed like every day she had some new surprise for us, like the first crocus of spring, or a new kind of homemade candy. But then my mother took to her bed. She did not complain of any particular pain, but would take only soup and a little porridge. After several days of this, she called Maggie and me to her bedside and asked us how we had enjoyed our time together. My sister and I, of course, gave an enthusiastic review.

"That is what I had hoped, to leave you with a fond memory of me. For two months ago I had a dream that I would have to leave you today, and I wanted to make sure I gave you all the love I could in the amount of time we had left."

Being still quite young, we had not envisioned such a tragic end to our weeks of fun, and we both began to cry. We knelt beside the bed and lay our heads upon the bump of our mother's leg beneath the covers. She stroked our heads in turn, and we must have fallen asleep like that, for when we next were conscious of our surroundings, we found her cold.

Although we mourned the loss of our mother deeply, Maggie's and my grief could not rival my father's. His was profound and all-encompassing; as we tentatively began to take pleasure in various activities again, he began to take pleasure in drink. And my shy father became an outspoken critic of town affairs, using the saloon stool as his pulpit. Maggie, only eleven, took responsibility for making sure he got home before a fight broke out. She took on the role of mother, cooking meals, mending clothes, and making sure I went to school.

When Maggie was fifteen a gentleman by the name of Beare came through our town; he was an investor sort, very well-off and handsome to boot—certainly no younger than thirty, though. Well, he had not been in town but two weeks when he disappeared abruptly—and my sister along with him. I suppose my father, being inebriated most of the time, did not mind Maggie as much as a girl of that age should be minded, and I, being young and ignorant of such things, did not really wonder about my sister's activities outside the house. I was only hurt that she did not take me with her. I overheard one woman in town saying it would be a blessing if Maggie were found dead, as it would save her the shame of having run off with a man. But I knew she was alive—I felt sure that if our mother could foretell her own death, that her children would be able to feel the worldly absence of the other.

My father's business had been in slow decline ever since my mother's death, and after Maggie ran off, its collapse was precipitous. We had few friends in the community where we had once had many; the church was not eager to help, as none of us had attended in years. My father was too proud for handouts, but I don't think he realized the extent of my hunger—he being used to filling his gut with grain of the liquid sort, and I a growing boy. Were it not for a schoolteacher who slipped me potatoes and heels of bread, I might have starved.

Perhaps it was my mother watching over us; perhaps someone back home had managed to reach my sister with news on how poorly we were getting along. Or perhaps it was coincidence. But however it came about, two years after Maggie had run off, we received a letter from her—or from a Mrs. William Beare of New York City; it wasn't until I opened the envelope and read the signature that I understood Mrs. Beare was my sister. But, having helped Maggie respond to condolences sent upon the death of my mother, I knew what the black-bordered paper implied.

Mr. Beare had done the respectable thing and married her, Maggie said, but he had taken ill with some kind of ague—there were too many people in New York City, and about three-quarters of them were sick at a time, she said—and he had died last month. When she went to the pension board, hoping for compensation as the widow of a veteran, the board had refused to acknowledge his service in the war. She had begun to take in boarders to support herself—no mention of where Beare's wealth had gone. But it was frightening being in the city by herself, and with strange men to boot. Would my father and I come to New York? I could help with meals and housekeeping and Father could probably find work nearby.

So that is how, at the age of fourteen, I came to live in New York, having prepared for the trip primarily by myself, with the help of one neighbor whom I suspect was glad to assist because she wished to be rid of us. But in fairness, she was nothing but kind to me in my last days there, and gave me a little money and food for the journey.

Not having left the state of Michigan in my life, hardly having left the town in which I grew up, I was ill prepared for the long journey. I had little sense of the timing of trains and stagecoaches. Once I had my pocket picked outright; other times I was swindled by greedy coachmen and innkeepers who saw in a young boy and his drunkard father an easy route to extra pennies. I had hoped our financial state would keep my father sober, but he had brought along a stash of whiskey and kept his taste for it, so that when his bottle went dry he wanted money for more, and when I wouldn't give it to him he struck me and took it anyway.

Somehow we made it to Maggie's house, nearly penniless and much the worse for wear. I had cut my foot at some point in the journey, and the wound had festered, so that I limped like a little cripple. Father was even more slovenly, wearing the same stained, foul-smelling clothing with which he had left Michigan. Maggie greeted us in a much tidier condition, but her clothes had had their share of wear, too. She had aged twenty years since I had seen her, it seemed. Tired and footsore as I was, I was grateful she had sent for us.

But Maggie was woefully ignorant of the realities of employment in New York. In any place where Father was qualified to work, an Italian or a Hebrew would work for less money, longer hours, and be sober to boot. Within a month he was dead, stabbed in a bar brawl, and my sister and I found ourselves alone.

Mr. Holloway stopped abruptly, as if someone had snagged him from behind and stopped him in the pursuit of his story. "Please forgive me. You ask me a simple question and I give you the longest answer possible. I am surprised you have not excused yourself already."

Alice shook her head vigorously. "No, please, continue. I'd like to hear the rest of your story." These revelations made her feel protective of Mr. Holloway; she wished she had been there when he was a small boy, to soothe him after the death of his mother, to make his sister realize the error of her ways, to wrest the drink from his father's hand.

"Well, at least I am at the point in the story where I was introduced to spiritualism," said Mr. Holloway, "and so I can directly address your original query."

A year or so after my father's death, a spiritualist came to board with us. He didn't announce his profession until he asked if he could use our parlor for a séance room. Maggie refused at first, but when he offered to pay double the usual rent for the privilege, she couldn't afford to say no. Sometimes the boardinghouse would be full and sometimes nearly empty, and we had only two other boarders at the time.

I took care of much of the housekeeping myself. When I went to clean the parlor one day, I noticed something different about the loveseat. Upon a closer look, I found that a battered volume of red leather lay there; its color had made it blend in with the faded upholstery.

It was a collection of verses, by a poet of whom I had never heard. I still remember the frontispiece and the title page—a pen-and-ink rendering of a woman sitting at her desk, bent over her writing materials, while a transparent man stood behind her, his hand on—or through—her shoulder. The title was simply *Poems*, by one H. M. Shaw, but the subtitle made up for its predecessor's brevity: *Being a Collection of Verses Produced by Spirit Communication with the Author, as Transcribed by Miss Cecelia Button, Medium*. I don't want you to think I was a worker given to distraction and procrastination, but this intrigued me, and the house was quiet. I do not know how long I sat there, transfixed by those poems—they were not the finest I'd ever read, and positively awkward in some places, but there was an essence they contained, a certain uninhibited emotion, that kept me turning the pages.

"Mr. Shaw has some talent, no?"

I looked up to see the spiritualist standing there, a not-unkind look on his face, but I must have turned completely red thinking of how to explain my indolence as well as my invasion of his private property.

"His," the man continued, "was one of the first spirit-written books I purchased, back when I was first starting out in my profession. Tell me, do you find more to like in the poems themselves or in their origin?"

Now, at this point in my life, I had not thought much of spirits. I didn't believe or disbelieve—it was simply a lack of consideration on the whole. After all, the most important spirit, my mother, had never reached out to me. And yet I was aware that she had foreseen her own death, and had always wondered how. "I think that there is something imperfect in the communication, but..." And then I tried to explain what the poems conveyed, just as I explained them to you.

He laughed. "You are very diplomatic, Mr. Holloway. Those poems are rubbish. But I felt the same way upon reading them as you did." He then mentioned that he was in need of an assistant of sorts. "I like to keep track of who has visited me—insurance against forgetting their names or those of their dead loved ones. I also need someone to take account of donations so that I might properly acknowledge their generosity. How are you at arithmetic?"

I told him I had always done well with sums.

"And do you know shorthand?"

I didn't, and felt a great disappointment—he would not want me as his assistant now. And I realized how quickly I had grown attached to the idea of helping him.

"It is no matter—I am sure you are a quick learner."

Maggie was again reluctant, but much less so once he offered compensation for my assistance. That is how I learned shorthand. And that is how I entered the world of spiritualism.

Mr. Holloway raised his eyebrows and held his hands out, as if to say, *That is all I have to offer.* But for Alice, it was plenty. Knowing nothing about love herself, save for the idealized version that appeared in novels, she had struggled with how to categorize her feelings. She had decided that she could not truly be in love with someone about whom she knew next to nothing. But with these revelations now in her possession, Alice gave her eager heart permission to admit it: she was in love with Thomas Chester Holloway.

Chapter 8

Alice pasted these conversations with Mr. Holloway into a mental scrapbook, and she made it her goal to add at least one memento each session. Her questions initially focused on his past, but she inevitably craved a rough sketch of his future; perhaps she would discover if it held any room for her.

"Will you be returning to New York at the end of the summer, or do you have other places to visit?" She asked this after a particularly productive session, hoping her success would encourage an honest reply.

"Oh, I am always on the move," sighed Mr. Holloway. "I tell people that my home is in New York City, for everyone must have some place to call home; else what makes you any better than a tramp? But to give the honest truth, I do not spend much time there. For the past few years, I have spent the majority of my time in the Midwest."

"Midwest?" repeated Alice. "Do you go back and forth between the big cities, then?" She pictured Mr. Holloway staying in the finest hotels of Detroit and Chicago and St. Louis, their lobbies adorned with sumptuous velvet curtains and chandeliers that burst into a thousand pieces of light.

"Oh, not very often. Really only for meetings, conferences, private invitations. I prefer to set up shop in the smaller cities and towns, places that might have been touched by the spiritualist movement but have few resident mediums. I take a vacant storefront, or a spare hotel parlor, and set out a sign. People in these places have...an earnestness, a sincerity, that those in the largest cities sometimes lack. That is not to say that there are no serious practitioners in the cities—there are plenty. But to those in the more rural areas, a séance is not a pastime or an evening's entertainment. It is an opportunity to ask questions that no one else has been able to answer for them."

The thought of traveling beyond established cities made Alice uneasy. Here in Massachusetts, rural areas were still a reasonable distance from Boston or Hartford or Providence. Alice had always regarded points further west with particular apprehension, believing you could travel for days without a sign of civilization—a land so vast that it could swallow you up and leave behind nothing but a mystery.

"I do come upon the occasional town that has been swindled by a previous visitor professing to be a medium," Mr. Holloway continued.

"His victims might not have abandoned their belief in spiritualism, but they are wary. Those few who come to me despite their doubts, I ask to talk with me for a while before I go into trance. Who in the town was tricked? How much money did they lose? Then I reach out to the victims and offer to sit with them privately, for free. There are inevitably a few whose faith cannot be regained, but most I leave with faith restored."

"When do you know when to leave?"

"I make it clear at the outset that my time in town will be brief, but I never commit myself to a certain number of days. Dr. Anderson tends to tire of a place when he is there too long. So I leave before he becomes ornery and begins to ignore my patrons' questions. I was worried about how to hold his attention in Onset. I am happy to say that, likely owing to your influence, that he has shown no restlessness, and has been very accommodating to the campers here."

"You must meet so many interesting people," Alice murmured. Do you make friends? Do they invite you back?"

"Oh, yes—I've met a number of people on the road whom I would care to call friends," said Mr. Holloway. "But I do not often return to a place within the course of a year—my philosophy being that there are many more towns to find anew, and more people who need my assistance. Also, that gives any agitators time to cool their tempers."

"Really? Out in those small towns?" Alice did not say that she thought all such people gullible enough to accept whatever a medium told them.

"Certainly. Usually they are gruff old men in threadbare suits, short on money, long on self-righteous intellectualism. They want everyone else to be as disillusioned with the world as they are. I find them less of a bother in wintertime, when they are less inclined to leave the warmth of their houses simply to stir up trouble. It is well that I am spending this warmer season in a community of spiritualists."

"But surely you don't pay much attention to the naysayers." Alice was suddenly angered by the idea that someone would harass Mr. Holloway.

Mr. Holloway shrugged. "I do if they try to ruin the experience for others with their unfounded claims—well, what man should tolerate such an insult to his profession? They *are* tickled by the thought that they drove me out of town, but I tell all my loyal visitors that it is not for some embarrassment of proof they have presented, but rather that the spirits will be less communicative if they sense that a nonbeliever is present. The spirits will try and convince anyone of their existence once, and then if the person is unconvinced they no longer waste their time.

"But then, enough about me and my detractors. Today," said Mr. Holloway, "I think we should try something different. I think you should try to put yourself into a trance."

Alice felt her pleasant mood of the morning wilt. And how would that affect their sessions, if she were successful? Would they be less frequent, or end altogether? "Don't I need your help for that?"

Mr. Holloway shook his head. "If you're going to be receptive to spirits, you must be prepared for them all the time, not just during our few hours a week. One ear to the other world, always. Soon it will come naturally. Now"—he took a seat across from her and turned down the gas to a flicker—"close your eyes and breathe deeply. I will not touch you."

Alice did as told, her hand holding the chalk above the slate. She waited for what seemed like ten minutes, trying not to be distracted by the muffled footsteps of the occasional passerby, her own heartbeat, Mr. Holloway's faint even breathing...and the realization that if she succeeded in putting herself into a trance, there might be no reason for them to have such frequent sessions.

She opened her eyes and shook her head. "I cannot do it. I think I need your guidance for a while longer."

"Of course. And you will have it." Mr. Holloway smiled. "After all, one may do anything in a trance. It is about surrendering control. Given the pens and pencils you broke during your first foray into spirit communication, perhaps it's best that I continue to supervise you."

Alice quite willingly closed her eyes again. She mentally took herself through Mr. Holloway's preparations and imagined his hands on her shoulders.

It took longer than she was used to, but eventually a cozy warmth, not the stickiness of summer air but the comfort of a winter hearth or a dry clear day, overtook her. It was like drinking a mug of chocolate in January, or how she imagined a salamander would feel, curled up on a sunny rock. Then she started, her heart pounding. Disrupted again—and she had felt so close this time! She was about to apologize to Mr. Holloway when she noticed that the slate was covered with script from top to bottom. Her hands were dry and dusty from gripping the slate pencil.

Mr. Holloway turned up the lamp. "You were in a trance for a good half-hour."

Alice blinked. "I felt as if I were asleep for only a moment."

"And that is why we mediums are rarely bored," Mr. Holloway said. "You can receive for three hours, have every ounce of energy sucked out of you, but the time will stop. You will not remember your exertions. Of course, some may think this an easy way to make a living, but they do not consider the toll on the psyche, nor the fact that the medium must relinquish complete control of their bodies and minds."

"Do you think your mediumship has hurt you?"

"Certainly. I have no outward signs of wear and tear, thank goodness. But only a decade and a half of talking to spirits and already I find it more difficult than I did at the beginning. I had an easy time of it then, but now making that first connection takes something out of me. That's why your communications have been so helpful. I still feel drained after a séance, but ready to fill up the well again. I do not want to seem ungrateful for Onset hospitality, not at all, but devoting a day to intense introspection and then needing to be a sociable creature at the supper table, well, it's a challenge. And then there is the occasional lecture on top of that, and meetings with you..."

Alice swallowed. Was she a burden to him? "We can meet less often..." she began reluctantly.

"I'm sorry, Alice—I did not mean to imply you were the source of my trouble. Did I not just finish saying what a help you've been?"

Alice nodded shyly—then realized that he had used her first name. Was he conscious of this? But Mr. Holloway—Thomas—took her hand, and she knew the intimate address must have been deliberate.

"It is not every medium—perhaps not any medium—who finds himself in the company of a superior medium, one who only wishes to help him."

"I am glad to be of service." Alice thought that in the dark tent, she must be aglow.

It was nearly one when Alice returned to the cottage, euphoria carrying her along the road and down the bluff. She carelessly slid her hand along the railing as she climbed the steps to the porch, forgetting what state it was in, and felt a poke in the fleshy part of her hand below the thumb, then a burn. She paused to examine the depth of the splinter; seeing a bit of wood still protruding from the skin, she scraped at it with a fingernail.

"Alice!"

Her father's voice broke her concentration. She glanced up to see his eyes steely behind their spectacles.

"Where have you been?"

"For a walk. I lost track of time." She looked down to see how the work on her hand was progressing, but the splinter had broken off below the skin, and she would have to fetch a needle and tweezers to finish the job.

Mr. Boyden tapped his fingers on the railing. "Perhaps containing your walks to under three hours would be beneficial to your academic progress." He held out several sheets of paper, which Alice recognized as the essay she had composed the night before.

"Your arguments are weak, to say the least."

Alice avoided her father's eyes and studied the chipping paint on the steps, light blue paint giving way to the silver-brown ash beneath. She knew very well that her paper was lacking in originality and intellectual heft, but she had only wanted to finish it in time for dinner. She should have known her father would not accept such substandard work. "Sometimes there are limited ways in which to make a point."

"Yes, if one has not put in the time to explore other arguments."

Alice reached for the essay. "I'll rewrite it today."

"No." Her father held the papers behind him. "You'll begin a new one today. Harvard won't give you the opportunity to redo a poor paper. You will only have the chance to redeem yourself with a superior paper for a different assignment. Which I have left on your desk."

Alice tried to tell herself that her father was only pushing her towards the excellence she needed to succeed in academia, and that it was good for her. But at the moment, she was not feeling particularly grateful for his help. "May I first have something to eat, at least?"

"I suggest you take your meals in your room today. Nora will bring you something. And for that matter, you ought to stay close to the cottage for the rest of the week. You will need at least that much time to compensate for your half-hearted efforts." Ignoring Alice's squeak of protest, her father reentered the cottage with a heavier tread. She heard the quite deliberate closing of his study door.

What would she do without Thomas for an entire week? Alice tamped down the sorrow welling and told herself not to panic—her mother would surely set things straight. Her lengthy "morning walks" had kept away the headaches, after all.

But her mother would not be back until evening, and likely couldn't save her from the new essay altogether.

Several discarded beginnings later, Alice found herself staring at a blank new page while her hand doodled on a previous attempt. Flowers, vines, trees. Alice had some talent in drawing flora and fauna and could produce a fair copy of the various bones and tendons found in her father's anatomy book, but somehow she had always had difficulty in drawing manmade objects. The particular pattern of a vase eluded her, as did the trinkets with which her mother adorned the cottage.

Perhaps botany should be her academic focus, and then she could sketch plants and flowers to her heart's content. But Alice could not shake her father's view that botany was a safe department in which to drop women interested in science, for upon their graduation they could go straight to cultivating a beautiful and productive garden for their husbands and families. Did she want to spend years of learning Latin names and the chemistry of soil so that she could have the right herbs for dinner, the right flowers to decorate her home for company?

The light of the waning sun shifted and illuminated the blank page before her. She wished that essay writing could be like spirit-writing—close her eyes, breathe deeply, awake to something she didn't remember having written.

Or could it?

Perhaps she should try, just try...

Entering the trance took some time, as the movement of her parents downstairs broke Alice's concentration more than once. Although the cottage was much newer than their house in Cambridge, its simple construction and minimal insulation meant every footstep translated into a sharp creak. A brief silence was soon punctuated by the sound of her parents arguing, and she had to restrain herself from trying to pluck words from the gibberish that made its way up the stairs. She had nearly given up when the now-familiar tingling came over her, and she relaxed into the syrupy warmth of unconsciousness.

Her eyes eased their way back open to darkness. The last light of the day had faded. She fumbled for the key to the lamp, which illuminated a line of blue ink on the page.

If we help you now, what hope is there for you on examination day? Spirits are not allowed in the examination rooms at Harvard.

Suitably chastised, Alice sighed and turned to a fresh page.

Chapter 9

To Alice's dismay, her father followed through on his threat, confronting her with calculus when she tried to slip away the next morning. She slunk back to her room with the assignment, but soon turned her attention to a note for Thomas. Surely her mother would be willing to serve as courier—it was only polite to explain her absence.

The occasion warranted a simple message, and yet four drafts lay in pieces before Alice realized why the task was so difficult, why the right balance of politeness and earnestness eluded her. Even the most eloquent missive could not convey her true feelings for him.

She was wondering whether to let her mother chance a verbal explanation when a spot of pain flickered behind her eye. It quickly disappeared, and Alice did not think much of it. But then it hopped back beneath her brow, like a tiny toad in peril, propelling itself beyond reach. Instinct always made her press her fingers against the spot that hurt, as if she had only struck it against something hanging from the ceiling. The gesture never made much difference, but at least it felt as if she were doing *something* to combat the pain—that she was not totally helpless against the headache.

But perhaps she did not have to be so helpless.

Alice locked her door and drew the curtains. She sat at her desk again and cleared it of everything except a notebook and a pen. Closing her eyes, she tried to reclaim that feeling of sunshine on her face. The pain—a sneaky creature with erratic movements, growing larger by the minute—threatened to kill her concentration, but she persisted, lifting her chin higher. And there it was, that seasonless warmth, starting on her brow and cheeks and working its way through her body. In her last moments of consciousness, she thought she felt Thomas take her hand in his, and she let her fear out in a sigh.

She awoke with her head on the blotter, staring at her hand, which she had somehow managed to scratch in her trance: dried blood beaded at the conclusion of raised pink lines. The page in front of her contained mostly scribbles, but a few sentences emerged towards the bottom of the page:

I had the good fortune of running across Stephen. I knew him by his marmalade coat. He wanted me to tell you that he would have died that day you found him if not for your care, and that the last of his days were wonderfully happy ones, and that his death was not your fault—his weakened heart just gave out, but it was filled with love for you at the end.

Outside of Thomas's tent and without his explanation, the message seemed nonsensical. Without his guidance, perhaps stray messages meant for others made their way to her pencil. But the headache had ceased to take hold, and Alice said a silent thank-you to Stephen, whoever he was.

The first day of August brought a sticky, buggy heat that surpassed the discomfort of any day since the Boydens' arrival. Alice had gone to bed hoping the night would cool things off, but the stationary air maintained its temperature, and she awoke in a sweat. Even the bay breezes, usually so dependable at cooling the cottage, were infrequent.

Mrs. Boyden had eaten lunch at the cottage perhaps twice this summer, as she thought the lunchtime séances were less crowded; she joked every year that she preferred spirits to sandwiches. But today she complained that the tents were too hot for séances, and joined her daughter's usually solitary midday table.

"You would think there were coals underneath the platform," said Mrs. Boyden. "Or Hell."

"Aren't spirits supposed to lower the temperature with their presence?" Alice asked innocently.

"Well, we still need to wait for them to appear, and it can be beastly until they do." Mrs. Boyden fanned herself for effect.

Alice pointedly returned to her book, attempting to show great interest, although her mother's interruptions had kept her on the same page for some time.

"I spent the morning in a séance with Mr. Holloway," said Mrs. Boyden, a minute later. "He asked after you."

"He did? What did he say?" Alice shut her book without even the pretense of keeping her place.

Mrs. Boyden looked pleased that her announcement had provoked a reaction. "He said that he hoped that your studies were going well, and that you would be available to visit again soon."

Alice's eyes wandered back to the cover of her book. "Well, if Father wouldn't keep such a close eye on me, perhaps I could escape one of these mornings."

"I hardly think you need to skulk like that."

"Well, yes, I do, if I am to keep the visits secret from Father."

"Oh, your father knows. I told him."

"You told him?" Alice swallowed, torn between her mother's betrayal of a confidence and relief that she was no longer responsible for initiating such a conversation with him. "When were you going to tell me that you told him?"

Mrs. Boyden shrugged. "I assumed he would broach the topic with you. Perhaps he has been impressed with your output and wishes to keep your focus a bit longer."

"You are both quite wicked," Alice muttered.

"Pardon?" When Alice did not immediately repeat herself, Mrs. Boyden continued.

"I told your father to think of the sessions as visits to a doctor. 'She's looked so well lately, hasn't she?' I said, and he could not disagree. And then I suggested he might feel more comfortable with the idea if Mr. Holloway came by for tea sometime. Perhaps even dinner. Then he can judge Mr. Holloway's character for himself, though I am sure he will find it as impeccable as I do."

"Father didn't exactly welcome him to Onset the last time that they spoke."

"Last time?" Mrs. Boyden looked confused. "Oh, yes, the dinner. I believe he was just cranky at being torn away from his laboratory for a social event."

"And yet he was so genial at first, when Mr. Holloway asked about his work. Whatever excuse he had, he was terribly rude and embarrassing."

Mrs. Boyden sighed. "You know your father's social skills leave much to be desired," she said. "But if you expressed your favor for Mr. Holloway, I'm sure your father would be civil."

"Even if he does not have a Harvard degree, or is not pursuing one?"

"Well, doesn't he have one from Michigan?"

"No, Mother."

"Oh." Mrs. Boyden was momentarily quiet, searching for an appropriate response. "Well, this country was built by self-made men and women. And plenty of intelligent people don't have the opportunity to go to college. I, for one, didn't have a tenth of the opportunities now available to you as a woman." This was Mrs. Boyden's favorite refrain. "If we have him to visit, perhaps your father and Mr. Holloway can find some common ground. I just think a visit would be proper, if he should be considered a suitor for our only daughter."

"*Mother.*" If Alice's face wasn't already red from the heat, it surely was now. "I am not sure you should think of him in that way."

"And yet you won't look me in the eye when you say it."

Alice finished a draft of her French essay before bed, thinking it a passable garden that simply needed to be weeded; she was frustrated to find a thorny thicket when she awoke. She had hoped to complete it quickly and then sneak away to a 7 a.m. session with Thomas, proving to her father—and herself—that she could balance her academic commitments with more enjoyable summer activities. But questions left partly answered and major themes unaddressed delayed her progress; another subpar essay might prompt her father to further restrict her activities. By the time she had revised and recopied to her satisfaction, the sun was too bright for anything earlier than nine.

Very quietly, she crept down the hall to her father's study and slid the papers beneath his door with a minimum of rustling. She held her breath as she stood upright again and was beginning to move away, hoping the creaking boards wouldn't betray her, when a gruff voice sounded from behind the door.

"Alice. Come in."

Alice winced, but her obedient hand lifted the latch before she had time to think through an escape.

"Where are you off to so early?" He kept his eyes on his papers, yet Alice still felt his scrutiny.

"I think you know." When her father made no reply, Alice swallowed. "I am going to visit Mr. Holloway."

Mr. Boyden's face remained impassive. "Do you think that paper will meet my approval?" He jerked his head towards the pages in Alice's hand.

"Yes, I do."

Mr. Boyden held out his hand for the pages and began to read—with deliberate slowness, Alice thought. She took a deep breath.

"The only time I've suffered a headache since beginning our meetings is this past week, when I was prevented from seeing him."

Her father pointed to a line at the bottom of the page. "Your argument would have been strengthened here by the consideration of Conway's work, though I don't suppose I brought him with me." A beat passed, and then: "You can imagine my displeasure at first. But your mother convinced me that these meetings were good for your health, and so I did not put a stop to them. This is not to say I don't consider them ridiculous. But the mind has managed to convince the body of stranger things, I suppose." He finally looked up, folding his hands and placing them on top of the essay like a paperweight. "I will not forbid you from something that eases your pain. I am a skeptic, but not an ogre. You are quite useless when you have headaches, besides." Something like a smile twitched his mouth. "However, your mother leads me to believe you may have an interest in this Mr. Holloway that surpasses your desire for medical treatment, and I wonder about the propriety of your meeting with him in private without a chaperone."

Alice blushed. "*Father*. I hope you would not think that of me..."

Her father held his hand up. "It is not you that I worry about. I have had only one encounter with this young man, which is hardly enough time to read the nature of his character. In addition, I had hoped you would ultimately fall in love with an educated man. Has he even completed secondary school?"

"Father! I have not said anything about love..."

"You may visit him this morning, but for an hour only. I shall have commentary on your essay when you return."

He returned his attention to the pages in front of him. Alice wanted to explain the situation further, but neither did she wish to give him a chance to rescind his permission. She closed the door slowly and quietly behind her, then hurried outside.

Alice found the flap to Thomas's tent closed but not secured, his usual signal to her that she might enter. And there he was, writing notes in the lamplight, seemingly unchanged from the last time she had seen him. She wasn't sure why she had expected to see a difference after only a week's absence.

"Miss Boyden. How lovely to see you. Have you been given a reprieve from your academic schedule?"

"Yes, at last."

"While I understand your father's desire to keep to a schedule, I was worried about your health. To commune with the spirits three or four times a week and then stop altogether—it seems a gamble."

Alice could not keep the pride off her face. "When I was ill last week, I was able to put myself into a trance. It helped me to avoid the worst of the pain."

Thomas's eyes widened. "Did you now?" he said, with the tone of a mother whose child had managed to dress herself for the first time. "And did you produce a message?"

"Yes. But it does not seem to be addressed to me."

"May I see it?"

Alice handed the paper to Thomas, watched him sort through and discard the incoherencies at the top of the page and then pause at the legible text. He stared at it a long time, stroked his mustache. She was surprised to see him look up at her with glistening eyes.

"Amazing. I have long wondered—but have never had proof of—animals moving on to the spirit world." Seeing Alice's quizzical expression, Thomas explained: "Stephen was a cat." He took a deep breath before continuing.

"I found him when I was six, after a heavy snowstorm. I was building a snow-fort when I heard a mewling from the bushes on the edge of our property. He was all skin and bones, hair matted with mud and frozen stiff. I took him inside and Mother prepared a warm bath for him in a basin, and I gently scrubbed him all over—which he didn't particularly like, but he was too weak to struggle much—and wrapped him in a towel when I was done and gave him some milk. From the grime I thought him to be a calico cat, but his fur was pure marmalade. I slept with him in my bed that night, and named him Stephen—I don't know why, I just liked that name—and nursed him for a week, thinking he was gaining strength. I never let him out of my sight, but one morning I woke to find him cold. I felt I had failed him, that if I had only been a better nurse he would still be alive. My mother tried to tell me that I had given him the best care I could, and that his body had been through a great deal, but I was inconsolable." He held up the page. "You would think, after knowing him only a week, that I would not care so much for an animal, and that it would certainly not matter years later, but—" His voice, cracking throughout the narrative, finally broke apart, and Alice watched him struggle against the tears that rolled down his face.

She had never seen a man cry before. The only man Alice knew well, her father, disliked such displays of emotion, and would never allow himself to enter such a state. But Alice's own vision blurred—for little Stephen; for little Thomas, so devastated; for the kindness of his mother, wanting to bring him news of Stephen's happiness; and for herself, the messenger, who had dismissed the words as meaningless.

"I've never known anyone to make contact with the spirit of an animal, since they cannot speak for themselves," Thomas said, in a steadier voice. He dabbed at his eyes and mustache with his handkerchief. "So, what a breakthrough this is—a human spirit speaking for an animal spirit! You cannot imagine what peace this has given me, to know that Stephen's brave soul has continued on, and that I did help him."

Alice shook her head and gave him a damp smile. No, she couldn't imagine, though the explanation of his mother's message was helping her build a peace of her own. Without it, she would have never understood the purpose of the orange cat who had torn her curtains during the fever. She looked down at her scratched right hand, saw how a set of small claws could have made such marks…

Chapter 10

"How are your preparations for the fall examinations progressing?"

The question startled Alice. They might speak of their pasts and the goings-on of the present in Thomas's tent, but they did not venture into the future, beyond Onset. To speak of September, or the Annex exams, might break the delicate bubble that encapsulated the summer.

"My arguments are not as groundbreaking as my father would wish, but at least I do not have the headaches to break my concentration."

Thomas did not reply to this, but began to study Alice with the intensity of a scientist intent on a new discovery, and Alice blushed to find herself under the microscope so.

"I know that you have been working towards Harvard all summer, but I sense that your heart is not in it."

"It's not." Although she felt that way, deeply, Alice surprised herself with how absolute her reply sounded. "Even if I persevere for four years, I'll have nothing to show for my studies but a certificate. I can't imagine we'll receive stellar instruction from professors who likely see us as either a burden or an extra source of income." The misgivings poured out as if Thomas had broken a dam. "You might think I'd warrant special treatment for being the daughter of a professor, but many of my classmates will likewise be affiliated with the Harvard community, and I suspect that a number of instructors do not like my father, anyway."

Thomas cocked his head. "He does not seem the type to cultivate false friends."

"Or true friends, either. He knows insects intimately, but has only a cursory relationship with his fellow faculty members."

Alice loved how Thomas's face changed when he smiled: the slight outer-eye creases pronounced, the lips stretched wide to expose fine teeth, the cheek-apples rounded to meet his mustache, the slight flopping of his hair as he tilted his head. She had not had much opportunity to observe him around others, but she wondered if he grinned as much for anyone else.

Thomas leaned forward in his chair, hands clasped together. "I would like to tell you about the arrangement I've been considering. I have, for some time now, sought an assistant of sorts. Someone to not only coordinate séance appointments, but to serve as sort of a warm-up medium, and do as you have done this summer—entrust my Dr. Anderson to complete and deliver fragments of previously collected messages. I have found it a most efficient way to work, and it ensures that someone with whom I sit will be satisfied with the experience. To that end, I was wondering if you, Alice, would be interested in accompanying me on my travels, and continuing our partnership."

Alice suddenly felt dizzy. Had Thomas just invited her to be his companion? As in, they would spent long hours together in exciting places, and she would not be trapped in a half-mile circuit between home and her Annex classrooms for the next several years?

And did he mean to imply that they had more than a strictly professional partnership?

"I know you are probably thinking of propriety." Thomas interrupted Alice's silence. "We would have different rooms, on different floors, if you like; we would avoid retiring at the same time; I could even call you sister."

Sister? Hearing the platonic title made Alice realize that she wanted something entirely different. She spoke from the heart, without letting her mind weigh in.

"You would not want to call me your wife?"

Thomas's enthusiastic expression froze then, and Alice wished the words were beads on a string that she could quickly wind back into her mouth, but they had fallen out loose into the tent and rolled into every corner. Would it be less humiliating, Alice wondered, to open the tent flap right now and flee, or to wait for an answer?

"Part of me is overjoyed that you voiced your affection, as I have been too afraid to speak of my fondness for you."

Alice's heart thrilled.

"...but part of me knows why I have not yet spoken to my feelings."

Why was he frowning?

"Dear, dear Alice. I do believe that the spirits have brought us together. I must assure you that I feel very deeply for you, and if your feelings are the same, I want to assure you how committed I would be to you." He caught her hands in his and took a deep breath. "But I'm afraid I don't believe in marriage, at least not in the traditional, legal sense."

"What?" Alice's voice was a squeak. Her mind slowed to sort through the sudden revelation while her heart continued its rejoicing, a beat behind in the conversation.

"Marriage does not honor the independence of women. It is a prison sentence for them. I think of myself as an egalitarian, and so long as a man and a woman are married they cannot be equal in the eyes of the law. Just because I reject marriage does not mean I am a rake or indeed anything less than a gentleman."

In that respect, Thomas's character was as Alice suspected—but why *this* radical philosophy? Why could he not be a follower of Graham instead, and eat crackers every day?

Why did his cause have to affect her happiness?

"You are a free-lover?"

Thomas cringed. "I do not like to use that term. It carries all the negative connotations of my stance."

"You cared for me, and yet...you could not tell me this?" Alice's voice came out as a whisper. She felt as if her throat had all but closed, and breathing, let alone speaking, was a struggle. She was an enlightened woman and should be open to his ideas of equality. But still...

Thomas cleared his throat. "There was never a time in which discussion of my beliefs would have been appropriate. And I am not one to share my beliefs for the purpose of converting others. I keep them to myself in order that I not be brought into debates. I find discussion of it at spiritualist gatherings to be inappropriate and distracting; people who have congregated to contact those who have no need for mortal regulations should not devote their energy to a topic that pertains only to the living.

"Alice, I take this stance not because I condone sin and wantonness and anything less than romantic commitment, but because I believe the legal institution is flawed, and people who are truly spiritual companions do not need laws to sanctify their communion. I frown upon those who use free love as an excuse for infidelity and promiscuity, for the whole idea is to aspire to a partnership so sacred that civil sanction is unnecessary."

His argument made sense to Alice's logical mind, but having contemplated marriage this summer for the first time, she was not prepared to abandon it so quickly.

"I did have a feeling that, despite all your learning, you are a fairly traditional young woman," he continued. "I must be certain of your conviction before creating a situation that could be socially damaging."

"Well," said Alice slowly, it is not a stance I have ever considered." She studied his face. "Your views will not shift towards the radical, will they? In years to come, will you want to take a mistress? Leave me behind?"

"No, no—I assure you, I could love no one after you."

It was the first time he had said *love*, and the sound of his voice wrapped around the syllable, the knowledge that he spoke it in reference to her, made Alice feel as if her chest were melting wax. She could not harden her heart against Thomas—not when he had occupied it all summer.

Her helplessness must have showed in her face, for Thomas rose from his seat, bent over her, and brought his mouth to hers.

Alice had long wondered what such a kiss would feel like. People often made love to one another in novels, but a description in black type had not prepared her for this. Thomas must have kissed other women before—his lips guided hers into a deeper embrace with apparent skill—but she could not think of anyone but herself having this same sensation.

"This is not fair," Alice murmured as their lips parted for air. The pronouncement did not have the resolve she wished it to carry, but Thomas looked stricken all the same.

"Of course. I am sorry."

He made a move to retreat, but this time Alice stood and sought his lips, concentrating upon them until just before they touched and then closing her eyes, as she had noticed him do. The absence of sight made the motion seem continuous and completely natural, as if their mouths were designed for joining, and they were one being, edges and boundaries of flesh blurred and indistinct. When she felt his hand on her cheek, she reached for his face, and let her thumb fall upon the bristle of his mustache. The little finger located some slight stubble where his beard might have been, if he had chosen to grow one. The other three fingers reached up and were rewarded with skin as soft as hers at the top of his cheekbone.

Alice pulled away. "I...need some time..."

"Yes, yes." Thomas nodded with excessive vigor.

"Although...there are only three days left in the season..."

"I will give you my address, and you can write me, when you decide." Thomas hesitated. "Though I hope to receive your answer in person…it is a serious undertaking, and to rush you would be inadvisable."

If indecision were agony for her, how would it be for him, waiting for an answer? "I think I will need to decide before camp is over. There is the clambake and final dance—the phantom ball—on Friday evening. I will give you my reply then."

Thomas looked relieved. "Very well. I will await Friday. 'Eager' is not strong enough to describe my state."

As she stepped out of the tent, Alice licked her lips, as though she would find honey there.

Without Thomas in her sight, however, being with him seemed less plausible. Alice did not think herself made for rebellion, and her parents would most certainly not approve. Even her mother, liberal as she was, denounced free love as a view detrimental to the spiritualist cause. Alice remembered her coming home from two weeks at the Lake Pleasant camp, years ago, when even the question of whether or not to discuss the topic had caused a stir. "They will think us altogether devoid of morals, when we in fact seek a higher morality than most," her mother had moaned.

There were limits to Mrs. Boyden's activism: first for abolition, then for woman suffrage, she was only loyal to the movement's core beliefs and unwilling to tolerate any offshoot that threatened to disturb its symmetry. And for all her rejection of laws and rules that trapped women under the thumbs of their fathers or husbands, Mrs. Boyden had been raised as a lady of society and did not wish to reject it altogether. She had never worn bloomers and always removed herself from picket lines and protests before arrests began. She cared deeply about her reputation in the community. Only a few months after Lake Pleasant, Victoria Woodhull rose to speak at a suffrage convention in Boston, and Mrs. Boyden had walked out. "I think you can agitate for the vote without ruining your reputation," Alice remembered overhearing her mother tell a neighbor.

"What reputation had she left to ruin?" the neighbor had said.

What was the value of Alice's reputation, compared to the value of a life with Thomas? No one would know her in the places they'd travel. Perhaps she could convince him that she should go by Mrs. Holloway to make them seem more wholesome to small-town folks. And as to her legacy in Cambridge and Onset, why should she pay it mind? Assuming her parents would not give their blessing to...well, the lack of a marriage; she and Thomas would have to elope—if elope was the right word, when there was no ceremony, not even a furtive one...

The situation was making her dizzy, and Alice sought refuge in one of the groves of oak and pine that the saws of cottage-builders had left alone. Only a few feet in, the breeze that blessed all the open land with its face to the water ceased to penetrate. Alice felt the cotton of her dress cling gently to her arms; the skin of her legs and torso, encased in their structural trappings, simply sweated within the muslin that surrounded them. As she walked across a carpet of rust-colored needles, the occasional disturbed beetle or spider skittered out in search of a safer spot.

She tucked herself in the nook of an enormous rock, chipped and smoothed again by natural forces thousands of years ago. The spiderwebs strung across the opening only gave her brief pause, as her hand involuntarily went to her face to brush away the sticky strands. Her fingers settled on a spongy, slightly damp patch of moss, and she laid her warm cheek against the cool stone. This was how Alice preferred to think of Onset—a peaceful refuge, far away from assorted Thatchers and the unsettling shrieks of mediums. If she went with Thomas, would she be welcome here again?

That night, between wide-awakefulness and fretful sleep, Alice dreamed that she was on a prairie, surrounded by nothing but grasses, sod, and sky. Unsure of in which direction to walk, she went with her instinct and progressed a few feet. Then she questioned that decision, doubled back, and proceeded in the opposite direction. But the path suddenly yawned open into a chasm, its lip invisible until Alice stepped forward and found nothing underfoot. Looking down yielded nothing but darkness; looking up revealed an ever-shrinking sky and the grasses waving goodbye. She woke feeling as if she had fallen into her bed.

Worse than dying would be to die without anybody you loved knowing, Alice thought as she waited for her heart to slow down. Worst would be if your loved ones thought your lack of communication was due to a character flaw, greed, or selfishness, or simply a desire to separate yourself from them. Such had been the fate of the Western settlers with whom she had been in contact—Mary Sawyer in Ohio, as well as two spirits who had gone beyond the Mississippi and fallen prey to the particular dangers that awaited them there.

The dream repeated itself once again that night, and Alice had not learned from her previous errors. She still changed directions against her instinct, still stepped into thin air. But as gravity took hold of her, she saw someone on the other side of the abyss.

Thomas.

Alice called out to him, reached out her arm, but the scene abruptly ended with her in bed, alone. She sat up, trembling.

Had he saved her before she had fallen out of reach?

Alice had arranged to meet her mother outside of one of the tents at noon, for a walk along the beach and then some lunch. She cautioned herself to pay attention to where she was going—left to her own thoughts, her feet would take her directly to Thomas's tent. And she could not go there, when she did not yet have an answer for him.

As expected, the flaps of the tent in which her mother sat were still closed, and a soft, high voice made muffled pronouncements behind the heavy canvas. Alice perched herself on a nearby bench and opened her book—a novel, a welcome respite from the mathematical theorems of the morning. But between pages, sometimes paragraphs, she found her gaze drifting upward to the trees, distracted by the rustle of the leaves. A courting couple passing by with a whisper and a giggle was enough to keep her in daydreams for several minutes while the book lay open on her lap, the corners fidgeting slightly in the breeze.

And, of course, she thought of Thomas, and of the session she had not had this morning. Alice wondered if he had arrived at the regular time and waited for her, just in case she had already made her decision. She stared at his tent, just barely in sight of her seat. After a few moments, the tent flap showed movement behind it, and Alice quickly shifted to the end of the bench. None of the newly planted trees possessed enough girth to shield her from the people streaming from Thomas's tent. She decided that the only thing to do was to turn her back on them and bend over her book in what looked like deep concentration. But she could not help but listen to what the sitters had to say.

"Why, I don't think I've ever been at a séance of a matchmaking nature," said one woman's voice.

"I wonder if Mr. Holloway came to Onset because the spirits had plans for him, or if it was simply good fortune."

At the mention of his name, Alice felt her breath catch.

"Or perhaps Dr. Anderson could just be out to spread a rumor. He can be such a scoundrel sometimes."

"I would have asked Mr. Holloway directly, but I did not want to follow such a pleasant séance with discomfort on his part. Especially since Dr. Anderson might have an entirely different idea of whom Mr. Holloway should marry than Mr. Holloway himself."

"Well, I don't know to whom Dr. Anderson could be referring. Mr. Holloway hasn't kept particular company this summer, as far as I know."

"I will ask Letty. They've had him over to dine several times."

"Then I wonder if Isabelle Thatcher is the lady in question."

Alice's stomach flipped around and she clutched the edges of her perch. *Those women don't know the truth,* Alice told herself. *They are only making wild guesses.* She had to ignore the gossipy parts and focus upon the nugget of hope they had provided—that Thomas might be willing to, intending to, pursue marriage after all.

Tomorrow night was the phantom ball, for which everyone mangled pillowcases and resurrected old white sheets to make themselves a costume. Perhaps the sheets over their faces would make it easier to ask Thomas about Dr. Anderson's announcement while they danced. She deserved to know his true state of mind before making a decision that could estrange her from the society she had known all her life. And yet, the more she thought of the way he looked at her when she awoke from a trance, the tenderness with which he had kissed her, the more resolved she became.

"Alice? I'm sorry to be late—Mrs. Hancock made contact with a great-uncle and he suggested that there might be something of value in the walls of her parents' house, so naturally we were all quite enthralled..."

Alice turned to face her mother, trying to stash the tension in her taut mouth behind a smile. But Mrs. Boyden frowned.

"What is the matter? Are you very hungry? You could have gone on without me..."

"No, Mother, I'm quite well," said Alice. "You just caught me deep in thought."

Luminaries lit the paths leading up to the auditorium, as if the building were not a giant lantern in itself. Alice held up the fabric of her skirt to keep it from knocking over the glowing paper bags. Inside each of them, a white wax candle melted into sand scooped from the beach.

She carried with her a doctored white sheet for her costume, folded into a compact but somewhat uneven rectangle by Nora. Alice spotted Thomas almost immediately from the back, his hair's distinctive volume contrasting with the pomade-pressed tresses of the other men in the food line. While people waited to gather steaming clams and ears of corn from a table of wicker baskets, he chatted with various families, teasing the young Henderson twins about braving their first taste of tripe, and offering some words of comfort to Mrs. Boone—only recently widowed and deep in mourning—as she smiled slightly and put away her cambric handkerchief long enough to spoon a few sweet potatoes onto her plate.

Mrs. Boyden, who had a great many friends to whom she had to pay her regards—had disappeared into the crowd almost immediately upon their arrival. Alice was thankful for that; she stayed close to her father, who would not bother to ask her if she had something on her mind, or encourage her to sit with the other young people. She needed only to listen to his dissemination of August's *Popular Science Monthly*—the lead article of which claimed that the locust was more of a culinary delicacy than a pest. Then, when an idea struck him and he began to scribble in his notebook, Alice was free to sit in peace and watch Thomas make his rounds.

Gradually, as the food line tapered and the bowls of clams and corn dwindled, those finished dining unfurled their carefully bundled sheets and began to hover around the dance floor, a row of white moths drawn to the warm glow of the wood. The pale skirts and trousers peeking from beneath the sheets made women and men discernible, but identifying someone beyond that proved more challenging. To that end some of the young, single women had pinned distinctive brooches or flowers to their costumes, so that men who found them desirable dance partners could locate them again. Alice had pilfered a pink rose from a silk arrangement in the cottage and pinned it to the part of the sheet that covered her neck.

The gathering did not immediately catch the attention of the master of ceremonies, still quite involved with his meal; not until a ghost with a Yale-blue ribbon and full skirts marched over to him and tugged on his sleeve did he take notice of the crowd awaiting his permission.

"Ladies and gentlemen!" Mr. Thatcher stood on the stage of the pavilion, drenched with the combination of heat, excitement, and alcohol. He waited for the room to settle, wearing a too-broad smile that turned his cheeks into plums.

"Yet another summer at Onset has drawn to a close. I wanted to thank you all for making this season our grandest so far. It is hard to believe that we were little more than a circle of tents only a few years ago, and now we have such a spectacular turnout."

A round of applause, somewhat muffled by sheet fabric caught between hands.

"And I wish to offer especial thanks to our newcomer and guest of honor, Mr. Thomas Chester Holloway. It has been a pleasure and an enlightenment to have Mr. Holloway with us this summer, and I hope he will not be a stranger to Onset."

Thomas ducked his head in modesty as his neighbors at the table fussed over him. It suddenly struck Alice that if he returned to Onset next year, she could be sitting next to him.

"Yet the evening is young, and we can prolong our farewells a little longer"—Mr. Thatcher wiped a bead of sweat from his cheek as if it were a tear, and everyone chuckled—"so for now, in the spirit of aiding digestion, I open the dance floor to those needing a bit of exercise."

Uniformed workers scurried to empty deserted tables of dinnerware and push them to the side, and the band began to play a vigorous tune. Younger married couples who had eaten their fill took up immediately, and the swirling of the ladies' sheets and skirts provided a slight breeze, much appreciated by those overheated from the exertion of simultaneous talking, shucking, and eating. Single folks took a little longer to sort themselves into pairs or find their promised partners, entering once the song was partway through. Older onlookers moaned about the heat and begged off dancing altogether.

Onset's association members had brought the tradition of a phantom ball from meetings at Lake Pleasant, where their dance floor was legendary, cited as one of the finest in New England. Alice had never seen Lake Pleasant's dance floor, but she thought that Onset could likely hold its own. The wooden boards had been freshly polished for the final event of the season, and gave such a gleam that they reflected dancers as they moved onto the floor. Phantom images of phantoms. Alice sometimes wondered if the neighbors on the opposite shore, seeing this yearly spectacle, thought the spirits who served the mediums had risen up and taken over the camp.

A number of the older people had opted simply to wear white clothes; Alice's mother, for one, claimed that her eyesight and mobility did not need to be hindered further. They decorated themselves with plumes and lace and floral corsages the size of an open hand. Mrs. Boyden had managed to find an arrangement of yellow orchids, which she had pinned to her bosom like a war medal.

Even Alice's father, who usually moped around the outskirts of such events until a chance to excuse himself appeared, wore a pale suit. Once the dancing began he moved further down the table, conversing with some of the fellows from his Harvard horseshoe team. Alice left the table to don her costume, keeping an eye on her father. He seemed to be enjoying himself, though Alice noticed something she hadn't before; his hair, though still thick, matched his suit. It made him look tremendously old.

Of course, he *was* old, and Alice felt a pang at the thought of how he would take the news of his only daughter's abandonment of higher education for a life on the road with a spiritualist. Would it be enough to interrupt the beat of his aging heart? Or would her separation from her parents be so swift that she would not have time to observe their reactions?

Alice was distracted by the exaggerated cackle of a group of girls in the midst of a flirtation. She wondered what poor stupid boy they had trapped with their ploy, and looked over. The way the sheet draped over the ghost of the moment suggested that he had a full head of wavy hair.

Her jealousy roared up in her like fire in a flue. To tamp it, she repeated to herself what he had told her: *I could love no one after you.*

On the road, this would likely be a common occurrence, and she could not let it get the better of her. After all, she too had been enchanted by him.

Finding herself surrounded by matrons at that particular moment, Alice debated whether she appeared as a more attractive partner among them, by comparison, or whether it was cruel to make a young man walk through a gauntlet of lilac perfume. Deciding the latter, she made her way through to the edge of the dance floor just as the first song ended.

"Miss Boyden."

Alice turned to see a ghost bowing to her. When he looked up, she saw that the eyes peering through the holes in the sheet were a familiar deep gray-blue. When he stood upright again she saw what the crowds had previously obscured: he had also pinned a pink rose to his sheet. "May I have this dance?"

"Yes, of course." She held out her hand, no longer jumpy at the touch of his. But as they began to dance, she found that her mind could not form the question she wanted to ask, although she had practiced it in front of the mirror with a slightly flirtatious, hopeful tone. She decided to say something innocuous until she had regained the necessary words.

"Tell me, since you have the advantage of height, is there anything interesting going on in the room?"

"Well..." Thomas surveyed the floor. "The pavilion workers seem to think no one can see them passing a flask...a few young boys are gathering empty corncobs, to make pipes, I assume...and Mr. Thatcher is hearing out his wife, although he appears in desperate need of an ice-bath."

Alice smiled into his shoulder, and found her eyes drawn to his pink rose. They were a pair. She took a deep breath.

"I must take this opportunity to ask you about something I heard attributed to Dr. Anderson," Alice told the boutonniere.

"Yes?"

"Well, I heard some women pass by who had been at your séance, and they said that Dr. Anderson had mentioned your finding a wife at Onset."

"Indeed. Some took the liberty of questioning me after lunch."

"And?"

"I admitted that I had indeed found a wife, and that I would propose marriage at the phantom ball."

Alice's feet stopped short. A gentle pressure from Thomas's hand on her back encouraged them to continue, but she no longer felt the floor beneath her feet.

"I have reconsidered my feelings in light of yours, and I have decided that the best way to make marriage equal is if we set a good example. In keeping with custom, though, I have asked your father for your hand."

Alice looked around, and spotted a crowd of matrons bubbling with excitement. One by one, people stopped to pause and stare at Thomas and Alice.

"So what this means, my dearest Alice, is that I would like you to be my companion in work and in life. Will you accept?"

Alice realized she had seen nothing of Thomas's face during the proposal, but it did not matter. The eyes were all she needed for confirmation of her feelings.

"Yes," she breathed.

Thomas hugged her and spun her around as the cheers and applause began. She tugged on his sheet to finally reveal his grin, and he flipped hers back over her head, turning it into a veil.

Chapter 11

Alice would have thought, with the Annex having existed for several years and women receiving private instruction for longer, that she would elicit fewer stares from professors and undergraduates on the Harvard campus, but still she felt eyes follow her from the moment her feet met the brick paths of the Yard. She chose to look straight ahead instead of paying the gawkers any heed. No need to acknowledge the looks of derision, or lewdness, or confusion.

At least in the Museum of Comparative Zoology, where her father had his office, she was a familiar face, and a few lady assistants and librarians meant she was not the only occupant in skirts. The secretary offered her a lemon drop in a conspiratorial whisper, something she had done for as long as Alice could remember. Alice tried to accept the sweet with the enthusiasm of receiving a forbidden treat, even though she was nearly twenty and could seek out her own lemon drops without fear of scolding.

Alice knocked on her father's door, hoping it was loud enough for him to hear, but not so loud that it startled him. She heard a shuffling of papers, then a gruff "Come in." Mr. Boyden always made a point of finishing whatever sentence he was writing before receiving visitors, which sometimes meant standing there for several minutes. Alice pushed the door open slowly so as not to upset any piles of books that might be stacked in front of the door. From practice, she knew that a steady movement would keep the stack intact, but shift it to a less precarious position. She wasn't sure if her father purposely put books there to keep visitors away—perhaps he thought they would be startled by the crash and slink off without bothering him—or if he simply tended to forget that there was a way out of his office and into the real world.

Indeed, Mr. Boyden immediately pointed at the door once she had made her way inside. "Will you close that? I do not want students to have the impression I hold open office hours." Alice obeyed and shifted a stack of papers to the floor so that she could sit on the one spare chair. She took a deep breath.

"Father, as you may have guessed, I have decided not to sit the Annex exams next month."

"Well, yes. I suppose you will be too busy organizing dinner parties."

"Father, I am hardly going to live the life of a housewife. We'll be traveling—we'll live in hotels—I'll be the opposite of a housewife, really! Please see this as an opportunity for me."

"You would leave America's hub of learning to engage with delusional country bumpkins?"

"Just because I don't plan to attend the Annex does not mean I'll stop learning. I plan to self-educate as many women have done before me—as I have done this summer."

"And all will be fine and well until you have a child…"

"Which ruined your lives, I suppose." Alice bit her tongue; now she was just being spiteful. But her father simply sighed.

"That is not what I meant. I only worry that you are jumping into this marriage too quickly. You see, from experience…your mother and I…well…"

Alice blinked at her father. "But I always assumed you had a long courtship."

"Why? Because we are old?" He went on without waiting for an answer. "We had been courting for a few months, and she went away for a spring trip, and suddenly a letter arrived declaring her love for me and saying that she wanted to be married. Not very conventional, but then Caroline Carr was not a conventional woman."

"Absence makes the heart grow fonder?" said Alice.

"So I thought. When she returned she was simply devoted to me. It was if she were a different person. When I asked her what had altered her attitude so, she said that she had decided she wanted to be married before the age of forty. Seemed rather silly to me, but I was willing to oblige her. It was April; her birthday was July. So we set a date in June."

Mr. Boyden cleared his throat. "That was 1863."

Alice thought about the wedding sampler in the parlor. Her parents did not have a wedding portrait on display—she was not sure they had even had one taken—but the embroidery bearing their names and the wedding date had hung on the wall there for as long as she could remember. The imperfections in the stitching made sense when one considered the initials in the corner: CCB. Alice's mother had always abhorred embroidery, and never required it of her daughter; Mrs. Connors was the only reason that Alice could thread a needle. She had taught her how to mend her dolls' clothes since, like their owner's, their dresses were always catching on branches in pursuit of specimens.

But why did she think the date on the sampler was 1862? Alice looked up at her father, whom she saw had anticipated her confusion.

"I—we were so old, and I did not even consider what might be causing her haste in the matter..." He shook his head. "This is entirely inappropriate for you to hear."

"Father," said Alice, trying to keep her voice calm as the mathematical exercise in her head failed to produce the expected answer. "You've always said that no information should be denied me because someone deems it inappropriate for a woman."

"It's not simply that you're a woman. It's that it's a private matter. But if you are to be married, I want you to know what happened to me. Your mother did not love me. I don't know that she ever has. But to avoid...trouble, she claimed that she did."

Alice had been born in November of 1863, at which point her parents had been married for only five months.

"My point is that too often people abuse the word love," her father, avoiding her eyes as she reached a conclusion. "They might be after something other than love, and they use the word because they know it has such power. I suppose when you have known someone for a long time, you can tell when they are bluffing. But your mother and I did not have that time, and neither did you and Thomas. If propriety does not require your hasty marriage—" he raised his eyebrows at Alice.

"No!" exclaimed Alice, reddening. "No, it does not."

"Then I would wait to marry this man until you are better acquainted with him. You are very young to be contemplating marriage. You have the time."

Her father was trying to sound sage, but Alice thought he had never had less authority on a topic. If his own marriage had not been a love match, then how could he know how she felt? Was there a touch of jealousy in his pronouncements? Mr. Boyden had thought his daughter would become lonely and miserable like him. But no, she had found true love at half her parents' age. Why could he not simply be glad for her, instead of trying to stoke doubts in her mind?

But anger turned to pity when she saw how fragile he looked, how terribly old.

"Father?"

"Yes?"

"Do *you* love Mother?"

He looked down at his blotter. "I did once," he said.

Alice watched her father retreat into his thoughts, but couldn't think of how to call him back. After a few moments, he waved her away. "Along with you," he said, without meeting her eyes.

The conversation was over; Alice felt the familiar distance between them begin to grow again. She closed the door quietly behind her. Far from making her reconsider Thomas, Alice's father had strengthened her resolve. She would travel, she would continue learning—she would be happy in love.

Chapter 12

Alice found that preparing for a wedding was both very similar to preparing for examinations and quite the opposite. Both activities demanded significant amounts of time, both were focused upon a looming deadline. But studying was all brainwork, and putting too much thought into wedding plans made her head hurt. So she listened and acted instead, driven in whatever direction her mother wanted to steer her: subjecting herself to measuring and pinning and the contemplation of fabric swatches, perusing hymn-books, assessing flower arrangements and cakes. Thomas's only request for the whole event was that a Unitarian minister friend of his perform the ceremony. Her mother had argued for the minister who had baptized Alice, but when Alice reminded her that he had not seen much of the Boydens since, she capitulated.

While Alice would not admit it to her father, the examinations were still on her mind. If a sporty-looking pair of girls walked by her on the street, Alice stared after them, wondering if they were Annex students. Sometimes, when it felt as if she could take no more of lace and petals, she found herself pulling out the course catalog and imagining, based on the brief descriptions, what her classes would have been like. Would she never be satisfied? The Annex seemed desirable only once she had made plans for another life.

But Alice endured, for at the end of all the preparations, she and Thomas were to be married. She savored that fact, turned it over and over on her tongue, like a sweet that would never quite dissolve.

It was that time of year when everything began to creak again—the floorboards, the naked branches outside, Alice's very bones—and every groan traveled clearly through the crisp, dry air, unmuffled by vegetation or even snow, for it was not quite cold enough for that.

But on their wedding day it did snow, and Alice hoped it would not delay the trains; she was eager to take her first trip as a married woman. She imagined receiving well wishes from strangers on the train when they discovered she was a bride—her outfit and her natural glow giving her away. But the flurries had exhausted themselves by ten, and the day settled on being clear and cold. Her mother surprised her with a white ermine muff and tippet. It made Alice feel as if she were bound for a Christmas sleigh-ride.

If she had worn fur on the sleigh ride last winter, would she still have become so ill? And if she had not become ill, perhaps the spirits would not have approached her. And if the spirits had not approached her, she would never have become so familiar with Thomas. The speculation made her dizzy, and she swayed towards the bedpost to steady herself. Nora asked her if she was all right, and Alice said she was, but Nora did not seem to believe her. She left the room and came back a few minutes later with an unmarked bottle of amber fluid and a glass that resembled an oversized thimble.

"Here, you drink a wee bit of this," said Nora, splashing more than a wee bit into the glass. Alice sniffed at it.

"Whiskey? Is this from my father's drawer?"

"No, it's from my medicine cabinet. Only for the aches and pains at the end of the day, eh?" Alice wondered what her mother would think about their Irish maid keeping spirits in this house of temperance, but she took a sip. The brief burning left a trail of warmth through her body that made the second sip more enjoyable. Before she realized it, she had drained the glass. She handed it back to Nora.

"Thank you, Nora. That was thoughtful of you."

"Another?" Nora held the mouth of the bottle to the empty glass.

Already Alice felt as if she had been dipped in maple syrup. "No, no. I think that's plenty."

"Of course, miss." She looked up at Alice with a mischievous grin. "Or missus, it should be?"

"Not for a few hours, Nora."

"Are you ready for your mother to come and help dress you, miss? I'll fetch her."

Alice nodded—but quickly realized what a fuss her mother would make if she smelled liquor on her daughter's breath. So Mrs. Boyden found said daughter sucking on a peppermint lozenge, which set her clucking with concern.

"Do you have a sore throat? Should I have Nora heat some water?"

Alice shook her head. "I'm fine, Mother."

The next half-hour was a flurry of arms and exclamations, none of which Alice bothered to try and connect with their owner; she was having a difficult enough time with moving her own limbs and answering questions when she was asked. The dress was laid out on the bed, but slithered to the floor; then it slid over her head. She imagined the pale, fine silk as a snakeskin, which she was donning instead of removing for the new phase of her life. It seemed as it would never take proper shape, requiring the buttoning of a hundred buttons, but when completely fastened it fit her as well as any skin might.

Regarding her fully clothed reflection in the mirror, the magnitude of her departure suddenly hit Alice full in the stomach, and she burst into tears. A blurry form advanced towards her, and Alice found herself in her mother's arms. She sobbed with abandon, only briefly concerned with dampening Mother's dress. After all, what were mothers for, if not oversized handkerchiefs?

"Dear Alice—there's nothing to fear. Mother's here."

"I don't want to leave Cambridge—not yet!"

"It's not goodbye just yet," said her mother, holding Alice's damp face in her hands. "It's but eleven, and you've two and a half hours before the ceremony, and there's dinner after that."

Alice reclaimed her composure and nodded, allowing herself to be led to the water basin. Mrs. Boyden held her by the shoulders as she bent her face to the water and cupped some in her hands. She gasped as it hit her face, and stood still in shock, eyes blinking, mouth open, chin dripping. The hot water Nora had poured into her wash basin not two hours ago had already taken on a chill. A small towel offered saved the lace on the neck of her dress from wilting.

"There, now—the cold air is good for something—warmer water wouldn't have helped the swelling."

"I'm still red," Alice worried, glancing at her now-dry face in the mirror.

"The blush of a new bride and besides, you've forgotten"—Alice's mother produced a layered veil of simple tulle and lace. She attached it to Alice's crown, flipping one layer over her face. Instantly Alice's features softened and her blotches disappeared.

"Oh," said Alice, without meaning to.

"Now, are you better?"

Alice nodded and watched the tulle bob with her movement.

She thought herself calm at last, but her stomach had not been informed of this decision, and still it flipped and flopped as she came downstairs. She heard the low yet insistent buzz of a group of people trying their best to be quiet, but not being able to resist a whispered comment to their neighbor.

Despite her mother's urging to look up, Alice stared at her white shoes against the strip of red carpet as she walked with her father, thinking she would lose her composure if she looked anyone in the face on her journey to the altar. Once there, she gave Thomas a quick smile through her veil, but she spent the ceremony focused on not fainting, staring at the minister's hand on the Unitarian prayer-book to keep herself steady. At last the voices rose in song upon his declaration that she and Thomas were man and wife. At this she could not stop smiling, her skin now calm and the veil lifted.

Alice remembered the rest of the day's events as a series of blurry photographs, where everyone shifted before the exposure had completed. She took hands and offered her cheek for kisses and smiled politely at well-wishers, but that evening could not say who she had greeted or how. There were snatches of hats and cravats and the feel of kid gloves and bare fingers, but the guests' faces had run together in an anonymous blur.

After what seemed like only an hour of eating and dancing—although her mother swore it had been several—Alice was ushered upstairs to change into her traveling suit. She stared at her newly beringed finger as her mother and Nora freed her from the lace gown and helped her into a sturdy one of green wool. The hand seemed to belong to a different person, an older, mature person, one who was used to referring to "my husband" and responding to invitations with, "Mr. and Mrs. would be pleased to..."

When the carriage came to take them to the train station, Mrs. Boyden began to cry. This startled Alice; she knew that mothers were supposed to cry at their daughters' weddings, but she did not expect it to be such a sloppy affair. Mrs. Boyden turned red all over, her nose ran, and her eyes puffed to slits. The dainty lace handkerchief that she had procured for the occasion did no good against the waterfall, and Mr. Boyden had to offer his own broad cambric hankie.

"My only child—going away forever!" she bawled into Alice's new fur collar. Alice squeezed her mother tightly, hoping that the action—or the pressure—would quiet her, but the collar only grew more damp. "Promise me you'll write often."

"Every stop, Mother. I promise."

"Caroline. They'll be late for their train if you don't let them go."

Mrs. Boyden then transferred her embrace to Thomas, leaving Alice standing before her father. To her surprise, the man who had not embraced her in years came forward and squeezed her against his chest with as much force as his wife had. And all of a sudden, Alice had a glimpse of the desperate homesickness that could lie ahead.

She squeezed him back, and Mr. Boyden leaned down and kissed her on the cheek. Then he whispered something curious into her ear.

"Prove to me what a bright girl you are, Alice."

And then Thomas was taking her hand and leading her out the door, and the other hand was waving at her parents and the lingering wedding guests. Alice recognized her trunk already on the back of the carriage, and her well-fed, well-wished person felt the snap of the evening air for the first time, sending an intense shiver through her whole body. But with the carriage door closed and the curtains drawn, Thomas's mouth found hers and Alice thawed again at his touch.

It was arranged that the newlyweds would spend their wedding night at Day's Railroad House near the Springfield station. The owner of the house pulled their key from a board behind her and told them that there were only a few guests now and that breakfast would be served from seven to eight. She rang a bell that summoned a lanky, sulky youth dressed in red coat and tassels, as if he were the bellhop at a Boston hotel. His outfit looked gaudy and clownish in such a modest environment.

The woman led them upstairs to their room, which was somewhat smaller than Alice's old bedroom, but tastefully decorated, and papered a soothing shade of dusty rose. When Alice looked closer, what seemed like a solid paper revealed a faint flower print. The woman bade them a simple goodnight, and the young man dragged their trunks inside the room with no word at all, only a slight bend that might have been taken for a bow as he closed the door. Somehow Alice had expected an acknowledgment of their just-married glow—she had included in the letter that it was their wedding night, had she not?—but she reasoned that the owner was most likely a spinster or a widow, and might not like to acknowledge the wedded bliss of others, as it reminded her of her own loneliness. For the first time that day, it dawned on her that she had escaped the first fate, and Alice felt rather smug in her victory.

But now, together in a bedroom with the man to whom she would devote the rest of her life, Alice felt suddenly afraid. She smiled at Thomas, so that he might not sense her discomfort, and yawned.

"I am terribly tired. I cannot remember a longer day in my life." She laughed, trying to strengthen her facade of happy laxity.

"I cannot remember a happier one." Thomas's smile was without guile, and Alice thought how much easier the day must have been for him, preparing himself without familial interruption.

Then he began to undress. Alice could not decide whether to look away or watch, and she ended up staring helplessly at his shoes.

"Alice."

She forced herself to move her gaze up. His coat lay across a chair, his suspenders hung limply from his waistline. He was looking at her expectantly. She bit her lip.

"You'll forgive me," said Alice. "I'm somewhat nervous." Her hands went to the buttons at the back of the neck, but they would not obey her command. "Would you turn the lamp down?" she whispered.

"Wait, Alice." Thomas came over to her and took her gently by the wrists. Alice realized she was quaking and felt suddenly sorry for him, upset that she could not be braver about the whole thing.

"We are man and wife now, and this should not be shameful or unpleasant. Will you let me..."

He began to unbutton the neck of her dress, and when he had undone several he pressed his lips into the hollow of her throat. Alice let out an unintentional sigh, and his fingers began to work the buttons that closed her dress over her back. She had studied his hands throughout the ceremony; his nails hardly extended over the quick. Was he well groomed to have trimmed them so, or did he bite them out of habit? She pictured Thomas with his impeccable manners gnawing at his fingers while breakfasting alone or backstage at a lecture hall, at home after retiring for the night.

Alice gasped as his fingers wriggled down the front of her bodice, and all contemplations of the state of his nails ran out of her head like sand. Thomas looked up, perhaps expecting her to stop him. Instead, she reached back and loosened her stays for him, cursing the number of hooks and laces and buttons left, desperate to have him explore elsewhere. She could not even remember having been afraid, just moments before.

Chapter 13

Looking in the mirror, Alice ran a finger along her cheekbone. Did her face look ever so slightly more angular and distinguished? Was that a more confident gleam in her eye? She looked down at her hand and wondered if the golden band would ever become familiar, or if it would take her by surprise every time.

Despite the success of the wedding (and the wedding night), and despite the fact that she had slept surprisingly soundly for her first time sharing a bed, ever since waking she had felt somewhat off-balance, mentally and physically. While fixing her hair she had stumbled and fallen into Thomas, who had been sitting on the bed and tying his shoes; he took the attack to mean she wanted something of him, and half an hour later she had to redo her hair entirely.

At the station, she was grateful for the gentlemanly support of Thomas's hand, guiding her up the steps of the railcar and to their seats. During her first travels as a wife, as an adult, she did not want her clumsiness to make other travelers think she would be prone to fits and faints.

Albany seemed to have a head start over Springfield regarding the topic of winter. The depot where they disembarked had a roof but no sides, and the snow did not seem to care which direction it blew in, so long as it accumulated in frosty drifts worthy of Christmas decorations. Alice tried to curl deep within herself, hoarding the warmth within her torso. But then Thomas stood to block the path of the wind, and Alice gratefully drew closer to him.

She suddenly found herself thinking of her birthday, which would be here in two weeks. Alice had only ever received gifts from her parents—maybe a few token treats from schoolmates, but never from a beau. She felt giddy as a child when she tried to imagine what Thomas might devise for a celebration.

Alice clung to Thomas's warm, steady hand as they picked their way around the snowpiles on the streets of Albany, roaming in search of a place to eat. It was not yet five but already the lamplighters had been out, anticipating the dusk that would quickly descend.

They chose a small, woodshingled place that opened directly onto the street. The dining room was still quiet, the only other occupant an elderly gentleman who did not look up from his soup or his book to acknowledge the new company. A rosy girl seated them, smiling as she pointed to the menu board; a woman who looked somewhat more pinched and sullen took their order. Alice realized the difference in temperaments and complexions must be due in part to the fact that the hostess had a seat near the fire. Thomas opted for lamb; Alice asked for chicken and potatoes. Once the waitress had departed Alice beamed at Thomas across the table. He grinned and took her hand in his.

"Now that I am an expert on married life, I can safely conclude that the state suits us both quite well."

Alice giggled. "Would you consider yourself to have earned a doctorate in marriage?"

"Yes. I would call it the most difficult to prepare for and the easiest to attain."

Alice looked down at his hand, his knuckles cracked by the cold. "I don't think I ever thanked you for revisiting your views on that topic—"

"Shhh," Thomas interrupted. "There's nothing to thank me for. You were the woman I loved best, and I knew where you stood."

When the waitress came with their meals, they reluctantly withdrew their hands in an effort to keep them from being caught under hot plates. Both dishes had a liberal dousing of floury gravy—Alice noted the lumps of white powder emerging from the brown dressing—but it was flavorful, and moistened the slightly dry meat beneath.

More diners trickled in, and she and Thomas ate quietly for awhile, allowing the chatter of the newcomers to dominate. Alice worried through her gravy—had they already run out of things to say to each other, having been married for twenty-four hours? Thomas glanced up after he had swallowed a hearty bite, and perhaps saw Alice's look of unease, for he leaned over and whispered, "You'll forgive me for my silence. I have a habit, perhaps a bad one, of eavesdropping on the conversations of people I encounter in a new place. It helps me acclimate myself to the society, being aware of people's concerns, the important figures in the community."

Alice nodded, and opened her ears to help. When she heard something particularly juicy, she leaned towards Thomas and started to tell him, but he put a finger to his lips.

"Patience, sweet," he said. "We'll share once we're back in the room."

After a few bites, Thomas waved down the waitress for a pitcher of water, and asked for ale for himself. He looked at Alice expectantly. Alice shook her head shyly.

"We're temperance people, don't you remember?"

"I know of your mother's beliefs, but I assumed, now that you have left your parents' house, that you are free to form your own beliefs. And perhaps you forget that I saw you take punch, the first day I met you."

Alice smiled now to think of that awkward clambake, and what it had led to.

"Perhaps you should have an open mind about the grain and the grape," Thomas continued. "Temperance advocates decry them as harbingers of sin and vice, but have any of them ever felt the pleasurable effects of moderate consumption? Not everyone who sips now and then will end up a gin-soaked beggar."

The waitress returned with Thomas's foamy mug, and he pushed it toward Alice. "Here—why don't you have a taste?"

Alice tried to expel her mother's voice from her head, warning her of the many dangers she might face should she even put her lips to the rim. She frowned. "But ale? Do women—respectable women—drink ale?"

Thomas considered this for a moment, and when the waitress brought water, he asked for a glass of port for his wife.

"You'll like it," he said. "It's not much different than grape juice."

Alice found a tiny goblet in front of her, brimming with ruby liquid. It looked very out of place, as if it belonged on a fine tablecloth next to gold forks and china plates, not on rough wood and placed amongst mugs and utensils of pewter. She took a sip and the sweetness coated her tongue; she swallowed and was left with a dry feeling in her mouth, slightly bitter but not altogether unpleasant.

"Good?" Thomas was looking at her expectantly.

"Strange. But I think I like it." She sat back in her chair slightly and allowed the warmth of the port to trickle down into her limbs and torso. She took in a deep breath and let it escape into a contented sigh.

Thomas drank a second ale with his meal, though Alice declined another port; she could already feel it spinning a top in her head. By the time they returned to the hotel she was quite drowsy. Thomas said he had to make some notes to himself, so Alice readied herself for bed as he scratched symbols into his notebook. At first she thought she would not be able to sleep with Thomas's light burning, but the softness of her pillow and the effects of the port quickly soothed her qualms.

In the morning, Alice woke to find a note pinned to Thomas's pillow: *Out for a walk. Back for breakfast.* She dressed slowly and began a letter to her parents, not wishing to sit by herself in the dining room.

Thankfully, when she did venture downstairs, Thomas was waiting for her. Over breakfast, he explained that on his walk, he had identified two possible locations for their office, two vacant storefronts. He would ask around town regarding their availability. Alice was to be a receptionist of sorts, and give people information about scheduling private sittings and times for group sittings. Thomas said she should suggest a dollar "donation" for a seat at the group table, five dollars for a private audience with the medium, and ten for a séance held in the person's home with his or her choice of guests.

"Donation?" asked Alice. "But what if they don't want to donate anything?"

"They will," said Thomas, "if for nothing else because their friends will, and they don't want to be seen as the cheap one. And clients respect the value of a medium's time, and know that a medium needs room and board if he or she is to continue in service to the spirit world.

"That said, we should only schedule a few group tables. Having so many in Onset—which I was obliged to do because of the sheer volume of campers—quite drained me, and I don't wish to risk exhaustion, not with so much travel ahead."

Alice nodded. "How long will we be staying in Albany?"

"Mmmm…four or five days, perhaps? We will see how many people are drawn to our sign—and how many messages you produce, my dear. If the spirits will us to stay longer, we will do our best to oblige them. But I find that being vague about the time we'll spend here, simply saying it is limited, makes people more likely to come as soon as they can. When new customers trickle off—when most are repeat visitors—we'll know it's time to move on to the next place."

"Would we charge more or less in different towns?"

"No," said Thomas. "Those are generally accepted rates throughout the States. To ask for more will make us look greedy, as if we were doing this for profit only—charge less, and people will think us amateurs who know little about the business."

Business. In Onset, the only word used to imply the medium had some amount of monetary reward was *profession*. Alice never saw money change hands at camp—most of it was paid in advance, from the pool of dues, freeing members and mediums from the undignified act of requesting and providing payment at the time of service. She was certain additional donations were given and received, but in private.

"However, I do wish to extend complimentary sittings to a few known spiritualists in town, as they are sure to not only bring us more business, but should be generous patrons themselves upon future visits. I will give you a list of names and addresses, and you're to write them a little invitation. You'll note that they should bring the card to their sitting. In the case that they do not bring the envelope addressed to them as well, you should make a faint, unique pencil mark on the back of each card. Savvy séance-goers do not always introduce themselves, lest a dishonest medium look them up in town records while they are waiting and falsify communications. But this way I shall be able to keep track of them, and appear as if I am well acquainted with them and their reputation. A bit of flattery will go far."

Alice perused the list, which comprised about a dozen people. "Where did you find them?"

"Some names are readily available in spiritualist journals; others Dr. Anderson makes known to me. Often all you need are the names of people who expect to hear from their spirit friends, to convince those spirits of your readiness and willingness to help."

Thomas set off to ask about occupying the vacant stores, and Alice returned to their room. She found the signs wrapped in a cloth bag in his trunk, stiff cardboard sealed with a clear wax that flaked onto Alice's skirt as she set them on her lap. The first said simply, "T. C. Holloway, Medium." The next proclaimed, "Thomas Chester Holloway. Spirit Medium. Very Limited Engagement. Public and Private Sittings Offered."

The trunk also revealed a hectograph machine, about which Alice had heard but never witnessed the use of. To test it, she printed the text of the sign, the name of the hotel at which they were staying, and the street on which the storefronts were located, and was rewarded with several sheets of purple text, some blurrier than others, but all legible.

The cards would require a personal touch, though. She cut rectangles from thin pasteboard and carefully lettered the person's name and address on the front and the invitation on the back:

Mr. T. C. Holloway, Spirit Medium, invites you to a complimentary demonstration of his abilities. Redeemable at the beginning of his brief visit: Tuesday and Wednesday.

"Always best to encourage them to come early," Thomas had said.

Chapter 14

As Alice was content with helping Thomas behind the scenes, she did not expect the excitement that the idea of her public role brought. She imagined herself seated at a desk in the window of the storefront, looking out and being looked at. She imagined greeting people and saying goodbye in a charming manner; having older men and women call her dearie; overhearing someone half-deaf try to say in a whisper: "That Mrs. Holloway is enchanting!" And Alice would smile to herself, knowing that her role extended far beyond keeping Thomas's schedule straight. At least it would, once the spirits decided to speak to her again. Thomas sat with her every day at seven in the morning, since that had been her usual time in his tent at Onset, but her trances produced nothing. She told herself she should be grateful she was not suffering headaches as a result of the spirits' silence.

Their very first visitors came bearing one of Alice's cards sans envelope. The husband-and-wife pair looked like a set of dolls, their torsos and limbs identically stuffed but fitted with different heads. As Thomas had instructed her, Alice took the card and bent over her drawer, removing from it a blank date-book, beneath which was the list of names and their symbols. Matching up the marks, she smiled at them. "I am glad you have availed of our offer, Mr. and Mrs. Higgins. Mr. Holloway happens to be free right now. Allow me to announce you."

And Alice left the astounded pair blinking their glassy eyes at each other, knocked carefully on the door, and poked her head in.

"Mr. and Mrs. Higgins here to see you." She could not help but grin at her successful trick, but Thomas's raised eyebrows suggested that she keep her expression neutral. "Tell them I am eager to see them," he said audibly, so that the visitors might overhear their invitation. Alice ushered the Higginses into the room and closed the door behind her. She returned to her desk, wrote their appointment in her date-book, and settled herself with Blake's *Songs of Innocence and Experience*—a book she hoped would be appealing to their mystically minded visitors. (Without input from Thomas, she decided that science texts might be off-putting to inquisitive customers.)

Upon emerging from the room, the grateful Higginses told Alice that Dr. Anderson had facilitated a long conversation with their ten-year-old son, who had died from the measles a decade ago. Despite their complimentary card, they insisted upon leaving a donation of ten dollars, which suggested to Alice that they were indeed experienced spiritualists. They were followed not five minutes later by Mr. Bertram, a middle-aged man who nevertheless walked with a cane (a carriage accident, Thomas had told her). Promptly at ten, the Misses Olson arrived, a trio of blonde spinsters who all wore identical brooches at their throats. Thomas later told her that the pale hair within the brooches was from their brother, who had squandered the family inheritance and died young with debts aplenty; he had begun to contact them often, wishing to express regret for his actions.

If others came while Thomas was occupied, Alice instructed them to come back in half an hour. ("Why half an hour?" Alice had asked. "Because it is an amount of time that seems neither too long nor too brief," he had replied.)

When the tenth visitor of the day had departed, leaving behind eight dollars' worth of thanks, Thomas came out of the back room. He asked to see the donation box, and Alice obliged. Before Alice knew what was happening, Thomas pulled her from her chair and kissed her full on the mouth. His lips remained there for so long that she finally had to pull away for a breath of air.

"Alice, I have never had such a successful day—" Thomas spoke in between kisses that he planted on her neck.

"Thomas, what if someone walks by?" Alice looked toward the storefront window but did not make any move to disengage herself.

"Then they will see how much I love my wife."

That night at the hotel Thomas ordered them steaks and champagne. Alice tried not to sneeze when the bubbles seemed to creep up her nose.

"Don't you think it's somewhat conspicuous for us to dine so well here?" she whispered to Thomas. "Will people think they were too generous in their donations?"

Thomas shook his head. "No, not at all. We must behave as if we are used to staying in the finest places and eating the finest things—on account of our steady and successful business." Seeing Alice pause, he added, "I know you were raised on a diet of Yankee frugality."

"Perhaps on my father's side of the menu," said Alice, thinking of her mother's profligate spending on mediums and her father's threadbare suits.

"Well, you no longer have to be concerned about your parents' habits. We are our own family now, and we seem to be off to an excellent start. Cheers." He clinked his glass against hers.

"Cheers." Alice smiled. Thomas's words—and the champagne—tempered her feelings of guilt and self-consciousness.

A successful week in Albany had spoiled them for Utica. Their business there was slow to pick up; whether because of inadequate advertising, a less convenient location (Thomas had only been able to find a vacancy on a road leading out of town), or lack of interest, they were not sure. The fact that it snowed intermittently throughout their visit did not help.

Alice had sent out the same elegant cards to spiritualists known to Thomas, but only one of the eight came by, and although he seemed happy with the séance, he gave only a fifty-cent donation and did not return again. A few unsolicited curiosity-seekers came to call, but were apparently not impressed enough to spread the word. Alice spent so much time on her Latin that she worried she might greet a visitor in the language.

She had been grateful for the steady stream of clients in Albany, as she thought it distracted Thomas from her unproductive trances. Although Thomas continued to tell her that her difficulty did not matter, that the spirits would return in time, each of his assurances seemed to hold a little less conviction than the one before. While months ago Alice had resisted the spirits' communications, now she tossed and turned over their silence. Perhaps this odd twist would amuse her if she had read about it happening to someone else.

Just as they were prepared to leave Utica and try their luck elsewhere, however, people began to call on a regular basis, and within two days Thomas's schedule was quite full. On Sunday morning Thomas was at a prescheduled house séance, the owners taking advantage of his daytime discount for such engagements (a half-dollar for every hour before noon, up to two and a half dollars). Alice had received no acknowledgment from passers-by other than churchgoers who sneered or laughed at the sign and peered in the window, perhaps not seeing that someone sat inside to witness their gestures. She wished that she had brought a more interesting book.

Then a shadow fell over her desk. Alice looked up and saw a woman in widow's weeds pushing the door open, wearing a veil that obscured her features. Unconsciously, she put her hands to her throat as pathetic protection. Was the woman here for her—to harm her? Had her sickbed hallucination been a premonition of her own death?

It was ridiculous, really; a receptionist for a medium should be used to people in mourning-garb. And this mourner, unlike her attacker, soon revealed her face: a pale thin hand drew back the netting to reveal colorless cheeks and strawberry-blonde hair that had likely once been carroty. The woman stood less than five feet tall and was swathed in black crepe, making her look like a piece of chalk accidentally dipped into an inkpot by an absent-minded scribe. The sight of her red-rimmed eyes made Alice's fear slowly dissolve into pity.

"I'm sorry if I have disturbed you," she said in a soft voice. "I was only looking for Mr. Holloway—but perhaps I have missed him? He has already left town?"

"No, he is still here, but he is already engaged for all of today, and is not certain of his whereabouts come Monday," Alice explained.

The woman's tiny shoulders slumped. "I at last overcome my trepidation about coming—and I am too late."

"Perhaps not," Alice hurried to say. "If he thinks he has had a particularly successful time, he might stay longer."

The woman nodded but still looked forlorn. "I was hoping to obtain a private sitting, and wanted to inquire as to the cost. My husband's death has left me without much money, but I do have this necklace." She held it out, let it sparkle against her pale hand. "It's real gold. I don't suppose Mr. Holloway would accept it as payment?"

Alice looked at the chain, and then at the woman, who seemed to be pressing her lips together to suppress the tears. She saw a brooch pinned at her neck that contained an ash-brown curl, presumably from her husband's head. Thomas had warned her about people who claimed poverty and then tried to pay for a private sitting with trinkets. "If they are truly indigent, they can come to a circle of several people and slip out without dropping a cent. But private sittings take a great deal of my time and energy, and the privilege of having one should only be extended to the generous. As time goes on, you will learn to read people as I have—grow more assured of their true meanings and intentions," he told her.

"I confess I used to be a skeptic, hence my hesitation about coming here," the woman continued. "But when my husband died—only a month ago, it was—I thought, if only I could contact him, if only I knew that the spirit world existed and that he wasn't completely gone from me, I would be happier." Her eyes filled up despite her efforts. "I've been to several mediums and they all give me some vague description of his appearance and profession. None convinced me that it was really him speaking."

Alice thought for a moment. She knew Thomas would never accept the necklace, but she hated the thought of turning the widow away. Then she had an idea.

"If you would allow me, madam, I am Mr. Holloway's wife, and I have sometimes been able to contact spirits myself. I could try to sit with you. I will not accept any sort of payment, as my spirit connections have been weak of late, and this could be a total failure. But I will try my best."

A smile spread across the woman's face, and Alice could discern prettiness through a veil of faint freckles.

"Oh, bless you, Mrs. Holloway!"

"As I said, I do not want you to be too optimistic." Alice led her into the back room, with one nervous glance back at the desk she was meant to be occupying—had she locked the drawer with the donation box in it?—and gestured for her to take a seat.

"I just cannot accept the *finality* of it," the woman said, settling into a chair. "And I know I should believe he's in Heaven, but is it really Heaven for him if he cannot be near his wife?" She wiped the tears from her left cheek in one fierce motion.

"I was a lucky girl. I have both my parents, all my siblings, still living. One of my sisters lost her hearing from scarlet fever, but that is the extent of my family's misfortune. I had never known what it was like to be speaking with someone one day and have them packed away in a coffin the next...but I suppose I should not be telling you this! To verify that you are indeed speaking to the spirits, really I should not speak at all. You can see how new I am to this business."

Alice smiled. "You needn't fear. I am not sly enough to have researched you ahead of time." The woman's lips turned up a bit in response. Her eyes were such a pale blue that the red around them burned with particular ferocity.

As Thomas delivered most of his messages through Dr. Anderson, Alice had to search in his trunk for several minutes before finding a slate and an adequate piece of slate-pencil. She urged the woman to sit as she looked. "You shouldn't be standing," Alice told her, not knowing why she did so. The woman frowned, but did as invited.

"There. Now, I suppose I'll draw the curtains and light the lamp..." She twisted the key and the floral motif painted on the glass threw an intricate shadow upon the table. The black curtains did an admirable job of shutting out the bright afternoon.

Alice knew that once she closed the door, there was no turning back. The widow was looking at her expectantly, both hands outstretched and flat upon the table. Settling herself in front of slate and pencil, Alice took the widow's hand with her left and picked up the pencil with the right. "I do not know how long it will take me to go into a trance, so I would ask your patience."

"Of course."

Alice closed her eyes and sought a bit of that seaside warmth she remembered feeling in Thomas's tent. But something seemed to be blocking the state of mind she needed. She bumped into and bounced off it as if she had encountered a wall made of glass.

Several minutes of this only increased her discomfort. What was she doing, holding a séance? Surely it was a dangerous venture, for her and for the widow. She had only sat with a professional medium whom she trusted, and by herself—and if she broke pencils in her sleep, could she not harm a sitter?

Alice's thoughts drifted to holding Thomas's hands—how warm and soft they were, fleshy pads shielding oversized bones, joints that flexed as they squeezed her hand tighter...

And then the widow's hand became Thomas's, and Alice was at peace. She didn't need to open her eyes to know that he was there. The chalk burned a bit in her fingers, and then her hand went numb.

Alice was suddenly aware of a soreness in the tip of her nose, and of something placing pressure upon it. She sneezed and hit her nose on what she realized was the tabletop.

Rising slowly, wriggling her nose to recirculate the blood, Alice fumbled for the key to the gas-lamp and loosed her now-sweaty left hand from the widow's grasp. Her right hand, still clutching the slate pencil tightly, began to relax.

Studying what she had recorded, Alice's frown turned into a slow smile.

"I don't know what all of it means, but maybe you can decipher Jacob's communication?"

The widow clasped her hands and brought them in front of her mouth, as if in prayer, muffling the request that came after. "Oh, oh, can I see it?" Alice slid the slate to the other side of the table, turning up the lamp further for the widow to see by.

TWO-BIT,

HOW GLAD I AM TO HAVE THIS OPPORTUNITY TO TELL YOU AGAIN WHAT A DEAR SWEET THING YOU ARE, AND THAT I LOVE YOU. I HATE TO SEE YOU CRYING INTO MY COAT; BE CONTENT, LOVE, FOR I AM ALWAYS WITH YOU. I KNOW YOU WILL TAKE THE BEST CARE OF OUR CHILD, AND HE WILL GROW STRONG UNDER THE BRAVERY OF HIS MOTHER.

A THOUSAND KISSES,
I AM YOURS, EVER FAITHFUL,
JACOB.

"It's him, oh, it's really him." The widow spoke in a whisper and raised her head to see Alice, although her fingers still hovered over the slate as if it were emitting the warmth of a coal fire. "My name is Elizabeth, though my family always called me Betsy or Bet. Jacob, my husband, called me "Two-Bit" because I was so small and because he thought he was being clever with my name." She smiled at the memory. "Somehow his coat still smells like him, and I hold it close when I miss him the most." Her hands went to her stomach. "I am expecting a child, but I have told absolutely no one. Yet Jacob knows!" She took Alice's hands in hers. "Oh, Mrs. Holloway, won't you sit with me again tomorrow, once you've rested?"

"I—I'm not sure I can," said Alice, suddenly shy. "My husband's the real medium, you see. I'm only the appointment-minder."

"Nonsense. Look what you've done here!" Betsy gestured to the slate. "Please tell me you will try to bring me another message tomorrow. You truly have a gift!"

Thomas returned to the shop after the sun had set. He did not stop to sit, but held his arm out to Alice.

"You must be quite hungry. Come, let's find you some dinner."

"Let me empty the donation box." Alice leaned down to unlock the drawer.

"Did anyone come by while I was gone?"

"Well, yes," said Alice, "one woman. A widow."

"Did you ask her to return later?"

Alice looked down at the donation box sitting in her lap. "I offered my own services."

"You what?"

"I did it, Thomas," said Alice triumphantly, the words spilling out. "I was able to contact her husband—she confirmed as much. The slate revealed her nickname, her habit of crying into his coat, and the fact that she was with child—which was not readily apparent."

"Why, that's fantastic!" Thomas gave her a firm kiss on the forehead. "So, you see, your powers have not faded as you had feared. Perhaps it's just taken awhile for the spirits in upstate New York to realize who you were. Perhaps we will need to devote more time to each location, give you some time by yourself—yes, even give you a separate room. Was she a wealthy widow? Did she donate handsomely?"

"Well, no," said Alice. "She had been brought to poverty by her husband's death, actually. Being an amateur, I thought it all right that her sitting be complimentary."

Thomas's eyebrows stitched together in a frown. "You left your post for someone who could not pay?"

"It was a slow time. No one had yet come by. And you were entirely booked for the day..."

"Don't you see? If that woman tells others that she saw you for free—and had a successful communication to boot—everyone will want to see you. Why should they pay five dollars to consult Dr. Anderson?"

"Can you not simply be happy that I have made contact with the spirits again?" Alice was on the edge of crying. "What does the money matter?"

She felt herself wrapped in Thomas's arms. "I'm sorry, my dear. It's been a very long day, and the group was not as generous as I had hoped. It's wonderful that you've made contact again. Why don't we return to the hotel and have something to eat."

After breakfast the next morning, Thomas paused in the foyer and gestured up the stairs. "Will you take charge of the trunks, while I gather our things from the office?"

Alice was confused for a moment. "But I thought we might stay one more day. I told Betsy I would meet with her again before we left! She'll be so disappointed."

"Alice, our next stop has a lot of promise. There are a number of prominent spiritualists there, all of whom will be eager to avail of my services. It could make the rest of our journey through New York quite comfortable. The idea is to leave a town while demand is still significant; else we are only wasting our time. The interested parties will still be here and willing to listen when we return another year—provided they have not themselves passed into the spirit world, of course."

He kissed her on the forehead, a sharp peck that acted as a wax seal on their conversation.

As she packed, Alice tried her best to reconcile herself to Thomas's way of thinking, but she could not help but feel guilty about Betsy. She thought to leave a note under the office door, but Thomas would be suspicious of her return to the place he had just vacated. She thought to write a letter, but she did not know the widow's address or even her last name. Best to forget about it, and not cause trouble for herself. Still, Alice stared out the window of the departing train until she could see the town no more, half-expecting to see the red-haired widow appear out of nowhere, waving her handkerchief in the air.

While Alice unpacked their trunks in Rochester, Thomas studied a map of the town.

"What are those?" She pointed to one of the small X's in blue and red ink that littered the map.

"I've marked out the dwelling-places of prominent spiritualists. It would be embarrassing to fail to recognize someone active in the movement—especially *here*, of all places—and thinking of the location of their house on the map somehow allows me to keep them straight."

Alice wondered what stories she would have for her mother in this spot, the birthplace of spiritualism, near the childhood home of the table-rapping Fox sisters. She had often heard them spoken of as frauds—that even at the beginning, when they were eleven and fourteen, they supposedly cracked their joints to imitate spirits rapping on wood. Kate Fox's inclination to drink and Maggie Fox's scandalous affair with the Arctic explorer Elisha Kent Kane had done nothing to reinforce their characters. But whether their powers were fake or genuine, they had prompted the development of thousands of mediums, fake and genuine. Alice suddenly felt guilty for thinking ill of the sisters, as without the movement they ignited she would never have met her husband. Perhaps she could find a postcard with the Fox girls' likenesses; surely her mother would appreciate such a token.

On November 15, Alice thought she might awaken to a bouquet of flowers or a delivered breakfast. When Thomas roused her, she looked around but saw nothing remarkable.

"Come now, dearest," said Thomas. "I have an eight o'clock sitting."

Alice yawned and stretched dramatically. "Don't you think I have a right to sleep a bit late?"

Thomas looked at her curiously. "Do you?"

He is only playing, thought Alice. *He has a lovely surprise planned for me and wants me to think he has forgotten.* She decided to go along with it and not say anything, but she did don a new green dress that she had been saving for the occasion, by way of a hint.

No flowers awaited her at her desk in the office, either, and Alice tried to conceal her disappointment. She knew that hothouse flowers would be particularly dear this time of year, and especially in the midst of daily snowstorms—but this was her first birthday as Mrs. Holloway. Was she so greedy to expect a show of festivity?

They returned to the hotel for lunch, but no cake greeted her at the end of the meal, and Thomas hardly spoke to her. He read and wrote notes in a little blue book that he seemed keen on hiding from Alice's view. Alice's heart beat more quickly as she realized that he must be writing some kind of poem for her—so she did not interrupt him, but instead read the lunch menu over and over again to keep herself occupied.

But as the day went on and Alice tired of waiting for the celebration to begin, she resigned herself to the fact that Thomas had forgotten—keeping a secret or pretending forgetfulness was not in his nature. Having cleared a little space in her memory in anticipation of the celebration of two decades, she felt as if she could not actually *turn* twenty without some amount of recognition by others.

She tried to think of what her parents did for their birthdays—and realized she could not remember the last time they had celebrated them. So perhaps this was normal: adults, at least not sensible ones, did not place any particular importance on their birthday. Perhaps a greeting, an expression of well wishes from close friends or relations, would be welcome, but presents and grand meals were not to be expected or even desired. Let the fond memories of past birthdays remain intact, but Alice had now left her teenage years behind her, and was a wife, and in no way could be called a child anymore.

Chapter 15

So many people felt the loss of their loved ones around the Christmas season that the Holloways hardly had one of their own. They only realized it was Christmas when they came home from a long day and saw that their normally quiet hotel dining room was full of wassail drinkers and holly-sprigged plum puddings. Alice's gifts from her parents—mother-of-pearl hair combs and a pair of oranges—did not catch up with them until a January stop in Niagara. Alice had meant to save one of the oranges for Thomas, but, entranced by their sweetness, peeled and ate both of them in a single afternoon. The hotel chef gladly accepted the peels to candy, but they did not stay in town long enough to see them reappear in a dessert.

Buffalo and their other Great Lakes stops blurred together. In Erie, however, a wealthy spiritualist met the train with his own private coach and invited them to dine in his mansion with a view of the water. By the end of dinner, their host had mentioned so many people he had promised to tell of their arrival that Alice wondered if she need send any cards at all. She felt perfectly revolting the next morning, thanks to the decadent meal and two glasses of port.

Thomas was sympathetic to her plight but still recommended that she write out some invitations, if she were feeling up to it later. He brought her tea and some toast with butter. Alice appreciated the thought, but then she imagined the butter greasing her tongue, wayward crumbs of crust turning to mush in her mouth—and her stomach turned again. It was all she could do to wait until Thomas left to be sick into the chamber pot beneath the bed.

Thankfully less nauseous by lunch but still feeling weak, she ate a light meal and returned to the room, intending to lie down again. But her pulse protested, insisting that she was awake now and should occupy herself with something more active. Perhaps a stroll in the crisp air would eliminate the last of the stirrings in her stomach.

Alice wandered down the hotel's street in the opposite direction of the office and took a left turn. She was not used to such straight, even streets and unobstructed views; Old Cambridge's streets had evolved around the property of early settlers and the Common, and therefore kinked and terminated at unusual points. Sometimes a street there would end, only to begin again after the interruption of a house and lawn or a grove of trees.

A wrought-iron gate, such as one she might see at home, came into view, and Alice saw that it enclosed a small cemetery. Time and weather had heaved some of the stones into strange angles, cracked corners off others. The text chiseled on many had faded along with the memories and lives of people who had known them. This was not a botanical showcase like Mount Auburn; only a few naked trees hovered over the dead here.

Someone had shoveled a path where no gravestones grew. Since its excavation it had been blanketed again by a few inches of powder. It seemed safe enough. Yet within her first few steps her foot caught on something, and she nearly pitched headlong into the snow.

Alice stooped to see what had tripped her, and saw a tiny stone. She used a gloved hand to scoop out the snow that blocked the inscription from view. It did not help that the stone was white marble and the lettering blurred, but she discerned four letters after some squinting.

BABY.

The word made her gut twist as she realized the source of her illness, and she vomited into the snow.

Back in the room, she washed her face and mouth, fed the fire a log and rubbed her tingling hands in front of it. Perhaps it was ridiculous to make such assumptions after only one bout of nausea, especially after an indulgent evening—but somehow, some deep instinctual part of her assured her that yes, she was correct. Alice shivered, and the watering in the back of her throat began again. She cast only one regretful glance at the blank cards on her desk before settling herself upon the bed, hoping that upon waking she would be herself.

But a continued inability to eat breakfast persisted through the week. Thankfully, she could still work in the afternoons; and they had been able to set up in a small parlor of the hotel, with the help of their patron. Thomas was concerned by her extended illness, and offered to find a doctor, but he did not seem to be aware of its cause.

"I am usually better by the afternoon," she said, after Thomas had protested putting off the doctor's visit for another day. Thomas summoned the doctor without her permission, however, and Alice worried that the doctor would tell Thomas (the one who would pay his bill) whether she wanted him to or not. Thankfully, the physician was a kindly man, and promised, with a little wink, to keep her secret.

But now that she knew for certain, the news proved too exciting to keep inside for long. Several nights Alice took hours to fall asleep because of the urge to shake Thomas awake and include him in the celebration. She finally spoke up during breakfast one morning, after an older fellow sitting beside them, possessed of a voluminous beard, had lumbered back to his rooms. The man had consumed his egg and toast at a snail's pace, getting half in his mouth and the rest in his facial hair. Alice made the mistake of glancing over at him and had to breathe deeply several times to regain control of her stomach.

"Thomas?" It took her ten counts of one-two-three to even say his name.

"Yes, my dear?" Thomas glanced down from his paper at the plates in front of him. "Oh, I'm sorry, I've kept the butter from you."

"Thank you." Alice accepted the plate offered her and obediently picked up the little knife to spread her slice, but realized the toast was already coated with a thick layer, and getting cold.

She set the knife down. "No, that's not it."

"The jam's closer to you..." Thomas seemed surprised at Alice's lack of ability to keep track of condiments on the breakfast table.

"I—I'm going to have a child." She reduced her voice to a whisper just as the maid came in to clear the bearded man's plate.

Thomas gave her a look of astonishment, then smiled more broadly than she had ever seen him before, and Alice wondered why her simple declaration had been so difficult. She had been certain—mostly—that his reaction would be one of great joy.

"A child," he repeated, and laughed and shook his head. "Darling, I didn't think I could ever be happier than we were on our wedding day, but you have proved me wrong."

And he scooped Alice from her seat, right there in the dining room, and lifted her off her feet, much to the astonishment of the maid.

"We're going to be parents!" he told her, as she stared with coffee cup in hand and mouth ajar.

"Thomas! One doesn't speak of such things in public," Alice hissed as the maid scurried off, but inside she was bursting to tell all as well.

The change in Thomas was immediate; Alice's relief at his embrace of the news made January feel like spring. When she presented herself for an attempt at spirit-writing later that morning, Thomas shook his head; she could not put herself through that strain now. Although she protested, secretly she was relieved to be free of her obligation, at least for the next several months. What was once pleasurable had become too much of a chore, and too much of a disappointment.

Thomas covered her with kisses morning and night, inquired after her health so often that Alice thought she should begin giving him hourly reports, and always studied their plates carefully in the dining room, making sure that she had the choicest meat and vegetables. Sometimes he fell asleep with his warm hand on her midsection, and Alice dreamed of that hand patting their son or daughter's head.

But it seemed as if she would never shake the nausea. Alice spent much of the ride to Cleveland feeling pale and clammy as a whitefish, clutching at Thomas with a sweaty hand whenever a wave of nausea struck her—but thankfully, she never went completely under, and did not embarrass herself in the railcar. She felt so grateful upon waking one day in February and feeling well that she consumed an enormous breakfast, surprising even Thomas, who subsequently pushed food upon her as if she were a prize pig to be fattened.

The doctor she consulted in Cleveland said that soon she should feel the quickening, the first noticeable movements of the baby. Thomas would be thrilled: his hand was already anticipating such movement, checking Alice's stomach himself from time to time—as if Alice was not listening even more intently, putting her own hand there whenever her stomach gurgled, disappointed when it proved to be only indigestion.

Thomas's Midwestern schedule was lining up nicely. He had secured a lecture spot at a large conference in Chicago, and in addition had been specially asked to preside over a séance hosted by a meatpacking heir. A successful evening there could lead to a week of such sittings and a fine compliment to the Holloway purse. Next they would travel to Kalamazoo, a name that Alice enjoyed saying to herself. There one of Thomas's friends was holding a conference for Michigan spiritualists and had promised Thomas a fine spot in their order of lectures.

Alice pulled out their rail map to locate Kalamazoo, but her attention was soon drawn to the Upper Peninsula and its French-sounding town names: Sault Ste. Marie, Marquette, Manistique. How could land so separate from the rest of the U.S.—floating in Canadian territory, above the lakes—still be claimed as part of the state of Michigan? It might have made sense enough for it to stay with Wisconsin, but it seemed as if the peninsula were Canadian in all but name.

'What would possess someone to live in such a remote place?" Alice wondered aloud, as Thomas worked on correspondence across the room. She made her head hurt by imagining the vast northern portions of Canada, the isolation and desolation of perpetual winter and darkness. As the comment had been more of a rhetorical question, she was surprised when Thomas answered.

"Why, Alice, you'd think you'd never set foot in America. Settlers up there would be after land, mostly, and a sense of adventure—a taste for breaking new paths and constructing towns from scratch and perhaps even naming one after yourself. If one lucky pioneer manages to keep his settlement safe from Indian attacks, famine, and the fickle hand of Mother Nature, his offspring and the offspring of his settlers might never want to leave."

Alice raised an eyebrow at Thomas. "Do you crave a sod house or a gold-pan and life in a place called Hollowayville?"

Thomas grinned. "Now, that's a mouthful, although it has no more syllables than Kalamazoo."

"You're not answering my question." Alice suddenly had a vision of waking and finding herself on a covered wagon bound for California, kidnapped during the night by her wanderlusting husband. Though that was silly; they would take the train nowadays.

"I suppose every man has a bit of it—every native-born American, that is. I won't lie to you; there were times when I dreamed of homesteading and roaming with the buffalo. But now, I have a wife, whom I promised I would consult on all such decisions."

Alice laughed. "And, may I remind you, a child on the way who will need something stronger than a tent to sleep in." Her index finger traced their westward path so far on the map. "Speaking such arrangements, does your apartment in New York have room for a cradle?"

Thomas spun around. "New York? Why should you want to know about New York?"

Alice was startled by his reaction. "Because it is where you have lodging and, presumably, a doctor. Because it is somewhere familiar where I can spend time in recovery."

"Well, it is not familiar to you."

"That is no fault of mine." Alice could not imagine why he found the idea so repellent. "I would like to be somewhere semi-permanent during my last three months at least."

"I told you before we began this journey that we would be traveling throughout the year."

"Yes, but don't you think this an extenuating circumstance? The safe birth of your child?"

"Just because some of the places we visit are small does not mean they do not have doctors experienced in delivering babies."

"I do not doubt their competence," said Alice. "But perhaps it is advisable for me to have the same doctor for more than a few weeks at a time."

Thomas was silent. Alice came over to him and wrapped her arms around his shoulders.

"New York is not your home," he replied, calmer now. "Perhaps better would be somewhere like Chicago, from which I can conduct day trips. I do not like holding séances in New York anymore. There are plenty of believers, yes—plenty of generous sitters. But all too often I'd find my sitting interrupted by a skeptic, claiming some falsehood and upsetting the other guests."

"But those people shouldn't bother you! You have nothing to hide."

"It does not matter. They will claim, for instance, that I have opened a sealed letter, when I have had no opportunity to. No one has seen me do it nor heard the slight sound that might come from breaking a seal. When I hold it to my forehead, the seal is not broken, and I pass it around for people to examine. But their very suggestion causes people to doubt, to second-guess what they have seen. They leave dissatisfied, even if I have told them exactly what they admit they wished to hear."

"But—they cannot do that! Why do you even let them in?" Alice felt anger percolate inside of her. How dare they threaten her husband's reputation without any proof, and spoil it for the others! And what suggestible people, to follow the skeptics' lead!

Thomas shrugged. "They do not wear a badge that says 'skeptic' or 'troublemaker'. And it is my policy not to deny entrance to anyone. It would be my hope that even those skeptical of my abilities would come with an open mind, and be converted by the proof I provide. But, alas, most come with a preconceived notion and will even invent something to support that notion."

"Oh, Thomas, I'm sorry," said Alice, resting her head against the back of his neck. "I had no idea the city was such a poisonous place for mediums."

"Quite," said Thomas. "I much prefer the humbler surroundings—the more modest donation—to the insufferable intellectuals who wish to make a joke of legitimate spirit communication. That is partly why we tend to stay in places only a short while—the longer I am there, the more likely it is that word will reach some self-styled investigator, who will take it upon himself to ruin the reputation I have carefully built. If I am harassed by a skeptic I must cross that town off my list of places to return, for I will not subject myself to such treatment again."

Chapter 16

When a headache persisted in the middle of February, while they were staying near Akron, Alice assumed it to be just another symptom of pregnancy. She dismissed it to Thomas as much. But these were deep, penetrating pains as she had not felt since the summer. After two days divided between searing pain and lethargy, she asked Thomas if they should try and contact the spirits.

"No, no! You mustn't, in your state."

"But aren't we supposed to be servants to the spirits? They seem agitated..."

"If you had produced anything of worth these three months, I would say that we might try a trance," said Thomas. "But I fear the gift has almost entirely left you, and I won't have you risking our child's life by deliberately entering a state of nervous agitation."

He had given up on her. Alice pressed her lips together to prevent from crying. The pain surged in her temple as if to taunt her. For what could she say to him? She could accuse him of being cruel, but he was also speaking the truth, and she too was worried about the effects of a trance—especially a successful one—on the child. She wished she knew a woman medium with whom she was familiar enough to speak of such things.

"I have offered to fetch the doctor. I can call for him at any time."

Alice shook her head, and Thomas threw his hands up in frustration. "Then, try to rest, I suppose."

She closed her eyes and stayed quiet as Thomas readied himself for the day, making more noise than she thought necessary. Alice thought she had kept the memory of how excruciating her headaches had been, but the memory paled in comparison to the actual experience. Knowing what she did about the spirits' connection, she imagined them inside her brain, trying to break their way out with a hammer and chisel.

Surely one attempt could only help her child—would he not be uncomfortable if his mother was. Alice had never attempted to go into a trance with a migraine this advanced—she did not know if the peace required could find any purchase amidst the chaos—but she would make the effort to bring her body, and therefore the baby, relief.

Alice settled herself at the desk, pencil and paper at the ready, and closed her eyes. Bright colors splashed across her eyelids; her head felt weighted, as if her neck could not support it for long. She breathed deeply. If only she could separate herself from the headache for a moment—remove it like a helmet, and gather herself, Alice was sure that she could put herself under. She pictured herself pulling the heavy armor from her head and holding it away from her body while her scalp enjoyed the respite…

A dream came, one in which someone had scribbled on her tongue with a pencil. Her mouth filled with the metallic taste of graphite. She licked the back of her hand and words appeared, but the writing was backwards. She tried licking the other hand, with the same result. She searched for a mirror, to help decipher the text—but then she thought of touching her tongue to paper. Perhaps the words simply wanted paper, and were appearing backwards on her skin only to be contrary. One of Thomas's notebooks lay beside her; she opened it to a blank page and dragged her tongue across the top of it. She tried to read what was there, but the script was still blurry…

Her eyelids fluttered her back to wakefulness; she felt the desk shake and wondered if a train were passing by. After a few moments, Alice realized that it was her own body trembling. She rubbed her stomach and took a deep breath to settle herself. The pain in her head was gone.

Her gratitude at the absence of the headache, however, was quickly overshadowed by the thought of what Thomas's reaction would be to the treatment used. Alice forced herself to look at the paper. Something was there—had been there, but it was so badly smudged that she could hardly make out the original strokes. The fingertips of her left hand were sooty with lead. Perhaps she had unconsciously made these messy marks herself, to address both her fears: that she would produce something, and that she would produce nothing. She quickly crumpled the page and dropped it behind the fire screen, where it flamed brightly, briefly, and then withered into ash.

Alice had just poured water into the washbasin when she heard the creak of someone outside the door. Thomas, already? For how long had she been entranced? She began to scrub her left hand maniacally, feeling rather like Lady Macbeth.

"Alice?"

"I will be right there." Alice rinsed her hands and rubbed them with a towel. Her fingertips still looked slightly ashen, but the tinge was not noticeable enough to arouse suspicion.

But Thomas had let himself in. "You are on your feet—that is a good sign, yes?"

"Yes. I was able to rest at last, and now am doing well."

"I am glad to hear. I was worried that we would have to delay our engagement in Chicago."

"Of course not." Alice gave him a confident smile, though it troubled her somewhat that the trip had been his primary worry. "I'll begin packing tomorrow."

"Excellent." He came forward and kissed her on the forehead. "You are a great help to me."

Alice tightened her cloak as she hurried through a dark, lonely progression of streets. She knew she was looking for Thomas in this unfamiliar town, but she had no map, no sense of which turns would lead her to him.

"Buy some flowers, miss?"

A bony hand appeared in front of her, clutching a bouquet of long-dead roses. Alice shook her head and tried to dodge the seller, but the man kept stepping in her path. He shook the bouquet, making a noise that combined the rustle of autumn leaves and the scratchy footfall of mice.

"Buy some flowers. Help a poor man out," he quavered. "Just… five pennies a bunch."

Alice gasped at the sharp pains that had taken hold of her stomach; she looked down to find the tines of a rake embedded in her abdomen.

"Five…pennies." The tone and the volume never changed, not even when Alice began to shriek. Although the man's face was still obscured by the shadows, she knew his hands, and the tool with which he had attacked her. Her mind flashed back to the crowd of intruders that had haunted her bedroom.

The gardener had returned for her.

"Be quiet! What the devil has gotten into you!"

A hand closed over her mouth; Alice tried to bite it, but the gardener did not flinch. It was completely dark now, and he must have knocked her to the ground, which was softer than she had expected…

"I won't let go until you're quiet. You've had a bad dream of some kind, that's all." The face came into focus, and Alice saw that it was Thomas restraining her. Had she only dreamed the gardener, then? The rake had disappeared…yet the pain continued, deep within. Gingerly, her hand checked her lower half, which was intact but sticky with something. She held up a darkened palm.

Thomas's eyes widened in horror. He drew back the covers; Alice followed his eyes down and saw the dark stain that had spread beneath her.

"Oh no, oh, oh, no"—Thomas stammered, and his grip on her loosened. "I'm going to take my hand away, Alice, but please don't scream. I'll go fetch the doctor. There's something wrong with…"

He broke off, but Alice knew what he had meant to say. As soon as she nodded, he bounded out of bed and began pulling on trousers and boots. "I'll be back as soon as I can. Stay calm; don't move."

"Please hurry," whispered Alice.

Thomas kissed her on the forehead and squeezed her hand. "You will be fine—I promise," he said.

"There, now. That's a good girl."

Alice swallowed the medicine the doctor offered, although she wished he wouldn't speak to her as if she were a child. After all, wasn't she being treated for one of the trials of womanhood? The doctor had told her that yes, it was a miscarriage, and ordered her to remain in bed, flat on her back. No propping up allowed, so Alice did not even have the luxury of reading comfortably.

"No travel for a week at least," the doctor told Thomas. "I recommend that you engage a nurse—I will give you a few names."

"Of course. We'll make arrangements to stay longer."

Somewhere in Alice's hazy mind she thought that they had only intended to stay a day or two more, because…because…

Alice gasped, and both men turned toward her in concern.

"Chicago! We're to be in Chicago in two days."

"I'm afraid that's out of the question, Mrs. Holloway," said the doctor. "Of course, Mr. Holloway could leave you in the care of the nurse if he wished."

"We will take as long as she needs," said Thomas, although the pause before his statement suggested to Alice that he had, briefly, considered the doctor's suggestion.

"That would be most advisable." The doctor placed a little amber bottle on Alice's bedside table. She stared at the little cork stopper that kept the medicine inside. Plugged up like Alice was now, with cotton in uncomfortable places until the bleeding stopped.

"Here is some chamomilla. I understand that mental excitement brought this on?"

"I—I had a bad dream," said Alice.

The doctor nodded. "Sometimes it's not even a conscious disturbance, but the body always knows." To Thomas, he said: "You're to mix twelve globules of this"—he tapped the bottle—"with three tablespoonfuls of water, and she is to have a teaspoonful of that solution every half-hour. Do that thrice and then repeat the dose every three hours until she seems to have gained. Should she go into throes, refrain from the chamomilla until they have subsided. Hopefully, though, the body has already done its work in that respect." He slipped his instruments back into his bag.

"Now, make sure you keep to bed, young lady. Taking the proper precautions now will reduce your risk of this happening again."

Again? Alice could hardly bear the pain now. She nodded at the doctor, if only to make him leave.

"That's a good girl," he said again. Alice watched Thomas dig around in his pocket for payment; he blushed as his fumbles became more and more frantic.

"The desk drawer, Thomas."

"Oh, of course." Thomas fetched the metal donation box and counted out several bills for the doctor. The doctor, who had been looking apprehensive about the adequate delivery of payment, turned sunny once the money was in his hand.

"Thank you. I think she'll mend nicely"—he dropped his voice, but Alice could still hear him—"just don't get her too excited. No upsetting news, no inflammatory literature. She's a frail one and more distress could endanger her life."

Inflammatory literature? Alice wished she had more strength; she wanted to berate the doctor for his old-fashioned ideas. But Thomas agreed to do as the doctor asked and shook his hand. The doctor donned his hat and tipped the brim at Alice.

"Rest easy, Mrs. Holloway."

Alice didn't want to cry again, but her body didn't seem to be minding any of her wishes lately. At least she held back until the doctor and his black bag had gone out the door.

"Thomas?"

Thomas was staring out the window at the newborn glow of the dawn, his hands clasped behind his back. "I do not know what else we could have done." He looked back at her. "I had you restrict your outdoor activity. I tried to make our travel as comfortable for you as possible. I have kept you from going into trances."

Something telltale must have flashed across Alice's face then, because Thomas began to scowl as he realized what had happened. "You *did* go into a trance."

"My headache would not stop. Surely it can't have been good for the baby for me to be in that much pain...I thought I would try just once, and it worked."

"It worked? You received a communication?" Thomas's voice was still wary, but brighter.

"Something, but it was too smudged to read. Yet my head was much improved..."

"You are keeping them from me, aren't you? Aren't you?"

Alice stared at him. "Thomas! Why would I do that? What reason could I have?" The fuzziness in her head made Thomas's hysteria even more startling. His pacing was making her dizzy. She closed her eyes. "Thomas, you don't really think this was my fault, do you?"

"I think your actions showed tremendous selfishness and irresponsibility, and that you are clearly not ready to be a mother."

Something inside Alice spasmed, and she swallowed deeply, trying to keep herself calm. "Please...the doctor said I shouldn't get excited and you're upsetting me."

But when Thomas fell to his knees and began to cry, the anger she had felt at his insult collided with pity and shock. She should go to him—no, she should leave him alone—no, he had done her a great wrong—but she was his wife, and who else could comfort him?—no, she was not supposed to get out of bed—

"Come here, Thomas." She was not quite sure how to comfort him, as she had only just regained control of her own emotions; but he came and lay on the bed next to her, and she held him as best she could while staying on her back. A little pain rippled through her abdomen as she shifted to accommodate him, but she bit her lip and made no sound.

"I never realized how badly I wanted to be a father until you told me I was going to become one," Thomas whispered in Alice's ear. "I had sworn to myself that I would be a better papa than mine had been."

"You'll have another chance, in due time," Alice said, though she had not five minutes ago doubted whether she would ever want to carry a child again. Even if she carried it to term, it could be born simple or deformed. It could die during the birth; she could die during the birth. She could be mangled by forceps or touched by fever, and never again did she want to lie abed for months, insensible to the world.

Yet she cooed in Thomas's ear about the fine boy or beautiful girl they might have in another year, trying to convince herself as well as him that things would go right in good time.

Thomas brought a nurse by the next day. A rosy-cheeked middle-aged blonde who must have been beautiful when young, she gently changed Alice's bandages and chatted as she worked. Alice was so grateful for company that she found herself asking all sorts of personal questions. A New Englander might have taken offense, but the Ohioan nurse answered Alice's queries cheerfully and thoroughly. Once, after taking her chamomilla, she dozed while the nurse knitted in a corner, and woke thinking that Mrs. Connors was watching over her again.

When her week of bedrest was up and her chamomilla doses were tapering, the nurse fixed her a warm bath and helped her in. Alice let herself slide down in the water so that her lips were separated by the surface. She blew bubbles and watched them swell and break.

Now would be the time to cry, when no one would question a wet and flushed face, but Alice found she hadn't the urge. She had kept herself from weeping ever since Thomas had broken down, in an effort to project a strong front, and the restraint had seemed to desiccate her tearducts. Certainly many Cambridge women she had known must have endured such a loss, but when their bodies recovered they returned to their lives, and the sympathetic whispers died down in due time. Some suffered from illness or melancholy ever after—but Alice told herself she would not be one of those women, even as her heart seemed to draw her down like an anchor.

Chapter 17

To pass the time during travel, Alice liked to make up stories about the homes she saw for a few moments before the train clattered past in a cloud of black smoke. She found abandoned houses and shacks the most intriguing, since there were no such structures in her carefully kept Cambridge neighborhood. Perhaps the owner of a dilapidated brick farmhouse had followed his true love out of their small town, she thought. Maybe a son had inherited the log cabin whose ragged white curtains now waved in surrender to nature, but the young man's dream was to be a newspaper reporter. He achieved success in the city and never returned.

Alice preferred to think that these buildings were abandoned for a happy reason. She knew it was probably not the case for most.

They were to stay at the Kalamazoo House two nights. The organizer had apologized to Thomas; overeager convention-goers had snapped up all the rooms in Kalamazoo's largest hotels for the conference itself, but he had made arrangements for them at a boardinghouse just outside the center of town for the remainder of their stay. It was run by the widow Kollner, who reportedly made very fine pies. But Alice, starved for company, had been looking forward to the possibility of mingling with other attendees. Thomas had not been very talkative as of late.

The hotel certainly made an attempt at worldly glamour, although the years had left it a faded beauty. Pink velvet wallpaper that must have been scarlet once and a mahogany front door only absorbed the flickering flames of untended gas lamps. A man at the front desk called for a young man with gold braids and epaulets to take the trunks upstairs in the elevator, and asked them to sign the guestbook.

Mr. and Mrs. Thomas C. Holloway, she wrote, and the pen obliged a smooth script without any skips.

Alice moved to follow their trunks, but Thomas held her back and steered her away from the stairs; he seemed to be drawn to the laughter and conversation coming from the parlor. When she looked in, the room's occupants—all male—stared at her as if they had never seen a woman before. Alice averted her eyes, feeling like a curio in some collector's cabinet, but as Thomas entered behind her the men sprang to voice and action.

"Why, Holloway, you've made it! I grant the snow was not too much for you in your travels, what with all your time spent in the East."

"Well, we have snow back there too, you know," Thomas said, shaking the hand of and embracing each man in turn. "Or maybe you don't. You did go to State, after all, and I don't know what they teach there."

Guffaws and back-slapping all around. The rivalry between Ann Arbor and the state university must be similar to that of Harvard and Yale back home. Alice stood quite still, but used a trick her mother had taught her when she was younger and naturally fidgety, and wriggled her big toes within her boots. "You have to channel the squirms down there, so people don't think you're so impatient," her mother had said once, after Alice's kicking boots at a lecture had connected loudly with the bench in front of them.

"Oh, forgive me, my dear. Gentlemen, this is my wife, Alice."

Alice bobbed her head towards the strangers, who all stood, bowed and spoke their names—quickly forgotten by Alice— and sat down again.

"It's a poor excuse, but I'm not used to the responsibility of introducing a lady. You see, we're only just married."

"*Just* married?" said the one with rusty hair. "Don't tell me this cad is bringing you here on your honeymoon. To the frozen village of Kalamazoo? Really, man, why not go further north to Canada, if it's tobogganing you're looking for, romance-wise..."

"Kalamazoo's a city now, remember?" said the shorter fellow with dark, sleek hair. "Incorporated just last year. Was the biggest village in the U.S. before that."

"Well, it still doesn't deserve the title," said Rusty. "Now Detroit, there's a city." He puffed out his chest like a proud rooster. "Have you ever been to Detroit, Mrs. Holloway?"

"I believe we passed by it on the train ride here, but I haven't had the pleasure of an extended stay."

"A pleasure it is indeed, and Thomas would do well to take you there once he's fulfilled his duties in Kalamazoo. I'm afraid I've left my own wife at home to take care of the little ones. At least you have not been wed long enough to be burdened with children."

Alice tried to smile at his comment, but she felt tension radiating from Thomas. She excused herself with the reason of wanting to unpack. Thomas held up his finger to signify his momentary return, and walked Alice to the stairs.

"I'm sorry if I haven't done a better job of including you."

"It's all right, Thomas." Alice patted his arm. "I would rather your friends be able to speak freely to you, and I don't see how I can fit into the conversation."

Thomas opened his mouth, but Alice shook her head. "I'm exhausted. Please—I'll just go up, get our things in order, and have a lie-down."

Thomas nodded. "Very well, then. And please don't wait up on my account—as you've seen, these fellows are talkative, and it may be a while before their motors wear down."

Alice's energy was flagging by the time she reached the third floor, and at the sight of the unopened trunks her face crumpled. She had to remind herself that her retirement this evening was entirely voluntary; that Thomas had asked her to stay. She did wish, perhaps unreasonably, that he had offered to leave his friends early so he could keep her company. But it was childish to expect Thomas to give up every aspect of his life before her.

The few times Alice and her parents had stayed in hotels, they had always kept to themselves during meals. Rarely were they in residence more than a few days, and so her father deemed it not worth interrupting the meals of others to introduce one's self.

"Just think—it might be their last day here!" Mr. Boyden had said when Alice, aged eight, had asked if she could play with a girl they saw at lunch. "They're trying to enjoy the little time they have left, and then another family interrupts their meal with introductions, which they are too polite to refuse, and not until their soup has gone cold do the intruders ask how long they are staying, and then excuse themselves awkwardly once they know. No, vacationers should be left in peace."

In fact, the other family had stayed just as long as the Boydens, but Alice had not been eager to point this out to her father.

In the dining room here, however, people waved Thomas over, inviting them to share their table. Alice was quickly introduced to Josiah

Hammerstein, Esq., William Todd, Dr. Amabel Inman (the title both impressed and intimidated Alice) and the Lindens, Joel and Clara. "He does full-on apparitions; me, I only have the talent for table-tipping," said Mrs. Linden, by way of introduction.

"Are you all from Michigan?" Alice asked politely, and was answered by a chorus of nods and head-shakes.

"Josiah, I thought you were in Lansing?" Dr. Inman asked one of the headshakers.

"No, no," said Mr. Hammerstein. "I've been in Chicago as of late. But the Illinois spiritualists are not nearly as organized as the Michigan ones, and I daresay I'm still close enough to enjoy the company of my compatriots here."

"Well, we are glad you have not forsaken us," said Dr. Inman. "I am in Ann Arbor." Alice presumed she had gone to medical school there, and wanted to ask her what it was like, but decided it was too early in their acquaintance for such a question.

"And we are from Detroit, as is Mr. Todd here," said Mrs. Linden. "We know that Mr. Holloway has roots in the same area, but where are you from, my dear?"

"Oh. Cambridge. Cambridge, Mass."

"Oh, lovely. We had a nephew who attended Harvard—went there for his graduation. Such a beautiful campus."

"My father teaches entomology there," said Alice, feeling proud.

Mrs. Linden gave a little grimace. "Well, he must have a strong backbone. And I'm sure you've encountered more than your share of skeptics in such an academic town?"

"A few." Alice realized she had never broached the topic of spiritualism with any Cantabrigians save her father.

Mrs. Linden shuddered. "They're always circling around these conferences, you know. Like vultures, or lions waiting for someone to fall behind. Some mediums avoid organized spiritualist gatherings for that very reason. They think it dangerous to make themselves such a target. I say they should not spoil our fun and fellowship." She sighed. "You also would think the spirits would warn us when there's a nonbeliever in the room, and sometimes they do, but more often than not our spirit guides wish to give anyone a chance.

"And these skeptics, these so-called investigators," she continued, her voice increasing in volume, "are often bigger crooks than they ever accuse us of being. Why, some are experienced pickpockets, and so can rearrange evidence while the rest of the sitters concentrate on the medium, and the medium is in trance. Some are simply failed charlatans who, when caught at their game, made a grand public confession and swore to combat similar chicanery, as a way of clearing his or her name. But they simply seek to bring down the network that would not stand by them while they soiled the term of spiritualist."

The soup had come during Mrs. Linden's speech, but Alice had not touched a drop of it. She suddenly felt as if her previous skepticism were a mark that lingered on her skin, and that Mrs. Linden could sense it.

"Come now, dear," said Mr. Linden, who had turned back to his wife, "you're wasting your words on discussing those parasites. I am of a mind that the more we ignore them, the less they will want to pursue us. It's no fun for them if the prey isn't game."

"I don't feel as if that matters to them—if they see a medium achieving success, they automatically assume he or she is using trickery to achieve results, and will dog their target until they have found, or are able to fabricate, some "proof" to support their claim," said Mrs. Linden. "Those mediums who seek to mind their own business are not necessarily safe from these people. But I'll speak of them no more. As I told Mrs. Holloway here, I'll not let them ruin my good time."

"That's the spirit, dear," said Mr. Linden. "Now, onto more important things, such as the consistency of this onion soup. Gelatinous? Viscous? Let us take a poll as to the most appropriate adjective."

As people at the table alternately sipped at their soup, made some variation of a face, and offered up the ideal descriptive word, Alice's thoughts were still mired in the idea of lurking skeptics. Thomas had been so loath to return to New York because of them. Would he be challenged here?

"And you, Mrs. Holloway? Do you have anything suitable with which to label our first course?"

Alice gazed into the murky depths of the soup, which she still had not explored. "Secretive," she said.

Everyone looked down at their bowls, stirred their spoons around, and indicated their consent.

"I think we have a winner!" said Mr. Linden.

Thomas, occupied by a meeting with the conference organizers the next morning, had asked Alice to handle the transfer of their luggage from the hotel to the house on Burdick Street. She was glad that the prospect of taking on such tasks, once a nerve-racking endeavor, had become quite familiar.

Alice had hardly seen her husband over the past two days; he seemed to have a great many friends here, or have made new ones, and his days were a blur of lunch and dinner engagements made continuous by other social calls and drinks. Always drinks. Alice had grown quite used to Thomas having a nightly ale or scotch, but now he poured himself into bed at a very late—or very early—hour, reeking of it. And he was inevitably ill-tempered in the morning.

From the window of the carriage Alice saw the storefronts of Main Street turn into the glorious homes of what the driver called Mansion Row. Each house was made even more romantic by the light snow that had settled on ornate wooden trims and stone statues holding court in empty fountains.

"Are all of these homes boardinghouses? They can't be," said Alice, answering herself before the driver, occupied with a particularly heavy trunk, had a chance to reply.

"No, ma'am," he confirmed, puffing a bit. "Mrs. Kollner is the only one that takes boarders. The other owners of these houses might have the room for guests, but they certainly don't need the money."

There was not even a sign out front, and at first Alice worried that the driver had deposited her at the wrong house. Although she and Thomas had stayed in other boardinghouses and small inns, she had never had such an acute feeling of paying someone a visit unannounced. She gave the knocker a deliberate thump and waited for a minute. No answer. Then Alice noticed the corner of what seemed to be a brass plaque, peeking out from a dusting of snow. She brushed it clean and read:

IF NO ANSWER, PLEASE ENTER AND RING BELL.

Alice tried the door, which was indeed open, and slipped inside, taking care to knock the bulk of the snow from her boots before treading on the carpet. The boardinghouse was light and airy where the hotel had been dark and curtained; even on this gray afternoon, it seemed lit by spring sunshine. The front hall and parlor probably owed their cheeriness to the fact that most of the decor was white, yellow, and pink, muted by age and sunlight. A more feminine place, certainly; the velvet and gilt of the hotel had had suggestions of a smoking parlor, but this was a home.

After some searching, she finally spotted the silver glint of the bell behind some books on a side table, and was moving toward it when the front door of the hotel burst open and a gang of flaxen-haired children came running into the lobby. She was wondering what guest would allow their children to behave like this when she felt something attach itself to her leg.

Alice was glad she had resisted the impulse to kick whatever it was away, for the clinger-on was a little girl of about four, her arms filled with Alice's traveling coat and skirt. Several other children had escaped to another room. When the child looked up and saw Alice staring down at her, her face collapsed in a frown and she began to wail.

"Oh, please, little one, don't cry, it's all right..." Alice bent down in an attempt to soothe the girl, but she only put a hand in her mouth and continued crying around the obstruction.

How could you have offspring of your own, when your mere presence makes others' children cry for no reason? said a voice in Alice's head.

"Eleanor? Is that you? What's the matter?" A bullet of a woman—slightly pointy head, the same width from her shoulders on down—in a smudged cook's apron ran out of the kitchen and looked around for the source of the crying. When she saw Alice, she frowned.

Alice realized that she still had not rung the bell to announce her presence, and straightened up. "I'm so sorry. I don't know what I did to upset her. She grabbed my leg, and then the tears started when she looked up at me."

The woman scooped up the little girl, who quickly quieted down when tucked into her mother's bosom (Alice assumed this woman was the mother) and patted on the back.

"She must have thought you were me." The woman's face and voice had softened. "Look."

She pulled her apron aside and stuck her leg out towards Alice. Puzzled for a moment, Alice realized that their skirts were an almost identical shade of brown.

"We're about the same height, too," the woman said once Alice had nodded in understanding. "From Eleanor's line of sight, we're just about twins."

Now Alice smiled at the thought of what the world must look like to the little girl. She remembered an observation of her own at the age of nine, how every year her father procured a smaller Christmas tree than the year before. Her mother had laughed at Alice's observation. "Your father makes sure to get the same height every year. He's very methodical about it. But come to think of it, haven't the windowsills in the parlor sunk, too?"

"Have you just arrived? I'm sorry—that was hardly much of a welcome. I'm Mrs. Kollner, but you may call me Thea. Everyone does once they've been here five minutes."

"Thea?" Alice echoed.

"Short for Theodora. Now you know why I shorten it, eh? This is Eleanor, as you might have heard. The sandstorm that I presume just blew by you consists of Maudie, Francis, and Ernest." Thea set the now-quiet Eleanor down, who waddled away happily, presumably in search of her siblings. "I permit a bit of horseplay down here during the winter months, when there's nowhere else suitable for them to stretch their legs, but they are not allowed upstairs on the guest floors—and if they are ever bothering you, anywhere, let me know and I will address the situation." She lightly smacked the spoon she held against her thigh for emphasis, or perhaps as a demonstration. "And you are Miss..."

"Mrs. Holloway." Alice found that she had finally mastered remembering her new name. Alice Boyden seemed a distant memory, the title marking another person altogether. "Alice Holloway. My husband Thomas is speaking at the spiritualist convention."

Thea's eyes widened. "Oh, yes, I recognize his name from the program. I don't hold much stock in this spirit-chasing myself—I'm sorry, was that dreadfully offensive?"

"No, it's all right," said Alice.

"Sometimes my tact just leaves me. But I am providing lodging for a few of the meeting-goers, and they gave me a program to help me familiarize myself with the names."

She pulled out a pink booklet held to her waist by her apron sash. It had already had a tour of the kitchen, Alice noted: dusted with flour and splattered with a sauce of some kind.

"Ah—here we are. Mr. Thomas Holloway, featured lecturer—you're in room three." She pointed to the number written in blue ink beside Thomas's portrait, the same that had graced the Onset program. Alice reflected that his mustache was a little longer now, his hair a little shorter. "Just come with me, if you please."

Alice followed Thea's round brown-clothed rump up the stairs. Aside from the dress color and height, they did not look alike at all. Thea's stick-straight, fair hair fit smoothly into a bun, whereas Alice was sure some of her own dark waves had already escaped their pins.

"My apologies for calling you miss before—you just look so young! I thought you might be here with your parents, or taking a look at the teachers' college." Thea said this over her shoulder as she puffed her way up the stairs.

Alice almost said, "I am young—I'm only twenty," but held back on the bare truth for some reason. "I've always looked young for my age."

"And what a blessing that is—or will be, once you have much age to speak of!" At the top of the stairs, Thea looked to one side and then the other, a finger tapping her lips, as if she were not sure where to go. A glance at the number on the key again, though, and she immediately turned down the right-hand hall.

"Here you are," said Thea, unlocking the door to reveal rose-patterned wallpaper, a bed with a coverlet in the same print, an armchair, and an armoire. "Will this suit?" She turned to Alice for a reaction.

Alice peered in. "Is there a desk? My husband has a great deal of correspondence to keep up."

"Yes, yes, it's in that little nook there." Thea pointed toward a narrow part of the room leading to a window. A simple straight-legged desk and its matching chair rested below the sill.

"This will be fine, then." As she spoke, Alice ran her hand over the footboard and felt dust stick to her fingers.

"Excellent, excellent." Thea pressed the key into Alice's other hand. "I'll leave a second key downstairs for your husband, should you choose to retire at different times."

"Thank you."

"And I'll have one of the boys bring up your trunks." Seeing Alice's startled expression, Thea quickly added, "Oh, no, not *my* boys. There are a few neighborhood teenagers that help me during busier times." She grinned, revealing a front tooth that resembled a gray pebble.

"Oh." Alice gave a relieved chuckle. Although she had not had a good look at Thea's sons—she had forgotten their names already—she remembered them being no bigger than the trunks themselves.

"Lunch will be served in about an hour. Shall I count on your husband to join you?"

Alice shook her head. "No, he'll likely be dining elsewhere."

"Very well. I shall see you at noon."

Thea smiled and left the room, leaving Alice to absorb her new surroundings. The wallpaper depicted an assortment of tiny idylls, framed by leaves and buds and thorns. Having spent her life in old Cambridge parlors, Alice knew toile prints well; this one was rather crudely drawn, and looked faded. But there was the shepherdess with her beribboned crook and two little lambs to mind; there was the young man reclining against a tree trunk, flute to his lips and hat cocked to keep the sun out of his eyes. The pastoral characters were old friends of hers—and she was grateful to see anything familiar at this point in their journey, seven hundred miles from home.

Chapter 18

She did not expect him for lunch, but as dinnertime grew near Alice wondered about Thomas's evening plans.

At four she checked the mailbox and with Thea to see if a note had come, but nothing.

From five to six she waited in the bedroom.

From six to seven she waited in the dining room.

Finally, at seven-thirty, after coaxing from Thea and losing willpower to the smells coming from the kitchen, Alice accepted the bowl of stew and the emptiness of the chair across from her.

The stew was one of the best Alice had ever had—hearty chunks of beef in a rich broth with bits of carrots and potato cooked to perfection. She tried to concentrate on taking moderate, not gluttonous, bites and murmured her appreciation to Thea when she emerged from the kitchen again, a compliment that Thea took as an invitation to sit down. Alice had seen other dinner guests come and go while she waited, making her the sole member of Thea's audience—save for Eleanor, who was hosting her own repast with a trio of dolls and not very interested in what the adults had to say.

"When the celery comes in the spring, my soups will be full of it. I'm afraid it's root vegetables for several weeks yet. Did you know that Kalamazoo is known as the Celery City?"

Alice hadn't known.

"They're all covered by snow now, of course, but further down South Burdick here you'll see a number of celery fields. They'll be a lovely light green in the springtime."

And so on, with the occasional interruption from Eleanor, who offered Thea and Alice imaginary desserts.

"Dowwy says the wemon tart is *delicious*."

Alice returned to her room feeling enlightened about the industries of Kalamazoo, but the silence she found there only reminded her of why she had spent her meal conversing with the housekeeper. Thomas was well aware that she was in an unfamiliar place, without even the casual acquaintances she had made at the previous hotel, and yet he had made no attempt to include his wife in his evening plans.

She lay wide-eyed in the bed for what seemed like hours. When she finally heard the door open, Alice tried to make it sound like an innocent statement, rather than a complaint. "I missed you at dinner this evening."

"I was dining with the other speakers at the hotel," came the sharp reply through the darkness. "My time is not my own here."

Alice propped herself up on one elbow. "I did not mean to imply that you should be dining with me alone. I only wish I could come along."

"No one else invited their wives to dinner." Thomas turned on the gas lamp without warning, making Alice squint in the sudden brightness.

"Yes, but they did not invite their wives along for the trip." Alice could not keep the increasing shrillness out of her voice now.

"You would not have enjoyed yourself." He spoke slowly and deliberately as he rummaged around in one of their trunks. "The only people there were mediums, and the only conversation about the peculiarities of our trade. The talk would have bored you."

So—he no longer even thinks of me as a medium, thought Alice. Of course, his dismissal of her former talents was justified—how long since she had produced some useful communication? Three months—or more? She let herself sink back into the sheets without a reply and closed her eyes against the light. After a few moments of silence, a muffled "Aha!" suggested that Thomas had found whatever he had sought.

"My friends are waiting on me and my cigars." Thomas gave her such a quick peck on the forehead that Alice wondered if she had imagined it.

Thomas insisted he was too nervous to take breakfast the morning of his lecture. Despite his behavior the previous night, Alice felt nurturing in the face of his vulnerability and gently pushed him to have at least a piece of toast. He murmured something about needing to warm up his voice and hurried off, leaving Alice sitting at the table with a half-finished plate.

"You could warm up your voice by having a conversation with me," she said quietly, in the direction he had gone. She returned to her breakfast, but found that her appetite had dissipated as well. Thea frowned when she came to collect the plates.

"Breakfast not to your liking this morning?"

"Oh, no, no," Alice hastened to say. "It's just that Thomas has a rather important lecture today, and, well, we're both a bit nervous."

"Ah," said Thea. "I should have looked at the schedule. I might have made you something less dense."

"I wouldn't have wanted you to go to the trouble."

"It's really no trouble at all," said Thea, stacking the plates carefully. "You may have noticed that you two rise earlier than anybody else staying here, so I'm happy to cater to you. And Thomas being a VIP and all."

Alice had taken note of the prominent place given to Thomas in the program and the number of people who sought him out at hotel dinners, but still she was not prepared for the crowd she confronted in the auditorium. Twenty minutes until the talk began, and already the hall was nearly full. She searched for Thomas, hoping he had reserved a seat for her, but she could not find him, and so she took a vacant aisle seat. She had never heard Thomas speak before an audience, as he had dissuaded her from attending his two lectures at Onset, saying that the presence of such a powerful medium might confuse the spirits. Now, he must have reasoned, she would be no distraction, no drain on his power.

"Have you ever been to a spiritualist convention before?"

Alice turned to her right. A small woman with a nest of grey curls blinked up at her through spectacles.

"Of sorts. A spiritualist camp. My mother is a member of the Onset Bay Grove Association." Alice felt a strange little ripple of pride when she said it.

"Was that where Mr. Martin belonged?" the woman asked her husband. He shook his head, and the woman turned again to Alice. "I'm afraid we're not familiar with Onset."

"Perfectly understandable; it's in Massachusetts," said Alice, although she had assumed Onset enjoyed a fairly wide reputation.

"Oh, so you're from the East, then? I knew it—Teddy, didn't I say she must be from one of the eastern cities? Or at least Chicago. You just have such a sophisticated air about you."

"Why, thank you," said Alice, keeping her own first impressions of these people to herself. "We've been traveling in the Midwest mostly, though our home is in New York City."

"What a world traveler you are! It took us until our children were grown to get as far north as Chicago. I'd love to get to New York before I die; I hear it's wonderful."

"It certainly has a great deal to offer," said Alice, not mentioning that she had still not been to New York herself.

"Will your husband be joining us? Should we shift seats?" The woman waved at her husband to occupy a vacant chair more toward the middle of the row, all the while craning her neck to peer down the aisle, presumably for someone who looked like Alice's husband, equally citified.

"Actually, he's speaking soon, so I needn't save him a seat."

The woman froze halfway between her seat and one further, blinking at Alice. "You mean your husband is Thomas Chester Holloway?"

"Indeed."

"Did you hear that, Teddy? We're sitting next to the wife of a celebrity." The woman clapped her hands and immediately reseated herself beside Alice, leaving her husband to shift yet again. "I'm Vera Haddon, and this is my husband Teddy. I am now well acquainted with the program after much study, and I said to Teddy, didn't I, Teddy, that Mr. Holloway must be a *very* interesting man."

Before Alice had a chance to answer, Mrs. Haddon threw up her hands with a laugh. "You must forgive my babbling. It's only that we're so excited for this event to be held right here in Kalamazoo, and not long after we embraced spiritualism, either. My daughter-in-law is the one who convinced us to sit in on a séance; a lot of hogwash, I felt at the time, but you see, we just lost a grandchild—a five-year-old boy, the Lord rest his soul—and Sadie, that's my daughter-in-law, was just prostrated by grief before she sat with a medium whose spirit control found Billy and bade Billy speak though the medium to his mamma, and she heard his little voice telling"—Mrs. Haddon was tearing up now—"telling her to be strong for the sake of his sisters, and that he was safe with God, but that his siblings on earth needed their mamma still. I sat in a circle at the request of my son and daughter-in-law, praying this wasn't some charlatan giving them false hope, but then what else could it be? The real thing?

"And then once we were assembled, we all held hands, and the lights were turned down, and the medium shut her eyes. What seemed like twenty minutes passed, and I was afraid that nothing would happen and Sadie would sink back into despair. When she described her conversation with Billy through the medium, she was happier than I'd ever seen her—even when Billy was alive—even on her wedding day.

"But then a high little voice much unlike the medium's own came through her lips, the voice of a small boy. And it said, 'Grandmamma and Grandpapa, I am so glad you came! Grandpapa, I wanted to ask if you would finish my project for me.'

"And indeed, Teddy had begun a woodworking project with Billy—a chair for his smallest sister. Teddy had been helping Billy cut the pieces and sand everything smooth.

"'Please sand it well, so she won't get a splinter in her finger,' said the voice of Billy, as that's how he always was, looking out for his sisters.

"And then—and this is the amazing part—he says, 'Grandmamma, I am honored that you wear a lock of my hair in your brooch—but do not forget the live children as well!"

At this point Mrs. Haddon broke down completely, and her husband, looking damp-eyed himself, offered her a handkerchief. Alice saw one of Mrs. Haddon's hands take the handkerchief and the other go to her throat, where a glass-domed brooch held a dark curl.

How could Alice tell this woman she had probably been had? Nothing the medium said without encouragement sounded specific enough to suggest actual communication with the boy. An unchanged child's voice was easy enough to imitate. The grandfather's project? A lucky guess, or else the father or mother had let something slip.

Instead Alice said, "It's wonderful, isn't it, the sense of peace you feel after such an encounter," and hated herself for saying it.

Mrs. Haddon looked up at Alice as if she had said something deeply profound. "Yes. Yes, that's it exactly. Why, perhaps you should be up there speaking with your husband!"

At that moment applause redirected everyone's attention away from their conversation partners and towards the stage, so that Alice did not have to respond. Mr. Whiting ascended the stairs, followed by Thomas. Both appeared to be having a good laugh about something.

"Oh, isn't he handsome," murmured Mrs. Haddon.

Alice squirmed though Thomas's introduction. This was the moment when the audience listened most closely, wondering whether the speaker would live up to their expectations, exceed them, or prove to be a complete waste of time. Some would have their own particular agendas, of course; there were those who would not be swayed from their opinions and merely wanted more fodder to support or disprove the speaker's thesis. These were the ones who rose with pointed questions at the end, questions that ended up being mini-lectures in themselves.

She would take comfort from the matching band Thomas wore—if she could see it; his hands were moving so quickly and the lights alternately illuminated and shadowed the figure on stage. Alice twirled her own around her finger.

Had he switched it to his right hand, for some reason? When both his hands lifted from the podium, Alice glanced between them, but neither hand seemed to be wearing any sort of jewelry. She scrutinized every knuckle—nothing.

She knew Thomas was speaking, but her own thoughts pushed every other word past her consciousness, so that he seemed to be transmitting some kind of code—a code that everyone else in the auditorium understood, as they nodded and murmured in reaction to his statements. How could he have forgotten his ring, on such an important day?

This is silly, she tried to convince herself, unsuccessfully. *He could not mean anything by it.*

She had not realized how completely she had been enveloped in this limbo of insecurity until Thomas stopped talking and took a bow. The auditorium erupted into applause and a chorus of conversation. Alice could not hear what was being said around her; all had melded into a buzz. She thought the Haddons might be speaking to her, but she could not turn her head to look at them. All the muscles in her body had tensed, freezing her in place. She felt a roaring in her ears.

And then Alice heard from someone in the crowd, as if the seas of talk had been parted—

"I wonder if he is married."

That, finally, propelled Alice from her seat and out the door into a windy gray day. It was not until she was halfway to the boardinghouse that she realized she had forgotten her coat.

Blue and shivering, Alice could barely move her fingers enough to open the front door. She had hoped to seek refuge in her room, but was almost immediately greeted with a motherly cluck of concern from

Thea. "Oh, my. Now, we all want spring to come, but you don't want to risk not seeing it by leaving off your coat, do you?" As Thea steered her away from the stairs, Alice's bare hands began to burn in their thawing.

"Come, come in the kitchen—it's toasty warm in there. I'll fetch a blanket."

Moments later, Alice was hunched at the table in a wrapping of gray wool, her rose-colored hands clasped around a cup of hot tea that Thea had dosed liberally with milk and sugar. Around her, Thea seemed to be doing three things at once: pouring her own tea, sweeping stray flour from the table, and setting out a plate of biscuits from which steam rose.

"Are men apt to forget to wear their wedding-rings?" Alice blurted. She could think of no small talk with which to ease into the conversation, but felt the need to say something, having been silent throughout Thea's ministrations.

Thea frowned. "I suppose some are. Men pay less attention to such things. But mine never took his off. He still wears it now," she said with a little smile. "Perhaps some more resourceful women would think to take it off and sell it before the body was buried, but I didn't think it right to deprive him of something that had been such a part of him. I doubt his very finger would have relinquished it."

Alice burst into tears. As Thea patted her back in sympathetic confusion, Alice found her mouth forming the words to her entire story—about her illness, their courtship, her marriage and miscarriage, sometimes jumping back and forth in time, but not stopping. She managed to slow her tears a few minutes in, realizing that her blubbering was making her difficult to understand, but fresh ones came when she mentioned the loss of her child. While she spoke she watched her hands break and butter two biscuits, biting them between explanations and swallowing without tasting a thing.

When Alice finished she realized that she had not had one friend since she was married, no one to whom she could unburden herself, and that this virtual stranger had received the pent-up confidences of several months. It made her sadder to realize that she had not actually spoken to someone in such a personal matter since Mrs. Connors was alive. Before she could be embarrassed by her openness, Thea had wrapped her arms around her in a hug.

"You poor, poor dear."

Alice leaned into the woman for what seemed like a long time. When Thea finally, gingerly, pulled away, Alice was surprised she could sit upright, unsupported.

"Oh, four o'clock already? I'd best get started on dinner," said Thea. Alice watched her wipe her hands on her apron as if she had just completed a round of dishes or a baking task, though her gestures did not suggest annoyance or unkindness. She wondered if the woman was a regular confidante for her boarders. "Please stay as long as you like. You've not finished your tea—but, then, it's likely cold. Let me fix you a fresh cup."

"No, no—I've taken advantage enough of your hospitality." Alice stood and carefully unwrapped the blanket. Her hands were still red and cracked from exposure, but they no longer shook uncontrollably.

"Being hospitable is my job," said Thea. She saw Alice studying her hands and went to the cupboard, which contained dozens of hand-labeled bottles and jars. "But I wouldn't want you to think that I've been listening to you out of a sense of duty—here." She handed Alice a jar of what appeared to be salve. "Slather your hands well with that—make sure it's especially thick before you go to bed, and you should wake with them much improved."

"Thank you so much," said Alice, clutching the jar to her chest. "And I hope the carousing of my husband and his friends last night did not wake you or the children."

"Oh, of course not." Thea shook her head vigorously. "We're all sound sleepers, and believe it or not, the servants' quarters are quite isolated from the sounds of the rest of the house. Are you sure you won't stay?"

"No, I'm plenty warm now. And I have some correspondence to take care of," although she had no such thing.

Thea looked as if she were about to say something, but simply smiled. "I'm glad. Now, I don't mean to be nosy—"

Alice blushed. She had already told this woman a lion's share of her secrets.

"—but I've noticed that while your husband has friends aplenty, you spend much of your time alone here. I know that I'm old and that my husband has been dead for five years, but I still remember some things about marriage, and about a few other topics as well. I want to repeat that you're always welcome here in the kitchen, or even beside me as I dust or polish silver, if you'd care for some company. Selfishly I'd like a bit of company myself. The older three are usually off at school, and Eleanor, bless her, takes long naps in the afternoon."

"I'll remember that. Thank you." Suddenly shy, Alice left Thea with a nod and a little smile, and retreated upstairs. At this point, Thomas would likely be surrounded by friends and inquiries and would soon be engaged in cocktails and dinner. She wondered if he was looking for her—but, then, they had never discussed where to meet after the lecture. And why should he suddenly want her company in the evening, when he had happily gone without it for days?

Alice appreciated that Thea never questioned the legitimacy of her feelings, never told her that it was silly to get worked up over something that was likely a harmless, mindless mistake.

At the sight of the toile wallpaper back in her room, homesickness slumped Alice's shoulders. She wondered if her absence in any way impacted the goings-on of Cambridge—perhaps only one less set of footprints in the snow of Brattle Street. She sat down to write a letter to her parents, but she could not think of how to begin. Next she sought distraction in the pages of a novel, but this one opened with the bickering of a husband and wife, and Alice had no taste for it.

The only other viable option was sleep, though it was not even dinnertime. Alice dozed herself into a sort of limbo between wakefulness and slumber, moments of peace interrupted by visions of Thomas being fawned over by his followers.

A gentle knock on the door roused her from her half-sleep, and it took a few moments for Alice to engage her arms and legs in an effort to answer it. When she finally reached the door, no one was there, but a tray of food had appeared. On it were mild but delectable things: some soft cheese, fresh bread still warm to the touch, a boiled potato with a pat of butter on top, just beginning to melt.

Bless you, Thea, Alice thought, and brought her treasure back inside. Cheered by the plate of food, she dug into her trunk and pulled out a text at random. It happened to be a book of geometry. If they had stayed very long in any place, if the book had had the comfort of resting on a shelf for awhile, it would have been covered in dust, but the marbling along the top and sides of the pages was still a pristine swirl of red, green, and yellow.

The food and the drone of the text indeed made her eyes heavy, and at eight-thirty she surrendered. While preparing for bed she kept looking at the door, but Thomas had not been home early these past two nights, and she doubted tonight would be an exception.

She woke at the creak of the door opening, combined with her husband's unusually heavy footfall. She knew it was Thomas from the shape of his silhouette, but also from the smell of whiskey he brought with him.

"Hello," she said softly.

The shape started. "Oh. I was trying not to wake you." The words were blurred ever so slightly, as if someone had brushed a hand across not-quite-dry ink. He sat on his side of the bed, and Alice wrinkled her nose at the peaty odor of his breath.

"Somehow I do not think those were the spirits you came here to uncover," she told him.

"Ah, my dear, the two sometimes go hand in hand." Thomas sat down on the bed and pulled off his boots. "They are excellent bedfellows—as are we, I should think—"

Alice twisted away from his inquisitive hands. "Why did you not wear your wedding ring at your lecture today?"

"My ring? I was not wearing my ring?"

Even without being able to see his eyes, the slight exaggeration in his voice made Alice doubt his innocent disbelief.

"No, you were not. And I want to know if there was a reason for it." *Though if you truly did not notice it missing, that is reason enough,* she thought.

"Mere human forgetfulness. I removed it last night, as it was chafing my finger, and neglected to replace it this morning. I assure you, it was not an intentional oversight."

I take no stock in your assurances anymore, thought Alice, but instead of speaking she turned to the wall and let the ire hover above her like smoke.

"Oh, don't *pout,*" said Thomas, climbing into bed. "You're no fun at all."

Chapter 19

"I have excellent news," said Thomas at breakfast the next morning.

Alice's heart thudded. Was their winter trip to be abbreviated? Was it time to return to the East Coast and go to housekeeping? She relished the idea of relegating trunks to a closet or cellar and giving a mattress time to mold to her shape.

"My lecture enjoyed such an audience that I have been engaged for at least a week more in the town for the purpose of conducting private sittings."

Alice stared into her bowl.

"A whole week of exclusively private sittings, Alice. We needn't set up shop anywhere—you will have no duties—they have come to us."

Her spoon dragged through the porridge, creating a lingering trough. She did not say that she would have been grateful for something to do, that she would rather travel again than stay put with no tasks ahead of her.

"What is the matter? Are you still upset about the ring? Look—" Thomas thrust his hand out towards her, so that she saw his beringed finger framed by the lace doily on the table—"I have it on now. I'll take extra care going forward, now that I know how much it means to you. And if you're unhappy about the alcohol—well, I daresay you have realized what a pleasant feeling it can create."

"It is neither," said Alice, even though the events of the night before rankled in her mind. "It is that I am homesick—"

"Alice," said Thomas in an exasperated tone. "I told you before we married that I would conduct my travels wholly in the Midwest until summertime. Then, I should hope we'll be invited back to Onset, and you'll be among the familiar once again. For they cannot deny that I was the most popular medium there."

Thomas puffed out his chest a little, and the red vest he wore made Alice think of a robin, overly proud to be the first sign of spring. From where had this vanity come? She had thought him quite humble, once upon a time.

"I don't necessarily mean that I am homesick for New England," she said. "I am homesick for a home—wherever that may be. I am tired of hotels, of packing and unpacking, of meeting so many people and yet never having the time to cultivate a friendship."

"I disclosed the extent of our travels before we married, did I not?" Thomas repeated. "It is only a few months until June. And have you not made friends here?"

Alice feared that he knew about her unburdening with Thea, but his eyes were without guile. She had previously told him that she and the housekeeper sometimes met for tea, and that was true. "Yes, *one* friend."

"Then you will be able to keep yourself occupied. I have also been made aware that there is a college in town—a Baptist college, but a college nonetheless—with a library of which you might avail; one of my clients is an instructor there, and so perhaps he could ensure your access."

"I could sit in on a class." Alice envisioned herself taking what she hoped was an inconspicuous seat in the back of the classroom, blending in as she should for someone her age, taking careful notes for future applications of knowledge.

"Ah, we will not be staying in Kalamazoo that long. I know you are eager to recommence your education, but I think it best that you continue to engage in self-study. Did you consider that your transient presence could disturb the learning of the other students?"

Alice frowned. "Is there some reason you do not wish me to interact with other people?"

"Why would I wish that? I do not dictate your movements and activities. You have had the opportunity to be more social, and you have chosen to remain in a solitary state."

"But you have not invited me to any of these social events." Alice's eyes stung. "And I am not wont to go where my company is not desired."

"I have not invited you because you are free to do as you please, and should not be constricted by the movements of your husband. Why, I am certain that some of the lady guests at the hotel would have been glad for your company, if only you were to offer it."

"Fine, then. I shall leave my card at the hotel for Mrs. Linden and Dr. Inman."

"Unfortunately, you have missed your opportunity to do so. They both depart tomorrow, as do the great majority of the lingering conventioneers. To the extent of my knowledge, I will be the only visiting medium left in Kalamazoo—hence my excitement. I'll be quite busy. And weren't you saying that you'd like a new dress?"

The grayness of the Michigan winter, the perpetual cloudy gloom that drove the sun away, leaked from February into March. Alice observed the town grow quieter, returning to its moderate buzz of activity after the swells of bustle brought on by the conference. She adopted the habit of dressing as soon as Thomas had departed in the morning and then taking a long walk, having come to rely on the grids of Midwestern towns to lead her back to her place of lodging.

Thomas briefed her on the contents of his day at breakfast every morning, but more in the manner of an announcement or a verbal date-book than anything resembling conversation. Alice, for her part, said little. She knew he would not return home until late, smelling of billiard rooms, jolly where in the morning he had been somber. She no longer let these moments of cheerfulness raise her hopes; experience had proven it was alcohol alone that had thawed the ice between them, for Thomas woke sober and scowling.

Alice longed for him to ask her about her recent attempts to reclaim her power of communication with the dead (brief and ineffective) or her renewed interest in self-study (still slogging through geometry; Greek also). She knew she should simply volunteer the information if she wished to stimulate a conversation, but at breakfast her tongue felt heavy and clay-like, and each time she made to open her mouth, Thomas would emit some sigh or throat-clearing that suggested a less-than-pleasant mood. Instead of speaking, Alice channeled her sentiments into an ever-deepening well of loneliness that threatened to hollow out her chest altogether. It was as if some gnawing hunger had moved from her stomach to her heart, but she had nothing with which to feed it.

When the sun emerged for the first time in days, it found Alice at her desk, determined to make it through some Greek exercises. The dappled light on her book sharpened her focus; it promised a walk in the hopefully warmer air upon the completion of her schoolwork. She lingered for a warming bowl of Thea's stew, then bundled herself up and set forth.

Alice had resolved to extend her walk today—perhaps wander the northern part of the city, which she had not yet explored. The wind was still biting, but instead of bowing her head against it, Alice raised her face to the chill. The shiver that traveled from her exposed cheeks to the rest of her body felt purifying.

Her platitudes to herself, the excuses and explanations that grew weaker every day, ran through her head. *Thomas's neglect is only temporary. He is still in mourning for the child. It is not even really neglect—did he not say that he wished you to be independent? It has nothing to do with your spirit trouble. He is disappointed for you, but not disappointed with you. How could his deep feelings for you have changed in the course of four months? He asked you to travel with him, be his companion.* And so on.

The laces on one of her boots had come undone, and she bent in the snow to retie them. As she stood up, brushing off the hem of her skirt, Alice noticed that she had come to the edge of Mountain Home Cemetery.

She had passed by the cemetery on most of her walks, but it had been choked with snow since her arrival in Kalamazoo, preventing her from taking a detour onto the grounds. Today's sun had melted the powder to reveal the names on some of the graves, and someone had taken a shovel to a few of the paths.

Alternately shaped by wind and thaw, the snow did not come flush with each stone, but sloped smoothly to meet the slate. Alice kept a sharp eye on where she stepped, not wanting to catch her toe on a leaning stone again. Her hand came to rest on a double grave, "Father" carved on one side and "Mother" on the other. Did Father and Mother have a contented love that lasted for decades, and would they have been pleased to have their bones interred together? Or was it wishful thinking on the part of one of their children?

When we return East, things will be better, Alice told herself. *We will only be stronger for this difficult time.*

As if issuing another challenge, the moderate wind that had sent snowflakes down in gentle pirouettes began to intensify, and Alice looked up to see dark clouds encroaching upon the sun, promising to add more fresh flakes to the smooth crust that surrounded the graves. She abandoned her plan to venture northward and instead followed Main Street back to Burdick, the wind at her back propelling her forward, hurrying her home for no reason.

Chapter 20

Alice opened the door of the boardinghouse to find Thea and two men in animated conversation at the foot of the stairs. None of them took much notice of the newcomer until Alice removed her hood and the man with a dark, wiry head of hair glanced over. He tapped Thea's arm and said something to her in a low voice, not taking his eyes off Alice. Thea nodded, and the man's blond friend turned to look as well. All three of them wore startled expressions on their faces.

In the next moment, the two men were bounding up the stairs. Alice looked down at her outfit—it was snow-sodden and muddy at the hem, and surely her cheeks were pink from the wind, but she must not look so out of sorts as to prompt men to flee.

"It's locked! Thea! The key!" one of them called.

Thea hurried over to her drawer of keys and, after a small cacophony of shuffling, unearthed the one she sought. The blond-haired man was there to receive it, and in several great strides rescaled the stairs.

"Damn it!" came a shout. Thea took a quick glance around, presumably in search of little ears to cover.

"Whatever are they doing up there?" Alice asked, wondering if the men were visiting from the insane asylum. She began to strip off her cloak and mittens and stomped her feet to rid them of snow. But the look on Thea's face was enough to tell Alice that something was terribly wrong.

The red in the stair carpet pattern beat before Alice's eyes, as if it had a pulse. Down the hall, the door to her room hung ajar.

"What is happening here?" Alice cried, finding the two men leaning out the open window beside her bed. "Why are you breaking into my room?" She turned to Thea, who had hurried up the stairs to stand beside her. "Thea, will you not ask these men to leave?"

Thea looked guilty. "I'm afraid I can't," she said. She gestured toward the dark-haired man. "Mr. Weissmann is my landlord. He owns this house."

"We did not *break in,*" Mr. Weissmann retorted, pulling his head back into the room and facing Alice. "We had a key. And if we had called the police, which we should have done in the first place, there would be no question of our legitimate entry. Of course, we would not have needed to intrude upon your privacy if your husband had not deceived us and made his escape from the window here."

Alice gasped. "Was he not injured?" She hurried to the window, expecting to see Thomas's tall form prostrate in the snow.

"That bush appears to have broken his fall," said the blond man, pointing to some broken branches visible amid the snowdrifts. "I'll follow the footprints," he told Mr. Weissmann, and moved to hurry out of the room, but he was restrained by his fellow.

"The way this snow is coming down, they'll have filled in by the time you get down there—and it's no matter. We have his wife now, and he'll have to return for her at some point." He surveyed the room. "We'll need to search for the money. My hunch is that he took it with him, but he could have planned to return for it during the night."

Alice's confusion flared into anger. "Search my room? What right do you have?"

"Every right," said Mr. Weissmann. "As a currently unwelcome guest, you are trespassing on my property and are possibly harboring ill-gotten money."

"Am I your hostage now?" It was the steadiness of Thea's arm in hers that made Alice realize she herself was shaking violently.

Mr. Weissmann studied her with a suspicious eye. "In a way, I suppose. It may depend on how much you know of your husband's doings."

"Will you not at least tell me what he has done, then?"

"Close that window; you'll freeze us all," Thea scolded, and the blond man obeyed. Thea began to rub Alice's arms; briefly, in a paranoid state of mind, Alice thought she meant to pin them behind her back, but then she realized that the woman was merely trying to keep her warm. "Can we all come down to the kitchen for some tea? I don't wish other guests to hear this fuss, and Alice is chilled."

"All right, then," said Mr. Weissmann, but he did not take his eyes off Alice.

As Thea guided her down the stairs, one shaky step at a time, Alice wavered between compiling a defense of Thomas and wondering if what he had done was worth defending.

For the second time in a week Alice found herself hunched over a cup of tea at the kitchen table, vacillating between pain and absolute numbness. She felt like a bag of sand: weighty and lifeless, yet shifting in all different directions at once.

"Adam—Mr. Weissmann—is brusque but harmless, and Mr. White is a dear," Thea whispered as the men conferred quietly in the doorway of the kitchen. "It's probably best to let them ask questions of you now, and then they'll leave you in peace later.

"Now," she called to the men, "I think you owe this young lady an explanation as to why you were in her room. Not to mention an introduction."

The blond man walked over with his head hanging like a chastised child, but the dark one kept his high, his bright, beady eyes focused on Alice. "I am Adam Weissmann. This is my cousin, Neil White."

Mr. White gave her a kind smile and polite nod. Alice realized her face must register some shock at the announcement that the men were related—broad-shouldered Mr. White looked to be of Nordic descent, while the slight Mr. Weissmann had the large nose and curly dark hair that Alice associated with Hebrews.

"We have had an eye on your husband and his...spiritualist activities"—Adam said this with some venom—"since shortly after his arrival in Kalamazoo. One of his clients here, a well-respected widow, told her children of the great success he had experienced in making contact with her late husband. When the children pressed her for details of what their father had said, however, she could offer nothing remarkable, despite having sat with Mr. Holloway multiple times."

Alice shifted in her seat. "That is not proof of anything," she said. Was vagueness their only charge against him?

"Perhaps not. But one of her children was concerned enough to contact me, knowing of my interest in the debunking of spiritualist frauds."

Ah. One of the so-called vultures about whom Mrs. Linden had grown so agitated. Alice pictured them walking in circles around the hall in which the lectures were being held, occasionally poking their heads in to see if anyone had collapsed in the aisles, perhaps waiting for the smell of decay before they attacked.

"This widow is a successful businesswoman of great integrity, liked by all, and we were not eager to see her taken advantage of. After a few colleagues volunteered to sit with him by way of reconnaissance and reported suspicious behavior, we took the liberty of engaging a few private sittings with Mr. Holloway, to test his abilities for ourselves, and were not very impressed."

"And so you ran him out of town, because you were not impressed with him?" Alice let out a stilted laugh to try and conceal her agitation. "Would you do the same to a restaurateur, or a craftsman, simply based on personal opinion?"

"No, not personal opinion. I simply don't know how much to tell you. His offenses are quite extensive."

Alice took a deep breath. "If they are severe enough that he would flee to avoid accusation, I think I should know of them."

"Very well." Mr. Weissmann interlaced his fingers. "I assume you are aware of his spirit guide, Dr. Anderson? Yes. Says he's a physician who was trained in Scotland and then lived out his life in the Australian bush. Mr. White here wondered how much of his medical knowledge he retained in death. Turns out, not a great deal."

"But Dr. Anderson diagnoses the living all the time," Alice heard herself say, and her statement dangled weakly in the air, unsupported.

"You need no medical degree to claim what is wrong with people. Treating those people, on the other hand—that is where you must fall back on your training. So we quizzed him on some basic medical knowledge. He recommended certain cures taken orally instead of hyperdermically. He had the doses all wrong—"

"Many of his "remedies" would have killed a patient outright," explained Mr. White.

"And could not name some of the most basic bones in the human body—"

"Sternum, clavicle, scapula," Mr. White rattled off. "I know that Scottish medical schools might have different requirements than American medical schools, and that the methods of fifty years ago might seem antiquated or foolish today, but surely they would not let someone graduate without being able to identify elements of the human skeleton. We had to be able to recite the bones our very first semester."

Alice did not doubt that—she herself had had to memorize the major bones for her father, and could remember them. So these two men were doctors? Would they not have introduced themselves as doctors?

"And," said Mr. Weissmann, "in what I think was a most clever move by my cousin..."

"Thank you," said Mr. White.

"...he asked what Australia was like in July. Dr. Anderson replied that it was beastly hot, and there was little relief until September."

"It is curious that he does not understand the seasons of the hemispheres," said Mr. White, "and believes that July marks the Australian summer rather than its winter."

"Perhaps Dr. Anderson has not brought that knowledge with him to the spirit world," said Alice. "Why should he need medical skills among the dead? Why should he bother with keeping track of seasons?" Even as she formed them, however, her excuses sounded ridiculous to her ears. A better question was, why had she never thought to question Dr. Anderson's identity, despite the uneasy feeling he gave her?

Because she had trusted Thomas.

"Well, that argument makes sense to *me,*" said Thea, "as much as anything about this spirit hoodoo makes sense."

"These missteps," said Mr. Weissmann, ignoring the two women, "as well as a few others that I will not explain until further investigation, including one in which he claimed that my cousin was dead—"

"You can see I am not."

"—prompted us to confront him about his fallacies. At first he denied us, fought us in every way possible—we had endeavored to lay traps for the spirits; we had warped their messages with our ill will and doubt; we had distracted Dr. Anderson from his purpose and upset him."

"He does not give the spirits much credit, if he believes them to be so impressionable," added Mr. White.

"We would not accept any of this, and told him we would take him to the police—unless he relinquished the money he had taken from our widow friend, and revealed to us the source of his information on spiritualists in town.

"He then accused us of trying to steal from him, and that he had no assurance that the money would be returned to her—you see, he soon gave up on defending his honor, but would continue to fight for his purse. I assured him I had plenty of money and had no need of his, but if he liked, I would ask a policeman to supervise the transaction.

"Finally, he broke down and said that if we followed him back to the boardinghouse, he would give us the money. He had spent some on room and board, but most was still there. We, of course, knew where his boardinghouse was, so we could ensure he was not taking us for a wander with the intention of flight. When we entered the house here, he begged leave to go up alone first. He said you had not been well and were likely resting, and that two strange men coming into the room would be too much of a shock, but that perhaps he could get the money without waking you.

"Not wishing to disturb or offend you, we obliged him." Mr. Weissmann snorted. "You might imagine our surprise, then, to see you coming through the front door when he had already been up there for several minutes, presumably calming you or sneaking around you while you slept. I grew up in this house, and thought I needed only to lock the door to the servants' stairs to prevent his escape. But we never thought about the window. Even considering it now, it seems an extreme measure for a moderate sum."

His caterpillar brows came together in a frown as Mr. White leaned over and whispered something to him. Mr. Weissmann shook his head. Alice found her eyes drawn to the men's hands as they conversed. Mr. Weissmann's tapped rapidly upon the table, but did not rise from it. Mr. White's hands were more active, but one of them did not have the range of motion that the other enjoyed; it remained curled in upon itself, as if it were sleeping and unable to wake. When the hand's owner caught her staring, Alice blushed and looked down at her own hands, which she could study without consequence.

Mr. Weissmann sighed deeply and reached into his coat. "He dropped this as we left the circle." He laid a notebook—Alice recognized it as one of Thomas's—on the table. "We had hoped that it would give us some clue as to where he would have escaped, but we cannot make sense of it." He opened to a random page and pushed it closer to Alice. "Can you read it?"

Alice did not answer at first because she was already reading. It had been months since she had studied Thomas's style of shorthand, but she could still stumble through it.

Mrs. Matthew Fayerweather (Lucy). Widow. Matt. died age 50 of heart trouble. Speaks of heart being intact in spirit world and longing for his wife. Good mark for private sittings, pays well.

"No," she told them, but a skeptical look suggested that she had lingered over the book too long to claim total ignorance. "Well, not really. It is in some kind of shorthand, though not a conventional one. I can pick out a few words—here is 'heart,' here is 'well.'" She shook her head. "I cannot understand more than that."

"How about these?" Mr. Weissmann turned to the previous pages. Alice made a face as if she was trying to understand, which she was—not the words themselves, but what they meant to Thomas.

Isaac Solomon. Spt. Dau. Rebecca, age 12, diphtheria, light. Spt. Fath. Mark Solomon, age 71, dark. Walked with a limp, now gone in the spirit world. Alludes to papers left behind for Isaac and younger son, Nathan. Dead easy!

Alice swallowed. "I am sorry," she said. "I cannot make anything of this."

"And no wonder," said Thea. "You've had quite a shock.

"Can't you continue your interrogation tomorrow?" she asked the cousins. "Can't you see that Mrs. Holloway is shaken?"

"It was no interrogation—we were simply curious as to her ability to read her husband's script." Mr. Weissmann slid the book back to his side of the table. "But it appears as if she knows almost as little as we do."

Alice did not look up. She knew her eyes would likely give her away.

"I'll fix you a plate and bring it up," Thea told her. To Mr. Weissmann and Mr. White she said, "You can speak to her again once she's had some time to rest. Alice will promise not to run off. Won't you, Alice?"

Mr. Weissman snorted. "And I am supposed to believe a promise from her?"

"She's done nothing wrong."

"So she says."

"Adam! You needn't be so rude—"

"I promise I will not leave," Alice interrupted. She tried to keep her voice steady as the realization hit her. "In truth, I have nowhere else to go."

As soon as she had closed the kitchen door, Alice heard Thea scolding Mr. Weissmann for his behavior.

"Just think, if you had been abandoned in a strange town by yourself!"

Alice realized that Thea meant well, but she had not yet used that word, *abandoned*, to refer to herself. It brought to mind the dilapidated houses she saw decaying along the railroad tracks. Feeling much like a wayward dog or a broken-down piece of machinery, Alice climbed the stairs.

In her room, it felt as if the window were still open, although the sash was flush with the sill. Water pooled on the floor where snow had blown in and met a quick end. Alice exhaled and watched her breath puff out in front of her. She was not certain she wanted to be by herself, but she could stand no more of Mr. Weissmann's judgmental glances. And she wanted to know if one of his suspicions were true. If Thomas in his haste had left without their donation box, he would need to come back eventually.

The drawer where they kept the box was empty.

Alice pulled out drawers and unfurled the clothing inside, hoping for bills to flutter free or coins to bounce off the floor and roll beneath the bed. She shook out Thomas's shirts and her underclothes, the linen and lace taking ghostly form as they billowed with air. She wriggled her fingers beneath the mattress and the base of the bed. She tore off the bedclothes and twisted the buttons on the mattress to see if any would give way to a hole. Thumbing through her books yielded nothing, no bills slipped between the covers or pages, not even a note. Thomas's few spiritualist books were equally bereft. She threw the last one back into the trunk and heard the faint crack of its spine.

Had he not even thought of her as he left? Had she not crossed his mind? Even in his haste, had he not considered that she would need money in his absence?

A steady, blazing fire was what she needed. Someone—either Thomas or Thea, likely Thea—had added a fresh log to the fireplace, and bits of paper as starters. Alice held a match to one of the balls of paper until the flames embraced it—and illuminated lines of typeset text inside.

She yanked it from the fireplace, scorching herself, and stomped it out on the hearth. It was was a printed list of names and descriptions—a hectograph, the type a blurry purple. Half was already ash, and embers had burned holes in the remainder, but she could still read the lines well enough.

—am Samuels, Spt. son Ephraim, 28, gold front tooth from fall —as a child.

Mrs. Carrington. Widow twenty years, no children. Did not get on with Spt. — Higgins in life, but is pleased to know she—

Alice sucked on her injured fingertips as she unfolded the other pages in the woodpile, all revealing more of the same purple type, the same guidelines and instructions. As an afterthought, she pushed aside the logs and prodded the ashes beneath with the poker. It struck against something solid.

She reached in and shoved aside the half-blackened logs to reveal several small notebooks. Thomas's notebooks. She would have unwittingly burned them all.

Ash clung to her fingertips as she opened the cover of one. The first three pages were blank, but the fourth rewarded her with marks in faint pencil. Alice carefully transcribed the text, trying to keep herself from stringing sentences together until she had made out each word. With sadness, but little surprise, she found more of the same.

Miss Matilda Cunningham. Spinster. Will join in two group sittings before requesting her own; at the close of the second, have your spirit guide ask her if they could meet in private. Looking for apologies, professions of love from fiancé, name of Lawton, who left her under mysterious circumstances. Spt. sister Ellen, age 23, typhoid.

Mr. and Mrs. Gerald Manor. Spt. sons Gerald Jr., 12, and Simon, 10, fell through the ice while skating. Speak of being cold, feeling warmer when talking to their parents. Both fair. Simon missing a tooth on the left side of his mouth, the space through which he whistled.

Mr. Dean Crawford. Spt. wife Isabella (Bella), 35, childbed fever. Smells of lavender. Speaks of visiting sons and daughters at night to sing them lullabies. Respected and wealthy man. DEAD EASY.

The first five pages were marked *Erie* in the top right-hand corner. Alice remembered all of them: sad Miss Cunningham who amazingly had more color after a day in a dark room; the Manors, who sometimes brought their old hound dog to the séances with them, and he slept by the hearth, his deaf ears undisturbed by cries from the séance room or jingles of the front-door bell; sweet Mr. Crawford, who once gave her a silk flower "with compliments from his Bella." She flipped through the rest of the book; the arrangement of the marks on the page suggested more of the same. Sometimes a star indicated a note at the bottom of the page; these often described a new death in the family—or a change in material fortune.

Perhaps he was simply making notes for himself after sitting with these people. But Thomas frequently claimed not to know anything about what Dr. Anderson had revealed during the séance, saying he could rely only on the testimony of those who had sat with him. And he would not have stuffed his books in the fireplace if they did not contain something potentially incriminating.

She looked again at Mr. Crawford's entry. *DEAD EASY.*

No, these were not postmortem notes. They were instructions. Scripts.

Alice remembered her concern about the Haddons at the lecture; she thought they had been duped. But perhaps she should have been concerned for all the people Thomas had seen in New York, Pennsylvania, and Ohio. All those to whom she had been friendly, who had trusted her and her husband, who had served them dinner and bought them gifts and donated generously. How many of them were in these books? How many of them had been deceived?

She wanted to read further, and yet she could stand no more. Only when she put the book down did Alice realize that she still had not built a fire. Her shoulders had tensed up around her ears from cold and concentration. No longer able to burn any of the paper—although part of her wished for it all to go away—Alice tore blank pages from her own notebook and stuffed them beneath the new log. She turned her palms to face the tiny flames, flexing her fingers as the joints tingled their way to warmth. Somewhere in these notebooks, most likely, was a section labeled "Onset." But she would not have the heart to decipher that section tonight.

Chapter 21

When she closed her eyes Alice saw a series of strokes and curves on the inside of her lids. The shorthand marks glowed red and green in the darkness, begging her to translate them. She tried to ignore them, but her brain could not help but pick out a few words. *Widow. Easy. Child-bed.*

Her dreams even invented descriptions of imaginary patrons, their proclivities and preferred spirits evolving from shorthand scribbles into actual characters. These patrons came to her desk, where Alice consulted her calendar.

"We have no more seats available at the table for this afternoon," she told them. "But for five dollars Mr. Holloway will give a private sitting at your home tonight." Then she would lean in and warn them. "He thinks you are gullible, and knows you will appreciate any news about your brother at sea, however falsified."

But the people would only nod and smile, as if she had simply told them to enjoy themselves.

Then she was in the séance room, in an arrangement that mirrored the one her mother had held for Mrs. Connors. A stuttering candle provided the only light. Her mother and father were both there, their eyes closed, hands joined. Then she saw that Mrs. Connors was in the circle as well, and—after her eyes adjusted—Thomas appeared.

"I will see if I can find her," said the voice of Dr. Anderson, and the room was completely silent. Then Thomas's body twitched in a spasm.

"It is me, Alice," said her voice from Thomas's mouth. "I am sorry to have left you so soon."

No, I am right here! Alice tried to tell them, but she could produce no more than a faint whistling sound. She put her hand on her mother's shoulder, and her mother jumped.

"I can feel her!" she cried.

Of course—I am present, and alive—but Alice's mouth refused to move.

"I regret running away from Thomas," said the Alice-voice from Thomas's lips. "The loss of my child made me so unhappy, so much that I did not value my own life. My husband did all he could for me, but I was beyond saving."

Then Alice dropped from a great height into in a tangle of bedclothes that pinned her legs together and caught her arms at strange, cramped angles. She looked down and for a moment was terrified that someone had wrapped her in a winding-sheet.

Alice could not fall asleep again after that dream, and by morning she had cried herself into a desert. Now that her face had ceased to leak, everything about her felt devoid of moisture: her nose bled, lips cracked, eyelids scraped down over eyes in desperate need of lubrication.

It had occurred to her not to get out of bed at all. Nothing positive awaited her outside of the covers: the two inquisitors would presumably be waiting for her downstairs; the evidence of Thomas's lies was piled on the floor; the floor itself would be icy cold with the death of the fire.

A soft rap on the door suggested that perhaps breakfast was outside. Alice allowed herself a brief smile of gratitude, and snuggled back into bed and her misery. But when the rap came again, and a third time, she realized she was expected to answer.

"Who is it?" she called, her voice crackling from its first use of the day.

"Thea," came the reply. A pause. "And only me."

Alice reluctantly extracted herself from her nest, donned a dressing-gown, and opened the door. Thea held out a tray on which rested a teapot and cup, some fresh bread, still steaming, and two little pots that Alice hoped contained jam and butter.

"May I come in?"

Alice swept her arm out to indicate an invitation. She clutched her dressing-gown together at the throat. "Please forgive my state of undress..."

Thea shook her head. "You needn't apologize. I would not have disturbed you but...but for some sensitive business that Adam urged me to discuss with you." She sighed. "It is the matter of accommodations here. Your husband paid only though Saturday."

Alice felt as if someone had punched her in the stomach. "And what day is today?"

Thea looked down at her shoes. "Friday." She dropped her voice. "Do you have anybody you can ask for a loan? I would give you the money to send a telegram."

There was the obvious option. But the mortification of asking her father for money to return home—when he had been skeptical of the marriage from the beginning—seemed worse than homelessness. She would rather commit a crime and be thrown in jail—mimic insanity and find herself in the asylum—than face her parents after only four months away, with a ruin of a marriage behind her.

Alice shook her head. "I can think of no one. I shall have to pray that Thomas returns today or tomorrow."

Thea looked uncomfortable. "Do you have anything to pawn—any silver, or jewelry, perhaps?"

Alice followed Thea's eyes to the gold ring on her left hand.

"Perhaps," Alice swallowed. "I would have to think on it."

Thea patted Alice's shoulder. "I'll leave you to eat."

Once the door had closed, Alice poured tea into the cup and cream after that. She removed the top from the sugar bowl and saw her ring glint in the sunlight. Thomas could return, at any moment...he could work things out with the cousins, perhaps give them money, they would let him go, he and Alice would continue on their tour...

And yet, knowing about Thomas's notebooks, how could she stand to watch him cheat those who trusted him?

Had she already added sugar to her cup? She took a sip, and tasting only the bitter tea and the cream, selected a cube with the tiny tongs and dropped it in. When she stirred, however, her spoon encountered two distinct lumps in the liquid: the first cube had lurked in the bottom while she took her exploratory taste. The resulting concoction was painfully sweet, and Alice set the cup down, her small comfort spoiled.

She wrapped her hands around the teapot for warmth and heard the clink of gold against ceramic. Once the band had been a symbol of assurance, in times when she doubted Thomas's love. Now it only spoke of uncertainty.

Thea reappeared mid-afternoon with a plate and a proposition. "I took the liberty of mentioning to Mr. Weissmann that you had no other recourse. The cousins have an offer of employment, and they were wondering if you would join them for dinner to discuss it." Secretly, Alice was grateful for a motivation to dress; she had tried several times during the day to encourage herself out of bed, but inevitably some memory of Thomas had sapped her intention.

She found the cousins deep in discussion at the center table; Alice had nearly reached them by the time they noticed her and stood to greet her. Mr. White pulled out her chair for her. Alice steeled herself for awkward small talk while they waited for their soup, but Mr. Weissmann produced the fallen notebook as soon as he sat down again.

"Thea tells us you do not have the resources to extend your stay here, nor travel back home."

Alice shook her head. His statement made her sound like a Dickensian orphan with no income or family. It was perhaps not fair or sensible to discount her parents, but she still had no desire to let them know of her situation.

Mr. Weissmann's bony fingers turned the pages. "As we had mentioned before, we would be very interested to know what this book contains. We think that with some study, perhaps you can translate this more easily than you first thought."

The notebook was open to a description of an "easy mark, eager to believe." Alice swallowed. "And what is your objective in having a translation? I doubt it would give any clues as to his whereabouts now."

"We are not so interested in this book telling us where he is *now*, as where he has *been*," said Mr. White. "It is in our best interest to prove that Mr. Holloway's chicanery did not begin in Kalamazoo, but in previous towns."

"You see—" Mr. Weissmann hesitated, then went ahead. "We suspect that in addition to his tricks of palming pellets, opening sealed letters, etc., Mr. Holloway obtained much of his preliminary information from a 'blue-book.'"

Alice gave him a blank stare.

"Don't know or won't say, eh? A blue-book is a sort of medium's travel guide, but instead of descriptions of locations it describes people and the deceased with whom they wish to be in contact. Mediums pool their information on "marks." Whether they prefer private sittings, or spirit manifestations, or go crazy for sealed-envelope tests. Whether or not they have any money, and are willing to spend it."

"Many skeptics and mediums alike know of and speak of bluebooks, but few have ever claimed to have seen them," said Mr. White.

"We ourselves had never seen one, and supposed it to be a thing of legend."

"Did you never consider that this might simply be a diary?" Alice asked. But her thoughts had wandered to the hectographed pages now carefully wrapped in her undergarments.

Mr. Weissmann shrugged. "Perhaps it is, but I should think there would be valuable information in a diary as well. We will pay you to translate this—say, the cost of room and board—for however long it takes. We ask that you help Thea in the kitchen as well. It's not very busy now, but come the thaw she'll have her share of travelers. And to keep you from dragging your feet, at the end we will pay for a ticket to anywhere you wish to go."

Alice brushed her fingers across the page. The marks for "easy" smudged slightly with the sweat from her fingertips.

"You are asking me to invade my husband's privacy."

Mr. Weissmann rolled his eyes. "A husband so considerate that he has left you in a strange place with no money."

Alice looked at her hands, at the gold ring and its perhaps empty promise. "I will do it." Her mouth spoke the words before she had much of a chance to think about it. *You could write something completely different than what Thomas has, and they would be none the wiser*, she told herself in her regret. *Remember that.*

"That was not so difficult, was it?" said Mr. Weissmann. He poured himself a glass of wine from the carafe on the table. He offered some to Alice, but she shook her head; she would abstain in the company of unfamiliar men. Then, in a motion so swift as to make Alice think she imagined it, he took an amber bottle from his coat, tipped a few drops into the wine, and returned it to his pocket.

Soon Thea emerged from the kitchen with the roast, and as the de facto patriarch, Mr. Weissmann took up the fork and carving knife, making little exclamations about the quality of the meal as he sliced and served. Alice reached for the notebook to protect it from wayward scraps of meat, but he snatched it back and tucked it into his coat pocket.

"We wouldn't want this to go missing. Let's agree upon a time for you to come to our office—it's just in back of the house—and work on it there."

Alice resented his distrust, but said nothing. After all, she would not really trust Mr. Weissmann but for Thea's assurance, and ultimately, wouldn't Thea's loyalties belong to her landlord?

"I suppose you miss New York," said Mr. White. Alice looked at him in confusion for a moment, then realized that Thomas would have listed his home as such in the program. To assume that his wife also resided there was not unreasonable.

"I've actually never been," said Alice.

"But..."

"We began touring as soon as we were married. We have traveled through upstate New York, but not yet through the city." Alice realized she spoke as if their tour would be continuing as planned.

"Where did you live before your marriage?" asked Mr. White.

"Cambridge, Massachusetts." A wave of homesickness hit her, and she had to take a deep breath to steady herself. Knowing the next question Mr. White might ask, she explained: "I met my husband at Onset Bay Grove. It is a spiritualist community on Buzzards Bay."

"Yes, yes, we know Onset."

"I was not a member," said Alice, "but my mother had brought me there since I was a teenager. My father is an entomologist, and had no interest in séances, but he did take the opportunity to study the water insects of the bay." She had no desire to share her beliefs regarding spirits—she was not even sure of them anymore—so she quickly changed the subject. "Have you both always lived in Kalamazoo?"

Mr. White shook his head as Mr. Weissmann nodded. "My parents met here in Kalamazoo, but I was born and raised in Grand Rapids," Mr. White said. Seeing Alice's momentary confusion, he pointed towards the ceiling. "It's a bit north of here. Mr. Weissmann, though, grew up here."

"Are your parents still here?" asked Alice. Mr. Weissmann shook his head.

"No. They both died while I was doing my undergraduate work in Ann Arbor. Hence my ownership of this house."

"Oh, I'm sorry." Alice regretted not using her skills of deduction to realize that this property must be an inheritance.

Mr. Weissmann straightened himself up. "Well, I've been lucky enough to cobble together a new family for myself—what with Mr. White and Thea and the chicks."

"The chicks?"

"Thea's children. Haven't you ever seen that fine, light yellow hair and thought of baby bird feathers? Also, when they're all together, they tend to follow Thea around as if she were a mother hen."

Alice pictured a hen dressed in an apron, clucking to her brood in wee frocks and tiny trousers as they circled the barnyard.

"My siblings are scattered," explained Mr. White, "and my parents prefer to stay in one place—but once I heard Adam was going to Ann Arbor for college, I wanted to do the same. We are really more like brothers than cousins."

Alice's eyes looked from fair Mr. White to dark Mr. Weissmann. Mr. Weissmann caught her glance and laughed. "Though we might not believe ourselves to be related at all, if we hadn't grown up visiting the same grandparents."

Mr. White explained that the Reform Jewish and Unitarian communities were very close in Kalamazoo, and that the Jews often went to the Unitarian church on Sunday for purposes of fellowship, even after they had their own temple. "But my father liked the church so much he stayed there—and he liked one of the other parishioners so much that he married her."

"Liked it so much he Anglicized his name."

Mr. White looked at his cousin with a grin. "Adam is jealous that I have fewer letters to write." As they smiled at each other, the family resemblance suddenly appeared in the particular upturn of their lips, the toothiness of their expression, and a slight squint around the eyes.

"Oh!" said Alice, remembering her scraps of German, "*Weiss* means White."

"Ah! *Sprechen sie Deutsch*?" said Mr. Weissmann.

Alice shook her head, somewhat embarrassed. "I know a few words from school. But I studied French instead."

"Ah," said Mr. Weissmann, sounding disappointed. "You won't hear too much French around here. Further north in trapper country, or near Detroit, perhaps. *Au nord et a l'est.*"

Thea joined the table at this point, and shook her head at the conversation. "You college boys, showing off all your languages."

"Don't get him started on Greek," said Mr. White. "He is intolerably proficient in it."

Sensing a challenge, Alice threw down a gauntlet of Aristophanes: "High thoughts must have high language."

"Impeccable Greek, too?" said Mr. Weissmann. "My, I believe we have a bluestocking on our hands."

Alice bristled. "You do understand, don't you, that it is common for women to be educated nowadays?"

"Of course he does," said Mr. White. "Many of our classmates at Michigan are women. Mr. Weissmann is only attempting to be provocative, as that is his nature."

"My father meant me for the Harvard Annex—the women's school," Alice said. "I would likely be there now if I hadn't married..."

Everyone was silent for a moment: passing judgment on her decision, Alice thought.

Thea began to collect the table's dirty dishes to make way for dessert. After a beat, Alice rose to help her, and noted that Mr. Weissmann, for all his praise of the meal, had barely touched the already small portions on his plate, merely shifting morsels from their original positions. No wonder he was so thin.

Dessert was a velvety caramel pudding, and everyone savored the first few bites in silence. Alice allowed the burnt-sugar flavor to fill her mouth before swallowing each spoonful. Even Mr. Weissmann of the birdlike appetite made a few divots in the smooth surface of his portion.

"I think my cousin had an ulterior motive in putting this house into Thea's care," Mr. White told Alice. "He knew he would eat well every time he visited."

"Cooking for you two is the least I can do," said Thea. She turned to Alice. "My husband died soon after Eleanor was born—the same typhoid that killed Adam's parents—and, well, I don't know what I would have done if Adam hadn't given me this house and let me rent the extra rooms. Starved, I suppose."

"An impossible alternative," said Mr. Weissmann, patting Thea's hand. "Thea was friendly with my parents at the temple—yes, she's Jewish too, you never can tell in these parts, you see—and while everyone gathered together some aid for her at the beginning, no one this proud can live on charity forever."

Thea blushed. "I'm afraid I don't go to temple much any more."

"I doubt anyone faults you, what with four children and a boardinghouse to run." Mr. Weissmann swept his hand around, as if to emphasize the extent of Thea's responsibilities. "But it's really my pleasure. Besides, what would I do with a fine house in Kalamazoo, when I am in Ann Arbor nine months of the year?"

There was a sudden silence, and Alice saw Mr. White and Thea exchanging looks. Mr. Weissmann seemed oblivious as he dragged his spoon back and forth through the pudding.

"And what do you study there?" asked Alice. From the others' reactions, she wondered if she ought to be questioning Mr. Weissmann about Ann Arbor—but she wanted to know.

Mr. Weissmann swallowed with a slight bob of his head. "Psychology. It's a relatively new extension of philosophy and physiology..."

"William James of Harvard is a prominent instructor in the field, I believe?" Alice interrupted.

Mr. Weissmann raised an eyebrow in a gesture of what Alice thought to be respect.

"Adam was accepted to Harvard for graduate work," said Mr. White, "but chose to continue his education in Ann Arbor."

"Why travel so far when you have such a fine institution right here in state?" mused Mr. Weissmann.

Alice thought she saw a little smirk from Mr. White. "And what do you study?" she asked him.

There was a pause. "Medicine," said Mr. White. "Specifically, surgery."

Alice's eyes immediately darted to the hand curled like a dry leaf on the table; its palm faced her, and Alice caught a glimpse of an angry red scar before Mr. White removed it from view. This time she knew he saw her staring, without even looking up. She wondered how the one virtually useless hand impacted his practice, but did not think he would welcome the question.

"What I don't understand," said Mr. Weissmann, on his own tangent and his second glass of doctored wine, "is how an educated woman like you could be tangled up with such a cad. How do we not know you are pretending to be ignorant of your husband's schemes? Really, it does not make sense to me. The person to whom you are supposed to be closest, and you cannot see them for what they are? If you are so intelligent, how did you not deduce what sort of tricks your husband was pulling?"

To Alice's embarrassment, tears filled her eyes. She pressed her lips together, trying to keep them from falling so she could say something in response. Then she felt Thea's hand close around her forearm, protectively.

"You, the bachelor," said Thea, "would not understand. She was in love."

Chapter 22

Alice kept waking to what she thought was a stone thrown at her window, or the rustle of a note slid under her door, but when she went to check there was no one and nothing there. Her dreams were filled with departures: a closing door, a train whistle that grew more and more faint. The broad bass tones of a ship's horn, its reverberations shaking some dock on which she stood, startled her to tears. And in no case did she know who was leaving, only that she was very much alone.

It wasn't until the wee hours that she succumbed to pure exhaustion and fell into any kind of slumber. Whatever rest she had cobbled together was not enough; Alice was still drowsy as she descended to breakfast.

The dining room was quiet save for some muffled clanking in the kitchen, and Alice at first wondered if yesterday—indeed, the past two days—had been a dream. Thea came out to take her order with no mention of the cousins, and so Alice ate her breakfast slowly, counting the rosebuds painted on her china cup and those on the plate once bites revealed new flowers. Since Thomas had not been much for breakfast conversation recently, she had devised ways in which to entertain herself.

As soon as her plate was clean, however, the door to the dining room swung open and the cousins entered.

"Thea made us promise to wait until you had finished dining before we set your task in front of you," said Mr. Weissmann. He had the book in one hand and loose papers and pencils in the other, and looked as if he were ready to clear her plate himself in order to expedite matters.

"Well, I appreciate her consideration," said Alice, a bit dryly.

"Adam's only eager to see what your husband wrote in his notebook," Mr. White apologized. "He does not mean to be rude."

Mr. Weissmann sniffed, as if he did not entirely agree with that claim.

"And you needn't do your work at the breakfast table," said Mr. White. "We have set up a desk in the office for your use, although Adam may have forgotten that in his excitement."

Alice followed the men through the kitchen to the garden door, giving Thea a small wave as she passed. Thea smiled from a face dusted in flour; her rosy cheeks gave the impression of apples covered in sugar for Christmas.

A narrow path led to a substantial building in back of the house, about the size of the Boydens' quite comfortable Onset cottage. The window in Alice's room faced the street; she had never even been aware of this structure.

"Was this a gardener's cottage?" asked Alice, taking in its two stories and elaborate wooden scrollwork. Mostly painted white, it seemed to melt into the winter background, creating the impression of floating black-bordered windows and pink trim. A brick chimney emerged from a roof rendered nearly undetectable beneath a layer of snow.

"My mother's studio," said Mr. Weissmann. "She was an artist. All of the paintings you see throughout the house are by her."

Alice thought of the river scene that hung on the wall outside her room. The boat looked so real she had more than once longed to seize it and paddle away. "She was very talented."

The interior seemed to absorb even the weak winter light, and the one fireplace kept the space cozy; Alice could understand why this would be a painter's oasis. However, there were no easels or even wall-hangings to be seen: only two desks covered in papers and one, which she assumed was hers, containing nothing but writing instruments and an inkwell. A deep-basined sink rusted and dripped in one corner. Bookcases along the wall had an assortment of volumes bound in colorful cloth and leather.

"We weren't sure which you would prefer—pen or pencil," said Mr. White. "So we brought both."

"Or would you prefer a typewriter?" asked Mr. Weissmann. "I suppose we could find one for you."

"Pen or pencil is fine. I am likely not as quick as I used to be on the typewriter," said Alice.

"I would think transcribing to be slow work in any case. But remember, the sooner you finish, the sooner you can leave."

Alice nodded, although the thought of leaving was frightening, when she wasn't sure where she would go.

Feeling somewhat rusty after two years of little practice, Alice wrote out for herself a key of standard shorthand. The tilts and strokes of the pencil stirred memories of notes on knitting-needles and butterflies that she had taken for her father. It was fitting, she had thought, that she described such creatures with marks that mimicked the head and thorax; the angle of a wing; one or two of the six delicate legs; an eye that, beneath a microscope, held many facets. Then she tried to remember Thomas's rules—which marks remained the same in his system, which were reversed, which changed entirely. She did miss those dragonfly-like hooks, which Thomas had replaced with something like a spear.

At first Alice confused the sounds indicated by a mark made light or dark, below or above the line. It would have been helpful to say the words out loud, but the cousins were silent in their own work. She made do with mouthing the words and scribbling possibilities on a folio reserved specifically for that purpose. An hour later, the first page was finally gray with pencil, and she turned to a fresh side.

As she moved her lips to piece together "undertaker," Alice looked up to see Mr. White staring at her. He gave her a bashful wave and returned to his own project. Given her prolonged curiosity about his hand—and the strange faces she was making—she felt his attention was only fair. His bent head revealed a patch on his head where the hair was already beginning to thin a bit, and Alice wondered how old he was, and how old Mr. Weissmann was. Did they realize she was only twenty? Alice had forgotten it herself.

It was easier to transcribe these Kalamazoo notes, about people whom she had not met. She could restrain herself from imagining them, and pitying them for their gullibility. But her mind drifted back to the Erie descriptions of people with whom she had conversations, whom she had been fond of. She saw their faces when they emerged from the séance room, tearful or joyful upon hearing the voice of someone they had lost. Little did they know that the voice had not come from the spirit world, but was conjured from a short biography in a notebook.

Alice was able to concentrate for a few hours, but after that the marks began to blur in front of her. She shook her head to refocus, pieced together a word, and then lost it in a drowsy nod. What she read was transformed by that brief moment of dreaming, so that she opened her eyes and expected to see an orange in her hand. When she discovered that she held only a pencil, she searched the shorthand for the fruit or the color and was puzzled to find no mention of either. Other items seemed to appear in front of her when her eyes were closed—a loaf of bread, a whole chicken—only to be gone when she jerked herself awake. The shorthand held no mention of food at all—not even a series of symbols that could be mistakenly interpreted as such.

A shadow slid across the notebook. "Mrs. Holloway?" Alice looked up to see Mr. White standing there. "Would you care to accompany me to lunch?"

Alice let out a relieved sigh, recognizing the cause of her hallucinations. "Yes—yes, I think I am much in need of something to eat."

"First, let us see what you have written so far." Mr. Weissmann extracted himself from his desk and came over to hers.

Alice wished she had more to show for three hours' work. "I have needed to refamiliarize myself with the symbols—Thomas's in particular—and I have not been sleeping very well. My level of concentration is not what it should be."

"I should think that's not surprising," said Mr. White. Alice looked up for Mr. Weissmann's reaction, expecting at least a scolding or an eyebrow-raise. Instead, she watched him fumble around in his coat. He drew a small amber bottle from his pocket and offered it to Alice, its neck pinched between his forefinger and thumb.

"Take a few drops of this in a little water before bed. I imagine you'll find it difficult to sleep tonight as well."

Alice stared at it dumbly, wondering if he thought murder would be the preferable way to evict her.

"It's not poison," Mr. Weissmann sighed. "Look." He opened his mouth, applied several drops to his tongue, and swallowed. "You can keep an eye on me if you like and make sure that I do not fall into convulsions, but I am not in the habit of killing myself or anyone else. It's only laudanum. I wouldn't recommend taking it straight like I do, but a more sensible dose is harmless."

Alice slowly held out her palm and accepted the bottle, still warm from being in Mr. Weissmann's breast pocket. The skeptical look must have lingered on her face, for he explained, "I have back trouble."

"I am famished," Mr. White announced, and gestured for Alice to precede him through the door. She caught his frown directed toward Mr. Weissmann, which did nothing to assure her of the safety of the drug, but she tucked it away. Mr. Weissmann returned to his desk, and only Mr. White followed her out the door.

"Is Mr. Weissmann not hungry?"

Mr. White shook his head. "He eats at strange times. Don't worry about him."

They filled their plates in silence, Mr. White gesturing for Alice to help herself first. As she took her seat, she thought, *There is no harm in asking.*

"I am curious as to what you two will do with the information I provide."

Mr. White hesitated for a moment, then apparently decided that Alice posed no threat to their studies. "Adam's goal is to make people fully aware of the various tricks employed by these people, so that they might not fall prey to them in the future. And finding an actual 'blue-book' would be treasure indeed—real written proof that mediums are sharing information and are out to take advantage of the people who trust them."

Alice nodded. Was she to be instrumental, then, in destroying her husband's profession and her mother's passion? "Your cousin said last night that he had caught Thomas palming pellets. What does that mean?"

Mr. White spread his napkin over his lap. "It means that he had people write the name of a dead person they wanted to contact on a small piece of paper, then compress it into a tiny pellet. While distracting them with some talk, he would slide them off the table and replace them with several blank pellets of his own. He then would unwrap the sitters' pellets beneath the table and read the names. It's a particularly effective tool when you already have the names of some of the people in the community, and know for whom they are searching. But any good conjurer can, based on a sitter's reaction, know how to proceed.

"Adam has been particularly diligent about visiting and recording the habits of pellet-readers. He writes a description of the medium's set-up, the way in which he directs the sitters, even the sort of paper and pen used. Sometimes I am along to distract attention from Adam, who, if anyone paid particular notice, does not always act like the most interested sitter. He is not very successful at faking enthusiasm, so that is where I enter."

He pasted an expression of mirth on his face and adopted a twang unlike his cultured college English. "I cannot believe it. Old Joe! It's been what, thirteen, fourteen years since I have heard from him? We were playing cards when he dropped dead, just like that. Hasn't lost his sense of humor."

"You could say that I study the sitters," Mr. White continued in his normal voice, "and that Adam studies the mediums. I have learned the scripts. I am aware of the response that a medium expects to a particular question—the additional information he seeks, just by the tone of his voice and the wording of the inquiry. I keep track of sitters' physical reactions and can mimic the stance of a man in mourning for a wife or a child, the swagger of the skeptic who then becomes a believer."

"Perhaps you should be seeking a job in the theatre, not in medicine."

"Heh. Perhaps I should."

"What is medical school like?" Alice asked. "Is it very rigorous? Do the girls have a fighting chance of gaining any respect?"

"Oh, certainly. Most of them rise to the top of the class, even though there are inevitably several who drop out because they cannot handle the operating theatre."

"I suppose, though, that some men cannot handle the operating theatre either."

"But the difference there," said Mr. White, "is that those men never try the course in the first place. They go straight into the law."

Alice laughed. "Do you mean to say that the law school at Michigan is filled with squeamish would-be doctors?"

"I speak only of individuals I happen to know," said Mr. White. "But they are missing a sublime learning opportunity. The thing about medicine is that the field is always changing. New discoveries can change doctors' entire approach toward a particular procedure or their understanding of how an organ functions, which might then affect their understanding of other organs."

Alice thought about this. "But literature is always changing, too. Why, new novels are published every day."

"Yes, but literature only moves forward, in that a book published today does not change the state of one published a hundred years ago."

"Novels, perhaps, but what of essays? A later essay might refute an earlier one."

"True. But that is *always* the goal of scientific papers, it seems—to throw your predecessors' hypotheses and methods into doubt." Alice, thinking of her father's composition of and reaction to papers in his field, had to nod in agreement. "To return to your original question—it is rigorous indeed, but exhilarating. To think that humans have always had bodies, and that in sophisticated societies there was always someone to whom you could go if your body went awry...well, I like to think of myself as part of a very old tradition."

"Then, may I ask why you are taking a leave of absence?" Alice pointedly looked at his face and kept her eyes away from his hand, but Mr. White avoided her gaze.

"Adam has been...ill. Too ill to return to school. And I am his closest family now. So I am looking after him. Thea would volunteer, of course, but she has four children and occasional guests to mind." He shrugged. "Psychical research has always been an interest of his, and he needed something to occupy his time. We discovered that Michigan's spiritualist convention was to be held here, and it seemed like the perfect opportunity to begin his investigations in earnest."

"Back trouble?"

"What?" said Mr. White, sounding confused.

"Mr. Weissmann mentioned he had back trouble," said Alice. "Hence his need to leave school?"

"Yes, that's it."

Alice did not understand how back trouble could interfere with one's appetite, but Mr. White did not seem to want to elaborate. She watched him work a slice of ham with the side of his fork until a bite-size piece came away. His curled right hand lay inert beside his plate, useless to wield a knife.

When Alice put herself to bed that night, sleep would not come. After she had lain there for what seemed like hours, her eyes unwilling to shut completely, her heart beating in her throat, she remembered the little bottle Mr. Weissmann had given her. Still wary of what its contents might do to her, she reasoned that there could not be a state much worse than the one she found herself in now. And the sweetness the drops brought to her water glass seemed to reassure her that it could only make things better.

Chapter 23

Alice woke to find her fire cold and the sun bright in the sky. She sat up slowly, and her head spun a bit but soon settled into a gentle daze. Moving unsteadily across the room towards her dressing-gown, she remembered the few drops she had taken from Mr. Weissmann's bottle the night before. She had not slept so soundly in months. A burst of gratitude for the strange little man lifted her through the motions of her routine and carried her downstairs with an eagerness to work.

Her desk was near the office hearth, a small kindness that she greatly appreciated when the wind whooped around the cottage and sent snow flying against the windows. Alice watched the stickiest flakes cling to the panes like shaving soap on a man's whiskers, and her nose was briefly filled with the slightly floral scent that lingered after Thomas had finished his morning shave, his brush and razor rinsed and left to dry on their own.

Her daily task made it a challenge to put him out of mind. When memories threatened to choke her progress, Alice tried to imagine herself as a medieval scribe, copying and translating sacred texts. She did not have to worry quite so much about the neatness of her handwriting, but neither did she have license to illuminate her manuscripts with colorful pictures as the tonsured monks had.

Mr. White sat across from her, his back to the wall of bookcases that blocked three windows. On a brighter day, when he or Mr. Weissmann would turn around and pull a book from one of the upper shelves, a briefly blinding rectangle of light would glow in its absence, a trapdoor to the outside world.

Sometimes, after a straight two hours or so of concentration, Alice felt pressure building up between her brows, and her eyelids felt as if they were lined with sandpaper. Self-conscious about taking breaks when her officemates worked steadily throughout the morning, she made a pretense of staring at the wall, as if puzzling over some combination of marks, when instead she studied the two men in the room.

Mr. Weissman's gruff demeanor clashed with a body that did not seem capable of supporting his moods. Sometimes, he would move around the office like a fly alighting on everything of olfactory interest it could find, propelled by a burst of frantic energy. During these times Alice had to bend low over her papers to keep him from becoming a distraction in her peripheral vision. Other times he stared at his books for hours, barely shifting in his chair, only raising a hand to turn a page or take a note. Mr. Weissmann was comprised almost entirely of angles; the constant narrowing of his eyes behind his glasses—whether in disdain or concentration or both—shifted even their relative roundness, and his ears had slight elven points. The sharpness of his body made his aggressively curly hair all the more startling, as if Nature's desire to curve the human form had channeled itself into only the spirals on Mr. Weissmann's head.

Alice was not certain that she liked Mr. Weissmann, but she did find him intriguing, and a bit frightening. Perhaps it was thanks to her mother and her militant brand of temperance, one that painted even infrequent drinkers as morally deficient and demonized those who developed a dependence on drugs, liquor, or both. The persistent use of narcotics was too horrible to speak of, Mrs. Boyden told her daughter when Alice was sixteen and secretly reading De Quincey's *Confessions of an Opium Eater.* Alice's occasional glasses of wine when dining with Thomas had convinced her that imbibing in moderation was harmless, but she could not quite escape her mother's idea that tipplers and opium addicts were potential murderers all, a knife or their bare hands at the ready to prey upon anyone who encountered them in a state of intoxication.

Thankfully, however, Alice was rarely alone with Mr. Weissmann, who spent several days a week away on some sort of fraud-finding business; he always returned with notes and papers that he then passed on to Mr. White. Mr. White was usually at his desk, broad shoulders and sandy head bent over his latest assignment. In contrast to his cousin, he radiated health; he was what Alice imagined a Midwestern man should look like. She had been slightly disappointed when he said that his father was a lawyer and not a farmer, having conjured up a romantic image in her head of Mr. White as a boy, working the fields in a pair of overalls and eating a breakfast of eggs plucked from nests that morning.

Every day, around noon or one, Mr. White's carefully tailored, decidedly unrural cuff would appear in her line of vision, and Alice would know it was time for lunch. He never spoke, never tapped her shoulder in an attempt to draw her attention away from the shorthand, only quietly, slowly, placed his hand on the desk. Perhaps he somehow sensed that the sight of Thomas's handwriting unsettled her to the point of jumpiness now, noted the unintentional glances over her shoulder from time to time, as if her husband could appear without warning.

After lunches with Mr. White, Alice donned an apron and transformed herself from a secretary into a maid—a role that ultimately proved more stressful than transcribing Thomas's notes. For once in her life, Alice wished she had received more of her instruction in the kitchen than the laboratory. She assumed that measuring cups and mixing would give her little trouble, given the precision required for scientific work, but the unmarked, miscellaneous spoons and vessels of Thea's kitchen erased her confidence. Thea hardly weighed or measured anything, instead knowing instinctively how much of an ingredient to add based on the level in her mixing bowl or the feel of the paste. Alice tried to pay attention to Thea's techniques, but whenever the housekeeper offered the reins to her assistant, Alice always shook her head. She was happy to be in the ranks of reinforcement but not the front line, and found herself most comfortable cleaning up after the preparation of the food, when she would not endanger diners with culinary missteps.

When Thea walked her through the cleaning and preparation of a guest room, Alice's lack of domestic training truly showed. She was all thumbs at making a bed from the mattress up; an attempt to clean a fireplace only left her looking like a chimney sweep. Soon Alice found herself back in the kitchen, rinsing the grease from a roasting-pan, while Thea's brisk footfalls sounded upstairs along with the echoing patter of Eleanor's. While the elder three were at school, Eleanor followed her mother around, chirping continuously. She and Dolly explored cabinets, sampled batters, and set imaginary tea tables with old, chipped china and mismatched silverware.

"Perhaps you think me mad, attempting to do all of this myself," Thea said as she demonstrated proper silver-polishing, Eleanor sitting at her feet in a spot cleared of flour. "Adam and Neil are always after me to get a girl. I did have a girl up until a couple of months ago; she tidied the rooms and sometimes minded the children." Alice watched Thea dampen a cloth with water and dip it into a powder, which she then rubbed vigorously on the belly of a teapot, revealing its hidden gleam. "But when Eleanor went into one of her fits—even though I had warned her about them, and told her exactly what to do when one occurred—she up and quit."

Though a hardy-looking child, Eleanor had a perpetual wheeze that intensified when she became excited or upset. The struggling for air, the barking cough came on suddenly. Alice had witnessed the procedure once, after a flood of tears precipitated by some unknown insult. Thea had held Eleanor over a basin of hot water ("to loosen the phlegm") and dosed her with a syrup from the cabinet, executing the process almost elegantly—but Alice did not really blame the hired girl for her panic in the matter.

"I make the syrup myself, from my grandmother's household book." Thea had shown her yellowed pages of spidery German. "I'm sure there's a more modern remedy, but not one of Oma's tonics has ever failed me. I gave this to Ernest when he had the croup something terrible as a baby, and thankfully it worked for Eleanor's trouble as well."

Though she was friendly, nearly flirtatious with Mr. Weissmann and Mr. White, Eleanor was still shy around Alice, usually sucking her thumb and clutching her mother's skirts while Alice assisted in the kitchen. Alice smiled at and greeted her whenever she entered the Kollners' domestic domain, but it was weeks before she received a smile from the girl in return.

Aside from the occasional conference, boarders were relatively rare this time of year. Travelers usually opted for the hotels in town or the small inns just along the railroad tracks, Thea explained. "We receive more of the overflow in summertime. But if they've stayed here once, they'll return the next time they are in Kalamazoo." One of these return customers, a textile distributor, was lodging for two days while he presented his offerings to stores in town. "Either the Burdick Hotel or the Kalamazoo House would have provided more convenient lodging," said Thea with a grin that showed her gray tooth. "But he said the breakfast alone is worth the longer walk."

Alice had volunteered to buy extra meat from the butcher one afternoon, always grateful for an errand that took her outside, but Thea insisted she needed the air. She left Alice with an empty tart shell and directed her to peel, core, and slice the apples to fill it. The thought of such intricate knife-work terrified Alice, but she had seen Thea perform the procedure half-a-dozen times now, and there was no excuse for her to refuse. Perhaps if she moved slowly enough, Thea would return in time to keep her from amputating a finger.

Thea addressed her younger daughter, who was conducting a conversation with her doll. "Will you stay here and play while Mama goes out for a bit, and mind Miss Alice? If you behave, there will be *apfelkuchen* for good girls tonight."

Eleanor looked apprehensively at Alice, then at the beginnings of her beloved pastry, and must have decided that the bargain presented was an acceptable one—for she nodded, and resumed chatting with Dolly. "It will take twice as long to bundle her up for the outdoors as it will take me to run the errand," she said to Alice under her breath as she left.

Alice watched the girl out of the corner of her eye for a few minutes, but Dolly was still listening patiently. Satisfied that Eleanor would keep busy for a while, she turned all her attention to the dissection of the fruit piled in front of her. *Peel first,* she told herself. She tried to remove it in a long, curling strip, but it broke more easily than she would have expected; the first peel came away in jagged red flakes.

"I tell Dowwy everything."

The announcement came quite suddenly, and Alice barely missed her thumb with the blade. But Eleanor was not even looking up—did she mean for Miss Alice to respond?

"Does she give you advice?" Alice hazarded a reply.

"Noooo!" Eleanor giggled and screwed up her face. "Dowwy isn't *real*."

Eleanor had an imagination, as evidenced by the yarns she devised for her own amusement, but still made firm proclamations about what was real and what was not. Alice wondered if all the children had been like this, or if being the youngest had made her more conscious of the world she and her siblings inhabited.

The quiet discussion with Dolly recommenced. Alice returned to her task, and was just finishing her third apple, the strips slightly less abbreviated, when she heard a yelp. Unbeknownst to Alice, Eleanor had risen from her spot in the corner and was now sitting in front of the stove, holding her right hand. Alice could see the fingers already beginning to turn pink.

Looking around for a salve, Alice located a pot of butter and gently greased the burned skin. "There now, that should make it feel better," Alice told her, grateful that she had once made the same mistake as a child and that Mrs. Connors had depended on the same remedy. But Eleanor continued to cry, her cheeks turning into cherries. Her eyes disappeared behind damp lashes and then opened wide as she began to gasp.

Alice panicked. Her first thought was to fetch Thea, but she must be all the way into town now, and how much time did she have?

She shoved a basin beneath the boiler's hot water tap as she had seen Thea do. "Come on, now." Alice begged the water to flow more quickly. She sat Eleanor by the basin and groped around in Thea's medicine cabinet. One of the bottles stuck to her hand, and she saw with relief that it was helpfully labeled "E."

"You will be all right," Alice told the child. She tipped some of the liquid into Eleanor's mouth. Half rolled down her chin and onto the front of her frock, so Alice dosed her again. Hoping to calm her, she stroked the girl's fine pale hair as they waited for the medicine and the steam to take effect. Alice nearly shouted with relief when Eleanor's breaths grew deeper and less desperate.

"Better?" Alice asked her. The tears were still flowing, but Eleanor nodded.

The door to the kitchen opened. "How are the apples coming?" Thea asked as she entered. Her eyes went to the small pile of peelings, and then to her daughter, sitting on the floor and covered in butter and syrup like a flapjack.

Alice realized for the first time that she was shaking. "She burned herself—and then she couldn't breathe—"

"Oh, my little one!" Thea pressed Eleanor to her, heedless of her sticky state.

"It was my fault—I looked away—I'm so sorry…" Alice realized she was close to tears herself.

Thea shook her head. "Eleanor should know by now—shouldn't you, Eleanor—that the stove isn't to be touched, ever. This isn't the first time she has burned herself." She kissed Alice on the forehead. "And you must not apologize—you saved her life."

The next day, when Alice entered the kitchen and asked the girl how she was, Eleanor wrapped her arms around Alice's legs and looked up with a smile.

"Mish Awish," she would say, "do you know what makes bread rise?"

"What is that?" Alice asked. She had at least learned from observing Thea that questions from Eleanor were not meant to be answered—they served as a demonstration of her knowledge.

"Yeasht."

Chapter 24

As consistently delicious as Thea's cooking was, Alice found herself feeling rather desperate for fish. Even salt cod would have done. But dinners rotated through beef and lamb and veal and beef again, with the occasional roast chicken or turkey dressed and bolstered by the remaining contents of the root cellar. Alice suspected that at this point in winter, everyone craved some vegetable besides one that had gestated underground and now was kept from sprouting in a similar, less dirt-smothered situation. But that was not to be helped, with the ground still frozen solid, trapping the spring's harvest for now.

Mr. White must have noticed the chagrin that Alice had tried to conceal, as he paused before depositing a lambchop on her plate. The chop hung from the tines of the serving fork, dripping brown gravy onto the table.

"Not interested in lamb this evening?"

Alice thrust her plate beneath the chop to save the tablecloth. "No, I'm sure it's delicious. It's only that I was thinking—I've missed having fish on a regular basis."

"Ah," said Mr. White. "See, I have never been accustomed to the fruit of the sea, and my sensory memory is short. So, although we had lamb but four days ago, my mouth is saying, 'Lamb! I have not had that in ages.'"

Alice giggled. "You must be a cook's dream."

"Indeed, I am not one to criticize food put in front of me. Especially when it is Thea's," he added, as Thea came out with a steaming pile of root vegetables, Eleanor tagging along beside her with Dolly in tow.

"Do you have something to say about the food, Neil?" said Thea in an indignant tone, although she was smiling.

"Only that is divine, as always."

Thea arched an eyebrow at his plate. "You have not even tried the chop."

"Yes, but I can *imagine* taking a bite, and I am sure that it will be delicious. The smell alone is making me feel full already."

Thea gave him an affectionate tap on the head and disappeared back into the kitchen. Eleanor, however, lingered, tugging on Alice's skirt. Alice scooped her up and sat her on her lap, carefully tucking her little legs beneath the table.

"Eleanor!" called Thea, who must have noticed her shadow missing. "Leave Miss Alice to her dinner."

"It's all right," Alice called back. She tried to put aside thoughts of flaky whitefish and instead cut into the chop, angling her arms around Eleanor, who soon grew bored and wriggled away. It was indeed mouthwatering, with some sort of peppery mustard sauce into which she dipped her potatoes as well, and she was instantly ashamed for wishing for something else. They chewed in contented silence for a few minutes.

"You must be homesick for things other than fish, I would imagine," Mr. White said abruptly.

Alice used the chewy meat as an excuse to delay answering. The steady routine of meals and work had served as a barrier against the tide of homesickness, but Mr. White's innocent comment had dislodged a sandbag, and the water trickled in.

"I am sorry; I should have waited until you had finished your bite," said Mr. White, just as Alice replied, "Yes, for some things."

"Would it make you suffer to tell me what you miss?" Mr. White waved his fork. "I do not mean to be cruel. I only wish to know you better."

"I miss my walks in Cambridge most of all," Alice decided.

Mr. White frowned, though his focus was on ferrying another chop to his plate. "But you walk here—are the roads of Kalamazoo not equal to those of Cambridge?"

"I have found some lovely routes here," answered Alice. "But in Cambridge I had a few particular paths that I had walked since childhood." She could name Mount Auburn specifically, but if Mr. White had never seen it, never meandered along its ant-tunnel paths with their whimsical flower names, how could he begin to understand her deep attachment to a cemetery?

Mr. White sighed. "Ann Arbor had havens like that—and, now that I think about it, there must be similarities aplenty between the two towns, as home to colleges and all the students and academics that come with them. Places for people who had both the time and the inclination to seek them out. There was a particular corner of the medical library, surrounded by windows giving afternoon light and set away from the busier stacks and stairwells. My boardinghouse had its share of noisy playboys, and while I was not against some carousing, I needed my quiet study time. That second-floor corner saved my grades many a semester."

He shook his head. "But we were talking about your particular attachments to home—not my musings on a town I've lived in for only a few years."

"Cambridge has a privileged way about it, as one might expect from a town partly built around a two hundred and fifty-year-old university, and I'm not going to say its inhabitants don't sometimes take their intellectualism too far. But I like being in a place where intelligence seems almost contagious." As Alice entered her teens, she had insisted on walking to Harvard almost daily, in hopes that the air enclosed in Harvard Yard would have some effect on her mental capacity.

"I would very much like to visit," said Mr. White.

An image flashed in front of Alice's eyes: she and Mr. White traveling east together, Mr. White keeping her occupied during the long ride, helping her step down from the railcar, meeting her parents in Cambridge... "I would be most happy to be your guide," was all she said.

"I would ask for no other."

Alice hoped she was not blushing too brightly.

"My father had always hoped I would go into the law, and he would have loved to ship me off to Harvard."

Alice laughed. "Imagine, a family disappointed that their son wanted to become a doctor instead. Not like my father, who has an excuse to be dismayed."

"Why's that?"

"I had the opportunity to pursue higher education, and did not." Alice swirled a piece of potato in the gravy. "I know I should not say this, but I almost wish my parents expected me to be conventional. They expected me to reject marriage in favor of education. But that I rejected education for marriage..." She trailed off. "I am disappointed in myself. Especially seeing how it has all turned out."

She had never quite admitted that to herself before, and she was surprised at how easily she confessed it to Mr. White.

"Perhaps you should use this opportunity to make a new start," said Mr. White. "You could write your parents and ask for money for your education, perhaps take a job as a professor's assistant at one of the schools here. I'm sure you could work out a lodging arrangement with Thea—she is so fond of you, I would think she'd let you stay as long as you're around to listen to her."

Although the transcription was going slowly, and she was fond of the company Mr. White and Thea provided, Alice had never thought that she might stay in Kalamazoo. She let his suggestion sit in front of her—not ready to pick it up, but willing to examine its various facets, see if she saw herself reflected in any of them.

Alice threw herself into the dependable rhythm of her routine—wake, breakfast, transcribe, lunch, help Thea, walk outside if the weather allowed, dinner. She had yet to see Mr. Weissmann at another meal, but Mr. White joined her for most lunches and dinners. He rose very early, he said, and so he ate a cold breakfast oftentimes before the sun came up. Often needing the assistance of Mr. Weissmann's amber bottle to sleep, Alice had become a later riser, but after one exhausting day she forgot the elixir and so woke before daybreak herself. She opened the curtains to see clouds hanging thick and purple in a slowly lightening sky, and she found herself wondering what Mr. White was doing, where he was in his routine. Was he dressed? Had he eaten? Was he reading fiction before turning to work, as he said was a common indulgence?

Certainly part of it was curiosity; she had not yet found the courage to ask how Mr. White had injured his hand. The deformity must have occurred recently, as he still seemed quite conscious of it; and would not a child whose right hand had been crippled from birth been dissuaded from entering the surgical profession?

Perhaps a month of interaction with no one else was to blame, but Alice was fascinated by these people whom she maybe trusted too much. And they seemed more trusting of her, too, more willing to let her in on their aims the longer Thomas stayed away. He had become an abstract figure to them—a specter himself, really. She did not notice exactly when Mr. White began to refer to her by her given name instead of Mrs. Holloway, and when she began to respond in kind, but it was one of those things she realized in the process of drifting off to sleep.

One morning, Alice came into the office to find Neil standing in front of his desk, staring at something she couldn't quite see, his hands on his hips.

"Good morning." Alice craned her neck to look around him. "What's that?"

"A present, apparently." He stepped aside to reveal a three-sectioned tube in gleaming brass, tied with a red ribbon. It looked like some kind of musical instrument, but with no finger-holes or slide.

"How lovely." Alice cocked her head. "What is it?"

"I was just wondering that myself." Neil picked up the tube and turned it around in his hands a few times. Then, with a murmured "Ah," he put the small end to his eye.

"It's a telescope—and a strong one at that." He shook his head and blinked. Alice wondered why this had not been her immediate conclusion—her father had owned one of a similar size. Perhaps it was the strange context—or perhaps it was because she had never seen her father's free of tarnish.

"Is it your birthday?"

"No. It's Adam. He's just fond of giving presents." Neil said this with some resignation.

Alice, who was very fond of receiving presents, couldn't help but ask what the matter was.

"Adam is often giving me things that he thinks might pique my interest," said Neil. "For Christmas it was an aquarium full of exotic fish. When I didn't immediately turn into a zoology aficionado, he gave me a collection of rare rocks and geodes. This month, apparently, I am supposed to take up astronomy." Neil sighed. "He means well, but when will he learn that nothing is going to seize me quite like surgery did?"

Alice was quiet. That further confirmed that Neil's injury had been recent—quite recent, most likely.

"We'll try it out after supper tonight," she said, perhaps a little too brightly. "Clear sky today."

Neil stared at the telescope and sighed. "All right. I likely know all of five constellations, but it will be worth the fresh air, at least."

They accessed the widow's watch via a narrow staircase at the back of the house; Neil offered to go first, to serve as the primary victim of the cobwebs lying in wait. There was still enough spider silk left for Alice, though; when she stepped outside, the moonlight revealed her cloak to be draped in silver thread. She clutched the flask of coffee Thea had insisted they take with them; she had protested that they wouldn't be there for long, but now she was grateful for the extra warmth in the chill March air.

The small balcony was covered with dead leaves, pinned beneath snowdrifts until recently. Neil cleared a spot for the lantern with his foot, then set about unfolding the tripod.

"Here, I brought you this." Alice drew a slim green volume from underneath her cloak and handed it to Neil. The moonlight was enough to illuminate the embossed title on the cover.

"*Half-Hours with the Telescope*." Neil grinned. "Where did you find this?"

Alice shrugged. "I offered to take care of Thea's shopping today, and while I was in town, I made a stop at the bookstore. A half-hour sounded like a suitable foundation on which to begin your new avocation."

Neil raised his eyebrows at Alice, perhaps trying to gauge if her comment was serious or sarcastic. But he opened the book and began to read out loud. "When it becomes necessary to clean the glass, it is to be noted that the substance should be soft, perfectly dry, and free from dust. Silk is often recommended, but some silk is exceedingly objectionable in texture..." He looked up, as if waiting for a signal to go on. Alice shook her head.

"I think you can become acquainted with the telescope itself once we are inside and warm."

"Of course," Neil murmured, barely keeping a straight face. "On to orientation, then. Mr. Proctor here says we must first find the Greater Bear."

The moon proved a better source of light than the lantern, though Alice was certain that their innocent stargazing would seem to have more sinister intentions to any passerby. As if they were enacting some ancient ritual, Neil held the book aloft, solemnly intoning directions, as Alice, giggling, spun around in search of the next guiding star. One directive brought her face to face with him, and the particular definition of his cheekbones in the moonlight briefly made her forget the tingling in her chilled fingertips.

It was only back in the privacy of her room that Alice felt guilt about her growing fondness for Neil. She was a married woman, after all...even if her husband had lied to her and abandoned her. But then, she told herself, why should she not make the best of her situation? Why should she not accept friendship when it was offered? Tonight, under the stars, she had felt some of her bitterness ebb; in its place, a gentle sweetness that she was almost afraid to taste.

March's slow shift from snow to rain left Alice feeling rusty. The creaking in her joints that had appeared with wet weather since last spring had intensified, her movements slower and more laborious. She managed to sit at her desk for two hours before pain in her wrist made her wince. Adam was out, thankfully, so she only had to address Neil.

"Neil, I'm afraid I haven't been feeling well. Do you mind if I take my walk early today?" She wasn't sure that a walk could help her, but at least she could transfer the pain to her hips and knees and curb the twitching in her hand.

"Of course." He put down his pen and looked at her curiously. "Are you well?"

"I will be all right. It's only that my joints become stiff when it's damp, making this work somewhat uncomfortable." She felt like an old woman, explaining her aches and pains to whomever would listen.

"You don't look old enough to be affected by the weather," Neil said, smiling.

"I had a bout of rheumatic fever last year"—was it only last year? Yes. The winter before Onset, before Thomas.

Neil's smile transformed into a furrowed brow. "Oh. I'm sorry—how thoughtless of me—"

"No, no." If Neil was anything, he was not thoughtless.

"You should ask Thea to concoct something for you. She is a regular witch doctor with herbs."

Alice was not certain she wanted anything like Eleanor's syrup, but perhaps a cup of tea would help. When she entered the kitchen, Thea jumped.

"Oh! I've been hoping you'd come in before lunch."

Alice looked at her curiously, and Thea beckoned Alice to the bread box, from which she pulled an envelope. "This arrived in the post this morning. I wasn't about to leave it out or bring it into the office, for fear that Adam would want to read it first." The letter was addressed to "Mr. T. C. Holloway, A Boardinghouse, Kalamazoo, Mich." Alice flipped over the envelope. On the back flap was a return address: "Mrs. M. Beare, New York, N. Y."

Maggie Beare—Thomas's sister. Her sending the letter to Kalamazoo suggested that Maggie was unaware of Thomas's current whereabouts. Perhaps there would be a clue for Alice to interpret, a mention of Thomas's next stop. She gave Thea a grateful peck on the cheek and hurried up the stairs to read the letter in private. Her eager fingers broke the seal before she had even turned the key in the lock.

Dearest Tom,

I've had a devil of a time trying to track you down. I know you'd prefer not to leave a forwarding address, but some approximation of your itinerary would be much appreciated. Thankfully, by chance I ran into Mr. Richardson, and he informed me he had just seen you in Kalamazoo. So I try you there.

Thank you for your last letter and the bills contained therein—Tommy has grown out of his boots in only three months, and he will be most grateful for a pair that does not pinch. I trust you are keeping enough money for yourself!

How odd that Thomas had never mentioned his nephew; Alice would think it would be a point of pride that the child bore his name.

It's been the usual routine at the boarding-house. We've not had much turnover of tenants lately—but when someone leaves, almost immediately someone steps in to take his place. One man in particular (you know which) has been lax about his rent payments again, but he only laughs when I threaten him with eviction, and I cannot very well pick him up and throw him out the door! Perhaps it is something with which you can assist when you return.

I look forward to your homecoming in May, as does Clara, of course. I worry about her—she's been as helpful as ever with the housekeeping, but I feel obligated to tell you that I have hardly seen her smile these past few months. You know I am not one for conversation whilst I am working, but a silent sister-in-law is a poor choice for your only companion.

Sister-in-law? Alice felt her heart skip a beat when she processed what that might make Clara—but no, Clara must be the sister of Maggie's late husband... The voice in Alice's head that attempted to explain the relationships mentioned in the letter was growing more faint. She was growing faint herself.

The single sheet of paper suddenly seemed too heavy for her hand, and Alice laid it on her desk. Her hands shook so violently she thought she might be having an attack of some kind. The explanatory voice had ceased altogether, realizing that its theories made less sense than the horrifying truth. Taking a deep breath, she forced herself to finish the letter.

Perhaps you will consider a summer conference closer to home? I know that you were successful at Onset, but if it means an additional two months' absence, well, would not a camp in Connecticut be preferable? We could visit you. Or perhaps Clara and Tommy would like to accompany you. While Clara has previously expressed her repulsion at sleeping in a tent, I assume you could find a nearby hotel—and she may not mind sparser accommodations, if it allows her to spend more time with her husband. Tommy has been naughtier than usual, and I cannot help but attribute his misconduct to his father's absence. You are very good about sending money and letters, but that cannot make up for seven months of no Papa.

Thomas not only had another wife—he had a child, too.

This was rage unlike any Alice had felt before. It stemmed from a furnace in her chest, which then inflamed her entire body. Deep breaths only acted as billows—for why should she even try to calm herself? She had been grievously wronged, and, perhaps even worse, made to look a fool. Adam's question as to why she had not noticed anything amiss in Thomas's professional affairs held a particular sting now, now that she realized she was just as oblivious to his personal affairs. Now it made sense that Thomas had shown such interest in their marriage officiant; he merely wanted a minister who would play along with his scheme.

The discovery had somehow greased her joints. Moving like a well-tended machine, Alice gathered up all the hectographed pages and the notebooks from their hiding place in the clothes-press. They still held the odor of smoke and ash, like how she imagined phoenix feathers might smell.

I don't know that you would like New York. Perhaps we should be on the lookout for somewhere more desirable to settle, he had said. No, Alice did not think she would have liked New York.

"What's the matter? What did it say?" asked Thea as Alice swept by her and into the garden. Alice entered the office without knocking and found Adam back at his desk and Neil bending over him, pointing to something in a book. Both jumped slightly. Adam frowned at Alice, apparently annoyed by the interruption.

"Mrs. Holloway? What is the matter—what do you have there?"

Alice dumped her armload onto Adam's desk. Adam grabbed the hectographed pages, knocking over his inkwell in the process. Neil managed to catch it but was rewarded with a black splatter across his pale green vest. He turned to Adam in protest, but Adam was focused on only one thing.

"A blue-book," he said, staring at the purple text, his voice taken with awe.

"I believe so, yes."

Adam flipped through the pages of one of the notebooks. "Are these all by your husband?"

"It appears as if he is not my husband," said Alice. "But yes, these are Mr. Holloway's notebooks. And I think you'll find plenty of evidence for your case therein."

A quick negotiation, and Alice had secured for herself not only room and board, but a small stipend in exchange for translating the rest of the notebooks. Adam was mesmerized by the notebooks despite the fact that he could not read them—flipping through them, running his fingers over the marks as though he could translate by touch. She thought he might cry over the hectographs.

Neil was the one to speak up about her confusing statement. "What do you mean, he is not your husband? I thought…"

"I also thought. But apparently he has another wife—and a child—in New York."

That prompted Adam to join Neil in an open-mouthed stare. "I knew he was a snake," muttered Adam. "But I would not have suspected him of bigamy."

The word flipped her emotions from anger to sorrow. Alice hated the fact that she was about to cry. Thomas did not deserve her tears, but they welled up despite her efforts. With as much dignity and composure as she could command, Alice said, "Please excuse me for a moment."

She turned and hurried out of the office before her vision warped and swam, and found her way back towards the house, ignoring Thea for a second time. The tears did not begin until she reached the landing on the stairs, and the gasps held off until her key had turned in the lock. *This is the last time I cry for him*, she promised herself, and half-screamed, half-sobbed into the muffling goosedown.

Perhaps Thomas was not simply threatened by Neil and Adam. He was eager for an excuse to leave her.

Chapter 25

With the absence of a schedule that spanned a week or two, no longer scrawling appointments in the blocks of a calendar in front of her, Alice had been losing track of the days of the week and then their position within the month. So she was surprised when, stepping around puddles made by the latest rainstorm, she saw a crocus boldly protruding from the ground beside the path to the office.

Alice bent to take a closer look, filled with the wonder that spring's first flowering produces after a grueling winter. In her admiration of the deep purple petals, their frosted interiors, and the bright yellow stamens that promised further growth this season, she suddenly realized that this was the first flower she had ever seen growing in Michigan. Its perfect resemblance to a crocus she might find sprouting during one of her walks through Mount Auburn filled her with a sudden homesickness. *This should make you happy,* Alice tried to tell herself. *See, it is not so different from Massachusetts here.*

"Is everything all right?"

Still in her crouching position, Alice turned to see Thea standing at the door to the kitchen, drying a pan and regarding her with concern.

"Look," Alice pointed, glad again at the opportunity to share her discovery. "A crocus, already."

Thea frowned. "Already? I should hope them to be up by April."

Alice tried to verify Thea's statement by sorting out the days in her head. April meant that she was nearly halfway to age twenty-one, that Easter was near if not passed, and that Thomas had not emerged or sent any kind of word during his monthlong absence.

She expected this realization to affect her as those regarding Thomas usually did: with a layer of grief, then anger, then grief again, then a short period of resolve before she sank into a sorrowful rage. But looking at the colorful crocus calmed her, and she forced herself to focus on its beauty. Part of her, with the human desire to collect and possess lovely things, wanted to pluck it and keep it at her desk so she could gaze at it when her mind wandered. But that would negate the flower's achievement and precipitate its death, and that Alice could not imagine.

Adam and Neil looked at her oddly when they found Alice at the door of the kitchen, pointing to something on the ground and telling them to be careful where they trod. But they obeyed, giving the crocus a wide berth. And Alice felt a little thrill of pride in aiding its preservation.

After the tease, however, spring exploded into existence almost overnight. Amidst the predominant grays of the morning, she noted the bright yellow-green of maple florets, color she prayed would not be torn off its tree at the whim of wind and rain. Not long after, when the sun woke her early one morning, Alice was surprised to find the maple leaves emerging dark and wrinkled, like butterflies from a cocoon.

Springtime meant the return of regular boarders and passers-through, and the extra housework made the time pass even more quickly for Alice. Neil and Adam were spending the first week of May in Chicago, looking into a levitating medium who had captivated the hearts and wallets of the city's meatpacking heirs. Although a small part of her longed to play hooky and forsake the office for the sunshine, Alice persevered in her transcription.

As she worked her way through the notebooks, and every page gave further proof of Thomas's deception, Alice could not help but doubt her own supposed interactions with spirits. She imagined Thomas hypnotizing her, then taking the pencil from her hand and inventing stories based on the scratches in his notebook. But then why would he have bothered? Alice found it difficult to believe that Thomas found her so desirable as to concoct such a scheme.

In the afternoons, she welcomed the opportunity to clear her mind of Thomas and run errands for Thea, sometimes taking a child or two off her hands. With Ernest and Eleanor in tow, quietly absorbed in the peppermint sticks that had been their reward for good behavior, Alice purchased another Richard Anthony Proctor book—*Easy Star Lessons*—on one of her trips into town. She planned to impress Neil with her knowledge of May's stars when he returned.

When the last dinner dish was dry, Alice excused herself from the kitchen and hastened upstairs to fetch a shawl. The stars would be out all night, but she would be lucky if her stargazing lasted half an hour. The last few nights she hadn't needed a drop of Adam's laudanum—the feel of a soft pillow against her cheek had been soporific enough.

Alice had only just affixed the telescope to the tripod when she sensed that something on the roof was different. She had heard no sound, seen nothing out of the ordinary, and yet she felt that a...presence had joined her. She clutched *Easy Star Lessons* to her chest as if it were a shield.

"Hello?" she whispered. But there was no reply.

Alice shook her head vigorously. *You are simply tired, and imagining things,* she told herself. She flipped to "The Stars for May"—*Toward the north, we now see the Plough, or Dipper raised directly above the Pole-star; the constellation of the Great Bear occupying a much wider region of the sky*—and followed its instructions through the lens, picking out the patterns that would guide the rest of the chapter's directives.

Suddenly, she pulled away from the telescope, wide-eyed. One eye struggled to adjust to the dim light, the other to the narrowness of human vision, the mundane earthly shapes of chimneys and gables.

"Who's there?" Alice tried to keep her voice steady as her mind raced through the possibilities. There was no sure footing on the roof beyond this little cupola; it was unlikely a boarder had found his way up here, so perhaps it was a squirrel, a particularly large squirrel...

There, out of the corner of her eye, a white smudge by one of the chimneys. When she turned to get a better look, it had already faded considerably, but still the outline of it was there. The outline of a man.

She had spent her share of afternoons in dark places, allowing an otherworldly force to take possession of her hand, but never had a spirit appeared to her, except...Automatically, her hand went to her forehead, to test if her fever had returned. But her fingertips found cool skin.

"Do you have something you would like to say?" Alice spoke to the shade with all the steadiness she could muster. "I would like to help you, but I have no paper."

As soon as she uttered the words, she remembered that yes, she did have paper, a little scrap on which to make notes of what she saw in tonight's sky. Alice sat down among the rotting leaves, trying not to wince as the dampness seeped through her skirts.

It had been so long since she had tried to reclaim this sense of quiet, and she wondered how long it would take, especially with her hand shaking so...

Then there was that sensation of waking too quickly from a dream of falling, and feeling the impact as she landed in her bed, except she was still on the roof with the night's chill seeping through her shawl, and her paper had two lines on it.

Please do forgive me for all the sorrow and worry I have caused you in the past. If I had returned, you would have found me a changed man.

Alice looked up, in the direction of the shade, but it had disappeared completely. She was the only being on the roof once again.

Were those words meant for someone in the house? She thought of Thea's husband, of Adam's father, and wondered how they might have disappointed their loved ones. Who else was dead, and owed someone an apology? And then the plain answer hit her so suddenly that she burst into tears.

Oh, Thomas.

The idea of Thomas's death threatened to open all the wounds that were just beginning to heal. But the truth of the matter was, she so ached for an apology that she found his voice in every bit of the message. And it gave her a reason as to why he had never even sent her a letter.

Alice packed the telescope slowly, trying to fill her thoughts with stars instead of with images of how Thomas had met his end. Back in her room, she took a drop of laudanum straight to the tongue.

Alice had no stomach for the blue books the next morning, or the one after that, and trusted that her steady efforts during the first days of Adam and Neil's trip would count for something. Explaining to Thea that she had hit an impasse in her work, she volunteered to do the tedious task of laundry every morning, attacking the washboard with a previously undiscovered arm strength. She no longer relished quiet evenings in her room, instead shadowing Thea until it was time to turn in. When the day's last cup of tea had been drunk and her door was closed, Alice allowed herself a little laudanum, and slept.

Suppressing her thoughts of Thomas worked well for a time, but when she looked out the window early one morning to see light spilling from the office into the backyard, Alice was overwhelmed with a desire to tell Adam and Neil about her experience on the roof that night. The impulse made no sense, when they had just presumably been seeking evidence to convict a fraudulent medium—she doubted they would welcome the two sentences from the night on the roof as proof of her legitimate powers. And they would have little sympathy for the passing of her not-really husband.

She instead turned to thinking of excuses for why her transcription work was sparse. Perhaps Adam had been up early, going through her work, and already knew—but when she entered the office, he was engrossed in something else. Her desk was just as she left it...except for the neatly wrapped, red-ribboned package sitting there. Was Adam attempting to steer her down some professional path of his choosing, too? If that were the case, though, the present's flatness and thinness suggested that he did not have much hope for her.

"Miss Boyden," Adam looked up barely long enough to offer a brief nod. Apparently not.

"Good morning, Mr. Weissmann." Alice tried to keep the smile out of her voice. The mere predictability of his curt response made her want to laugh. "Where is Mr. White?"

Adam began to answer, but then the door creaked open. He gestured with his pen. "Right behind you." and went back to work, but not before Alice detected a smirk on his sallow face. She turned to find a slightly out-of-breath Neil.

"Alice! I had hoped to make it here before you, but Thea caught me and wanted to hear all about Chicago, and, well, you know." Neil was animated in a way she hadn't seen him before. "Look, I brought you a little something."

"What's this?"

"Oh, a souvenir from our trip. Open it."

Alice carefully untied the ribbon. No man besides her father had given her a gift before. Not Thomas, certainly.

"Go on." Neil was acting like a child giving his mother a long-worked-on present. Alice tore open the paper to reveal a book: *Picturesque Chicago*.

"Before we left, you mentioned that you had never been to Chicago. So I thought I'd bring it to you."

Alice flipped through the pages—beautiful engravings of the pavilion in Humboldt Park, Lake Shore Drive, the Union Stock Yards. Of course she hadn't mentioned to Neil exactly what had prevented her going to Chicago—just that plans had fallen through.

"Is something wrong?"

Alice realized that her face must have betrayed her thoughts of Thomas and the baby. "It's lovely, Neil. I just hadn't realized Chicago was so beautiful." She closed the book and held it to her chest, hoping her eyes were not too watery, that her voice was not shaking too much. "It's perfect."

Neil relaxed visibly. "I'm so glad. I would have tried to find something more personal, but our leisure time was rather limited." He stood there awkwardly for a moment, then appeared to gather himself; his hands flew up and he turned as if remembering something. But all he did was resume his normal routine: hang his coat on the hook, take out his notes and pen. Alice watched him out of the corner of her eye, and smiled. The gift-giving had thrown him off his morning track, and it had taken him a moment to line up his wheels again.

It was then that she realized how much she had missed Neil in his absence, in spite of all the strangeness on the roof. Dead or alive, Thomas had still abandoned her, and she must not forget that. Neil had thought of her on his travels. And Neil had come back.

Chapter 26

Alice accepted that her transcription work, requiring such concentration, would bring on run-of-the-mill headaches. The pain focused itself right in the middle of her forehead, emanating from the space between her eyes. But unlike her migraines, they came without nausea and could usually be treated with a cup of tea and some rest. If Neil looked over and saw her fingers pressed against her brow bone, he insisted that she retire to her room for the afternoon, and expressed hope that he would see her well again at dinner. Perhaps it was his confidence that made the headaches pass more quickly.

So it came as a shock when olive drops began to spatter the page in front of her. She tried to ignore them, but the pain arrived soon enough, gathering like storm clouds on the left side of her head, giving Alice little room for denial. She stood up slowly, but a thunderous boom by her ear made her stumble.

"Alice? Are you all right?" Neil was by her side in a moment, supporting her.

Alice could not speak at first, but knew that nodding or shaking her head would only exacerbate the situation. So she merely blinked at him, hoping he would understand.

"Alice?"

She found that moving her arm was possible, and she raised her fingertips to her forehead.

"A headache?"

"Yes." Alice thought she produced the word herself, but it sounded strangely distant from her lips.

"Here. I'll help you to your room. Do you need me to carry you?"

Alice considered this. "No." Although the image of being lifted in Neil's arms was comforting, she imagined she could better steady herself on her own two feet. She was nearly blind in one eye now, however, and leaned heavily on Neil, allowing him to determine the pace and placement of her steps. As they passed through the kitchen, he asked a concerned Thea something about medicine, but Alice felt as if she had already been drugged. Every moment without pain was a blissful valley amongst the vicious peaks, and she imagined herself cradled in a bed of grass, comfortable until she shifted her head and banged it on a rock.

The stairs seemed a mountain to climb, but she had Neil on one side and the bannister on the other for support. He helped her down the hall and onto the bed, where Alice gratefully closed her eyes. "Thea will be up soon with some concoction; I'm sure she will help you undress…"

Alice waved a limp hand in protest. "Are you not in medicine? Surely you have seen a woman's undergarments before." She desperately wanted the extra comfort of a loosened bodice, but the thought of undoing all her tiny buttons and her laces was more daunting than climbing the stairs. It occurred to Alice that she should think of propriety, modesty, but they seemed inconsequential right now, mere details next to the main topic of pain.

There was a pause, and Alice wondered if Neil was leaving to fetch Thea instead. But then she felt a trembling finger brush the underside of her chin and her neck was freed from fabric. He hesitated again when he reached the buttons that ran between her breasts, but just slightly.

Neil cleared his throat. "The stays as well?"

"Yes, please."

Alice could not concentrate on what his fingers were doing; all her concentration went into staying afloat as the waves of pain crashed over her. But when he stopped, Alice took a gratefully deep breath.

"Neil?"

"Yes?"

"Thank you."

Neil said nothing in return, but Alice felt the gentle brush of his lips on her forehead.

First Alice was back in her bedroom in Cambridge. The cast of characters was mostly the same; they floated in and out of her vision as if they were set pieces on wheels. The woman she believed to be Mary Sawyer was there, still helping herself to the pink roses on the bedspread, but pausing to sweep one across Alice's forehead, as if blessing the spot where Neil had kissed her. Mrs. Connors sat in a rocking-chair in the corner, knitting something out of lilac yarn. She saw Alice watching, smiled kindly, and turned back to her work.

Alice sensed someone standing at her shoulder. Her mother, come to nurse her? Panicking, she realized it might be the people in black who had robbed her of her breath—but paralysis, whether from fear or illness, had set in and she could not turn her head enough to see. She breathed a sigh of relief when it was Thea that appeared, although she could not understand what Thea was doing in Cambridge.

She must have awoken fully but briefly then, as she found herself back in the Kalamazoo bed. Thea tipped up Alice's chin and held a spoon to her mouth.

"Can you open?"

Alice, feeling like a toddler, obeyed. The syrup was sweet and noxious at the same time. Alice could not help but screw up her face.

"I know. It's not the most pleasant, but I think it will work." Thea held a tin cup of water from which Alice was more willing to sip. "Now. Try and sleep."

Alice wanted to obey Thea, who had been so kind to her. This was motivation enough to coax herself back into slumber.

The pain in her head remained when she next woke, but it was slightly duller, a knife that had not seen a whetstone for some time. Alice's panic was reserved for the next sensation, or lack thereof: it seemed that her feet had disappeared. No, not quite missing; now she felt them burn and tingle, as if they had been packed in ice like so much meat.

She wiggled her toes to speed their warming, wondering where her quilts and flannel stockings had gone—until, pulling herself upright, she realized that her nightgown was not flannel but cotton lawn, and the weight of her blankets suggestive of a spring evening on the edge of summer. She tried to move her dry tongue around in her mouth to moisten it, but gagged on some sort of fuzz. She spat out something that tasted like a combination of dirt and lint.

Alice brought the gas light up too quickly and blinked blindly for several moments before regaining her sight. She studied the oddity expelled into her hand. At first she thought it was a patch of some rough lace, but in poking it with an index finger it fell apart. She realized it was lichen, though less robust than any she noted as a child while playing at the base of green-spattered tree trunks. Had she been sleepwalking and chilled her feet that way? Had she wandered outside and somehow decided that the growths on a nearby tree looked like an appetizing snack?

Now that it was late May, Thea had packed away the heaviest of blankets. Alice unearthed a spare quilt from the press and cocooned herself in it, then applied a double layer of flannel to her feet before returning to bed. It was enough to regain some warmth, but she must have some kind of ague—her shivering did not stop with the addition of flannels. Surely the chill would take a turn as she slept and the fever would break into sweats.

The next thing she knew, someone was shaking her awake.

Alice's eyes twitched as if ready to open, but her lashes remained gently brushing her nose and cheekbones. Her mouth hung slightly ajar; she moved her dry tongue to her broken lips, though it did nothing to soothe them. Was it Thomas? What was important enough to rouse her from such a precious sleep?

But a glance to the right told Alice that Thomas was not there, reminded her that he had not been there for months now. Instead, as her eyes adjusted, she discerned a stranger at the foot of her bed, glowing faintly.

Alice yelped and skittered backwards, crablike on her feet and hands, until her back smacked against the headboard. Seeing what state the man was in, however, her fear began to shift to pity. He was hardly older than Alice and could not be much taller. She certainly outweighed him. The moonlight cast shadows where his cheeks should have been. Two eyes burned a pale blue from dark sockets. The flesh that remained on his face was gray. He wore a sealskin coat; the fur at his wrists and encircling the hood of his jacket had turned sharp and white with rime. It was her quietest fever apparition—the one who had never bothered her.

Alice pressed her head between her hands, as if to squeeze out the vision that instinct told her was not real. But when no amount of closing and reopening her eyes cleared the man from the room, she sought to address him directly.

"Who are you?"

No response. He made no perceptible movement but a blink.

"Why have you come here?"

Still no acknowledgment that he was being addressed.

"Why have you come to me again, after so long?"

Suddenly the man shook his head as if he had just awoken from a trance. He raised his head to look at Alice again and opened his mouth...

Alice found herself staring at the armoire against the wall. The figure had disappeared without a saying a word.

The migraine, or Thea's syrup cure, was making her see things. Without the man to focus upon, her body recalled how desperately tired it was. Having edged forward to confront the visitor, Alice backed into her pillow again. Something buckled within her stomach, and nausea made her salivate; she clutched the nearest bedpost until it passed. She wiggled her toes from their flannel wraps; now they were burning hot. She realized that she was drenched in sweat. At least it seemed the fever had broken.

When she woke several hours later, the sky had turned from pitch black to purple, promising sunrise soon. Her first thought was to see if Neil was at breakfast, and tell him about her midnight vision. *It was the strangest thing,* she would say. *I don't know if my feet have ever felt so cold.*

She had nearly resolved to put the starved man out of mind, but when she turned the gas up, she noticed a piece of paper lying on her desk blotter. In a strange hand. In what appeared to be German.

Alice found both Adam and Neil already in the office, working away at their respective desks. They both looked up at the opening of the door.

"Hello," said Neil, smiling at Alice, though she saw shyness creep into his face, perhaps at the thought of his assistance the day before. She returned a smile that she hoped displayed her gratitude and put his mind at ease.

"Alice. I hope that you are much improved?" said Adam.

"Yes, thank you." Alice hesitated, then almost took her seat as usual, but the paper felt as if it were burning her hand.

"Adam, would you be able to translate this for me?" She placed it in front of him. "It is in German, and so I cannot read it."

Adam scanned the page once with curiosity. When he started again at the beginning, his mouth fell open slightly. Unnerved by his silence, Alice started talking. "I suppose I should give you some background. You see, last winter I was very ill with a fever, and I would see... apparitions...people...who were not there. When I recovered, I was left with these tremendous headaches..."

Dark eyes looked up at her and narrowed. "You wrote this?"

"Well, I did not *compose* it." Alice swallowed. "What I mean is...I have reason to believe that is a spirit message."

Adam cackled. "I have spent the last five months investigating frauds, and you expect me to believe this to be from a spirit?"

"But you know I do not speak German. And that's not my handwriting at all—see?" She took up one of her transcriptions that lay on his desk and held it next to the page that Adam had in his hand. The scripts were notably different—hers sweeping and bold, the German letters elegant yet delicate, as if the author were trying to conserve ink. Adam did not acknowledge the difference but abruptly tore the page in half, then in quarters, and let them flutter to the floor, ignoring Alice's little cry of protest.

"I do not know what you're playing at, or where you obtained this, but this did *not* come from your hand. Do you suffer from similar delusions—or moral failings—as your husband, and have simply been hiding them from me?" Alice found herself retreating until she was pinned against Adam's desk, and still Adam was snarling right in her face, waving his hand around. Was he going to strike her? She closed her eyes.

A hand touched her and she flinched—but it was a gentle touch. Slowly, she opened her eyes again and saw that Neil had stepped between them.

"What is this?" said Adam's voice, slightly muffled by the obstruction, his face hidden. "Did Neil have a hand in this?"

"I have not even seen what she's written…" began Neil. Alice saw Adam's bony finger poke at Neil.

"I've seen what eyes you make at each other. I wouldn't doubt you have an alliance. For all we know she could still be in touch with Mr. Holloway, who is plotting his return…"

"You are being positively paranoid," said Neil.

"Am I? And why should I not be? Why should I be anything but skeptical, when our investigations yield nothing but trickery and deception? You think I trust this woman?" Adam jerked his head to the side to see around Neil, and Alice thought his eyes might burn through her own. "For all I know, the discovery of your husband's other wife could be a ruse to make me let down my guard."

"Adam, I think you should leave," Neil said, his voice level.

"This is *my* home, *my* office. Why should *I* leave?" Adam roared, but after one pointed stomp on the pieces of paper, he tore open the door and slammed it shut behind him.

Alice had not realized she had stopped breathing until her lungs demanded a big gulp of air.

"Are you all right?" Neil turned to her and took her hands. "This is not the restorative day you needed, I am sure."

"I'm fine," said Alice, although she knew he could feel her pulse tell a different story.

Chapter 27

Alice and Neil arranged the pieces of the message on the desk and stared at them for a few moments.

"So you truly don't know German?" said Neil.

"No," said Alice, a bit exasperated. "Don't you know any?"

Neil shook his head. "I can sing Christmas carols in German, but this does not appear to be 'O Tannenbaum' or 'Stille Nacht.'" He looked a bit sheepish. "My father thought we would have an easier lot in life the more American we were. So he pressed very little of his heritage upon us, and the only time I heard him speak German was with my grandparents." A look of triumph suddenly came over his face, and he snapped his fingers.

"Thea. Thea will be able to translate this for us."

Alice followed him out the door and down the path to the house, but she was still haunted by the look in Adam's eyes.

"Neil?"

"Mmmm?"

"Do you think Adam would have hurt me?"

Neil was quiet for a moment. "He's stronger than you think."

They found the kitchen deserted, though sweet and savory scents of breakfast still lingered in the warm room.

"Thea must be upstairs," said Neil. "I'll go find her."

"Wait, wait." Alice gave the kettle a quick tap with her hand. Still hot. "She won't be away long. Why don't we have some tea?"

Neil looked at her strangely. "Don't you want to know what the message says?"

"Of course I do," said Alice, filling two teacups. She watched some of the dregs flow out into one of them; she would take that cup for herself. "But I also want to know what the trouble is with Adam." This seemed like the best opportunity she'd had yet, and she did not want to squander it.

"Well, we can't really guess until we have a translation..."

"What his general troubles are." Alice pushed open the dining room door with her shoulder and set the cups and saucers on the table. The cream and sugar had not yet been cleared from breakfast, and so Alice settled herself and gestured to Neil to do the same. "Is the laudanum to blame?" she asked outright. It was past the point of being careful around the topic.

Neil looked down into his tea and did not answer.

"You needn't deny that he's dependent on it—no one carries a bottle around in his shirt pocket unless he's a bonafide opium eater, despite his excuse about the injury." Alice cocked her head. "Shouldn't I know if he's a danger?"

Neil held up his hand for her to stop. Alice could see him bringing out the scales in his head, weighing action against consequence, so she sat patiently.

"You're right—you deserve to know the circumstances. You deserve to know the background, too."

Alice kept her eyes trained on him as she sipped.

"Adam was the top psychology student at Ann Arbor as an undergraduate," Neil began. "We all thought he would continue his studies out East, most likely at Harvard, but he surprised us all by staying with the Michigan program. It certainly wasn't for want of money that he remained, or by request of family—both his mother and father had died by that point. And he was sincerely admiring of William James, with whom he certainly would have studied. So with the obvious obstacles nonexistent, we could only surmise that he stayed out of fear—fear that his head-of-the-class status would no longer hold at a New England school, fear of being lost in the race. He's also not terribly fond of big cities."

Alice laughed at this. "But Cambridge is hardly a big city."

Neil shrugged. "Yes, well, he didn't have the benefit of any natives who could explain that to him. But mostly he liked being top dog, liked that showing up others came easily, and that he could produce standout work with time left over for recreation. I don't want you to think the program wasn't rigorous—it was, certainly. But no one wanted recognition more than Adam, and most of his classmates were content to step aside and let him have the bulk of it."

"So what happened? Did he simply become too complacent and fail his classes? Or was he in the laudanum even then?"

Neil cringed. "He was originally prescribed the drug for a sprained ankle, and he would say that it was a slow heal. When he gave you the laudanum, it was the first time he had used the excuse of a back injury. Less apparent than a limp, I suppose.

"We came to the end of the semester, when no one is quite in their right mind...everyone has their eye on the December break and would much rather be wassailing and trimming trees than studying and writing papers. So they procrastinate, indulge in less and less sleep, perhaps turn to wassail early and thus exacerbate their delicate state...my point is that none of the students were quite themselves, and so Adam's increasingly strange behavior only made him blend in with the other scattered souls on campus.

"We knew he had been given laudanum for his ankle in the spring, though he continued to dose himself regularly over the summer, sometimes adding drops to his drink right in front of us. But once the school year began, he seemed to have put the bottle away, and we figured he was back to business. In reality, he had simply become secretive about his self-medication. He'd excuse himself early from social events—to study, we thought."

"But he was spending time with his amber bottle."

Neil nodded. "I suspect that he did intend to study most evenings—the few times someone asked him about laudanum, he would reply that it sharpened the mind and speeded the learning—but in truth the drug distracted him, for he would often become fixated on something other than his textbooks. I once found him in the midst of writing an epic poem about a spider dangling from the ceiling. His pupils had dilated to the size of pin-heads. He must have thought he was Coleridge, writing *Lyrical Ballads.*"

"Sounds as if he would get along with my father," Alice murmured.

Neil frowned. "Is your father fond of laudanum?"

"No, of spiders." She shook her head. "Go on."

"I tried to get other friends to help me confront him, but they were wrapped up in their own end-of-semester assignments. Adam had been a calm soul through October, but November saw him comparatively moody. The smallest things sent him into tirades—when the dining hall ran out of something, I can't even remember what, that he had planned to have as lunch, he couldn't stop muttering about the administration's lack of consideration for its students' nutritional needs.

"I decided that the only thing to do was to take his supply away from him. While he was out one day I found his bottles—we shared the floor of a roominghouse, and he never locked his door—and poured them down the drain. Certainly he could afford more, but I hoped, in my desperation, that the loss of an easily accessible bottle might make him pause before seeking another.

"There was a study group scheduled for that evening. Adam appeared when we hadn't planned on him being there, and I hoped he was returning to his senses. But he had no books on hand, and did not remove his coat. He seemed shaky; I thought he was simply cold. He asked to see me in the hallway, but we weren't even out of the room when he grabbed me by the collar and demanded to know what I had done with it.

"'With what?' I asked, trying to keep up an innocent front, but he wouldn't let go. 'You know,' he said.

"One of our friends came in at that point, asking what this was all about, but Adam was focused only on me. I saw his hand go to his pocket but couldn't imagine what he was reaching for. In the next moment I was holding up my hand to keep a knife blade from my face."

Alice gasped.

"I remember a few moments of excruciating pain, and then I think I went into shock. I wouldn't have wanted the police called for Adam, but I was incapable of voicing my opinion—and I think the other fellows, as much as I'm sure they would deny it, were afraid for their lives. I did not wish to prosecute, but the school became aware of it and expelled Adam. They are generally tolerant of their brightest students' failings, but this they could not ignore. They offered to put him in an asylum as well"—Neil jerked his head in the direction of the state hospital—"but I refused to allow it."

"But he crippled you!" exclaimed Alice. She dropped her voice once she realized what decibel she had attained in her agitation. "Why are you taking care of him?"

"Cripples are those who need a cane or crutches, in my opinion," said Neil, his voice clipped. "I don't count myself among them. And he's a family member who needed help. He has no parents or siblings to turn to. There was only me. Do you know of Charles Lamb?"

"The...essayist?" Alice's mind reached back to her readers and recitation books, and pulled the name out of the table of contents.

Neil nodded. "A friend of Coleridge, actually. His sister Mary, much older than he, taught him to read. He owed his education and eventual career to her instruction. But one night she suffered from a fit of mania, and stabbed her invalid mother to death. She was released into Charles's care, and he looked after her for the rest of his life. Such was his love and gratitude."

Alice met Neil's steady gaze. "But Adam is not mad per se," she said. "His disturbances have a chemical component. Why is he still—"

"I know he isn't," said Neil, a rash of irritation reddening the words. "But I doubt it is a good idea for me to take the laudanum away from him again, and I would not sacrifice anyone else to the task. Would you volunteer?"

When Neil laughed, Alice realized she must have flinched.

"He eats enough to survive, keeps us both lodged and clothed—you as well, remember. He realizes that he has taken my livelihood away, and while he cannot repair my hand, he can provide for me, and give me work. He leaves me those presents to encourage me along another career path. You've seen his temper flare up from the imbalance that's produced in his system if he doesn't have enough of the drug, and although he's not hurt anyone since, I'd rather he be calm and docile.

"If I really wanted him to be rid of this habit, I could put him in an asylum. Even a nice private one—not the state place down the road. But in either case, while it is easy to commit someone, it is often quite difficult to convince the institution to let him go. And Adam's not insane. He likes his liberty. He wouldn't go quietly, and he'd hate me forever. And if there was no one to greet him when he finally was freed—if he ever was freed—don't you think he would go straight back to his one comfort?"

Alice looked down at the floor. "I do have some sense of what it's like to be confined to one room all day." Of not wanting to sleep for fear of nightmares, but not wanting to wake up to the dull day that stretched ahead. Sorting her books by color, then alphabetically by first line, when she grew tired seeing them grouped in the usual ways of title, subject, and author. Alice wondered if one was even allowed to have books in an asylum. Most likely there was a common library, a shelf or two of dingy, thumbed-through castoffs donated by the staff or by people who considered themselves charitable—giving away a book they themselves would never read again or recommend to any friend. She imagined that the collection was also likely purged of inflammatory political treatises, controversial religious texts, or any biographies that might prove appealing to a delusional soul searching for a new identity.

"How much does your family know about Adam's...troubles?" she asked.

"My parents think that Adam was ill, and they know I'm looking after him, taking a semester of leave. They don't know he attacked me. My sisters are older, with their own families, and I see them only on holidays."

"They did not see your hand over Christmas?"

"I haven't been up there to visit since last summer—a convenient snowstorm prevented my traveling north to Grand Rapids for Christmas. I thought for certain the story would leak out when students went home for their winter break, but I've heard nothing to indicate that they know the whole story."

"And they don't mind that you're taking time off from school?"

"They think I'm returning in the fall."

Alice raised an eyebrow. "And you're not?"

Neil snorted. "Look at me!" It was the first time that Alice had seen Neil angry, and the contrast between his usually calm demeanor and his face now was stark. "Look at this claw. How can I be a surgeon if I can barely write? No one is going to come to me when they know of my handicap, even if I did manage to bumble my way through the rest of school." His face drooped. "I downplayed the severity of my injury, hoping they would allow me to take responsibility for Adam. A classmate sewed up the wound, but not well, as you can see. I didn't realize the extent of the damage until I removed the bandages."

Without asking, Alice took Neil's curled-up right hand and twisted it to expose the palm. He tried to pull away, but she held fast. The scar tissue ran from the heel of his hand to the webbing between forefinger and thumb. The fingers trembled at her touch, as if the hand itself were distrustful of Alice's motives. She laid her other hand over to comfort it.

The creak of the kitchen door made both of them jump, and Alice quickly reclaimed her hands. "Ah, Thea," she said, turning away from Neil. "We've been looking for you. Would you help us translate something from the German? Adam has gone out for the day."

Thea's expression suggested that Alice had not been quick enough; her smile seemed too broad to refer to a translation request. "Why, of course." Thea glanced down. "Where did it come from?"

"It is an alleged spirit-writing, sent to Adam by a skeptic." Alice was surprised by how easily the lie came. "We are impatient to know what it says."

Thea beamed at the thought of being useful. "I'd be glad to help. Why don't we have a look." She accepted the message from Alice, raising her eyebrows at its fragmented state. "Looks like someone was not pleased with their composition."

Alice felt something at her ankles, heard a titter, and looked down to see Eleanor dusting her shoes. They were admittedly a bit dirty from walking through the garden. When Alice reached down to tickle her, Eleanor squealed and wiggled away.

Thea squinted at the writing. "Eleanor, will you fetch my spectacles? They are in the kitchen somewhere." Eleanor dropped her plumage and soon returned wearing a little pair of wire spectacles, giggling until her mother noticed her.

"You only wait until you have to wear such things, and you will not laugh then, I assure you." Thea carefully took the spectacles off her daughter's face and settled them on her own. "That is better. Now then.

"In Switzerland there lived an old count, and he had only one son, but he was dumb and could not learn anything...Ah! *Kinder- und Hausmarchen.*"

Alice gave Thea a blank look.

"*Children's and Household Tales.* The Brothers Grimm. There is a copy in the nursery. This one is...let me think... 'Die drei Sprachen,' or 'The Three Languages.'"

"Oh," said Neil. "My sisters and I read the tales as children..."

Thea looked confused. "And you did not recognize this?"

"In translation," Neil finished, looking a little sheepish.

Thea tsked. "Your father, the Americanizer!" To Alice she said, "All good German children know these tales...my dear Frank loved them especially, and would read them to the children in the evenings. I have not opened the book since his passing"—she paused and rubbed her eyes underneath her spectacles. "This reminds me that it's time for Eleanor to hear some. I shall avoid the more violent ones for her, of course." She looked at the page. "This isn't the whole tale, though; it's only the first passage. It doesn't include the happy ending!"

"What is the gist of the story?" asked Alice. She hoped it would give them some clue as to what had upset Adam.

"Well, a Swiss count thinks his only son is stupid, and sends him to three masters in the hopes that the son will learn something. He comes back knowing what dogs say when they bark, what birds say when they sing, and what frogs say when they croak. The count, not pleased with the results, orders his son to be killed, but the executioners set him free in the forest instead. His knowledge of the animals' languages allows him to perform various good deeds, he comes to be adopted by a lord, and is eventually made Pope."

Alice looked at Neil, who shrugged. "It may be worth a look at the original," he said, "to see if this is a verbatim transcription, perhaps implying it was simply copied from the book. If not, it suggests that the writer knows German and is retelling the story from memory."

Thea and her children occupied the servants' quarters in the back of the house. Neil said that Adam had long been after her to take some of the guest rooms as her own, but Thea insisted that her family did not need much space, and besides, those were rooms that could be let to provide more money for her children. The nursery, not much bigger than a closet and probably meant for such, sat between the girls' room and the boys' room.

It did not take long for Alice to find the stout tome in the compact nursery bookcase, its caul of spiderwebs intact. "Proof that I have not consulted this book," she said, and sneezed as she blew off the dust.

"*Gesundheit*," said Neil. "That really is the best of my German."

They both sat awkwardly on the floor, as the nursery lacked adult-sized chairs, and Neil read a few paragraphs aloud to the best of his ability. Alice was grateful that German was a mostly phonetic language as she checked the words against the book, circling any inconsistencies in faint pencil. At some point Neil looked over his shoulder, and Alice wondered if he thought Adam might sneak up on them.

"Well, there are enough differences to suggest that it was told from memory," said Alice. She stared at the handwritten German, its strange ligatures and umlauts, and cleared her throat. "Adam didn't give me much of a chance to explain, but you should know that this has happened to me before."

"What has happened to you? The unexplained appearance of German text in your sleep?"

Alice took a deep breath. "Last summer, when I me
was having...episodes. A migraine would hit me and I wou
in my room, and when I woke I found messages in handwriti
not my own. Most of them were illegible or made no sense,
decipher a word here and there. Thomas told me they were from spirits, and helped me control when I served as their secretary." She looked up at Neil, expecting him to be close to laughter, but he was listening with apparent sincerity. "Perhaps it was mere hypnosis. I have—I have thought of many explanations over the last few months. But since this latest incident occurred after a migraine, I cannot help but wonder if someone is trying to communicate." She almost mentioned the two sentences dictated to her on the roof, but perhaps it was best to explain one supernatural occurrence at a time.

"Were you ever going to tell us about this?"

"After you exposed Thomas as a fraud, I did not think it particularly wise," said Alice. "And I didn't think it relevant. I thought I had lost the ability. Thomas certainly seemed to think I had." Alice focused on her lap. "I had no desire to be a medium myself, and so I simply gave the messages I received to Thomas, who shared them in his séances. He said that he was using them as a sort of introduction to the spirit—that it would help him establish contact. I now realize he was likely using my communications to fill in where his blue books left off." She ran her thumb along the page edges of the Grimms' book until it turned gray with dust. "I thought you'd both think me terribly gullible for letting him get away with such a thing for several months."

"I think love can blind people to a multitude of sins." Neil cleared his throat. "The truth is, and you may not know it to speak to us, but we do think there is something to these psychical phenomena. With perhaps not spirits, but telepathy at the root of it. We have seen many frauds, but few mediums that gave us pause; hence our focus on debunking the pretenders. And the way in which Adam reacted to this...well, he is most likely afraid it is genuine. Either you read his mind and touched upon something very personal, or you are in touch with a spiritual correspondent he knew in life."

"Could he think it from his mother? Did she read him fairy tales?"

"Most likely, so there is a possibility."

"Any close friends who have died—perhaps in childhood?"

Neil thought about this. "Adam has been at the university several years longer than I, and I'm sure he has lost a couple of classmates lost along the way, but no one particularly dear to him. I was probably his most frequent playmate as a child..."

"Or maybe it is someone who he does not know to be dead—hence his reaction. Anyone who lives in a cold region—Canada, perhaps?"

Neil's face suddenly looked as if someone had bleached it. "Why do you ask?"

"Last night I saw—or dreamed—of a man wearing heavy furs, as if he were an Eskimo. But it was a white man, with a gaunt face."

She watched Neil swallow before he spoke. "Adam has a dear friend who joined a government expedition to the Arctic in 1881. They have not been heard from in over a year."

Chapter 28

Neil rose from his seat and replaced the book on the shelf without a word. Alice followed him downstairs. Thea was waiting for them in the kitchen—she gave Alice an expectant look—but they only bid her good afternoon and went into the garden. Alice felt somewhat guilty, but neither did she feel much like explaining, especially when she herself did not quite understand what was happening.

Alice waited for Neil to say something—to explain how someone as homebound as Adam had befriended an Arctic explorer, for instance—but he was silent as they walked toward the office. The bees were hard at work among the hyacinths and the daffodils, and one buzzed past Alice's ear, startling her into a yelp. Neil whipped around, perhaps expecting to see that Adam had reemerged, but seeing only Alice atremble, he took her hand and led her along. The warm pressure of his fingers entwined with hers let her regain some control, take a deep breath.

Adam apparently had not returned in their absence, as his books and papers were untouched. Alice thought again about the fury with which he had advanced upon her, and pictured Adam doing the same to Neil, but with a knife. She shuddered.

"Here, sit." Neil had brought a chair behind her, and guided her into it with a gentle pressure on her shoulder. He rummaged around in a desk drawer for a few moments before extracting a little pot and a brush, then settled himself at the desk with a fresh piece of paper and began to smooth out the pieces of the message with his good hand.

"Why go to the trouble to mend that? It's not entirely illegible."

"I have a feeling that Adam will regret, may already regret, destroying this. Besides, I like to put things back together," Neil said simply.

Alice felt pity for him then, and his lost career of putting people back together.

"Will you not explain to me from whom you think this comes?"

"Edward Israel. Michigan '81, top of his class. Adam and Ed were childhood friends here in Kalamazoo. Even though Ed was several years younger, I believe he was Adam's intellectual equal, if not superior, from an early age." Neil held the reassembled message up proudly, like a child with a drawing.

"You mean, then, that Adam thought someone more intelligent than him? Now that I find more difficult to believe than spirit communication." Alice, seeing a wrinkle, took a heavy book from the shelf and pressed the paper between the last page and the back cover.

"Well—he may never have said it out loud, but no one could deny that Ed was a genius," Neil said. "Although, you would never know it to meet him. Quite wealthy as well. But you wouldn't know about that, either, until you went to pay your bill at the tavern and found that everyone's had been taken care of and that Ed had quietly disappeared. His family owns M. Israel and Co., on Main Street. "

The bold lettering on the store's awning came to mind. "Oh! Of course."

"The leader of the expedition, Greely, had written Professor Harrington at Ann Arbor—head of astronomy, and director of the Detroit Observatory—asking for a recommendation for an astronomer for his Lady Franklin Bay expedition. Professor Harrington suggested Ed, who had not yet completed his senior year. They gave him his degree in absentia, as he had to leave before graduation for training in Washington.

"The whole town here eagerly followed news of the expedition at the beginning—their native son, not yet twenty-two, about to become a famous adventurer! It probably didn't hurt business at the Israels' store, not that they were lacking for customers. However, when last year's supply boat failed in its mission—the captain, the idiot, returned with nearly all the provisions intended for the party because he could not decide where to leave them—the excitement began to wane, and fear took its place. His mother, a widow, has four other children, but everyone knew that Ed was her favorite." Neil paused and stared at the floor. "Another supply ship has since failed to reach them. Needless to say, they did not bring with them three years' worth of provisions."

Alice tried to imagine being stranded in an uncivilized part of the world, unsure of when help would come, or if it would ever come. Even being outside of a proper town unsettled her, the very openness a threat, as in some ways as oppressive as a too-tight space. Rather than seeing only one or two avenues for escape, or for help, the possibilities could be limitless. The watching alone could drive one mad.

"I'm sure that Adam, and others who had loved ones on the expedition, must be losing hope for their safe return. But all the same, no one wants to acknowledge death without a body." Neil stared at the paper, as if simple study would allow him to comprehend the other language. "That this message would be from Ed makes sense. It is in German, and the Israels and the Weissmanns were all Prussian Jews. It is a children's tale, one with which both Adam and Ed would have been familiar." He turned his concentration to Alice. "I don't imagine you would have lied about your German skills from the very beginning, although sleep could have unearthed some subconscious familiarity with the language."

"But I've never even heard of this story," protested Alice. "And I assure you, my German is rudimentary at best."

Neil nodded. "I believe you. And judging from his actions, Adam believes you as well, despite his natural skepticism about...well, nearly everything."

"He is a scientist, and I grew up with a scientist in the house," said Alice. "It is an attitude with which I am familiar."

"Perhaps I would have been better served in medical school if I was the same," said Neil. "My classmates never forgot that, as a freshman, I fell for their trick of sewing different animal parts together and proclaiming it a new species. I finally realized my folly when I performed the dissection and found its stomach full of colored marbles." He shook his head. "You would think that incident would make me particularly careful of medical marvels, but the truth is I'm just as inclined to believe in the freakish and the odd. I've studied the human body and how it works. It in itself is a freakish orchestration."

Alice thought for a moment. "Neil, do you believe in spirits?"

"What?" He seemed caught off guard.

"You are helping your cousin in this new field of psychical research, one much maligned by skeptical scientists. You admit a willingness to believe in the strange. You must think that there is some promise of life after death, no?" When Neil said nothing, she continued. "I took note of the apparition of Edward because when Mrs. Connors—my family's housekeeper—died, I saw her. I saw her in the door of my bedroom, I saw her open her mouth as if she had something to tell me. But the room went dark before she could speak. Later I discovered that she had passed that same day. When I began to receive communications a few months later, I was disbelieving at first. But ultimately, I think the circumstances with Mrs. Connors made more receptive to them than I would have been otherwise."

Neil was still silent. Alice suddenly worried about her openness, if it had been too much. She wanted to curl the confession back into herself. Her shoulders hunched forward as if she could trap it against her chest. There were certainly times during the last few months when she had doubted her ability to make contact with the dead—had wondered if Thomas's intoxicating presence had given rise to hallucinations and delusions. But now, she was accepting her mediumship as truth, in front of someone who had no reason to believe her.

"My oldest sister died when I was twelve," Neil said finally. "She was more like a mother than a sister, as my mother was often ill, and Cecily would look after us in her absence. We had a cook and two maids and a nurse, none of them terribly efficient, but Mother and Father were never around to witness their transgressions, and Cecily too kind; she simply picked up after them. She possessed a hardy constitution, so it was a complete surprise when she was felled by a fever at twenty-two—and yet my mother, for all her ailments, survives still."

Neil's eyes always grew darker when he went deep into thought; perhaps it was an illusion, but Alice liked to think of the many thoughts crowding the front of his brain, waiting to be expressed. "Wouldn't you like to talk to her again?" she asked.

"I would love to talk to her," Neil said wistfully, but shook his head. "But I place too much importance on the physical self. Without the appearance and actions I associate with her, I don't think it would really be Cecily.

"I know the details of the human body by heart. I know that the brain plays a role in thoughts, actions, and speech. To imagine an intangible spirit—or soul, or however you wish to define it—to imagine those mental functions separate from a body I know to be no longer functional is to take a substantial leap of faith, even for me. And for months I have been studying the tricks and stunts of people who purport to be in touch with said spirits, but who are no more mediums than I am. How am I to believe that there are genuine practitioners out there?"

"I can try and make contact again," said Alice. "Then you might believe in me."

Neil considered Alice as if he were a dog pondering the mysteries of humans, his head cocked slightly to the side. Then he moved to Adam's desk and began to rummage through his drawer of papers, occasionally extracting one and immediately replacing it once he saw that it was not his target. Finally, he drew out a newsprint clipping and held it in front of Alice, thumb and finger obscuring the names in the caption.

"I'm only curious," he said.

Yellowed and smudged with age and handling, it was a photograph of two rows of men, one standing, one sitting. The heads of similarly slicked hair and mustached faces made it difficult to discern between them at first glance. But Alice's eyes were soon drawn to the only clean-shaven man of the group. His mouth was set in an attempt to be strong and serious, but his legs were crossed and his hands were clasped over his knee, suggesting a more casual demeanor. The face of the man in the photo was fleshier, of course, but the eyes were the same as those she had seen at the foot of her bed: solemn, focused. When he sat for this picture, did he have any idea of the fate that awaited him?

"Yes, that's him," she said, pointing. "That's who I saw."

It was past nine, and the sun was struggling to push its last light through the clouds that had descended over Kalamazoo. Alice realized how she had missed the longer days of summer. However, the sun would greet her again before five, the thought of which made her wince slightly. Last night's interrupted sleep was beginning to wear on her, and she did not know if tonight would bring more of the same.

She slid the latch on her door, even though she didn't expect to be bothered by anyone in the house. Somehow it made her environment feel more contained, as if anything that happened within would be of her own creation—or the creation of something to which locks and walls did not matter. Alice told herself not to fret; if she could not achieve a trance, or if she could but nothing came of it, she would leave the pen and paper and maybe a message would appear as it had the night before. Perhaps a drop of laudanum to help her along—but the thought of its sweet taste and release was suddenly broken by an image of Adam lunging at his cousin, completely crazed for want of the drug.

Could she trick her body into calm? It was certainly worth a try. Alice thought of the calmest things she could—the color blue, white feathery clouds in the sky, a brook trickling through a field of flowers.

After several minutes of running through this litany, she felt her skin prickle and cool. Her head became entangled in a mess of cobwebs, but rather than struggle, she let the soft sticky strands blur her perception. While she had a vision of polishing the bannister of a fine staircase, her head dipped in a nod. Rather than letting it recoil and wake her again, she leaned into the nod and held on to that drowsy sensation with all her might.

At first, the effort caused little explosions in her eardrums, as if the pressure within her head were uneven. Alice heard a faraway hum—although it might have been very close; her ears were still recalibrating. Then it did indeed come closer, and filled her ears as if with bees. Just when the noise had grown to such a volume that Alice was certain she would be stung by the sound itself, or her eardrums would explode, another sound began to pare it down. The last thing Alice heard was the scritch-scratch of the pen on paper.

When she came to, a paragraph of elegantly written German lay on the blotter, her hand resting contentedly beside it. Alice felt a triumphant thrill as she looked over the message, appreciating the penmanship though unable to read it.

"Thank you, Mr. Israel," she whispered, and slept a sound sleep without uncorking the amber bottle.

No one was in the breakfast room save for a chubby carpet salesman with thinning hair who had taken rooms for a few days. His first morning he had been especially friendly toward Alice, enough to make her nervous, but after seeing her dine with Neil he had lost interest. Now the salesman seemed intent on his newspaper and cup of coffee, so Alice did not feel obligated to keep him company. And Eleanor was fussing more than usual, so Thea had to keep herself and her appendage in the kitchen rather than lingering in the dining room to chat.

Alice found Neil and Adam in the office after breakfast, Adam notably subdued from the day before and clutching a cup of tea in his bony hands. A brown folder, bulging with some kind of documentation, rested upon his lap. Neil kept an eye on Adam as a mother might watch a newly tottering child, prepared to jump forward at any sign of distress.

"I am sorry for how I behaved yesterday." When Adam looked up at her, Alice saw smears beneath his eyes like the purple in quahog shells. He clearly had not slept as well as she, and she wondered how much laudanum an addict would need to sleep at night. The whole bottle? "I know that Neil has provided some background...and that you have presumed the message to be from my friend Edward, as did I, of course.

"You see, I assumed that you were playing some sort of cruel trick, but I don't know how you would have achieved it..."

"Yes," said Alice. She was glad to hear Adam's acceptance come so easily.

"...unless we attribute it to some sort of unconscious telepathy, which is the hypothesis I have reached upon reflection."

Alice glanced over at Neil, who shrugged as if to say, *I warned you of this.* Adam stood suddenly and began to pace back and forth. "Neil, we must develop a plan—look at some of the experiments done by Crookes, Wallace, Sidgwick. You will supervise some of the trances while I distance myself from the subject, to decrease the possibility of telepathy. I will ask Ed to provide information that I might not know, but that his family or other friends would." He snapped his fingers. "Barrett—Barrett has a study on thought transference, done a few years ago. Do you recall which journal, Neil?"

"A few years ago I was too concerned with my physiology course to dabble outside it," said Neil, with not a little sarcasm. Adam seemed to take no offense, however; his fingers were playing his bookshelves like a piano, tapping some volumes only briefly, lingering upon others. Those tomes he apparently thought promising were tossed in a pile on his desk. Alice resisted the urge to drag him to a chair and press down on his shoulders to keep him seated; his frantic energy unsettled her. Instead she drew from her pocket the paper that she had left on her blotter the night before. Edward's fine, neat strokes seemed to burn into her fingers. She laid it out like a treasure map on Adam's desk, smoothing the creases and stepping back, and waiting for Adam to take notice.

"Here—here is a study—" Adam returned to his desk with jerky steps, engrossed in finding the right pages of the journal, but the paper still caught his eye. "What is this?"

"If you had let me say anything, you would have known several minutes ago," said Alice. "It is another communication that I received last night. This time I put myself into a deliberate trance, and emerged at the other end with this."

Adam's hands shook a bit as he picked up the paper. She held her breath as he read, mouthing the German silently to himself. He set it back down on the desk.

"Neil, will you bring me that candle over there? And a match, please."

Neil gave his cousin an odd look, but retrieved a candlestick from the mantle and a matchbox painted in gaudy blues and purples, perhaps in imitation of the heart of the flame.

Alice snatched the message from the desk. "Don't destroy it! Have you no faith…"

"I'm not going to destroy it," said Adam. "But I do need it back, for purposes of comparison." From his folder he extracted a slender envelope, still sealed. "Allow me to preface this by saying I know nothing of what lies in this envelope." It contained only a lone, blank sheet of paper. This he held over the flame, just out of its destructive reach. Slowly, Alice saw brown letters begin to appear.

"Lemon juice," she breathed. But Adam was intent on his task, not pausing until an entire paragraph was visible. Alice returned her message to him, and he laid the pages side by side. The writing was identical, although slightly less elegant in the lemon-juice missive, and it was in English, not German. No one moved as Adam compared the two.

"They are the same," he announced. Then Adam, brusque, unsentimental Adam, burst into tears.

Neil, looking confused—Alice realized that this might be the first time he had ever seen his cousin cry—offered his handkerchief, but Adam waved it away and instead gave a loud snuffle. "If the elaborate ritual you just witnessed did not make you aware, I have been expecting something like this…an experiment that I hoped never to perform, but something for which the foundation was laid three years ago." Adam's teacup shook as he raised it to his lips. At the first sip he frowned and slowly lowered it to his saucer. He looked back and forth between the creamer and the sugar bowl before settling on the sugar, carefully extracting a lump with the tiny tongs, seemingly unaware—or unconcerned—that Alice and Neil were anticipating his story.

After what seemed like five minutes of listening to the scrape and tap of his spoon against the china, Neil cleared his throat. "Go on?"

Adam tasted the tea again, then, apparently finding it to his liking, wrapped the other hand around the cup. "I've known Edward Israel ever since I can remember," he said with a voice still on the verge of shattering into pieces. "His older brother, Joseph, was closer to me in age, but as we developed our own personalities, it was clear that Ed and I were of a similar drive and temperament. There weren't a great many Jewish families in Kalamazoo when we were very young, but it was the Israel family who had traveled back to Germany and encouraged more Jews to emigrate to Kalamazoo and take advantage of the opportunities, and the temple came about when we were in our teenage years.

"The Israel children held a certain superior status in the community—particularly in the Jewish community, but also in Kalamazoo at large, as time went on—as the first Jewish family in Kalamazoo and the heirs to one of the town's most successful businesses. As a child, I assumed the temple was called B'nai Israel in honor of Ed's clan—perhaps it was, in a way. Edward never puffed up about his family's comfortable situation, but he did take himself very seriously, as I imagine a smart aristocratic child in old Europe might. He was far and away the brightest fellow in his class—as I was in mine—"

Alice glanced over at Neil then, remembering what he had said about Edward's intelligence in comparison to Adam's. She found that they were both raising their eyebrows.

"People expected Joseph, who became the man of the household at eleven when his father died, to take over the store. So Edward never tried to be a businessman, but was determined to distinguish himself in his own way. His mother was a bright woman herself, one who should have gone to college had the opportunity been available. And Edward was clearly her favorite, so sure and determined. She missed him terribly during the four years he studied in Ann Arbor—letters, packages arriving all the time. They were very close. Perhaps you've already made the connection, but Ed's mother, Tillie, was the one whom your hus—whom Mr. Holloway defrauded."

Alice felt as if someone had run a finger down her spine. "No. I had not made the connection." Admittedly, she had not thought of that anonymous widow in some time, having focused instead on her own suffering, and she felt guilty for it.

"You can understand why I was so protective of her. A dead husband and a missing son? And one of the sweetest women you'll ever meet. Besides, I had promised Ed that I would look after her if he—if he—"

Adam's voice cracked again, and he stared into his cup. Setting it down, he fumbled in his drawer and withdrew a bottle. For a brief moment Alice thought it a particularly large bottle of laudanum, but the label revealed it to be whiskey. A glug went into the cup, and Adam sampled it without stirring. He took a sip and grimaced briefly, then cleared his throat.

"The tale you handed me was one of which we were both especially fond. One of the less popular tales, which somehow made it more attractive to us. Our early fascination with science extended to the animal kingdom, and the thought of being able to communicate with dogs, birds, and frogs seemed the ultimate fantasy. From time to time we would sit outside and listen to the creatures, inventing our own translations.

"With more of a focus on human language now, I have ceased trying to translate the language of fauna. No one else but Ed would have known of my fondness for this tale, not even Neil."

"I mostly liked the story of Hansel and Gretel because of the gingerbread house." Neil shrugged.

"Neil was a bit overfond of sweets as a child," said Adam, and received a glare from his cousin.

"Before Ed left," he continued, "I made him a rather morbid request of him. I had just begun to take an interest in psychical matters—they did not even have that label, psychical, until later in the year—and saw, forgive me, an opportunity in my friend's future isolation. If something happened to him, would he attempt to contact me? I had him write a message to me in lemon juice, seal it in an envelope, and swear not to tell anyone, including me, what it said. I would use it as confirmation that it was indeed him speaking. I do know his message was much briefer than this fairy tale you produced yesterday, so after my panic I realized it could have been a simple case of telepathy and nothing more. While I have not thought of *Die drei Sprachen* in some time, I have been thinking about Edward, as I inevitably associate him with the cycle of the school year.

"This is a message I have never seen, and yet it matches the one in the envelope. Even if you had somehow found this folder, which I kept in a locked box, and steamed open the envelope, you could not have read the message without making it appear." Adam drank the tea over which he had labored in one gulp, and a grin stole over his previously somber face. "Bless you, Alice. This is the case study for which I have prayed!" His eyes, which only moments ago had been filled with tears, now gleamed like those of a boy who had just been given an armful of toys. "My friend has broken through the barrier between the worlds of the living and the spirits in order to facilitate my return to science!"

Neil and Alice looked at each other. "But what of Thomas's notebooks?" Alice asked. "I have more to transcribe—"

"Hang the notebooks. We have already devoted too much attention to that charlatan. No, we need to focus on you. We must optimize your skills of spirit communication. I want to test the depth, the length of your trances. Tell me, has this happened before?"

"In Onset, last summer," said Alice. "I wrote in trance every day, and gave what messages came to Thomas. He used them in séances. However, on our journey west, I produced almost nothing." She glanced over at Neil, who had already had the benefit of her explanation.

"If you had such experiences, why didn't you tell us of your gift before?" asked Adam.

"Well, I tried to yesterday, with less than positive results," said Alice, raising an eyebrow. "And, at that point, I wasn't sure if believed it myself."

That night, Alice sat on her bed and stared at the wall, following the wallpaper roses as they climbed up to meet and disappear into the white paint of the ceiling. How should she spend her evening? *Perhaps some of that studying you're supposed to be doing*, she told herself.

No. She knew her motivation for retiring early, as she had the night before—she simply did not wish to admit it. Doing what had frightened her, then eluded her for so long. It was as if a gentle hand pushed her towards her desk, compelled her to sit, arrange the paper, pick up the pen.

This time, there were no violent bursts of noise, only a growing fog of peace, like the trances undergone during Thomas's watch. The thought of him broke her concentration, and she briefly considered abandoning the attempt. But she breathed deeply and headed into the mist.

Alice was surprised by how easily her set of quiet thoughts came out of storage, all on well-oiled wheels as if they were summoned on a daily basis. Standing at the lake in Mount Auburn, unable to see anyone else or be seen. In a similar position of invisibility, beneath the hedge in the back of the house, her child-legs in their shorter skirt curled beneath her. In the grasses on the bluff at Onset. Now, a new comforting memory joined the others: the warm weight of Neil's hand over hers. Just before the calm gave way to unconsciousness, she realized that it was her only scenario in which she was not totally alone.

Entranced for what the clock told her was an hour and a half, Alice was disappointed to find only a few lines on the page. In some places the writing was too flat or the letters too close together to be intelligible, as if she were writing in the dark, or with her eyes closed. "You *are* writing with your eyes closed," she told herself. But to her relief, the message was in English—and it seemed to be addressed to her.

Now that English...my command, I wish to introduce...My...Edward Israel—Sergt. Edward Israel, of the U.S. Signal...may...whose hand I...using? I'm sorry it has taken me...to put together a proper introduction. You see, I've only just...into the spirit world. I'm afraid I don't understand my situation yet, and this...communicating with the living is especially confusing. I first wrote in German because...before I did English, although I was never far ahead of the other in learning. Dying is not quite like being reborn, but...returning to your earliest days, struggling to absorb and retain information and piecing together a brief string of memories...the situation.

He must want an answer before continuing. Never had Alice interacted with a spirit in this manner—they always seized control of her hand as they liked, not caring to take the time for an introduction, or even acknowledge her at all. Did she speak her answer? Write it? She decided to do both.

"My name is Alice Hol—" She paused, scratched the letters out. "Boyden." Was there something else she should say or ask, in order to keep the conversation going? Unaccustomed to directing a spirit communication, she was not quite sure how to proceed. The brief communication had apparently come at great effort, both on Edward's part and on hers, as her arm ached. Perhaps they should both rest.

But she could not resist. "Please, make use of my hand for whatever you need," she wrote and whispered. "I am listening."

Chapter 29

Alice considered bringing the previous evening's correspondence with her down to breakfast, but she folded it up to pocket-size only to decide against it. After all, the message was meant for her, not Adam.

Within a moment of opening the office door, Alice could tell that Adam had a plan—and that he had stayed up all night to work on it. Now the skin under his eyes looked as if someone had left a thumbprint of plum juice there. She sat where she was told, too curious to question his actions at this point, watching him as he hurried back and forth across the room. Neil sat at his desk with his arms crossed. His mouth suggested a slight amusement, the corners quirked, but there was a worry in his eyes.

"Thank you for joining us, Miss Boyden." Adam regressed to formality from time to time. "I cannot tell you how excited I am to begin testing your abilities."

Alice suddenly had a vision of Adam forcing her to run on a wheel, poking and prodding her and taking notes on her reactions. "I am excited to be doing something other than transcribing shorthand," she said drily.

"I think we'll begin with some exercises that will reveal your capacity for telepathic communication. I am in the process of determining what those exercises will entail..."

Alice frowned. "But don't you wish to talk to Edward? For that I simply need to enter a trance."

"Of course I want to talk to Edward." Adam paused. "But after significant study and contemplation last night, I have reason to believe that long-distance telepathy could be at the root of the messages, meaning Ed is still alive."

But he speaks of his world and the world of the living, thought Alice, and she wondered if she should show him last night's message after all, just as Neil stepped in with, "Adam. You yourself said he had written the message he had agreed to send in the event of his death. What is the point in putting Alice through the additional strain of whatever you are plotting?"

Adam wagged a finger. "Or perhaps he only thinks he is dead."

Alice stared at him. Neil let out a great sigh, as if he had been waiting for this disappointment.

"Perhaps he is simply in an unstable mental state," Adam continued. "In sleep he comes to believe he is dead. We cannot discount such a phenomenon. We must be open to all possibilities."

"Will you listen to yourself?" Neil interrupted. "Do you see that your theory is even more unbelievable than the option which is now presented to you? I would believe that Alice is in contact with Ed—a dead Ed—over what you propose."

"You *would* believe *her*," Adam retorted. "I'd think you'd believe anything that she says."

"This again? Look, has he not communicated the message in the envelope as agreed upon? Do you think a dear friend would deceive you so? And to what end?"

"I said that he is doing so *unconsciously*," said Adam. "And I'm saying that you cannot keep your eyes off her. You're becoming a distraction to the experiment. Indeed, I think you need to excuse yourself from further sessions."

"That's unnecessary. I am your partner in this. When have I proven myself unprofessional?"

Adam glared at him. "I anticipate such a time."

"You anticipate such a time."

"When your relationship with the subject may interfere with her concentration, with results. I fear your amorous inclinations will prevent us from achieving an ideal environment."

Neither of them were looking at Alice, even gesturing towards her, and she felt oddly disconnected from herself, as if she, too, were looking at Alice Boyden as no more than a title and initial in a scientific study. *"Miss B." a twenty-year-old female of fragile health and questionable mental stability, purports to receive messages from an Arctic explorer missing in action. Will seek to determine whether the messages are the result of telepathic communication or acute hysteria.*

Alice folded her hands primly and rested them on her lap. "You may have forgotten, but I am still here," she said. Indeed, both cousins looked at her in surprise.

"Well," said Neil, rising from his chair, "I have long wanted a day to myself. Perhaps this is my chance." Perhaps purposely not looking at Alice, he marched out. She did admire Neil for his self-restraint; on more than one occasion Adam had made some comment about this being *his* field, not Neil's, and had criticized his performance. This always provided Neil with the opportunity—and the provocation—to remark how Adam's actions had perhaps destroyed *Neil's* career, but he never bit.

Once the door had slammed shut, Alice turned to Adam. "You argue as if you were my parents."

Adam smirked. "I've long said a professional relationship is like a marriage, but without the obvious benefits and with all of the pitfalls. In this instance it is further complicated by the natural combativeness of blood relatives. But, then, I have never been married myself, so perhaps I should not make such comparisons." He looked at Alice, as if she could confirm or deny his statement, and shivered slightly, although the May day was already warm.

"Technically, I have not been married either," said Alice. "My knowledge is as a twenty-year observer of marital discord between my parents, who ought never to have been married in the first place. I should hope they are not all like that."

Adam sighed. "My parents were very happy together. If they had disagreements, they conducted them well out of my sight and earshot. It sounds as if your parents were not so considerate."

"Considerate? My parents? No, they are positively selfish. It did not matter what I heard—I'm sure they considered it a learning experience. Prepared me for classroom debates."

"Do they know of—have you written explaining—what happened with…him?"

Alice's eyes widened. "Neil? Oh, no, goodness. I don't know how long you think—"

"I meant Mr. Holloway."

"Oh." His name sat like a heavy weight on Alice's shoulder. "I suppose you can't put the cart before the horse. No, they don't know about any of it." Too late, she realized that she had just played into what Adam suspected about her and Neil.

Adam did not press the subject, but folded his hands and leaned back in his chair. "Well. With that out of the way, perhaps now we can embark on more serious wo—"

"Is it true?" If Adam knew that Neil was on her mind, she might as well confirm something for herself.

"What's that?"

"That he cannot take his eyes off me."

Adam bared his yellowish teeth at Alice, revealing what looked like two rows of corn. It took her a startled second to realize that he was smiling.

"I can tell without looking up," he said.

At lunch Alice found Neil sitting by himself, shoveling peas into his mouth as quickly as possible, losing some off the side of his fork. One green marble bounced off his knee on the way to the floor, but he paid no mind.

"Do you always eat like this when I am not around?"

Neil nearly choked on his mouthful of vegetables when he saw Alice standing there. He rallied to chew and swallow, then held his napkin to his mouth as if he feared it was covered in pea fragments.

"I would have waited for you," he said, his voice muffled by the cloth, "but I did not know when Adam would allow you out. And since I am not welcome there myself..."

Alice took the chair across from him, waving away his offer of assistance. "That was a silly argument and we all know it."

"What part was silly?"

"What do you mean?" Alice shook out her napkin.

"My expulsion or..."

"The topic?"

"Yes." Neil became very intent on smoothing his napkin across his lap.

"I think I can maintain a professional composure with you in the room, as you can with me."

Neil nodded, a little too vigorously. "I agree."

"And I doubt Adam will exclude you from future experiments. He needs someone to order around."

"That is true."

"Perhaps we should view it as something on which he can focus his attention. Something to occupy his time until he is faced with the undeniable truth." Alice took her plate and assembled a sandwich from the materials on the sideboard. As an afterthought, she added a scoop of peas.

Neil colored slightly when he saw the vegetables on her plate; he had not touched his since her arrival. "Without company, eating is a very mechanical thing for me," he explained.

"As it is for me," said Alice. "I welcome someone to provoke conversation and interrupt the process."

Neil speared one pea with a tine of his fork and held it up as if studying a precious jewel, frowning and examining it from every side. Very slowly, he brought the fork to his mouth and closed his lips around the tines. When he withdrew the utensil, the pea had vanished. For some reason, Alice thought this riotously funny. At the same time, she felt an urge to the kiss the lips that had just performed the disappearing act.

By dinnertime, Adam had fleshed out the bones of his proposed study and made a rare appearance at the table. "Thea, this is a divine roast," he told the cook, although he only ate a few bites of it. He poked holes in his mashed potatoes, making them resemble a pile of snow pierced by falling icicles. Alice resisted the urge to scold him for wasting food.

"Barrett, Gurney, and Myers propose that thought-reading experiments be grouped into four categories," said Adam, tapping the blue paper cover of a journal. Alice leaned over to examine it. *Proceedings of the Society for Psychical Research, Vol. I. Part I.* "There's transference with hands touching, and without; also without visual or auditory contact, since both can influence the recipient, whether such influence is conscious or unconscious. Lastly, there is the instance of communication between minds far apart, which is what I believe is happening here."

"But I was of the impression that subjects in the latter instance were invariably close—if not related, then married, or the best of friends," said Neil. "How would Edward be able to contact Alice telepathically, when they have never met?"

"Perhaps because hers is the most receptive mind near someone to whom he *is* very close," said Adam, pointing at his chest. "That is my hypothesis, at any rate—he has not yet told us that he is dead."

"But she has received only two communications from him," said Neil, looking at Alice with eyebrows raised. "Perhaps you need to grant him more time to..."

"Listen to this." Adam interrupted, reading from the journal. "'One of us has, moreover, successfully obtained from the maid-servant a German word of which she could have formed no visual image.' You pose more of a challenge, Alice, having encountered some German in your education."

On and on he went, quoting from the study, adding his own personal commentary, until Neil interrupted him.

"You say you'll begin tomorrow?"

"Yes. Miss Boyden, please arrive at your usual time..."

"Then let us discuss this tomorrow," said Neil, sounding like a father in his authority, "and let Miss Boyden rest her mind."

Adam sniffed. "I have a great deal of work to do before then, anyway." He returned outside to the office, while Alice accepted Neil's offer of a glass of port and his company in the parlor.

"Edward would not be making these efforts to contact me if he did not have something important to say, and yet Adam is focused on theories and exercises. He has lost all his reason." Alice savored the port; it had been some time since she had indulged in a glass.

"Adam's way of coping is to create a structure around something amorphous and unknown." Neil held a small level of whiskey, served neat. "His physical and mental state are already fragile. He cannot just let the waves crash upon him. He has to build a barrier, however full of holes."

Alice tilted her port gently from side to side, watching the legs linger on the sides of the glass. "I did not show Adam, but Edward introduced himself to me last night, in a message."

"In English?"

Alice nodded. "He explicitly said that he was in the spirit world, and that it had taken him a while to regain his use of English. I think I must continue to try and reach him, regardless of what Adam thinks."

"Edward, I must tell you that Adam is having difficulty accepting your death," Alice wrote that evening, wanting him to be apprised of the situation.

She began as she had the night before, whispering and writing a question at the same time, but the next thing she knew, she was curled up in bed in the pitch black. Had her efforts failed? Had she given up so easily? Alice forced her drowsy self to sit up, then stand and reach for the lamp. She stubbed her toe in the process, and needles of pain burned their way through her foot—she pursed her lips tightly to keep from making a sound. But her discomfort was forgotten when she realized that her blotter was covered in sheets of narrative, the prose this time clear and continuous.

I should explain to you my agreement with Adam. At the close of the school year, right before I was scheduled to depart for Washington, we spent a few days in Ypsilanti with some friends—that's a town near Ann Arbor where students tend to go on the weekends. There we picnicked, boated, that sort of thing, and I enjoyed myself very much. I think even my close friends were surprised to see that I was in an excellent mood—I was anxious, certainly, but more excited than anything else. Excited to begin my official training and then put my studies into practice at last. I had also never left Michigan, and so to travel to the nation's capital, on the coast, was a significant step—let alone the journey I would make once training was complete.

But the event of my departure proved more difficult for my friends than I had anticipated. We would be laughing about something or other, and then one of my fellows' faces would grow pensive, even apprehensive. This usually proved contagious, and Adam was not immune. My jokes had some success but I could find no permanent solution. On Sunday, when Adam and I were alone in the rowboat, he confessed that he did not think I would return.

I tried to laugh it off, saying that I knew he thought me a weakling, and that this rowing was part of a prescribed plan to toughen me up. But his frown only deepened, and I realized he was quite serious.

"If you are confident in your survival," he said, "I have a favor to ask of you." And he reminded me that he had recently taken an interest in Spiritualism.

I had no belief in spirits at the time. I knew enough of God to believe in His miracles, and maybe He was behind all the coincidences and premonitions that psychics claimed arose from their own honed abilities. I thought it dangerous and potentially blasphemous to eliminate the possibility that these messages were not from Him.

But I was a scientist as well as a child of God, and I understood obsession with a topic of research, the way it insinuated itself into your life and throttled anything competing with it for attention. I could not blame Adam for forming an attachment to a new field that presented such mysteries—and anyone who joined the field in earnest now had the potential to be viewed as a pioneer in later years. Some might think my field relatively young as well, but I had plenty of forebears stretching back through the ages. I appreciated how their accomplishments, made without the technology of my day, kept me humble.

So I agreed to his plan: that if I were to die during my journey, I would attempt to contact him. When we returned to Ann Arbor he had me write a message in lemon juice and seal it in a sturdy envelope. It is a sort of pact that perhaps many have made before, but likely few have fulfilled. When I first tried to contact you, my English had not returned to me, and our beloved children's tale was all I could produce initially, the first thing connected to Adam that I could grasp and transmit.

I admit surprise at his skepticism, yet I will be patient. More frustrating is the ability to transcend space like this and communicate with an American, and yet have no means of securing help for my fellow explorers. Even if any government officials were to believe that my spirit was ready and able to steer rescuers towards the party, the ship sent to relieve us is out of range of communication. Now that I know I can communicate, I have tried to find her myself, hoping someone on board would listen. But I have had no luck, and we are running out of time. Thirteen of us remain—that is, of twenty-five—with the rest failing fast.

Alice stared at the last sentence to make sure she had read it correctly. Half of them, already gone. And how many would there be when the rescuers finally came?

Chapter 30

They began the day with a deck of cards. Alice dutifully stepped outside while Adam picked a card, then reentered after a count of ten. Once she became distracted by an inchworm carefully making his camouflaged way up the stem of a white rose, though a yell from Adam reminded her of her task. She was allowed three guesses, after which Adam reshuffled the cards and asked her to step outside again. In two hours, only once did she pick the correct card on the first try. At that Adam's face lit up, but she was unable to reproduce the phenomenon.

"You must *concentrate.*"

"I *am* concentrating," said Alice defensively, although to herself she admitted that she was allowing the idea of Edward to distract her. She felt so helpless, knowing the plight of his fellow explorers and yet able to do nothing. Muttering something about her difficulty as a subject, Adam nevertheless allowed her to escape for lunch.

She returned with Neil in tow after begging him to provide support. Neil hesitated at the door, ready to leave if Adam made a fuss about his presence. But Adam barely glanced at him. He had a new task for Alice and was entirely fixed upon it.

"Now, Miss Boyden, you must try to keep your mind completely blank. Pretend you are a simpleton."

"But then I will be thinking of myself as a simpleton, and that defeats the purpose." Alice knew she was being cheeky, but Adam had honed her frustration to a sharp edge.

"You will go outside and wait several seconds. Then you may reenter, keeping your eyes fixed upon the floor, not even a glance towards me or Neil…"

"But it's beginning to rain again."

"A few seconds merely, Miss Boyden. This will be a number under one hundred. I shall give you a maximum of three tries to determine that which I have written down."

Alice left the office as told and walked several paces from the door, ducking her head against the fat drops that fell from above, focusing on the cobblestones that formed an uneven tread for her feet. Then she attempted to clear her mind and let a number float into the void. When one appeared, she reentered the office.

"Eyes on the floor," Adam commanded, and Alice dipped her head in an exaggerated bow. "Now, what number do you have?"

"Eight," said Alice.

"No," said Adam. "Another try?"

Alice shrugged. "Twenty-four."

"No. Once more."

"Three."

"Correct."

Alice looked up. "Correct?"

"Yes." He recorded the result in his notebook and held up a slip of paper, on which was clearly written the number 3. "And I can see your thought process—eight, then times three—twenty-four, then divided by eight—three." He paused for a moment, then wrote something else in his notebook. "Very interesting. Shall we try again?"

Alice took a deep breath and stepped back outside. The rain had begun to fall harder.

She called out whatever numbers pushed their way forward in her mind, but she could not tell if they came from Adam or if she had produced them herself. She simply waited until one floated to the surface, then skimmed it from the top and said it out loud.

After five trials with the same result—the first and second guesses were always incorrect, the third correct—Alice was about to return to the drizzle when Adam called her back.

"You can look at me."

Grateful for the chance to stretch her bent neck, and thinking that she had done well, Alice was surprised to meet Adam's narrowed eyes.

"I hope you are not deliberately misleading me."

"Now what reason have I for that?" Alice rubbed her hands together, feeling the warmth spread over them like gloves. "I do not particularly *like* standing out in the rain. I do not like disapproving looks, or being wrong in general."

"These are all simple math problems. See here—fifty-one, seventeen, thirty-four. It is almost as if you know the answer from the outset, but you have to deduce it."

Alice shrugged. "I say whatever comes to my mind. I don't know if you put the numbers there, or if I have any say in it."

Adam frowned over a book from the pile on his desk. He passed another to Neil. "Neil, would you take a look to see if Barrett speaks of sums and figures at all?" The two men went silent, the only sounds in the office those of pages turning.

"Nothing here." Neil closed his book after a time.

"Nor here." Adam returned his volume to the pile; Alice watched his hand straining with the weight of it. Despite being dark, his skin was almost translucent in places, the yellowy bones of his knuckles about to poke through their covering. "But the girls whom he studied were simple. Perhaps they could do sums, but I don't think that they were clever enough to multiply and divide in their heads. Something to ponder for tomorrow, I suppose."

Alice looked at the clock. It was only two in the afternoon. "Am I done for the day?"

Adam raised an eyebrow at Alice's surprised tone. "Yes. I don't want to wear you out. That's not to say that I won't be working, but..." He gave a dramatic little sigh. "You, too, Neil. Take Miss Boyden for a stroll or whatever you youngsters do."

Alice stifled a laugh. Adam was only in his late twenties, and yet he liked to play the role of the elderly curmudgeon.

"Gladly," said Neil. His voice betrayed no evidence that Adam's declaration to stay and work aroused any guilt. "A walk to whet your appetite, and then perhaps you will allow me to take you to this fine restaurant I've heard about." He offered Alice his arm. "It's called Chez Thea, and the address is Burdick Street. It might be our best option in such temperamental weather."

Alice giggled. "I would love to try it."

"Very well." Neil opened the door for her. Alice inhaled deeply of the late spring perfume: wet grass and fading flowers. She looked back at Adam, to wave goodbye, and wished she hadn't. In his chair, slumped and skinny, he looked much older than his age.

"Adam runs me through these ridiculous tests and then accuses me of toying with him when the results do not correspond with his expectations," Alice complained to her notebook that evening. "Perhaps it's *his* fault. Perhaps *he* is transmitting the wrong numbers, intent as he is on proving something that is not true."

She realized this sounded more like a diary entry than a message, but still she hoped Edward would respond. "Have you any advice?" she added to the end of her rant, then closed her eyes. It took her some time to control her heart rate; even when it slowed, she knew that she had not created an optimal environment for a trance. For a moment, she thought she had achieved the perfect calm, had it trapped in her hand like a butterfly, but when she took hold of the pen, the butterfly slipped away. She nearly growled in frustration, until she glanced at the paper in front of her and realized that she had received an answer.

I know about the tests. I suggested the numbers to you myself. I am very sorry he was cross with you as a result—but I thought it might alert him to my presence. He knows of my particular penchant for rearranging numbers so that they form a complete equation.

"You gave me the numbers? Does that mean you can read my mind?" Alice felt herself flush; she must have, at some point during the morning, let her mind wander to romantic thoughts of Neil. Those were occurring more frequently these days—although she had tried to corral them on the slender chance that her mind and Adam's did make a connection. She had never bothered to account for Edward, however.

No, not in the slightest. I can no more read your mind than you can mine. But I was able to establish some kind of connection, as I do with your hand when I use it to write. Unfortunately, it seems as if my efforts were for naught, if he simply dismissed the patterns as a trick of yours.

Perhaps I can devise another plan—and give you fair warning, of course. But I feel as if I no longer know Adam as well as I once did, and cannot determine what will reach him. That might happen with friends separated three long years—though it should not affect his memories of me. Something seems to have changed him. I cannot always see what you see—sometimes I catch glimpses of scenes from the perspective of the living; other times it is as if I am extremely myopic, with everything blurry; still other times I am completely blind. But I did notice that Adam has lost a great deal of weight. You would think he was up here, living on tiny shrimps and lichen like the rest of the outfit.

Lichen. Alice recalled the rough, crumbling sensation of it on her tongue, the night Edward had appeared to her. This evening she had eaten a delectable tart Thea had concocted, filled with meat and egg and fresh vegetables from the garden. She suddenly felt guilty for complaining about the neverending supply of root vegetables in early spring menus, while Edward had apparently depended on a pale green moss to fill his stomach.

You'll have to forgive me—there's no need for me to describe what's happening up here. But sometimes I forget my audience, forget where I died, even believe that I am still living in that ragged hut on Cape Sabine. The experience of Camp Clay was something I'd not like to remember, and yet it was the last place I do remember. I would prefer to recall the auroras, the graceful gray wolves we saw in the distance before we went so far north that even they became scarce.

But Adam's frailty frightens me. My father suffered from cancer of the liver, and I remember how thin and yellow he was at the end. What is wrong with my friend? Did the strain of his thesis undo his health? Please tell me.

Would the truth not make him feel even more helpless? Alice did not feel as if she owed Adam her silence, but she was reluctant to heap another burden on Edward. She looked down at her hand. It quivered slightly as it awaited a reply.

"I will tell you. Perhaps you might be able to help. Perhaps he will listen to you."

June washed in on a week of constant rain, and even Alice, who was not averse to a little water, was kept from her daily walk by the downpours that came without warning. The lack of exercise made her particularly impatient with Adam and his experiments. Most days began with a squabble and ended with sharp criticism. She was ever grateful for Neil—Alice needed only a smile from him to regain her sense of calm during tense moments.

After an unsuccessful morning, Adam waved Alice off to lunch, and she happily abandoned the exercise. Neil opened the door to a curtain of water streaming down from the overhang. He stuck his umbrella out the door ahead of him and motioned for Alice to step beneath it. She gazed out at the ring of rain that surrounded her and was momentarily unsettled to be dry when her hand held no protection. Was this what it felt like to be a ghost in an earthly deluge?

But then she felt Neil's protective hand rest lightly on her shoulder, reminding her of her flesh-and-blood status. With the rain drumming on the umbrella skin and literally drowning out other sounds, Alice allowed herself to emit an audible sigh of happiness. Lunches with Neil were, more than ever, a refuge from the borderline insanity that filled the office.

Every evening, Alice used the excuse of the day's experiments to retire early. And every evening, she sat at her desk in her dressing gown and contacted Edward. He was her responsibility now, and she must keep the connection with him until Adam came around—even if she only produced a few lines each night.

At the beginning, Alice would come to in the wee hours, momentarily confused by the unexpected number on the clock. However, that clock confirmed that each night, the story was taking less time to unfold. She felt a certain amount of pride at her control over her trances, after thinking herself so rusty. Edward seemed more comfortable in his role as correspondent, and so did Alice. She insisted that he refer to her by her given name.

"Do you mind being called Edward? I realize that Adam and Neil refer to you as Ed."

Not at all. Only my mother and sisters call me that, but please do so if you prefer it.

"I do somehow. To me, Edward suggests nobility, while Ed is too abrupt. Eddie makes me think of a child."

You are doing me a great service by the loan of your hand. I should think you may call me whatever you wish.

Alice did not ask about the state of survivors at Cape Sabine, and Edward did not offer any information. She found it unusual that he asked no more questions about Adam, after being so insistent that Alice apprise him of the situation. Perhaps he had recognized the futility of convincing Adam to leave the laudanum alone. Instead he answered her questions about physics, astronomy, his discoveries up north.

My duties as astronomer revolved around pendulum readings—a Professor Pierce of the Coast Survey lent his own chronometer to the expedition, and trained me in the reading of it. In order to obtain an accurate measure, I needed to take into account the temperature of the pendulum as well as the general uniformity of temperature.

Alice found Edward the smart and humble person that Neil had described. But her mind longed for more personal details than the scant ones already provided. "Did you ever feel overwhelmed by your situation?"

If my thoughts were grounded in numbers, they were less likely to wander into contemplating the many unknowns that the Arctic held for us. When collecting readings, there were always plenty of calculations to keep me engaged. When I was on watch, sometimes I worked math problems in my head, or simply attempted to count the stars.

"But how did you keep your mind sharp, especially when you were cold and hungry?"

Nothing at first, and Alice wondered if it was a question Edward deemed too personal. But eventually her hand rocked the pencil tip back and forth, then began to write.

Actually, it helped to have a task that required such a level of concentration. Manual tasks kept me warm, but they always invited my mind to wander. When rations grew thin, I was tempted to use that time to feel sorry for myself. But why should I feel that way, when I had the opportunity of a lifetime? Whenever I wanted to complain about the cold, I would think of the quiet I felt in my very bones when on nighttime watch, knowing that everyone else in the camp is fast asleep, and that the next closest people, hundreds, perhaps thousands of miles away are also asleep. Or some marvel would come to distract me. How can you pity yourself for a slight chill when an aurora is filling the sky with living rainbows?

I hope that you might see an aurora someday. I wish Rice, our photographer, could have captured its brilliance on film! Once Gardiner, my fellow meteorologist who was on night watch at the time, shouted for us to come see a particularly gorgeous one. I was the first to the door despite the early hour, and the brilliance was such that I had to close it as soon as I opened it. I told the puzzled crowd behind me that it looked as if the sky would strike me in the face, and they all had a good laugh at the expense of the young astronomer and his unnecessary excitement about celestial matters. But when they left the shelter all were in agreement. It was as if we could touch the lights, which had come alive in the sky. The needle did not settle for three whole days. It was like an opal broken and spilled over the canvas of the heavens.

My, I have gone on a tangent. I apologize for my babbling.

Alice glanced at the clock; it was eleven. She had been writing on and off for several hours, but it hadn't seemed that long. "I hardly think the description of an aurora counts as babbling, Edward," said Alice. "Remember, I am here to record what you wish to record."

Yes, but then I find myself wanting to tell you stories instead. Perhaps it is because I spent the last three years talking to the same twenty-four men? Soon enough they'd heard all my good stories and jokes, and I had exhausted the discussion of my college curriculum.

Alice laughed. "I imagine that might be part of it." But she liked to think it was because she was a worthy listener—and that she was helping distract him from the horrors he had endured.

Perhaps now was the time to ask for his help with something that had been on her mind for a while. "Edward, I must ask you a favor, if you do encounter others in your world at some point. I have reason to believe the man who was my husband"—here Alice paused, decided it was too complicated to explain the whole story, and continued—"has passed on. His name is Thomas Chester Holloway. About a month ago, he sent a brief message from the other side, but I have not heard from him since. I suppose I only want to let him know that I am open to listening, if he should have more he wants to say to me." She pulled out the scrap of paper she had used on the roof in May and read it out loud. "That's all I have from him."

While I would be happy to pass along your message, I don't believe your husband wrote those lines. You see, I wrote those exact words in a letter to my mother, some weeks before my death. Perhaps I was near enough death at that time that you heard me, somehow.

Alice stared at the paper with...relief? No, strangely enough, it felt more like disappointment. It was easier to believe that death had prevented Thomas's apology.

Chapter 31

In just a week, Edward had come to mean as much to her as a living friend—and indeed, sometimes she found herself distracted from in-person conversations by the thought of something he had written the night before. They had an intimate connection, after all; he was dependent upon her for communication, and she looked forward to their time "together" all day. Alice's life had been defined by her dependency on others for the past few months. Now she was the one needed.

One night he did not come at all, despite her entering three separate trances, and the empty silence made Alice fidgety, kept her in a state too agitated for sleep. She took to pacing the carpet between her desk and the door, but the brevity of a lap made her only more on edge. She thought to prepare herself some tea in the kitchen, but did not wish to wake the sleeping chicks with clanging and whistling. After eliminating the prospect of a sojourn downstairs, Alice undressed in the hopes of convincing her body that it was time for bed.

She shivered slightly as she slid her bare feet between the cool sheets, and could not help but imagine what sleeping must have been like for Edward—how did one nod off in that perpetual cold? Or perhaps the men grew used to it after a time. And they must have slept in warm, thick skins and furs, not delicate sheets that retained the nighttime chill.

Alice lay down and closed her eyes, but her heart continued to behave like the crickets she used to trap in nets and coax into jars for her father. All she could think about was Edward, and she could not shake the feeling that he had something to say. She gave into the urge and slipped out of bed, entangling her foot in the covers and nearly falling in the effort to reach her desk.

Alice, I have a great favor to ask of you.

The message appeared almost immediately after her eyes closed. Alice was surprised she didn't hear the final scratch of the pen.

"Of course, Edward," she wrote. "What do you need from me?"

As soon as she put the question to paper, her hand began to feel strange, as if she had held it too long in a bowl of cold water. She tried to flex her fingers to warm them, but they did not do as she wished. Instead they shifted in search of a better grip on the pen than came from her usual position. Alice had always written with a knot of fingers curled around the barrel, but now her index finger lay so straight along the pen that the nib seemed to extend from beneath her nail, and her hand itself had become a writing instrument.

It was as if she were surrounded by a halo of static electricity, every nerve alert but her brain dull, so that no mental direction to move—if she could form it at all—translated into actual activity. Her attention was focused entirely on the conversation developing on the paper before her.

Many of the men here kept a diary in which their true and honest thoughts could be expressed—some in a book completely separate from their official records and observations. I imagine there was not much self-censorship, and I fear that, with all the tension present in the camp during our times of trial, some characters may not be portrayed in the best light in the accounts that survive. Perhaps I was one of the few, or maybe the only, who had no complaint with anyone. And yet there are still elements of my own diary...I thought very highly of my fellow men, but sometimes observed less than honorable behavior amongst them. While I am not one for gossip, I did write about my reaction to these incidents, intending the text for my personal recollection only.

Was this state she currently inhabited even possible? Every medium she had ever spoken to or read about claimed to be completely unconscious during trances. Their only knowledge of what happened during these trances came either from a written record or from the testimony of sitters and observers.

Her hand paused, as if waiting for her to scrawl a reply. But Alice had no control over the pen—how could she answer Edward? Unless...yes, her mouth still obeyed her directions. She moved her lips and pushed two words through them.

"Go on."

I hope that eventually, rescuers will reach Cape Sabine and recover our bodies and our records. Provided that no human or storm destroys them, there will be quite a collection. But nothing, I fear, that focuses upon the true heroism of all the men, regardless of certain flaws that I and others may have fixed upon. If you would be so kind as to lend me your hand, I would like to write a brief sketch of each man, highlighting some action or characteristic that gives a positive impression. There are stories of friendship that I never put to paper, believing that those friendships would endure beyond the expedition, and those stories told time and again.

Unless this was a hallucination, here she was, perfectly aware of the strange handwriting flowing from her possessed hand. Perhaps mediums hid the truth for their own protection. If one admitted to being awake during the séance, people could easily accuse them of interjecting their own thoughts into the speeches of the spirits—if they were even speaking to the spirits at all.

Focus on the conversation, not on theories, Alice told herself. To Edward she said, "But as a scientist, don't you value an accurate report over a rosy one? Surely they were not all angels, particularly at the end."

The pencil began to write something, but quickly scratched out its previous marks, and wrote instead:

No, not angels. But all of them made great sacrifices in the pursuit of scientific knowledge. All of them were heroes, and deserve to be remembered as such. I died peacefully, thinking that I had not an enemy in the world. I ought to repay somehow the goodwill shown to me by my fellows.

"But, Edward? How could this book I write for you be accepted as genuine? What do I write to the government, or to your family, or to whomever should receive it? 'Dear Sirs: The spirit of Edward Israel spoke through me and charged me to write this portrait-book.' They will think me mad."

You do already know my handwriting.

"But even if it is in your handwriting, how could I have come into possession of it?"

You needn't worry about that just now. Adam will take care of things later.

Alice frowned. Had Edward forgotten what she had told him, that Adam had become a hopeless laudanum addict? Not to mention that he still denied his friend's death…

You would be doing me a great service.

"Well, I will help in any way I can," said Alice.

Her hand jumped then, as if the connection had been interrupted; the pen dropped to the desk but her hand remained frozen, unable to retrieve the instrument. It hung there for a few moments, suspended, and Alice began to worry that she would not be able to regain control. But then her hand picked up the pen and resumed writing as if nothing had happened.

To make this book appear authentic, you might go to my parents' store and purchase the same sort of notebook I used. Anyone who has worked there for a few years will know that those are my favorite notebooks, and may comment on that fact. I cannot promise that they will give you a clue, of course. But it is worth a try.

"How will I know exactly which sort of notebook is yours, aside from saying I would like the same notebook that Edward Israel brought with him to the Arctic?"

I think you will know it when you see it. Notebook-makers must assume that if you want red leather, you also want all sorts of elaborate tooling and stamping. My books are quite plain, save for a small gold fleur-de-lis in the middle of the cover.

Now, your hand must be tired. Why don't you rest it, and perhaps tomorrow you can pay a visit to the store.

"I will do that. Good night, Edward, or is there no night where you are?"

It is always light and yet always dark, perpetual night and then perpetual day. It is like the Arctic in that way.

"You seem rather gloomy today," said Neil, poking his words between mouthfuls of stew that had seemed perfect for the chill morning, and was now unsuitable for a house baked in the sun for hours. "Is there something the matter?"

"I suppose the sudden change in weather has unsettled me," said Alice. But she realized that the excuse would likely not hold water with Neil. They almost never talked about anything as dull as the weather, once agreeing that older folks and graceless young people just coming into society had the monopoly on such discussions.

"Not gloomy, just preoccupied," she added. Then, not wanting Neil to ask about last night's conversation with Edward: "I have an errand to run in town."

"Would you like me to accompany you? I suppose I need a suit of a lighter weight, now that summer seems to have announced itself."

Alice hesitated. She did not want Neil to ask too many questions about her purchase, but he looked so hopeful, like a small child wanting an adventure.

"Only if you are the one to tell Adam I'll not be available for an afternoon session."

"It is done," said Neil.

Although the walk was not a long one, and the sun tried its best to beat them back inside, Alice found herself grateful for Neil's company. She was somewhat nervous about her errand—what if Mrs. Israel were there, and somehow knew her connection to Thomas? But no—Tilly Israel would not know Alice, at least by sight.

Neil took the lead, but when they reached the center of town he spun around to face her.

"Where to?"

Alice swallowed. "Israel's. I need a new notebook." She was unsure whether Neil's odd look had to do with the abundance of notebooks available in the office, or her choice of store, given her experience with one of its heirs—but he simply followed her lead.

When she saw the sign for M. Israel and Co. Dry Goods, she must have tightened her grip on Neil's arm, for he stopped and turned to her.

"Is something wrong?"

Alice sucked in a breath through lips pressed tightly together and shook her head. She thought to say that there was something wrong with her ankle, or that a stone had become lodged in her shoe, but she had not stumbled to make those excuses viable.

A bell tinkled when they entered M. Israel and Co. Dry Goods, as if they were entering a small country store. But to her surprise, the interior resembled a department store in Boston more than anything—not a barrel in sight, examples of clothes neatly organized. "I'll stay out of your way," said Neil, tipping his hat to her and disappearing into a forest of men's clothing in drab colors. Alice instead found herself drawn to the women's department and the colorful dresses there.

How long had it been since she had had a new dress? Alice fingered one in a plum color and compared her own frock: the fabric thinner, the color faded. Once upon a time, she had expected new clothes from Thomas, but that was before she realized Mr. Holloway was not as solvent as he would have people believe.

Suddenly, she realized exactly what dress she was wearing. Had it really been only a year since this blue frock was forgotten in a trunk at the Wareham train station? It was June now. Her parents had probably made their way down to Onset for the summer already, and she felt a jolt of guilt for how much time had passed since she'd written them. She had sent several letters from Kalamazoo, but all had avoided any specific mentions of Thomas. Would they be expecting to see her there with her new husband?

"May I help you, miss?"

Alice looked into the face of an eager clerk who so resembled the picture of Edward, it was all she could do not to gasp.

"I'm just looking around, thank you," she said automatically, as she did in the Boston stores. This was usually a sign to the shopgirls there that she would not be opening her pocketbook today, and they would walk away with a nod and a sniff. But this clerk only smiled, unfazed by what Alice believed was a universal rejection.

"Well, please let me know if I can assist you in any way," he said, smiling and turning back toward the front desk.

"Thank you," said Alice, surprised by his friendliness. The Boston shopgirls were paid to plaster false smiles on their faces, but really they had no interest in you if there wasn't a commission to be had, and they would mutter something about you to the other girls once they thought you were out of earshot.

Perhaps Alice should examine the dress more closely; what would it hurt? She went to lift the frock off its rack and the price label fell out. Her cheeks flushed and she replaced it. Now that Alice was earning and managing her own income, every cent was a serious matter. And this was a very serious dress.

She glanced up to find the clerk looking at her curiously, but he quickly averted his eyes and pretended to be engrossed in his ledger books. She located the stationery section herself, but she felt the urge to give this young man—he must be Edward's brother—the impression that he had made a sale through his genial manner.

"Excuse me?"

"Yes, miss?" The youth looked up.

"I'm looking for a particular sort of notebook or diary—bound in red leather, about this tall"—she indicated the size with her hands—"and moderately thick, perhaps two hundred pages. Minimal decoration."

The clerk stared at her for a moment, and Alice worried that they no longer carried the item she was seeking. What would she tell Edward? But then the clerk's smile returned.

"I think I know just the book you're looking for," he said, and lifted the counter to let himself out. Alice followed him to a display of beautiful journals, many bound in hand-tooled leather. He hesitated before the few red books—only one spine was plain, while the others were ornate with vines and gold-stamped seams. But in the end, he picked up the plainer one and handed it to Alice. Even before he asked if it was the right one, Alice knew.

"Yes," she said. "This is perfect."

The clerk breathed a little sigh of relief, although he continued to stare at the book as if he wanted to take it back.

"My brother favors those same books," he blurted. "I can't tell you how many he took with him to college. He always said that if notes were intended as references for later study, they ought to be presented neatly and in an attractive cover."

"Did he now?" said Alice, but it came out with a patronizing tone that she did not intend, so she tried to continue the conversation in which she already knew the clerk's replies. "And is he still at school?"

"He's graduated now, and working for the government." Alice thought she saw a little puff of the chest. "He is serving under Adolphus

Greely in the Lady Franklin Bay expedition, to the Arctic." He motioned her over to the cash register to ring up her purchase.

"You must be very proud of him," said Alice, praying the tears that stung her eyes would hold. It would make no sense so weep for someone she had supposedly just heard of.

"Yes, we are," said the clerk. "And he should be home soon. We miss him a great deal. Indeed, it is his birthday in two weeks, and we shall have cake in his absence."

The revelation struck Alice a blow. The hopeful face of his brother bore no trepidation, no worry that Edward would not be celebrating his next birthday, or any other. The contents of her purse blurred, and she fumbled for the right change, desperate to complete the transaction before tears fell.

"Good afternoon," she managed to say, keeping her head down.

"Good afternoon…miss," followed her as she sought Neil in the men's section. Alice had escaped without giving her name, and she preferred it that way.

"I've purchased my notebook, and I'm in need of some air," she told Neil, trying to keep her voice even. "Will you meet me outside the door?"

Neil's eyes remained on the fine tan suit he was examining. "You may be best off in here, given the temperature outside—" Neil broke off when he saw Alice's face. "I'll find a suit another time."

Quickly, but not so quick as to alarm the clerk, Neil lead Alice out the door and into the adjacent alley, where there was shade and privacy if not cooler air. Alice buried her head in Neil's shoulder. He wrapped his arms around her and said nothing.

"He…looks…just…"

"I know," said Neil, and held her tighter as she wept.

Chapter 32

Neil led her back to the house and to her room. "You should rest awhile," he told her, and Alice gave him a little smile through her tears. She was grateful that he had not tried to talk her out of her grief, perhaps remind her that she had never known Edward in life. Rather than disrobe after he closed the door, however, she took a seat at her desk. Try as she might, Alice could not keep the brother's hopeful face from her thoughts. Did all of the Israels share that level of optimism, or were some more resigned than others? Did they speak of Edward often, or was it easier not to speak of him at all?

But she could not sit and cry while Edward was waiting for her, eager to begin his project. Alice let go of Neil's handkerchief, now deeply wrinkled by her unconscious wringing of it. She opened the red notebook, hearing the crack of its spine that both made her wince and satisfied her. Ever since she was young, Alice had had a conflicted reaction to opening a new book. Occasionally she would delay the reading of it, instead revisiting an old favorite to give it a stay of execution. And yet, those old favorites had exposed string and visible glue, covers with frayed edges, pages with soft corners and faded marbling. A book could not move into that treasured position on the top shelf without sacrificing some of its fresh-from-the-bindery perfection.

Alice turned the first page, leaving that alone for whatever introduction Edward cared to write. As an afterthought, she lay a loose wide-ruled folio beside the notebook, and positioned the pen over it.

"In case you need to collect your thoughts first," she said to the air. Almost immediately an involuntary shiver made her body twitch, even though the room was overly warm from the day's insistent sun. Alice had come to look forward to the temporary paralysis, the relinquishing of control. She was not responsible for what her hand wrote while Edward had control of it, and she somehow found the sensation liberating.

Greetings, her hand wrote on the folio. *How are you today?*

"I'm well, thank you, Edward," Alice replied. Her words were slow at first, issuing from numbish, tingling lips. "I spoke with your brother today. Is he fifteen, sixteen?"

Goddy was sixteen when I left, which would make him nineteen this year? But he's not yet had his birthday, so eighteen. We all look rather young for our age.

Alice recalled the picture of the expedition members, Edward obviously a boy among men. "He looked very much like you."

Yes. Yes, I suppose he would—we resembled each other somewhat when I left, but as he is now of age, I suppose the resemblance is even stronger.

"When I purchased the notebook he said his brother favored that type and color. So you can be assured I found the right one."

He's always eager to help. It was hard to leave him, with Joseph already gone to New York, and Lillie at college in Ann Arbor, and only Mother, Mollie, and Carrie—that's Mother's hired girl—back home. I wondered how he would fare in the store, though; he's terribly shy.

"Well, he was very friendly, and not aggressive about a sale. I'm afraid I've had mostly poor experiences with Boston store employees."

I am glad. Perhaps being a clerk has helped with his shyness.

Alice smiled, her afternoon distress dissipating. At least for her, Goddy's brother was still alive. "With whom will you begin, Edward?"

With my fellow Signal Corpsmen, but first with George Rice, who was very dear to me. I have no doubt that he has received unanimous praise in the diaries of the other men, as he was a clear favorite, always ready to lighten the mood with a joke and optimism. But George and I were particularly close—perhaps because neither of us were Army men to begin with, but came about it by way of training in a different profession. Both of us enlisted specifically for the expedition and had little idea of the lifestyle that awaited us.

Alice watched her hand rock back and forth, a motion that she did not understand until she realized that it was trying to switch to the notebook. She was just about to suggest that she exit her trance, move her hand of her own volition, and reenter the trance, when she saw it lift ever so slightly and come to rest on the pristine first page of the book, which Edward's elegant writing began to fill.

A Portrait of Sergeant George Rice.

Rice originally hailed from Nova Scotia, and had a bit of college—law school, I believe—but then emigrated to Washington, D.C., where he operated a photography studio with his brother Moses. He used to joke that we were countrymen, Michigan being "almost-Canada." When I pointed out that, indeed, Kalamazoo sat three degrees further north than Nova Scotia, he stared at me a moment, then slapped me on the back and said, "I'm glad you're our navigator, Ed." I think of the world in terms of latitude and longitude, and when Greely commenced his lectures on each of the thirty-eight states, it was Rice's custom to ask me for the featured location's coordinates. My accurate reply never ceased to elicit a grin and a slap on the back from him.

Immensely talented at his work, he documented the animals and plants of the Arctic with great skill. It cannot have been easy to develop plates in such cold, but he made do. With his keen eye, he was assigned as lookout when we sought a break in the ice to move forward. He never complained of this assignment, although it required him to perch on the icy stern of the boat with the threat of one false move spelling a fall into the icy water.

I can also credit the man with helping to save my life: while skating, which was a popular pastime and source of exercise for many of the men, I had the misfortune to break through the ice. Unable to climb out myself, my limbs almost instantly numbed, I would have perished save for Rice and Brainard's quick reply to my cries. Rice was swift to sacrifice his own coat and stockings so that I could don dry ones as soon as possible. This reminds me of his cleverness in later months, as our clothing frayed and begged replacement: he urged us all to take our long stockings, cut off the leg at mid-shin, and sew one open end to make a toe, thereby doubling our supply.

Particularly toward the end, it seemed as if he considered it his personal duty to save us all. He labored for unknown hours as our shrimper, netting the tiny creatures that were far more shell than meat so that we might have something to put in our mouths. Brave Rice, who had no more energy than the rest of us, again and again pleaded with the commander to let him go after the stores in a small cache some fifteen or twenty miles away. At last he was permitted to set out with Frederick to try and recover this meat. Before he left, he came by my bag—I was completely useless at that time—and joked that if I did not adhere to frequent exercise, women would think me sickly and I would never get a wife.

I told him I could only hope that one of the women who surrounded him upon his heroic return to society would settle for me.

I cannot tell you how broken my heart was to see Frederick return not only empty-handed, but alone. I hoped I was simply suffering from hunger-induced hallucinations, but the look on Frederick's face was all too telling. One of the men began to wail upon hearing the news; the others tried to hush him. I sank further into my bag, knowing I would like to scream, too, and feeling more hopeless than ever before.

Rest in peace, my dear friend.

Alice waited for Edward to shift her hand to the folio and follow up his contribution with commentary addressed to her, but nothing more came. Eventually she tried to move one of her fingers, found that she could, and realized that Edward was gone, perhaps sapped by the effort of narration. She also realized the time—that Thea must be well into dinner preparations by now, and Alice not there to help. Aside from a few days of illness, she had not neglected her afternoon chores. Though Thea had made many solo dinners before Alice's arrival, Alice couldn't help but feel guilty for denying her an extra pair of hands.

Rice in his cheerful self-sacrifice reminded her of Thea, whose company she had been neglecting between time spent with Adam, Neil, and Edward. Lost in her own thoughts, Alice had been quiet lately while helping with the early summer harvest or preparing the vegetables for a meal. They had not managed a good talk in the kitchen in some time. After determining her facilities were back to normal, she headed downstairs, following the savory scent of soup.

Thea seemed surprised by Alice's immediate apology upon entering the kitchen. "No, no—Neil told me you were indisposed. I did not expect your assistance this afternoon, so I called another helper into service."

Alice realized that little Maudie, standing on a stool, was doing Alice's usual work of scrubbing the root vegetables and chopping them into whatever size a recipe required. Maudie seemed to be achieving what took Alice two months of practice: perfectly cubed potatoes and carrot rounds of equal thickness.

Maudie greeted Alice with a bright smile. "I like to help, Miss Alice." Alice wondered if Maudie still saw kitchen tasks as novelties, games in which she was allowed occasionally to take part, as young Alice had when the cook allowed her to stir a bowl or roll a pin.

"My little apprentice," said Thea, smiling at her eldest.

And Alice realized then that Thea was preparing Maudie for her almost inevitable profession: housekeeping, whether it be for her husband or for boarders. Thea expected her daughter to go to school, of course, but might steer her towards home economics rather than Greek or Latin. In contrast, Alice had been dissuaded from taking any practical classes, her secretarial course the main exception. She was learning how to keep house now, but that would never be her primary, all-encompassing activity.

Alice heard a meow and found Eleanor crawling around in the flour on the floor, doing her best imitation of a cat. Trying not to laugh out loud, Alice petted the kitty, who arched her back and yowled.

As dinnertime grew closer, Alice felt suddenly shy about seeing Neil again. She did not want to act as if she had been cured completely of the morning's sorrow, especially with the new sad story dictated to her by Edward, but time in the kitchen with the very alive Thea and Maudie and Eleanor had taken her from morose to simply meditative. She washed the plates more slowly, as if she could prolong the afternoon by doing so, leaving Maudie waiting impatiently with the cloth to dry them.

They had three actual boarders this evening, all middle-aged salesmen fresh off the train. Alice had not mastered the art of pulling conversation out of nowhere as Thea had, but she had become less timid about delivering the plates by herself. This time she was followed by Maudie, who managed to collect a sweet from each man's pocket simply by her presence. The natural friendliness of the salesmen (perhaps it was an act for them, as part of their profession, though Alice preferred to think of their demeanor as genuine) distracted her from worry about Neil. But the sound of his voice out in the dining room as she spooned herself some stew made her freeze. She quickly fixed another bowl and handed it to Maudie.

"Maudie, dear, would you bring this to Mr. White?"

Maudie did so without complaint, but Alice could feel Thea's eyes on her. Once Maudie had gone through the door, Thea clucked.

"Did the lovebirds have a falling-out?"

"I'm not sure what you mean." Alice pretended to be very interested in the contents of the stew.

"You never miss the opportunity to take Neil his dinner. If you won't tell me what's wrong I'll need to make up my own tale."

As Alice still hadn't explained that she was in contact with Kalamazoo's own Edward Israel, she could not tell Thea the truth. So she told a version of it. "I wasn't feeling well today, and I dislike Neil seeing me so weak."

Thea rolled her eyes heavenward. "But your migraines—he expects some illness, doesn't he? Any woman, really, is bound to have her fainting spells. All the fault of these, I'm sure." She tapped her side for the hollow sound of her corset. "He's clearly fond of you, and when he came to tell me you wouldn't be able to help fix dinner, there was no sense of annoyance or disgust about him—only concern."

"I still find it embarrassing. I played the invalid for some time, and I don't wish to do so again."

Thea convinced Alice that she should bring Neil his dessert. She stepped too quickly at first, and the mold quivered so violently she thought its own motion might propel it off the plate—an accident that might have sent Alice retreating to her room with red cheeks. But she slowed her pace, and the wobbling calmed, and when she saw Neil's smile, Alice returned the expression.

She wished she could sit with Neil in the parlor this evening, but she feared she would be poor company, perhaps falling fast asleep in her chair. So once her serving duties were done and her own blancmange devoured, Alice retreated to her room, wondering if she should try to contact Edward again or let them both rest.

At first she thought that she had walked into the wrong room, for she did not remember leaving a dress laid out on the bed. Alice checked the number on the door, the proximity to the stair. Yes, this was the same chamber she had occupied for the past three months. She had not recently given any of her laundry to Thea. But when she opened the curtains, the still-light sky revealed the dusty plum dress she had coveted in Israel's. With the end-of-day's sun catching and illuminating the pearl buttons, Alice thought the gown was one of the loveliest things she had ever seen.

She picked up a sleeve and fingered the fabric as she had in the store, admiring the frog closures and the smooth piping along the seams.

The details blurred slightly, and Alice realized the gift had brought tears to her eyes. She carefully undid the hooks and buttons of the blue dress, letting it fall to the floor like a pile of rags, and pulled the new treasure over her petticoat. After she had buttoned all the buttons and smoothed the skirt, she eyed herself in the mirror. A perfect fit. Was Goddy already that talented with sizes, even where women were concerned?

From the door came a knock so soft that the swishing of her skirts nearly obscured it; at that moment Alice realized from whom the gift must have come.

"May I come in?"

"Neil, it's beautiful," she breathed, beckoning him inside. She saw him look up and down the hallway before entering and closing the door behind them.

"I noticed your admiration for it at the store," said Neil, beaming and looking quite proud of himself. "Truly, I did need to buy a suit today...but I confess"—he took a deep breath—"I could not stop thinking about how beautiful you would look in this dress." Then, a declaration: "How beautiful you look, right now."

What happened next seemed perfectly natural: a thankful kiss on the cheek leaked into one on the lips, her arms went around his neck, his wrapped around her waist. Only up close did Alice realize that pale blond bristles ran along Neil's jaw. His chin, which had looked so smooth, scraped against hers. Thomas's dark beard had always given her fair warning when it went unshaven. But somehow she did not mind the discomfort; it convinced her that Neil was real, that this was happening.

Chapter 33

The next morning, Alice took longer than usual at the mirror, smoothing any wrinkles in the plum dress, admiring it some more in the early light. It had been some time since she had felt the desire to impress someone. She descended to breakfast hoping that Thea wouldn't immediately deduce the source of her glow. For now, she wanted to keep her joy all to herself.

"No, not yet, Maudie," she heard Neil say, presumably keeping her eager little hands from taking his plate. On seeing Alice, Neil rose quickly to pull her chair out, and his napkin fell to the floor. He had waited for her.

"Hello," Alice said shyly, slipping into the seat Neil offered. "I am sorry to have taken so long. I do hope your coffee is not cold."

Neil smiled. "I had a very attentive waitress refill it for me." Once said diminutive waitress had disappeared into the kitchen, he murmured, "You look radiant this morning."

"Why thank you, kind sir," said Alice, blushing. "My mother once told me that this color flattered my complexion."

At that moment, Maudie came out with a plate of breakfast, and Alice realized that Thea might be listening at the door. "Do you know what Adam has in store for me today?" she asked Neil, a little more loudly than necessary.

"I haven't the faintest. I haven't yet been to the office—opted instead for a later breakfast."

"For which I am thankful," Alice whispered. In a normal voice, she continued, "How long do you think he will persist in these experiments? I have not delivered stellar results, not in the least. I should think he'd be sick of devising these schemes, and then having them fail."

Neil stared into his coffee, stirring it with a spoon even though Alice knew he took it black, and therefore had nothing to stir in. "He has been keeping busy. You are good to humor him."

Alice wanted to ask Neil when she should stop humoring Adam and let him face reality, but something stopped her. Edward had become her pet project, and although he had never suggested she keep his correspondence a secret, she selfishly had no desire to share it with anyone. Adam had already had two opportunities to accept Edward's death, and he rejected them both. Let him continue with his silly experiments; Alice would keep Edward company in the meantime.

Neil finished his coffee and Alice her breakfast in silence, their eyes focused mostly on their plates as Thea came in and out, clearing dishes and resetting places, perhaps with less speed than usual. But several times she and Neil glanced up simultaneously, and the connection between them was so palpable that Alice thought it must be visible to others, perhaps manifested as a shining light in the space between them.

When Alice had consumed her last forkful, Neil lay his napkin beside his plate and stood up. "Shall we? The mad scientist will be waiting."

Each evening for the next few weeks, Alice wondered if she would be able to concentrate on her correspondence with Edward. Her mind was full of Neil, and dealing with Adam's experiments left her drained; it did not help that her lack of focus kept him in a foul mood. But Neil always found ways to make the day tolerable; he especially liked to creep into the kitchen after dinner and steal a kiss while she stood with dishwater up to her elbows. His mischievous smile would make her heart lift again, and she was able to sit down at her desk in a state of peace.

Not that that peace lasted long, once Edward began writing. Certainly, he recounted cheerful events during the expedition—the celebration of birthdays with an extra quart of rum for the lucky fellow, the issuance of the witty *Arctic Moon*, which Edward thought to be the most northernmost newspaper ever published. But inevitably the story would conclude with a recounting of his friend's last selfless action before his death.

One night Alice asked Edward if he had encountered any of his fellow explorers in the other world, imagining that their companionship might give him some comfort.

One would assume there to be some order to this place—people who knew each other in life grouped together, or even those who died in the same place or at the same time. I have not yet found one familiar face. But, then, there are many shades here, for the dead never move on as the living do.

"Is it not dreadfully claustrophobic?" asked Alice with a shiver.

Our concept of space here is quite different. When one no longer consists of actual matter, cannot breathe nor feel any physical sensations, comfort becomes a wholly mental state. In large part, it hinges on whether or not you are comfortable with the decisions you made while living, or the communications made from here. The proximity of another anonymous spirit has no particular effect on me, and yet I believe that the closeness of one I knew while I was alive would be comforting.

As had become commonplace when the connection was broken, Alice's hand flicked the pencil away in a spasm; it clattered upon the floor and began a slow, audible roll beneath the bed. When the tingling left her body, she would go after it. She always found herself wanting Edward to stay longer, especially when he had written something particularly upsetting—but she knew how draining the process was for him. Imagine writing biographical sketches of your friends, only to have each one end tragically.

Her own friends were few. Thea, Neil. Adam, she supposed. As her wits came back to her slowly, she thought to look at the clock.

Eleven. Would Neil, the early riser, still be awake? She found herself longing to feel his flesh-and-blood hand in hers.

Each step on the stair made her heart beat a little faster. Alice peeked in the parlor to find the lights dim and Neil asleep, a book sprawled across his chest, an empty glass beside him. No one else seemed to be stirring, so she kissed him full on the lips. Neil awoke with a start, but his surprised expression melted as he realized what was happening. He closed his eyes and pulled her towards him. The mere pressure of his hand on her back excited her. When they reached her room, it was as if she could not lock the door fast enough.

Chapter 34

Meeting Neil in the parlor after her communication with Edward became a ritual, and Alice let romance carry her through the days. She had never had this sort of courtship with Thomas, having gone from clandestine meetings straight through to marriage. She also knew that their living situation afforded them a freedom that would be envied by other young women her age. Alice loved seeing Neil's face, loved hearing him talk, loved feeling his kisses on a regular basis.

But one morning Alice woke to her head spinning from something other than love. She had hardly gotten to her feet before she was on her knees, sweating and shaking. Crawling across the carpet, she managed to make it to the bathroom down the hall and lock the door before retching into the toilet.

With her face against the cool tile of the floor, she wondered what was wrong. She hadn't taken even a sip of Neil's whisky last night, had not eaten anything particularly risky for dinner. Slowly, slowly, she pushed herself to a seated position, then used the washstand to pull herself up to standing. When she wiped off her mouth in front of the mirror, she found that her skin had taken on a peculiar, particular shade of green.

"Oh, no," Alice said aloud, then remembered Neil, back sleeping in her bed. "No, no," she whispered to herself.

What of the prophylactic that Neil had sheepishly produced during their first night together, mumbling that a classmate had distributed them during a class on the reproductive system? He had since procured more. It must simply be some unfortunate illness going around, brought to Kalamazoo by one of their boarders. Surely Thea had something in her bottles and jars that would settle her stomach and prove it a passing ailment. The more likely reason she tried to keep at bay, pushing it back in her mind with a wedge of denial.

She decided to risk the possibility that other guests would be up at this hour, and tied on only a dressing gown before hurrying downstairs. Thankfully, no one seemed to be stirring yet, for she was sick into the urn by the stairs while her feet rested on the last step.

She squeezed the edges of the urn's mouth and took deep breaths, trying to compose herself again. Looking up, she met the startled eyes of an older man coming out of the dining room, a boarder who had just arrived yesterday. She smiled quickly and hurried through the dining area and the kitchen door, not waiting for any awkward expressions of concern he might produce. Maudie would need to serve his meals for the rest of his stay.

"Thea!"

Thea turned around with a bowl and spoon in hand and almost dropped them both at the sight of Alice half-dressed, standing in the doorway.

"Good gracious, what's the matter?" Thea put everything down and wiped her hands on her apron.

"Thea, has anyone been sick from the food?" Alice tried to breathe through her mouth, in order to moderate the normally pleasant smells of the kitchen.

"I should hope not. Why? Did you poison it?"

"I'm feeling terrible this morning." Alice felt another wave of nausea come on; she pushed her way past Thea and out into the garden, but it was a false alarm and passed. Still, Alice had to grab hold of the fence to steady herself. She tried to focus on the way the blood rushed from her knuckles, turning red and then stark white.

"If I didn't know better," said Thea from the doorway, "I'd say you were with child."

Alice ground the heels of her hands into her eye sockets. She would not cry, but she could not look at Thea.

"Oh, Alice. Here. Let me fix you some tea." Thea pulled a few jars down from her shelf of herbs, examined the labels, replaced a few, chose a few more. "I'll send you up with this, and you send Neil down for breakfast."

The mere mention of breakfast nearly made Alice gag. "Why would Neil be in my room?" she managed to say, but she knew from the moment the words came out that no weight supported them.

Thea raised her eyebrows. "I may be an old widow and occupied with other matters, but I am not blind. As a boardinghouse-keeper, I do not comment on the sleeping arrangements of guests, as long as they do not distress others; as a woman, however, I am perfectly aware of who is in my house and where." She tied the herbal mixture into a small pouch of cheesecloth and doused it with hot water from the kettle.

"Do you want me to carry this up for you? You don't look particularly sturdy."

Alice held out her hands for the teapot. "I'll be careful. I think Neil would be startled if—"

"If I walk up to your bedroom door and he happens to come out."

Alice nodded.

"Very well," said Thea, replacing the stoppers in her jars. "I'll pretend I know nothing."

Alice made it up the stairs with only one scare, and then she managed to set the teapot on the landing before dizziness overtook her. Willing herself not to vomit again, she concentrated on the teapot's painted lilacs. *Your favorite flower. Aren't they pretty?* She spoke to herself as if she were a child.

Neil was still lying in bed when she entered, but his eyes were open. "You're up early, my dear," he said. He propped himself up on his elbows, and his brow wrinkled in concern. "You don't look well."

"I'm not," said Alice. Seeing him, and thinking of telling him why she was ill, made her stomach lurch again. She nearly dropped her tea in an effort to reach the bathroom for another round of coughing. Curled up on the tile again, she felt the floor vibrate slightly as Neil's stockinged toes made an appearance outside the door.

"Are you—are you all right?" His voice wavered through the wood. She could tell he had never cared for someone in this state before.

Alice closed her eyes to stop the room from tilting like a ship. "Thea has fixed me one of her teas. I just need to rest."

"If you need me—"

"I'll spare you," said Alice. She could almost hear Neil's sigh of relief as he retreated back to his room.

Once the quaking had calmed enough for her to stand, Alice shuffled back out to her own room. She built a sort of soft fortress for herself out of pillows and sipped at Thea's concoction. As the tea warmed her insides, Alice began to feel drowsy. She set down the cup and closed her eyes, thinking a short rest would not hurt...

Then she was upright again, walking through the zoology museum with her father. Against the wishes of the curator, who yelled protests after them, Alice's father opened the door to a room that usually housed specimens of birds. It had been replaced by a collection of underterm fetuses pickled in jars of preservative, filling a central display case and lining the walls. Each jar was labeled with the age of the fetus and the abnormality suspected to have caused its abortion—for a moment, before her eyes focused on the actual words, Alice thought some cruel scientist had named the creatures suspended there, as if they were museum mascots. One tiny three-month fetus in particular caught her eye—its cranium comparatively huge, froglike hands and feet wrapped into itself, gills still visible on its neck. Alice stared into its flat eyes, which eventually *blinked.* And suddenly Alice realized that this was *her* baby. How had they found it, after she had left it in Ohio?

She looked around; her father had disappeared. Surely they would not notice one specimen missing—one specimen that she wanted desperately. After all, it should be hers to keep! She wrapped her arms around the enormous jar and gently slid it off the shelf, but the weight was much greater than she expected, and the jar slipped from her grasp. She closed her eyes, waiting for the sound of shattering glass—but instead, she found herself back in bed, in Kalamazoo, drenched in sweat, the nausea replaced by a different sort of unease.

After a short, fitful drowse, Alice opened her eyes to see a pair bluer than her own, staring at her from the side of the bed. She started.

"Mish Awish," Eleanor lisped in a practiced manner, "Mama says dere is something the matter wit your tummy, and when I have something the matter wit my tummy, I ask Dowwy to fix it." She held out her bedraggled doll, today clad in a green dress that appeared to be dusted with flour. "And I eat these cwackers, and they make me feel better." Her other hand held up a plate of the crackers, but at an angle, so that one of the crackers fell to the floor. Alice heard the faint sound of it splintering on the wooden planks.

"Oops." Eleanor placed the plate on the bedside table before she could lose another one. Alice tried to make sure that her smile reflected more gratitude than amusement.

"Oh, Eleanor, thank you so much. But won't you miss Dolly?"

Eleanor shook her head. "I have udder toys. You need her." She reached over Alice and carefully propped Dolly against the adjacent pillow, then left without so much as a goodbye.

"Thank you," Alice called after her. She studied her new bedfellow, never having seen Dolly this close before. The doll's right ear was gone, the victim of a chip in the porcelain, a triangle of white showing through the peach-colored paint. A blue smudge showed on one cheek, likely the result of some artistic collaboration involving paint or pen. The bleached horsehair had tangled itself into three distinct clumps, two on the sides of the molded head and one sprouting from the back.

She must have dozed off during her survey of Dolly, but a soft knock at the door woke her. Alice sat up and straightened herself, wondering if it would be Neil. "Come in."

But it was Eleanor again, looking sheepish.

She mumbled something at the floor.

"What's that, dear?"

"I—I wondered if I could have Dowwy back now."

"Oh, Elly, of course you can." Alice handed the doll to the little girl, who hugged it close to her chest as if they had been separated for weeks or months. "She told me that she missed you."

Eleanor smiled. "I missed her too."

"I feel better now," said Alice, for in fact she did feel less shaky. "Will you thank your mother for the crackers? And thanks to you and Dolly."

"Well," said Eleanor, sounding grave, "if you have tummy trouble again, you can bowwow her again."

"That's very generous of you." Alice lay back in her pillows, thinking that if the child inside her was anything like Eleanor, she could be a contented mother.

By lunchtime, Alice was feeling better, though still unsure if she wanted to chance eating something. She decided to venture down to the kitchen anyway, but nearly tripped over a tray that had been set in front of her door. Of course Thea would leave toast and another pot of tea; Alice realized she should have expected no less.

Alice had not planned to contact Edward that evening, with thoughts of what a terrible strain a trance could be on her body. She should focus on catching up with kitchen work instead. But when Alice brought her lunch tray down herself, Thea had shooed her from the kitchen, despite her protests of wellness.

"If you're not going to tell him yet, he should at least believe you have something consistent. He was in medical school, after all; I suspect they give the students a fair explanation of women's bodies and symptoms, and an unexplained illness, worst in the morning, will likely not pass over his head. Go back to your room before he sees you."

Sufficiently warned, Alice obeyed, but found herself sitting on her bed, staring at the wallpaper, wanting to see Neil. She missed him, but Thea was right—she needed to act as if this were not just a morning malady.

Unless she simply told him. But no—no need for him to have this same terrified fluttering in his chest. After all, there was a possibility—however slim—that she could be mistaken. There was a possibility, too, that this would not be a long-lived condition, given what had occurred in February.

For the next few days the tray became a routine. The noontime buttered toast and tea settled nicely in place of the breakfast Alice's stomach rejected and a heavier lunch that she could not bear to consider. When Thea came to collect the tray, she studied Alice's face with a frown, then quickly pinched her cheeks—one side, other side—before Alice even had a chance to protest.

"Your overall color is much improved, but a little bloom in the cheeks never hurts. For a time there you were looking like an oyster."

Alice's stomach lurched. "Please, Thea, don't mention oysters. In fact, I would much appreciate it if you didn't mention food of that sort at all."

"Well, please believe me that you do look better." She glanced over her shoulder and lowered her voice. "Are you planning to tell him this afternoon?"

Alice sighed. Thea had asked the same question each day. "I am hoping to regain a little more strength before I speak with him." She wanted to be steady when she told Neil, that was true. But in addition she could not help but think of all the ways he could react, and she could imagine the negative ones far more vividly. Alice remembered how Thomas had rejoiced when she told him about her pregnancy. But that was an instance in which the parties were (supposedly) married, and conception was a favorable outcome. Would Neil yell? Would he cry? Would he disavow his responsibility?

"Hmmph," Thea replied, and left without further comment.

Alice entered the dining room that evening to find a new boarder and Thea engaged in conversation. Thea kept one hand on the fair head of her youngest, who kept trying to interrupt with a tug on her mother's skirt.

"And what do you sell, Mr. Beattie?"

"Oh, tonics, medicines of all kinds." He paused when Eleanor growled, "Mama!" and gave the fabric a particularly strong jerk, but Thea simply patted the girl's head and motioned for him to continue. "I like to joke that my collection even includes water from the Fountain of Youth, but truth be told, most of my wares are meant to help you grow old." He took notice of Alice's presence then, and stood to greet her. Thea turned and smiled. A smudge of flour had clung to her forehead.

"Mr. Beattie, this is Miss Boyden."

The man beamed with pleasure, as if he had been presented with a special secret. "I'm very pleased to meet you, Miss Boyden."

"Likewise."

"Alice, would you mind fetching him some bread? And"—Thea lowered her voice—"taking the little one?"

"Eleanor?" Alice said brightly, reaching out to her. "Would you be able to help me in the kitchen?" With what exactly, Alice wasn't sure—but the wrinkles and redness of frustration disappeared from Eleanor's face, and with a giggle she accepted Alice's hand. Thankfully, a pile of shelled walnuts greeted her as she walked into the kitchen.

"I need you to count those nuts," Alice said, pointing to the little mound. Eleanor did not know all of her numbers yet, but counting out sets of ten would keep her busy. "Could you do that for me?"

The girl clambered up on the stool and immediately went to work, counting loudly: "One, two, fwee…" Alice found a fresh loaf of bread and a knife. She couldn't help but listen through the door as she sawed two slices.

"How many children have you?" she heard Mr. Beattie say.

"Four. Eleanor is the youngest."

Mr. Beattie frowned. "Well, Mrs. Kollner, I hate to bear this news, but I am trying to keep ahead of a diphtheria epidemic that has been targeting children in Grand Rapids."

Alice froze. She imagined Thea's eyes widening at the thought of facing one of a mother's most feared diseases. Although Alice had never witnessed anyone in the throes of diphtheria, she knew of its symptoms and torments from her father's medical books. But the books' descriptions of the mucous membrane, ecchymosis, and oedematous swelling did not include the horror of a child fighting for breath and a mother unable to help. And what terror could it wreak upon Eleanor, with her already weak lungs?

"I have a preventative tonic—Wells's Throat-Coat—that has seemed to protect the children who took it before the disease visited their town. I believe it has saved many young lives."

Without being asked, Eleanor reached up for the bread plate and brought it out to the dining room, just as Alice heard Thea say, "My youngest has difficulty breathing from time to time. I fear she would never survive...Oh, thank you, sweetheart, for bringing that out." The praise was echoed by an overly enthusiastic Mr. Beattie. "I might have something in my pocket for good little girls," Alice heard him say, followed by a little squeal from the girl in question.

Eleanor reentered the kitchen, clutching a sweet of some kind, visibly pleased by her performance and the treat that followed. She attached herself to Alice's leg and gave her a glowing smile.

"What do you have there, Elly?"

Eleanor studied her prize. "Wemon dwop," she declared triumphantly.

Alice scooped the child up and squeezed her tightly against her chest as if she were a baby, and only let her down when Eleanor began to wriggle. Once free, the girl scuttled off to her stool in the corner and popped the sweet in her mouth.

"I want you to have a bottle for free," Alice heard Mr. Beattie say. Over Thea's cluck of denial, he insisted. "I've just put money in your pocket. I'll not take advantage of your situation. And what heartless fool would not want to protect that little angel?"

Alice realized only then that her hand had come to rest on her stomach, as if to protect the child inside.

A week later, Alice entered the kitchen before lunch to find Thea there with an odd look on her face.

"I know!" Alice threw her hands up. "I will tell him...I just need the right time."

But Thea did not reply immediately, and Alice realized she was focused on an envelope on the counter. She held it up but did not offer it to Alice. "I did not leave it in your room—did not want Neil to see it before you. I don't think he would invade your privacy so, but..."

Thea looked at the envelope again, shook her head slightly and handed it to Alice.

"From your mother?" There was doubt in her eyes.

"Yes, most likely," said Alice. She stared at the envelope, at the last name she had finally begun to leave behind her. She knew the handwriting.

"Don't you think you ought to tell them about Mr. Holloway's... departure?"

Alice forced her lips into a smile. "Perhaps now is the time. After all, I have given up hope of hearing from him."

Alice tore open the envelope as soon as she reached her room, fingers trembling. A pink ticket fluttered to the floor as she unfolded the two pages of a letter.

Dearest Alice,

I do not know how to begin, not being sure if you will even read this far. You must have recognized my handwriting from the envelope; I would not blame you if you threw it directly in the fire or tore it to pieces. I deserve as much.

I suppose that I should first apologize for the abominable way in which I have behaved. I cannot tell you how grateful I was to hear that you were well and apparently happy in Kalamazoo. I assumed you would have returned to Cambridge by now—but, now that I consider it, you are too independent and proud to run back to your parents. Perhaps you have had money from them, or perhaps you are teaching to earn your keep. I would not have run if I did not believe you would be better for my departure. The truth is, before being confronted by those skeptics, I was unhappy with myself, and knew I could not make you happy. I had hoped to send for you when my temperament had improved.

Now business has brought me to Detroit—no, not a spiritualists' convention or a private sitting, for I have left that all behind; I am now a salesman of tangible goods—and I find myself in the same state as you once more. I write because I would like to see you, having missed you dearly these past months, and also because I have a matter concerning our marriage that I need to discuss with you.

If, after all I have done to you, you will still permit me to explain myself, I will be staying in the Michigan Hotel for the next several weeks. You need only have the front desk alert me to your presence, and I will meet you in the dining room at 6 p.m. You will recognize me; I look much the same as I did six months ago, save for a shorter mustache. I have even taken the liberty of enclosing a train ticket, and have secured—separate—accommodations for you at the same hotel. I will also pay for your return ticket, if you do not wish to remain with me. If a meeting in person is not what you desire, a letter from you would be treasured.

Yours still,
Thomas

Alice had to read the letter several times before she could begin to parse its meaning. At first the placement of the words did not make sense to her; they were simply an artful collage with no particular intent. Slowly she began to extract and sort the facts in her head: Thomas was here in Michigan. He was sorry. He wanted to see her. She studied the ticket, which was for first-class passage. He must be doing well in his new line of work.

How strange to hear him refer to "the skeptics" as an anonymous duo, when they had become so familiar to her. She suddenly realized that she had lived with Adam, Neil, and Thea longer than she had with Thomas.

Not a few of the sentences struck her as suspicious. How had he "heard" of her remaining in Kalamazoo? Alice did not often leave the house, and she did not consider herself to be well known in the community. He must have some spiritualist friends still in the area who had passed the information through their twisted network.

She was startled by how his words on the page affected her, even after his long absence and his betrayal. A stirring of affection came unbidden and unwanted—how could she consider his offer with memories of March still fresh in her mind? She could not possibly meet him in Detroit. From Maggie's letter she already knew his revelation about their marriage, or lack thereof. And why should she put her budding relationship with Neil in jeopardy? She would burn it all—the ticket, the envelope, the letter—and forget about it.

But something besides stopped Alice from looking for a candle. She opened her trunk of books and dug out a chemistry text long neglected, its spine still stiff and fresh. The papers slid neatly in between some of the later pages of the tome. Perhaps it would be gratifying to look back on them someday and know that this time, she was the one who had left him without an answer.

Alice tried to follow her normal routine on the day she decided to tell Neil, but every nerve was on edge with the waiting. She pretended to be busy with cleaning the kitchen when he came to dine in the evening; her hands and voice shook so badly she thought he would certainly take notice.

She found him alone in the parlor after dinner, a book in one hand and a glass of scotch in the other. Alice watched him finish a page before he looked up to see who had entered.

"Miss Boyden. I hadn't expected to see you until later."

The playful formality of his address, given their intimate relationship, made Alice even more shy. She tried to respond to Neil's smile with one of her own, but a twitch at the corners of her mouth was the best she could do. Neil's own brow wrinkled in response.

"Alice, what's wrong?"

She could not look at him as she spoke and instead studied her hands, fidgeting with her fingers as if they could twist off. Alice had thought of many ways to approach the topic, but in the end simply whispered, "I-I have reason to believe that I am with child."

"Oh, Alice."

The words descended into a disappointed tone, and she cringed. But then she felt herself being pulled down to a seat on the couch and crushed into Neil's chest. His hands caressed her hair, and his mouth planted a garland of kisses across her forehead.

"Dear, dear Alice," he murmured into her ear, "will you marry me?"

Alice's relief at Neil's reaction almost said *yes* on its own, but she paused—remembering Thomas's jubilation, and then his sadness and anger when she lost the baby. That was when she lost Thomas, too.

What if this baby died in the womb, just as her first had? Would Neil regret his hasty proposal? They had, after all, known each other for a few months merely. She had had no reservations about marrying Thomas, after knowing him for even less time. But she was foolish then—and could be just as foolish now. And she herself was a child born of this sort of situation, and because of her, her parents lived a life without love.

"I need some time to ponder it, Neil."

Neil released her from his tight hug and stared at her. "Some time to ponder it? Why, the window must be closing for the baby to arrive at a proper time."

"I don't mean that I need much time. A few days, perhaps. You must remember that we have only known each other for four months—also the amount of time my husband has been gone—"

"I thought he was not your husband?" Neil stood back from her now, arms crossed.

"He was my husband as long as I believed him to be," said Alice defensively. "I married—or thought I married—him within four months of our meeting. And as you can see, it did not endure." She decided it was unnecessary to mention her parents' tale of woe as well.

Neil laughed and shook his head. "I do not understand how you can compare me to that charlatan who left you with nothing."

"I do not want to compare you. But he is the only model I have."

"Are you still in love with him?"

"No," Alice said vehemently. She knew that was an answer on which she did not want to pause.

Neil studied her, his lips pursed tightly together. "Are you in love with Edward?"

Now it was Alice's turn to laugh. "Neil, Edward is dead."

"But you spend as much time with him as you would a living person."

"Neil, are you jealous of a *spirit?*"

Neil remained serious. "Should I be?"

The truth was, Alice did love Edward—just in a different way than she loved Neil, of course, more affectionate than desirous. But Neil did not seem in the mood to have things explained to him. "Other people and things will always occupy part of my time. I am not the kind to devote my entire life to taking care of a man." She shook her head, amazed she had taken the explanation this far. "I asked for a few days of contemplation merely. A few days. Many women take more—"

"It did not take you long to invite me into your bed," muttered Neil.

Alice's mouth hung open. Sweet Neil, who only a moment ago had been covering her in kisses, had turned sour. She tried to respond, but all she could do was shake her head and flee.

Alice did not remember going upstairs; it was as if she had been dropped onto the bed, facedown into the pillow. Somewhere she heard knocking and her name being repeated, but it did not seem to have anything to do with her. While she breathed wetly into the feathers, her fingers sought the seams of the pillowcase; somehow they seemed to promise the stability that she desperately needed.

From the beginning of their relationship, Alice had never compared Neil to Thomas. They were completely different beings, in appearance, profession, temperament.

But now she felt as she used to after an argument with—or worse, silence from—Thomas. It was as if a large creature had settled upon her chest to effect her slow suffocation. It did not matter which way she lay on the bed, or whether she sat up or stood up; she could not seem to shake its claws.

Chapter 35

By morning, Alice had made a decision. It took her some time to locate the carpetbag, but finally she found it stuffed under the bed, rumpled and dusty. Shaking it out only made her cough, so she abandoned the look of the outside and began to fill it. Her savings, of course. Her hairbrush, and extra pins. A book to make the train ride pass more quickly. One dress, folded several times. With a light load, could she slip out undetected?

Before she closed the bag, she realized what dress she had picked: the plum one that Neil had purchased for her. But it was her nicest. She did not want Thomas to think her a ragamuffin, mired in last year's fashions.

Then there was Edward's notebook, and all his writings to her. Did she leave the notebook here, since Adam was meant to have it? Did she take it with her, in case...She thrust her hand into the carpetbag and pushed the brush into a corner, making just enough space for the notebook. At this moment, she could certainly leave Neil behind. She could leave half-mad Adam and even her friend Thea, who had pushed her to tell Neil, only to have this happen. But she could not leave Edward. She would finish her assignment, her promise to him, wherever it might take place.

Despite her best efforts, the sweat and dust of traveling had left Alice so disheveled that she gasped upon seeing herself in the reflection of a train station window. Thankfully, the hotel was easy to reach—perhaps a five-minute walk, though it felt like longer. How had her bag grown so heavy?

After so many months of keeping mostly to Burdick Street, it startled Alice to see a ceiling so high, ringed by elaborate molding, an open staircase carpeted in red velvet, clipped in with brass rods. Pedestaled plant and flower arrangements seemed like a nod to the Hanging Gardens of Babylon. Gold and crimson brocade hung heavy against the tall windows, opened today to let in any chance of a breeze. But the hotel staff looked pristine despite the heat, and they made no surreptitious moves to fan themselves with a receipt. Alice tried to tell herself that they were used to seeing people who had traveled much further than she, and that her red cheeks and loose locks would make no negative impression upon them.

She tried to approach the desk with all the confidence of one who was used to solo hotel stays, implying that this was one of many in her adventurous life. Alice's pulse slowed slightly when the desk confirmed that they did have her room reservation—she was glad she had thought to ask for Mrs. Holloway first instead of Miss Boyden, though perhaps she ought to have brought her wedding ring to make the title more believable. She was so grateful at the porter's haste in bringing her bag upstairs that she tipped him perhaps too generously, exposing herself as a novice traveler after all.

A face-wash and extra hairpins greatly improved her outlook on the evening. Alice locked the door and felt gleefully risqué as she stripped off her travel-worn gown and walked around the room in her corset and petticoat, investigating every drawer-pull, sniffing the small soap beside the washbasin that had given her skin such a nice smell. The single layer of clothing kept her much cooler, and she debated leaving her dress off until the last moment, but the buttons could sometimes be troublesome. It would not be well to arrive too late, in case he grew tired of waiting for her.

Alice wondered if Thomas had asked after her at the front desk yet, knowing approximately when she would have arrived on the train. She hoped so—she hoped he had been nervous all day, wondering whether he should anticipate her arrival or set himself up for disappointment. She imagined herself floating into the dining room in her plum dress, heads turning, Thomas standing up from the table with a gleam in his eye and his hand outstretched for hers.

Of course, she knew who Thomas was now, of his life before her. But this opportunity for closure, when everything else in her life seemed unfinished, had been impossible to pass up.

The attire of the other women in the dining room came as an utter shock, and Alice realized how wrong she was to think that a cotton frock would be sufficient. Waists nipped in by silk ribbons and ivory buttons, broad hats such as Alice had not seen since her Cambridge days. But Thomas would not care, she told herself. On the occasion of their first meeting, at the clambake over a year ago, she had been in far shabbier a state.

It took her longer than expected to find Thomas, and she stood awkwardly in the doorway of the dining room. As soon as the maître d' came over to ask if Miss needed any assistance, she spotted him—Thomas had seen her as well, and was standing at his seat, a smile on his face. It made all her reservations about meeting him fall away.

"My dear Alice," Thomas said when she arrived at his table, and kissed her hand. Were those tears in his eyes? Alice could not speak for a moment, merely smiled and gave something approximating a curtsy. Perhaps in her mind she had made him ugly after his abandonment, but truthfully he was as handsome as ever.

As soon as she had settled herself in the seat he pulled out for her, the waiter was there with menus. Thomas ordered a bottle of wine for the both of them, and Alice entertained fond memories of their meals in restaurants, early on. She felt his gravitational pull, was tempted to release herself into his orbit, but she had resolved to begin with the question that was first on her mind.

"I am curious as to how you found me."

Thomas chuckled. "Have you recently had a boarder by the name of Mr. Beattie?"

"Yes, for a night."

"A good friend of mine. We dined here in Detroit two weeks ago. He agreed to visit Kalamazoo and look for you. I did not imagine you would actually be in the same boardinghouse."

No wonder Mr. Beattie had seemed oddly excited to hear her name. Alice watched Thomas as he buttered a piece of bread for her and one for himself, a small ritual about which she had forgotten. "I took work there in exchange for board."

Thomas's bread paused in its ascent to his mouth. "Work? As a *domestic*?" The disdain in his voice surprised Alice; did his sister not take in boarders, same as Thea? Did he not help her with chores in his youth?

"I had little choice," said Alice, her teeth clenched. "You left me with no money."

A bite had to be chewed and swallowed before Thomas could reply, but he waved his bread around in a gesture that Alice took to mean, *No, you misunderstand me.* "I express surprise," Thomas said, once his mouth was clear, "not out of disapproval of your vocation, but because I thought you had little to no training in the domestic arts."

Alice lifted her chin a little higher. "I learned by example. I am a quick study, you know."

"I remember that about you."

"And your work?" she said, not willing to divulge any further information about her new home. "Do you sell tonics and potions as Mr. Beattie does?"

At this excuse to talk about his new occupation, Thomas beamed. "Oh, no, no. Paper goods mostly—but not just any paper. Embossed stationery, leather-bound notebooks, handmade sheets with flowers pressed into the weave, as well as other desk essentials—wax seals and gold-tipped fountain pens and paperweights." Alice half expected him to open his coat and reveal an assortment of sealing wax and pens tacked within. She was tempted to ask him if he had any blue books, but there was no need to arouse his suspicion on the matter.

This simple description of their current engagements seemed to ford the river between them, however, and conversation streamed easily from bank to bank. Alice had her soup without recalling its flavor; she noted the meat to be tender but forgot whether it was steak or venison. She managed to contribute to the conversation without indicating that she worked for anyone but Thea; since Thomas was uninterested in tales of disastrous desserts or aphids in the garden, Alice surmised, he did not pressure her for more details of her life in Kalamazoo. When she mentioned her apprehension about serving boarders at dinner, though, Thomas's face suddenly darkened.

"I do hope those men have not bothered you since. There was a tall, blond one, and a skinny Hebrew."

"No, they've not bothered me," she told him. *In fact, they have been more considerate than you.* She thought of Neil's pleading apologies outside her door the night before, and a sudden sadness squeezed her heart.

"I have sometimes regretted leaving spiritualism, but I have not missed the skeptics. And those two were the worst sort—bent on researching a medium and planting information and props to frame him in a fraud. Mercenaries, they were. And you should have seen the gleam in that Jew's eye when I told him I'd return his friend's money—if there were ever a "friend" in the first place."

"So you were not performing those tricks that they accused you of," said Alice. She reminded herself that she could win this game in several ways—such were the cards in her hand.

"Of course not! It saddens me that you would think that of me." Thomas pressed his hand to his heart, its thumb holding his knife away from his breast as the four fingers spread. "But I was not strong enough to stand that virulent sort of skepticism. It pained me to walk away because of a few detractors. But I decided it was not the life I cared to lead."

And yet, he had never consulted Alice in this decision, to ask her what sort of life she cared to lead, if she minded being left behind. The spell that she had come under when first seeing him was beginning to wear off; she felt it slipping from her shoulders like a cape. "Then why did you run?"

"Because I had the feeling that justice would not prevail in this case," said Thomas. "Because I should have paid heed to the rule that a medium is welcome anywhere but home. I should not have accepted the invitation to Michigan in the first place, and I stayed much longer than I should have dared—it's only that the people were so starved for the information I could give them, and I felt I could not leave them while the spirits had more to say."

Or when the victims still had money to give you, Alice thought.

"And—" Thomas stopped for a moment and stared at his empty plate, as if not remembering that he had eaten its contents; he opted for a healthy sip of wine instead. "You cannot imagine the pressure I faced to produce evidence of a spirit," he said in a low voice. "People are less patient with spirits than they used to be, when I began my training." Thomas shook his head in the manner of an elderly man ashamed at the state of youth. "And so sometimes I would...bypass Dr. Anderson, if he wasn't cooperating, or if I could not achieve the level of calm I needed for a trance. I would imply that the communications were coming through him, but really I was conscious of it all."

"So you admit that you made up the communications!" Alice said, perhaps a little too loudly.

"*Some* of the communications," Thomas said defensively. "All mediums supply a little filler to keep the clientele happy. It never hurts, often helps. I didn't need it while you were communicating with the spirits, though. They always opened up to you when you wanted them to. I mean, until..." He trailed off, looking at Alice with something like sympathy.

"I never gave you anything fabricated. Anything false."

Thomas sighed. "No. No, you did not."

They were distracted then by the dessert cart. Thea made fantastic but very basic cakes and pies, and it had been some time before Alice had encountered such confections. After staring at the plates as if they bore crown jewels, she opted for a plump cream puff sitting contentedly in a puddle of raspberry coulis, waiting to be split by a quick strike of her spoon. Thomas took a ramekin of crème brulée and gave it a similar sharp blow.

But once they had cracked open their selections and taken a taste, Thomas did not continue his thread of conversation, but doctored his coffee in silence. Alice decided it was time to ask.

"You had mentioned needing to discuss something that concerned our marriage."

Despite presenting it as their need to meet, Thomas seemed startled by the question. His spoon dawdled in the sugar bowl, and his words came out slowly, like syrup. "Our officiant did not follow the proper procedure for submitting the marriage certificate—and therefore, we are not legally married in the eyes of the Commonwealth."

Alice stared at him for a moment, then let out a laugh that startled the people dining next to them. "But even if he had filed the papers properly, it still would have not been legal. For I know that you had another wife before me, in New York, and may still."

Thomas looked briefly shocked, then smirked, his eyes low enough to completely avoid hers. "I don't understand what you mean."

"I meant exactly what I said."

Thomas leaned back in his chair. "Well, I don't know where you obtained that information, but I assure you it's an utterly preposterous idea. Why, I haven't even been back to New York in over a year."

"I have it from a very reliable source," Alice pressed on, determined to wring an honest word from him. "Your sister wrote you a letter, and it was delivered to the boardinghouse. She mentioned your wife, and your son, and that they missed you—that you had not paid them a visit since September."

She watched his face go pale, his features sink in horror. When Thomas regained the power of speech, he could not piece together a whole sentence. "I—she—never loved—the boy—" He swallowed and tried again. "Alice. I fell deeply in love with you last summer. I felt as if you were my kindred spirit. I told you that I did not believe in marriage because it had not worked for me. She—that other woman was never my ideal mate. I wanted you so much, but she would have fought me tooth and nail for a divorce, I know she would have. And then there was the boy..." Thomas gazed off into the distance, as if his son were waiting on a wall of the dining room.

"Yes, the boy," said Alice. "When we were in Akron"—she paused, wondering if he would remember the significance of that place, but the look on his face answered in the affirmative—"you told me hoped to be a better father than yours had been. And yet you had already had such an opportunity, and had squandered it."

"My father was a decent man while the woman he loved was alive," Thomas said softly. "After meeting you at Onset, I could not live like that, with a woman I did not love. I would have been a miserable parent because I myself was miserable. So I decided to start over. I thought we could have a spiritual marriage if not a legal one. I thought, with you, I had another chance to be a father—a good father. But when that opportunity did not come to fruition—I felt that it was God's warning shot, that He was telling me that perhaps parenthood was not advisable. And so I tried to distance myself from you, and thought that was the best option." He hung his head. "The best option would have been honesty with you."

"Yes," said Alice. "It would have. You do realize that it is difficult for me to believe anything that you say?"

"I have never been more honest in my life when I say that I love you."

She had expected some sentiment of the sort. But the tense of the verb caught her off guard.

"You still love me?"

"Of course I do." He seized her hands, clutched one on each side of the floral centerpiece. "Perhaps we could stage a return, under new names. I'll completely cut contact with New York. We could marry legally—you would select the officiant this time."

"You would cut contact with your child?" Alice asked.

Thomas winced. "I would provide for him. But he has likely already been corrupted by his mother, and does not love me as a father. And perhaps"—he smiled at her—"there will be other children, after all."

Alice bit her lip. He did not realize how soon that might be.

While alone with her thoughts on the train, she had wondered how she would respond when he asked her to join him. Although she was still angry with Neil, and annoyed with Adam and Thea, she felt a pang at the thought of never seeing them again. She had left things unfinished—weeding in the garden, a book she had been reading to Eleanor. And what if Edward was no longer willing to correspond with her after she abandoned the house on Burdick Street and its inhabitants? She tried to imagine being with Thomas again, but her imagination did not comply. It rolled through scenes from happier times and sped past the unhappiness, but the future was an overdeveloped photograph, a white blur that told her nothing.

Yet instead of being afraid of the mist ahead of her, Alice felt strangely liberated without a plan. It robed her in confidence and gave her an unfamiliar feeling of freedom. Her acceptance of this uncertainty would propel her forward into something positive, she felt, but that would mean not dragging bits of her past into her future. It would mean leaving Thomas behind for good.

Alice reclaimed her hands. "I'm afraid what you propose is impossible."

Thomas stared forlornly at his half-eaten custard. After a few moments, he said, "I suppose that is your prerogative." Alice was almost offended by his lack of protestations, as she realized she had plenty of arguments to counter them. Suddenly she longed to tell Thomas about Edward, tell him that *her* gift was alive and well, that she was engaged in an important project. She was not only a housekeeper's assistant; she was a dead hero's amanuensis, and he depended on her.

"Would you at least do me the favor of breakfast tomorrow?" Thomas finally said. "We can meet as friends? Then I promise, I will never trouble you again."

Perhaps that was merely to give him time to think of another tack. But Alice nodded.

"Lovely. Then I will meet you here again, at 9?"

"Very well." She told herself that this was benevolence. A lesser woman would have quit the dinner long ago, but she was strong, and kind, and she pitied Thomas where before she had pitied only herself.

She rose from the table, and offered him her hand. Thomas stood and kissed the back of it. "I believe I had forgotten how beautiful you are." He let go but paused, as if waiting for her to reseat herself. Alice smiled but stepped back.

"I will see you tomorrow, Thomas."

Disappointment rippled over his face, but a moment later there was a bow and a smile. "Yes. *À bientôt.*"

Alice thought she stood a little taller as she ascended the staircase, although perhaps it was only that the glass of wine had lingered with her throughout the meal. The quiet emptiness of her room made her droop again, however. It made her briefly rethink her decision to part with him and reunite on the morrow—his presence had temporarily submerged, but not drowned, the desperate loneliness she had carried with her to Detroit. Perhaps a night with him would distract her further—but she told herself she was not that cheap.

Alice thought of contacting Edward, by way of keeping herself company, but decided she would do well to have one night alone. She hoped he would not mind too much. Lately, wrist and finger twitches had been waking her in the middle of the night. At first she had thought they indicated that Edward was trying to communicate, but after several instances of coaxing herself from bed and returning to her desk with pencil in hand, she realized the involuntary movements were nothing more than overworked muscles unable to get a proper rest. Edward was too polite to interrupt her during the wee hours.

Usually it took some time for Alice's thoughts to wind down, especially after an odd night such as this one, and so she imagined herself sinking into various stages of conscious rest until she slipped into the void of sleep. But her next conscious thought after settling her head on the pillow was that someone was shaking her awake.

Alice briefly wondered if she had dreamed her rejection of Thomas, if she had had more wine than she thought. But she opened her eyes to see not Thomas, but a little blonde head peering over the edge of the bed, eyes wide as if she were surprised to see Alice.

"Elly!" Alice sat up and rubbed her eyes. "Why are you awake? Did you have a bad dream? Where's your mother?" But Eleanor did not reply. She continued to stare at Alice, squeezing Dolly in her arms.

"Oh, here," said Alice, and went to pick her up and scoop her into her lap. But when her hands seemed to be on either side of the girl, they grasped only air. As Alice in her sleepiness tried to understand what was transpiring, Eleanor vanished before her eyes.

And Alice realized that she was in a hotel room in Detroit, not her own room in Kalamazoo. Eleanor could not be here.

The implication of what she had just seen hit her full in the chest. Alice moaned in terror.

"Oh no, no, no."

She continued to grab at the space where Eleanor had been, as if massaging the air with her fingers would bring the little girl back. But she knew the truth: she was completely alone in the room. And something terrible had happened.

She had to get back to Kalamazoo.

Alice packed her things with shaking hands, thinking that perhaps an early-morning train to Kalamazoo was not unlikely. Thankfully she thought to ask the concierge before running out into the dark, who regretted to tell her that the earliest train west was not until 7 o'clock in the morning.

An attempt to read the book she had brought along did no good in the way of distraction. She sat at her desk—maybe a trance could take her through the night.

"Edward, I think something terrible has happened."

She waited for some time, but her hand never moved. She shook it out, wondering if it was some fault of her muscles, if they were suddenly unreceptive to Edward's command, but still nothing came from the pen. And suddenly Alice was unbearably angry. How dare Edward leave her at such a point? She wanted to scream.

Her restless night and terror only magnified Alice's morning nausea, as did the jarring motion of the train and the heat of the early day, but she bore it by forcing herself to think of how Thea must feel at this moment. Surely worse than any known physical pain.

Alice placed her hand over the part of her stomach that would soon swell, if all went well. She had already become attached to what was growing within, even though its appearance would bring her nothing but shame.

And yet Neil had offered to spare her that hardship. His words against her still stung, but Alice admitted she had thrown him into a difficult situation. And then she had turned him down.

She reminded herself that they—she and Neil—were not like her parents. Neil had had almost as much schooling as her father, but he had wished to put his to real use instead of writing papers that no one but his few peers would read. And she was not her mother.

Especially because Alice, in contrast, loved the man who had put her in this situation—didn't she?

Neil was a very different man than Thomas—that much was certain. And perhaps that was all she needed to know—that she could close her eyes, take his hand, and he would lead her safely the rest of the way. She leaned her head back against the seat and let her eyelids fall. Perhaps something could be done to mend the rift they had created.

But that could wait. Alice knew who would need her the most upon her arrival.

Alice was greeted at the Kalamazoo train station by a hot, eye-watering wind that made her stumble as soon as she stepped off the train. When the conductor went to fetch her baggage, Alice shook her head and pointed at her carpetbag. Just this.

A pointed corner of something inside the bag jabbed her leg with every step. She hurried toward Burdick Street nevertheless, feeling her cheeks flush and her neck grow damp. At the end of the road, she might find herself completely mistaken, or facing a horrible truth.

By the time she reached the house, she had almost convinced herself that she had dreamed everything, that her fears were totally unfounded. She imagined the thrill of seeing Eleanor alive and well, and it caused her to practically throw herself down the front walkway. She wrenched the knob to open the door, but it resisted her, and she stood back in shock. Thea never locked the door. She rattled it again, but the golden orb did not budge, only taunted her with empty clicks.

Suddenly the door opened from within, and there was Adam, holding a No Vacancy sign in his hand, without his jacket. Alice had never seen him in his shirtsleeves before, as he had a perpetual chill owing to his thinness, but now his cuffs were pushed up to his elbows. His eyes widened at the sight of her, but the lids fell back into a droop almost immediately, as if they had grown too heavy for the muscles to support. It was common for his eyes to be red, but Alice saw that they were damp, too, and her heart fell into her stomach.

"Alice." The exhaustion was clear in his voice as well. "Where have you been?"

Alice grabbed his arm. "Eleanor?"

As if in reply, the keening came: an uncontrolled wail that decrescendoed into breathless sobbing. Adam tried to say something, but could only nod. Despite the hours of knowing and her efforts to prepare herself on the train, Alice felt as if she would melt with grief.

"The diphtheria...are the other children sick, too? I thought Thea was planning to dose them with that throat-coat before it got much closer..."

"She gave it to Eleanor last night, but the diphtheria hasn't come yet. It was the cure that killed her. Thea went into the bedroom this morning and she wasn't breathing. One whiff and you could tell that tonic was full of morphine or something similar, but of course Thea wouldn't know that, being used to only herbal remedies. She never woke up."

It was Alice's turn to be speechless. Tears ran from her eyes into her open mouth, but she did not bother to brush them away. She had been mourning a child who had died of disease, not medical quackery. That peddler—if he had not stayed here to observe Alice—if Thomas had not sent him—if *she* had not stayed here...

Thomas was at fault for Eleanor's death...no, it was *her* fault.

"Neil took Francis and Ernest by rail this morning to his sister's house in South Haven—Thea is in no shape to care for them. We were going to send you, but you were nowhere to be found." He gave her a stern look. "I'm keeping the guests away for now." He tapped the sign against his leg, and Alice saw his eyes widen suddenly.

"Wait—how did you know—?"

"I saw her at the foot of my bed last night. When an apparition comes to me, I know that person has just died."

Alice fixed her gaze on Adam, willing him to absorb the information. She watched his shoulders slump, as if he had lifted a heavy pack onto his back. She made to go into the house and leave him with that thought, but Adam grabbed her arm.

"Alice." His voice was a whisper. "I don't know where you were last night, and I don't care. It is none of my business. But for God's sake, don't bring your own troubles into this house. It's too full of them as it is."

He let go of her arm and carefully hung the sign on the door. And Alice suddenly realized why Adam seemed different. He was sober.

Chastised by his request, Alice did not even pause to remove her duster or set her bag in her room. She went straight through the unnervingly silent kitchen and up the back stairs to Thea's room. The wails had dwindled to whimpers; the grief was sapping Thea's energy. Alice rapped on the door.

"Thea, it's Alice. I'm home."

The noises quieted for a moment, then continued without further acknowledgment. Alice slid down the wall and came to a seat in front of the door. She rested her head upon the wood and cried silently until she thought her head would break open.

Chapter 36

The two functioning adults in the Weissmann manor shared in the planning of Eleanor's funeral, and Adam explained the rituals of shiva—what would be expected of him, of Alice, of Maudie, of Thea. Alice coaxed Thea into a black dress as she might a child, and she and Adam took Thea in the buggy to the temple. Alice could not remember much of the service, partly because she did not understand Hebrew, and partly because her head throbbed throughout from crying and from the cloying, morbid smell of lilies. If it had been lilac season, she would have demanded that purple sprays decorate the little white coffin instead.

After the funeral, the community walked Thea around the block. They came into the house bearing dishes of all shapes and sizes. Ever-responsible Maudie tried to help by directing guests to the kitchen and then to the parlor, but it was not long until Alice saw her begin to tremble. Alice sent her to the nursery with a slice of strudel and took over front door duties while Adam sat with Thea in the parlor. A torn black ribbon was pinned to Thea's breast; she wore cloth slippers in place of her usual boots. She wore her hair down, letting it form a golden curtain around her, though it grew limp with grease as the week progressed.

Thea occasionally spoke in soft tones to those who came to sit with her, but often she sat in silence with her eyes closed; sometimes tears streamed down her face, sometimes she let out soft moans. The visitors cried with her, held her hand, spoke well of Eleanor. They never offered platitudes or told her to be strong. Alice had never liked how Christian mourners insisted that the deceased had "gone on to a better place." Eleanor belonged here, with her mother, and none of the visitors would try to convince Thea otherwise.

During the course of the next week, women came during the day, bearing more food. Always food. The men came after work, hats in their hands, expressing hope that the dishes their wives had prepared had been satisfactory. While waiting for Thea to engage them in conversation, visitors took the opportunity to welcome Adam back to Kalamazoo, asking if he had another year at the university. Adam smiled at the innocents and said yes, one more year. Alice they weren't sure what to do with—was she Adam's betrothed? No—her crepe was not fine enough, and she wore no jewelry. Perhaps she was a cousin. No one asked. It was just as well, for Alice had no idea how to explain her presence in the household.

Alice tried to work with Edward in the mornings now, being too tired to bring pen to paper at night. He was seemingly unaware of what had happened, and Alice preferred to keep him ignorant of the situation. He had his own mourning to do, expressed in the portraits that Alice continued to pen for him.

Three mornings into this routine, before sitting down at her desk, Alice found that a note had been slipped under her door.

I understand if you do not wish to meet this morning, but I find that adhering to my routine is the only way I can keep myself from remembering that everything is different now. Also, I have a particular favor to ask of you. Adam.

The house was always rather calm in the early morning, but now there was no bready smell wafting up from the kitchen, no little feet pattering in pursuit of a forgotten schoolbook, no older gentleman guest talking to himself. She supposed the house would always feel like this if Adam had never invited Thea and her family to occupy it.

Hoping to pass through the kitchen as quickly as possible, to avoid the memory of little hands covered in flour and doll conversations in the corner, Alice was startled to see someone standing there, regarding a glossy loaf of challah bread. Adam looked up at Alice with the sheepish grin of a child with his thumb in the pie. "It is so lovely, I hardly want to cut it."

"Well, I am certain that there will be more today, judging from the rate at which food continues to appear." Alice took the loaf and lopped off two thick slices. "Someone brought a lovely jam yesterday—here, I'll fetch it."

Adam's first slice was gone before Alice had even touched hers; she cut him another, choosing to refrain from comment on his returned appetite. After his third slice had disappeared, Adam stood up and nodded to Alice; she took her last bite and followed him out to the office.

She had not been in the little house through the garden for several days now, and was somehow surprised to see it unchanged. Why she thought anything would be different, she wasn't sure. Adam was not one for redecoration, or even rearrangement; every book and pile of notes had its place, and it unnerved him to see anything out of order.

But when Adam crossed to his desk, Alice realized that something *had* changed—there were no special cards on her desk, and in their place were a few sheets of looseleaf, a pen and ink bottle, and some sharpened pencils. She had correctly surmised what the particular favor was.

Adam pulled out her chair for her. "I didn't know if you preferred pen or pencil."

"Generally pencil," said Alice, taking a seat. "The consistency of ink is somewhat erratic in subzero temperatures." She looked at Adam to see his reaction to her comment, but he merely nodded.

"I take it you've had more correspondence with him than of which I am aware."

"Yes—he has contacted me every day for more than a month now."

Adam's deliberately passive expression only made it more obvious that he was struggling to contain his emotions.

"Do you need to be alone to enter a trance?"

"What? Oh, no. I mean, I don't think so. But I haven't attempted anything like this with someone in the room." Thomas did not count, she figured.

"Well, then?" Adam made a gesture that said *Get on with it.*

Would it take longer for her to go into a trance with Adam present? At what point would he become impatient? Alice told herself that she didn't need to worry about any of this. Edward was ready to talk to Adam, and Adam was ready to listen; all she needed to do was to coax herself into a state in which Edward could take over.

Yet it took longer than she would have liked. Alice was about to make an excuse—that it was a different desk, a different set of writing materials, or perhaps Adam's presence was disruptive after all—when the little finger on her right hand twitched slightly. Then her ring finger went slightly numb. The tingling spread to the rest of her fingers, the palm, the wrist, then suddenly vanished. When the hand was no longer under her control, Alice watched the fingers adjust themselves around the pen and touch nib to paper—at first it created only a bleeding black dot, then it began to scratch letters.

Adam. If you are ready to listen, I have some favors to ask of you.

"Yes, Edward." Out of the corner of her eye, Alice saw that Adam was leaning forward in his chair, as if listening to the written message. He folded his quaking hands in his lap. Her hand pressed on.

I have already set aside some money for a man who survives the expedition to visit and console my mother, and some for any survivors to indulge themselves on the journey home. Also some money for the families of the two Esquimaux men who were such excellent guides. I am afraid that in the rush to compensate the families of the white men, they will be forgotten.

"Of course."

If no one should return from the expedition—if the rescuers should not find the camp in time, or at all, I ask that you look after my mother in my absence. I hope it gives her the feeling that I am with her still, and will always make sure she has the best of care.

"Yes, yes." Adam's head bobbed almost spastically in Alice's peripheral vision, like a scarecrow whose stuffed head had worked itself loose from the stake.

And if you could call on Professor Harrington in Ann Arbor—I am certain, being the man that he is, that he will feel some guilt for nominating me for this position. But you must assure him that I feel only gratitude for his consideration, and for this opportunity. Please tell him that I had intentions to return and continue my studies, with the hope of becoming a professor of astronomy some day.

Alice tried to imagine how this instructor who had so endeared himself to Edward felt about sending his protégé on such a dangerous mission, and how he would react to the news that Edward would not be coming home alive. Certainly her father must have star students, but he never mentioned them by name or noted their distinction. She thought that Professor Harrington, in contrast, sounded like the type who would boast of his best students to his wife and children.

And, most importantly, I have been working on a project with Miss Boyden, one in which you will play an essential role. I determined that while I had a willing scribe, I should pay some tribute to the men with whom I spent the last three years of my life. I do not want their sacrifices to be forgotten. And I have a plan for how you should get it into the right hands.

If my body is recovered, I expect that my mother will send some of my friends east to accompany the coffin back to Kalamazoo. You will no doubt be one of them, Adam. Presumably then you would have the opportunity to hide the notebook amongst other artifacts from the expedition. Miss Boyden writes in the same sort of notebook I brought with me, and she writes in my hand. I doubt it would arouse any suspicion of being a forgery, as long as you are clever in how you plant it. And I know you are clever.

Adam did not readily assent to this as he had to the other requests. He sat silently for several minutes, leading Alice to wonder if he had somehow, in this intense scene, fallen asleep or fainted.

"How did you die?" This came as almost a whisper. The question escaped in a breathless tone suggesting that after his two-word responses, four words had proven exhausting.

Some time in May I had resigned myself to the fact that I was going to die. I had already written a farewell letter to my mother on the 6th, when a violent storm kept us all inside during the morning. But Ralston's passing, while he lay between Lieutenant Greely and me in the sleeping bag, brought death to such an immediate point...soon after that, I made it clear to Greely that I had precious little time remaining. Like a glutton, I begged for soothing rum that might have better served one in superior health. But I did not demand any more food than was my infinitesimal ration, comprised of so many small things—crumbles of moss, and tiny shrimps that were mostly shell.

We'd already spent months straining to spot a relief party that we were not sure even existed. I had periods of extreme apathy, when I wanted nothing better than to remain in my sleeping bag and close my eyes until the end came. Other days I was determined to keep myself occupied with measurements, and I did that until my emotions got the better of me and I collapsed into something resembling a crying fit, but my body had not enough in the way of fluids to produce tears. Towards the end I saw meals made by my mother spread out on the snow, once a perfect Passover seder of lamb and matzoh...I entreated my fellow survivors to join me: we were saved as God's faithful had been! I could not fathom why no one would come: had they all lost the will to live? Only the commander accepted my invitation, and we ate heartily, although the deprivation had robbed me of my sense of taste; everything tasted like water merely, and made my mouth cold. I told the commander, I cannot taste a thing, but I hope you are enjoying it, and as the leader of this expedition it would behoove you to keep up your strength. Commander Greely then said it was the finest meal in memory, and to compliment my mother on her skills in the kitchen, but there was a strange sadness in his eyes that I could not explain.

Alice saw Adam pulling at her arm out of the corner of her eye, but she did not feel the pressure of his grip, nor did her arm budge from its bent stance over the desk. The pencil—or the presence that drove the pencil—was determined to keep to the paper. While Adam would be the first to admit he was not particularly strong, he would have been able to twist Alice's arm under normal circumstances. But hers held fast in its position as if her bones were made of metal, and she felt nothing of his bony fingers. Adam gave up and sat down hard in his chair, whose legs screeched slightly upon impact.

And then there was the question of where Mother had gone. She had to be camped nearby in order to prepare and serve the dinner, but I could find no tracks. None of the men had seen her. One of two laughed at my question. I wasn't sure why they had to be so cruel. Surely they would want to find and keep their mothers safe if they were out in this desolate place. Perhaps they missed their mothers, or maybe moreso their wives and children. Many of the men had wives waiting for them at home, and thought of them to keep going. They wrote letters every day, some of them. I had that last letter to my mother, and I meant to destroy it when her food appeared, as I was safe and the note was no longer relevant, but I forgot in the activity of searching for her. I was prepared to go out on my own, but the commander steered me back to the shelter. Then I reasoned it was smarter for me to stay put, and then she would be able to find me again. I crawled back into my sleeping bag to wait for her, and I told Commander Greely of the other marvelous things my mother could make in her kitchen. But the talking made me tired, and so I slept. And I didn't wake up in that bag again. I had gone to the spirit world.

When I next awakened I was aware of floating above the camp. Below I saw my body quite stiff and cold. Lieutenant Greely stood over it with a Bible. I noted he read only passages from the Old Testament. He was very respectful of my beliefs in that way.

"They gave you a proper burial, then?" Adam whispered.

They have not yet buried me; I would not desire them to. They should not use up a bit of their precious strength on me, who cannot help them any longer.

I can only hope the camp will be found sometime this year, but I do not know that there will be anyone to greet the rescuers. I thought there were some nearer death than I when I last went to sleep.

"If I—if your mother—if someone had only persuaded you not to go..."

No one could have persuaded me. Of course I would have liked to make it home again, marry, have children. But I could not refuse such an opportunity—to be of real use to an important scientific program. I could use so much of what I had learned in school. Even now, knowing of the incredible physical hardships involved—clearly I, the newly minted college graduate who had spent more time on indoor than outdoor pursuits, was the weakest of the lot—the mental strain of isolation, monotony, and an uncertain future, I would still accept Commander Greely's offer. I like to think that my trek was not in vain, but will encourage a greater understanding of the Arctic. Perhaps my navigation even extended a few lives—that if they did not ultimately survive they still had time to write farewell letters to their families. Of course, it's easy to think of what might have been, now that one outcome has already been established. But I consider my life if I had turned the commander down. I think I would have been tortured by the might-have-beens. Even if the expedition had ended up in the same predicament, or worse, I would have been at home, wondering if my skills could possibly had done anything to help. No—my choice to join the expedition was the right one, and I do not regret it.

"I will help you in any way I can," said Adam, his voice full of tears. "You are my friend and I love you." Alice felt the sudden urge to wrap her arms around Adam and comfort him, but her muscles were not yet her own, and she sat there like someone Midas had touched, gilded by the trance.

Adam stood then and paced around the office, in and out of Alice's field of vision. She expected a sentiment in return from Edward, but her hand was still. Behind her, she heard one sob, and Adam's measured steps came more quickly.

The door slammed, jolting her from her trance. Her body went into spasms, as if someone had dunked her in a tub of ice-cold water.

Her fingers splayed suddenly and dropped the pencil, which rolled off the desk and landed with a hollow plink on the floor. Only then did her arm begin to throb. Having regained physical control, she rolled up the sleeve of her dress to find the pink impressions of Adam's bony fingers, like drops of blood seeping into snow.

That evening, Edward was slow to respond to her preparation for a trance, and Alice wondered if she had worn him out for the day, or if he was upset about Adam's reaction. She hoped he was only conscious of Adam's words, and not of his subsequent flight and seclusion. But just as she was about to give up, her hand took on that now-familiar tingle. It wrote four words, then froze at the punctuation.

We have been found.

Alice felt an ache in her chest. "How many are alive?"

Seven remain.

Alice heard the thump of the brass knocker on the front door while she was scrubbing a dish clean of noodle kugel remnants. She ignored it at first, but a second knock spurred her to dry her hands. Surely no one would call on Thea this early in the morning; it must be someone looking for lodging. Did they not notice the sign?

The third knock had begun by the time she pulled the door open. "We've no vacancies," Alice started to say, trying not to snap at the persistent visitor, but then she realized who was standing on the step: Neil, his hair bright in the sun and in contrast with a somber suit; Francis and Ernest dressed in new mourning garb.

"It seems as if Adam did not tell you we were coming back today," said Neil.

"No, he did not," said Alice. "I have not seen Adam today." He had avoided her ever since Edward had addressed him, even going so far as to hide when he heard her coming, and leaving her and Maudie to greet visitors and attend Thea.

Looking at him there in unfamiliar dark clothing, Alice realized that her heart had ached to see Neil more than she had realized, and an ordinary reply was her only defense against breaking down and jumping into his arms. But then she looked down at the boys, wondering if her response had affected them. Both stared blankly ahead, as if they had adopted Maudie's serious manner. Although it was their house, with their mother and sister inside, they waited on the step as if wanting an invitation.

To keep herself from embracing Neil, Alice bent down and wrapped her arms around the pair. Stiff at first, their bodies seemed to relax. Little Ernest put his head on Alice's shoulder, and she cupped her hand around the crown of his blond head. "Your mother has missed you very much. She will be happy to see you."

She released them, and it was as if that had given them license to go inside, for they filed in, leaving Alice to face the last arrival. She waited in the doorway, trying to make her face look as if it were open to an apology. After all, he had called after her as she stormed out, and after a week of separation, wouldn't he want to admit his wrongness?

But he simply stared at her coldly and walked by her into the house.

It was as if he had stuck a knife in her chest as he passed. She could not physically draw breath for a few moments, staring open-mouthed as if her lifeblood were spilling out on the stoop.

Once the steady stream of food from the community had slowed, meal preparation and clean-up proved to be an excellent outlet for Alice's frustration and grief. She kneaded bread furiously in the morning, chose dishes that required plenty of chopping for luncheon and dinner, and scrubbed the crustiest of pots. Her hands, the moisture sucked out of them, bloomed with red splotches and broke open at the knuckles. Alice rubbed lanolin into them at night—since she was sleeping alone, the strong smell of oily sheep's wool smell.

Maudie fetched Neil for dinner and served him at Alice's request. The three children ate perched on stools in the kitchen, as they often did under their mother's auspices. Neil was civil and thanked Alice when she took the plate away, but he did not look at her. Her heart screamed for just one tender glance.

Once the children had finished with their meal, they gave their dishes a preliminary scrub and filed up the back stairs to the nursery. Alice would check on them once she had completed her tidying in the kitchen, but sometimes the cleaning would take longer than she thought, and the children would be nodding over their books and games by the time she had hung up her apron. Once she found Ernest curled up on the nursery floor, sound asleep. Alice gathered him into her arms, trying not to grunt under his surprising six-year-old heft, and managed to tuck him into bed without waking him.

With no visitors to greet, Thea had been keeping to her room. Alice prepared plates of food for her and brought them up on trays, trying to repay the kindnesses Thea had shown her. As Alice removed a dinner tray one evening, she heard a faint voice from behind the door.

"Alice?"

The voice sounded rusty from disuse or tears or both. "Yes? Do you want me to come in?"

"Please."

Alice left the tray in the hall and opened the door to reveal a slouching Thea propped up in bed like an invalid. While she had still not washed her hair, at least it was tidy, gathered into a long braid.

Thea smiled faintly. "I asked you in because I have an apology to make, and also a favor to ask—so I'll confess first, and then you may decide whether you'll consider my favor." She gestured toward a chair in the corner, which Alice brought to the bedside.

"What's wrong, Thea?"

Thea hung her head. "I admit to eavesdropping on some of your conversations with Neil."

"Oh." Alice wanted to laugh—both she and Neil were well aware of Thea's curious ears, and so spoke of more private matters in soft tones. But perhaps Thea's hearing was better than she thought—and she looked so solemn that Alice dared not make a joke of it.

"It's only that—well, I took such an interest in your relationship...I wanted to hear how it was progressing..."

You could have asked me, thought Alice, but she simply said, "It's all right, Thea."

"Once I heard you discussing spirit communication—legitimate spirit communication, not what Mr. Holloway practiced. You said that you were in contact with someone, and that Adam would not accept that person's death."

"Yes, that's right." Alice paused, thought, and figured Thea's knowing would do no harm. "It's Edward Israel I'm helping."

Thea nodded, her eyes sad. "I guessed it was. Adam has missed him these three years, and I could not think of any other classmate or friend to whom he was so attached. Ed is—was—one of his oldest friends. I can imagine he'd have some reluctance to letting him go.

"But to my request. I know I have expressed skepticism of spiritualism in the past, but..." Her voice wavered as if it had lost its footing; once it had regained its balance, she resumed. "I would do anything to speak with her again."

Thea looked at Alice hopefully, awaiting a response. Alice felt as if she had been ambushed. "I have not communicated with anyone but Edward in some time, and I cannot predict the outcome," she replied. "We might receive nothing."

"I think you are too modest," said Thea, taking Alice's hand and giving it a little squeeze. She smiled at Alice, but Alice felt the nervous tremble in her hands.

"I may not be the right medium for the job," Alice hedged. "I am a spirit-writer—and Eleanor could barely write. Even if I am able to make contact with her, she may not be able to communicate."

Thea shook her head furiously. "Then see if she can speak through you. And I would not trust another medium. Even if you tell me of her presence, I think I will derive comfort from that." She held her hands out on the counterpane and closed her eyes. "Is this how it goes?" she asked.

You might make something up, and she would never know, said a little voice in Alice's head. *You know Eleanor well enough. You could easily say something she would say.*

She stared at Thea, whose shut eyes were dripping tears, her hands trembling in front of her. And suddenly she understood the sort of temptation Thomas had faced, and how someone with a sympathetic heart—or a ruthless one—could be motivated to dissemble night after night for clients in desperate despair. How he could have convinced himself that dissembling was better than disappointing people.

Alice took a deep breath. "I will try my best, but I cannot promise anything. Do you understand?"

"And will you lock the door?" Thea asked, already focused on her hope. *Against whom?* Alice wondered, but she obeyed.

Alice wiped her sweating palms on her skirt before taking Thea's hands in her own. How theirs had reversed—Alice's red and wrinkly from washing and cooking, Thea's white and smooth from the unprecedented break in domestic labor. Yet Thea's showed their age more than ever now—knuckles bony, veins blue-green and bulging beneath the skin.

"I want to know if she forgives me," Thea murmured.

"Forgives you? For what?"

"For poisoning her."

Alice's guilt weighed inside her like a boulder. Again, if Thomas had not been looking for her...but she could not unburden herself to anyone, for to do so would be to admit the reappearance of Thomas. Their dinner in Detroit seemed months ago, and she could not conjure up even a seed of the affection that had bloomed again that night.

"Thea. You gave her the medicine because you wanted to protect her. Her spirit cannot hold that against you." *If there is anyone to blame, it is me,* she thought.

"But you don't know that, do you?" snapped Thea. "You've not even bothered to consult with her."

Thea did not seem as if she were in a state of reason, so Alice did not answer. They sat in silence, eyes closed, for maybe ten minutes, but Alice felt no tingle in her hand, no itching for a pen and paper, no enveloping fog that would usher her into a trance. She opened one eye slightly and looked at Thea. The housekeeper was breathing deeply, eyes wrinkled shut in a squint Alice thought looked painful to maintain for such a period of time.

The sharp knocks startled Alice, and for a moment she thought it was Eleanor, ready to communicate through rapping. It took her a moment to realize that the sound was coming not from the walls or the bedside table, but from the door.

"Mama?"

Thea squeezed Alice's hand as if she would break it. "Eleanor! Eleanor, Mama's here!"

But Alice knew that voice; it was not Eleanor, but Ernest, his question full of tears. Alice expected Thea to realize this, to jump up from bed to see what was wrong. But Thea held Alice's hands as tightly as ever, and said nothing.

The knob clicked but the door did not open, the lock holding fast.

"Mama, I've had a bad dream. Please, I want to come in."

Only silence from Thea.

"Thea," Alice hissed, not caring to keep the ruse of concentration. "Ernest needs you."

"I want to hear from Eleanor," said Thea, her voice devoid of concern.

"We will try again later. I'm not receiving anything—"

"Ma-ma!" The first syllable shrill, the second sinking into despondent. Alice wrested her hands from Thea's grip and rushed to unlock the door. No sooner had she turned the key than Ernest pushed into the room. Blinded by tears, he at first rushed toward the dresser; then, spying his mother in bed, threw himself at her side and tried to put his head in her lap.

Thea did not look at him as she pushed him away, and Ernest fell to the floor with a little yelp.

"How dare you interrupt me!"

Alice had never heard Thea speak to her children—or anyone else, for that matter—in such a tone. Even when they were naughty, her scoldings were tempered by a good-natured request for better conduct. And if one of them so much as squeaked, Thea was there with whatever treatment was needed, be it a bandage or some warm milk.

His mother's reaction stunned Ernest into silence, but soon enough he began to whimper and hiccup. Alice helped him off the floor, although he dragged like a dead weight and did not offer any assistance. She gritted her teeth as she carried him down the hallway, being careful not to catch her toe on a curled-up rug.

Alice's heart raced with exertion and anger together. How could Thea ignore a living child in favor of a dead one?

The news came to town the next day, while Alice was at the market, gathering up the components of meals for seven. When she approached the potato barrels, she came upon the conversation of two older ladies whose deaf ears must have convinced them that they were whispering.

"Poor Tilly! Though, I assume the family must have been bracing themselves."

"Still, to lose a child in that way, and one so promising! Why, he wasn't even twenty-five."

Quietly, Alice abandoned her items by a box of apples and walked out, digging her fingernails into her palms to keep herself silent. She had known of his death for a month and a half, and still the official word rent a new hole in her stomach. But no one could deny it now.

Edward was finally coming home.

Chapter 37

As she returned empty-handed to the house, Alice realized that none of her housemates were likely to have heard the news. Was it then her responsibility to bear the bad tidings? The proper phrasing of it suddenly seemed the greatest challenge. But they already knew that Edward was dead—how startling could it be?

Perhaps she needn't say anything just yet. First she would go into the kitchen and see what sort of lunch she could create from the meager pantry offerings she had hoped to supplement today; she could also conquer the breakfast dishes she left to soak in the sink. But she opened the door to find Thea already preparing lunch, whipping something with vigor, the dishes cleaned and dried. Ernest jabbered away to his mother, a push of his chubby fingers providing the fuel for a small metal locomotive. Its bright, unchipped paint made Alice think it a gift from Neil or his aunt during their time away, for the nursery toys tended to show the effects of time and rough love.

Thea looked up at Alice with a weak smile. "I thought it time that I spell you in the kitchen. And I promised Ernest I would make his favorite for lunch."

"Cheese soo-flay," Ernest clarified, taking extra care over the words. He made a whistling sound. "South Haven," he said in a voice as low as he could muster, trying to mimic the confident rumble of a conductor.

Ernest seemed to be suffering no ill effects from yesterday's neglect, so Alice resolved to avoid mentioning the whole ordeal. But then Thea seized her son and hugged him to her; Ernest bore the embrace, but his eyes remained fixed on the train, and he returned to his role as conductor as soon as he was released. Alice watched this with horror, and Thea must have noticed her expression, for she came over and said in a low voice, "It's not unusual for a boy who is almost six to avoid shows of affection, if it is not of his choosing."

And Thea had already raised one boy to age eight. Alice smiled, quite embarrassed by her lack of understanding about children. At least she had her own experience as a girl-child to draw upon when trying to understand the actions of Maudie and—a lump gathered in her throat—Eleanor. Boys were still a mystery. She told herself to observe the children more closely in future months, so that she would better know what to expect from either sex.

"Well, I'm sorry not to clean up after breakfast," said Alice, "but I wanted to go to market on the early side, in anticipation of making dinner."

Too late she realized she had nothing to show for her trip. Thea looked questioningly at her empty hands. The news was there in Alice's mouth, ready to be spread, but still she could not say it. "Strangely crowded for the time of day," she lied. "And too hot to endure such a crowd. I thought I would return later in the afternoon, when it might have thinned somewhat."

Thea looked at the sunshine blazing through the window. "Only going to grow hotter from here. But here—I'll go after I've fixed lunch. It's been a long time since I have shopped at all. And I know of someone who likes to scoop beans, and who likes a sugar-stick for his efforts." She looked slyly at Ernest, who stared at her with his mouth a big O.

"Get your shoes, and your brother as well," she instructed, but Ernest had already collected himself and the locomotive and was making his way up the stairs to the nursery, yelling to Francis. The locomotive made an occasional whistling sound as it chugged valiantly up the sides of the stairwell walls. Thea turned to Alice. "Ernest is wanting to tie his shoes on his own now," she explained, "so it will occupy him until lunch is ready."

Alice would have protested, but Thea seemed genuinely excited at the prospect of leaving the house, and she had no real desire to face the marketplace again. There, Thea would likely hear the news herself, and surely she would share it with Adam and Neil. Alice stared out the window; from where she stood, only one white corner of the office building made itself visible. The pale pink trim and slate shingles of the roof formed the uppermost boundary of her frame of vision. She had not been there since contacting Edward for Adam.

Thea came to stand next to her, wiping her hands on her apron. "The roses are doing quite well this year."

Alice shifted her gaze from the office to the crisp greens and vivid yellows, pinks, and reds of the rose bushes. "They're lovely."

"Perhaps you could go out there and inform them of the lunch schedule?"

Inform the roses? thought Alice at first. The comical image of offering soufflé to the bushes outside amused her—but then she realized that Thea meant for her to inform Adam and Neil, and the smile vanished from her face.

"Oh, no, I'd rather not," said Alice in a small voice.

Thea put her hands on her hips. "What is the matter with you two? I assumed you must have had a spat of some kind before"—she swallowed—"before he left, but have you not managed to make amends by now?" She frowned. "Surely he did not refuse to marry you in your... situation? Or have you still not told him?"

"I told him." Alice hung her head. "He offered, but I—I was not sure I wanted to accept."

Thea tsked. "Whyever not? You love him. You'll be having a child together. Marriage certainly seems appropriate on both counts."

"You may have noticed that my first marriage, if one could call it that, did not work out," Alice said defensively. "I tried to explain my reservation, but Neil would not hear it. Bitter words were exchanged. I thought that time would have tempered the tension between us, but he has hardly looked at me since his return from South Haven. I was so glad to see him, and he looked at me like I was poisonous." Alice bit her tongue, hard—what a poor choice of words on her part.

"It sounds like one of you needs to step forward and apologize." Thea looked down and twirled a string of her apron around her finger. "Eleanor liked the thought of you two together," she said softly.

The words burned Alice like a cattle prod. Her eyes wandered to Eleanor's favorite corner. She was glad that she had thought to hide the little stool where the girl used to sit before.

Alice opened the door to the garden without further comment. She did not care if Adam were there as well. Surely he was not ignorant of the situation. And perhaps Neil would be less likely to say hurtful things in the presence of someone else.

She knocked, but received no answer. Alice pushed the door open slowly. First she noticed Neil's empty desk, then no sign of him at the bookshelves. But Adam was there, sitting in his corner. His head was on his desk, his face turned away from her; a brown bottle lay beneath his limp hand. Alice picked it up. It was empty.

Had Adam already heard the news and taken it badly, or was this just coincidentally the day of his inevitable relapse and decline? She poked his foot with her own: no response. Staring at his unconscious form and the cause of his stupor, her fists clenched. While Edward—who had an excuse to indulge in drink, thought Alice, being far from home in an unforgiving landscape, sleeping in a frozen bag on the ground perhaps—might have taken a bit of rum to dim the constant morning and dull the constant cold, Adam wasted what could have been much-needed medicine to some, all while warm and with ample food—even if he did not choose to partake of that food—at home. He had no concept of true suffering, and yet his doses implied that his whole body and soul were in pain.

"Adam? Adam!" Alice picked up the bottle and slammed it against the edge of the desk, near his head. It broke at the neck; the heavier bottom tarried on the desk, and the rest of the glass rained to the floor in shards. Adam stirred slightly and made a small noise. Alice took him by his bony shoulders and shook him as hard as she could. His spectacles, already crooked from his position on the desk, let go of one ear entirely and swung drunkenly from the other.

"You will *not* do this!" She found herself screaming, her voice cracking with the strain of the volume. "We have already had one poisoning in this house. There will *not* be another!"

Alice dug her fingers into his curls and yanked him upright in the chair. Adam groaned but still did not open his eyes. "Look at me," she demanded, and when Adam did not comply, she slapped him on the cheek. His spectacles lost their final grip and clattered to the floor. Adam let out a surprised snort, and his eyelids fluttered.

"Thea needs no one else to look after," she hissed. "And Edward is depending on you. His last wish is for you to deliver this notebook for him, and how do you think you'll get to the rescue ship now? Do you think they'll allow someone who has to carry a bottle around with him to carry the coffin of a hero? He would be ashamed of you. *I am ashamed of you.*"

"Alice?"

She turned to see Thea and Neil in the doorway, alarm on their faces. Alice realized she was panting. Untangling her fingers, she let Adam go; he fell back to the desk with a thud and another groan.

"I am done with him," she told them, and pushed past them to the garden, where she sat herself in the middle of the bench tucked amidst Thea's extensive herb collection. She looked away from the sight of Neil and Thea half-carrying, half-dragging Adam between them, and made no move to assist. Only once the three of them had disappeared into the house did she look down and realize she had cut her hand on the bottle in her frenzy, and had not felt the pain. Beads of blood trembled on an angry red scratch.

She would not help Adam, not in this state. He could only help himself.

Alice kept to her room the rest of the day, in hindsight a little embarrassed by her display of emotion. The savory smell of the cheese soufflé wafting up the stairs—miraculously, Ernest's special lunch had not been ruined by the interruption—nearly drew her from her self-imposed seclusion, but with her hand on the door handle she hesitated.

She wondered if Edward knew that the news had finally reached his hometown. It somehow made her hesitant to contact him, even though, according to Alice's count, Edward had five portraits yet to complete. Three were unsavory characters—the food thieves, Connell and Henry, and the inebriate Cross—all of whom Edward had begun to write about, but then decided that more careful consideration of his words was necessary. Then there were Pavy and Greely, the doctor and the commander, whom Edward had described as "at odds" and "complex characters." She and Edward would have perhaps two weeks to complete the notebook—although, given Adam's behavior today, Alice wondered if there was any hope for his sobriety by that time. Should she warn Edward, if he wasn't already aware of his friend's overdose?

After sitting at and rising from her desk a few times, Alice planted herself and took up the pencil. "Edward, I feel I must tell you about a possible wrench in our plans."

I know what Adam has done. I believe it was a momentary weakness of which we are all capable from time to time.

"But this is a weakness he has nursed for months," said Alice. "Are you not worried about his ability to become sober—*stay* sober?"

Adam will recover in time to fulfill his promise to me.

Alice thought of the almost impenetrable stupor in which she had found Adam, and Edward's confidence confused her. "Edward, do you know what the future holds? Do you have that ability?"

No. But I do know people and their tendencies. My situation has given me great faith in the prevalence of human integrity.

Despite knowing that Henry would gorge himself on others' rations? Alice nearly voiced this observation aloud, but realized that the comparison was not warranted. As Edward had said once, no one who had not been part of the expedition had any right to criticize its members—for how could they know that they would not have behaved the same, or worse?

Late that night, Alice woke to a strange, high-pitched sound. Worried that it was one of the children, she stumbled out of bed and into her dressing gown. Once in the hall, however, she realized that the sound was coming from the opposite direction of the servants' quarters. As she advanced toward it, a pounding came from within the walls, making her jump, and the ghostly wail increased. Alice's heart pounded as she contemplated supernatural explanations—could the ghosts of Adam's parents been summoned by the turmoil here?

"He's drying out. He may might be like this for a while."

The figure in a white sheet standing behind her made her gasp; the realization that it was Neil in his nightshirt made her stomach drop further than if she had seen a ghost. "You're not weaning him of it gradually?" she managed to say.

Neil frowned at her, and Alice realized that as a student of medicine, of course he would have thought of that. "While Thea and I were in the process of searching his room for an opium stash, to take control of it, he woke up. He told us that the bottles were all tucked in his clothes press, and asked us to dump them out. We told him that we needed to reduce his dose gradually to minimize the effects of withdrawal, but he was adamant that we pour all of it out the window. So we did. Then he told me to nail the windows shut and to lock his door."

Alice nodded but was silent. What was there to say? At last Adam was taking responsibility for his state of body and mind, but they would have to listen to him suffer through it.

"I know why you went away."

Alice was surprised by how icy her blood could turn in this stifling night. "I can explain myself..."

"How could you!" he hissed. "Without consulting me? Do you have no faith in us at all? Was the time you desired to think about the proposal really just a complete rejection?"

"No, no! I tried to explain..." Alice felt herself sinking; she wanted to melt completely, disappear into the carpet at her feet.

"I did not ask you to marry me simply because of the...situation. I want you to know that. I had—I had hoped to make you my wife eventually. But I cannot forgive what you have done..."

Suddenly Alice realized that they were not talking about the same transgression. She grabbed Neil's hands. "Oh, dear Neil. Do you think I've gone and...rid myself of the baby? No, not at all. What could have given you that idea? I—really...I—I was—"

She struggled for the words to explain herself, but suddenly found her mouth muffled, pressed into the soft fabric of Neil's dressing gown.

"It does not matter to me where you were," he whispered. "I am sorry that I thought you capable of such a thing. I was in a sad state of mind after Eleanor's death, and being away from you gave my mind license to think the worst...Even if you do not give me an answer at all, know that I will be here for you—for *both* of you."

Part of Alice protested, unsettled by the hurtful things that had twice now come out of Neil's mouth. Part of her chastised herself for her own sins, for her actions and her silence. And part of her simply settled into the hug and sighed contentedly, grateful for the protection his arms provided. She let the warmth of his embrace wash over her. The fleeting electricity of Thomas's touch was nothing compared to this.

Now that Thea had reclaimed her kitchen kingdom, Alice laughed inwardly at the idea that her own dishes were beginning to reveal dormant culinary talents. She still had no success with improvisation, was a poor hand at cakes, looked at certain ingredients from the garden with utter bewilderment, and slightly scorched every other dish. Thea, on the other hand, knew instinctively when a dish was ready to be removed from the oven, and the opening of the door never revealed anything but the perfect shade of gold or brown. The delectable dishes now emerging from the kitchen suggested a reversal of her extreme introspection. Maudie, Francis, and little Ernest no longer tiptoed around the house; the youth had been restored to the rhythm of their steps, and their chatter filled the nursery and the kitchen.

Occasional moans or delirious babblings still seeped beneath Adam's bedroom door, but the acute agonies seemed to have subsided. Alice was in a better place to pity him now; last night's reunion with Neil had tempered some of her own bitterness. She had even offered to nurse him, but Thea waved her off. Thea was the nurse in the household again, and Adam didn't want to see anyone but her—even Neil received a reprimand from the patient when he tried to enter.

When Neil gained access at last, Alice hovered around the door, listening for any cry of distress. She tried to tell herself that there was no knife in there for Adam to wield, even if he had the strength, but then she had never been inside Adam's room. He could have a fire poker, a statuette, an overlooked shard of glass from a bottle.

To her relief, Neil emerged intact, a bit pale but not bleeding as far as Alice could tell. He gently stroked Alice's hair with his good hand.

"He was asking for you."

Alice must have looked at the slightly open door with apprehension, for Neil took her hand and squeezed it. "He can hardly move," he whispered. "He won't harm you. I'm sorry I can't open the drapes to brighten the place up, but the light hurts his head."

A gentle push on the small of her back helped Alice move forward and push the door open. But the heat and the smell nearly drove her back. Entering with squinted eyes, her first impulse was to open a window, but the sash wouldn't budge. Then she remembered that Neil had taken nails and a hammer to them upon Adam's request.

"Otherwise I might have leapt out the window and eaten the laudanum-soaked dirt." Adam feebly waved a hand toward the window, seeing her futile efforts. "After Eleanor's death, I forced myself to decrease my dose, and—you saw—I had more of an appetite, and few ill effects." His face had gone sallow and gray at once, making the skin look like a faded bruise. "Faced with the task that Ed had given me, I gave myself a little extra for fortitude. And a little more. Then I heard the news that

Ed's body had been found, and I drank the whole bottle before I knew what I was doing."

"But why did you want to stop all at once?" Alice found if she took deep breaths through her mouth and not her nose, she felt less nausea from the miasma that emanated from the bed. "You didn't have to. Neil could have measured out a decreased dosage for you."

Adam gazed beyond her to the closed windows. "Penance, I suppose? A desire to rid myself completely of the stuff before I paid a visit to Mrs. Israel? Maybe I thought that the sorrow of the past week would flow out with the drug.

"I realize that for someone who professed to be researching supernatural phenomena, my reaction to your communications with Ed did not make sense. But it was just..." He swallowed, and Alice thought she could hear the rasp of his dry throat. "But Ed was a dear friend, and my friends are few. You may have noticed that my prickly demeanor does not lend itself to social grace. Without Ed to bridge the gap between my attitude and the college community, I was the island that Donne spoke of."

"It's all right," said Alice, and she patted his hand, forgiving him a little dramatic expression. "You have a chance to redeem yourself now."

She heard a throat clear behind her, and looked to see Neil in the doorway, a hammer in his hand. He gestured toward the window. "Isn't it time, Adam?"

"Yes," Adam replied. He held Alice's gaze as he said it.

Four days later, scrubbed and shaven, Adam went to pay a visit to the Israel family. The fine suit tailored to his already thin build hung from a now skeletal frame, and his pallor had not subsided much, but Alice assumed that if anyone asked, he could attribute it to the shock of losing his friend.

Not long after Alice and Neil had sat down to lunch, Adam came into the dining room with a little more color in his visage and a half-smile wrinkling his cheeks. As had been expected, Mrs. Israel had asked Adam to travel to New York with several of Ed's college friends and accompany the coffin back to Kalamazoo. He would leave in a week, with the notebook in hand.

The next few days were a blur of preparation. Alice wrote down Edward's remaining portraits and scuffed the corners and cover of the notebook, to make its supposed trip to the Arctic and back more feasible. Thea considered it her personal duty to fatten Adam up for the journey; there were plenty of meats, potatoes, pies on the menu. Adam still ate sparingly and avoided breakfast, but Alice and Neil took full advantage of the bounty. Alice wondered if she owed the increasing snugness of her dresses to the baby or to Thea's return to the kitchen.

The morning that Adam was scheduled to leave, Alice moved tentatively, walking around the bedroom in her nightdress, moving her gaze from side to side. Nothing. She sat at her desk, put her head down as if to read, then looked up at the ceiling. Nothing. She thought of food, and the only reaction was...hunger. She clapped her hands together with relief.

"What? What's wrong?" Neil cried, sitting up and looking around in confusion.

"Nothing is wrong," said Alice, and she gave him a big kiss on the cheek. "That's the lovely thing. How would you like griddle-cakes for breakfast?"

Neil kept her company as she measured, mixed, and poured, despite the fact that the stove turned the already warm kitchen into a larger furnace; when he thought she wasn't looking, he pulled a handkerchief from his pocket and gave his brow a quick swipe. Alice was so pleased by the continued absence of nausea that she sweated almost happily.

The moment she had finished, sleepy little ones began to trickle down the back stairs, lured by the smell of cakes and syrup. Alice doled out the golden disks to each according to their size. Their mother followed soon after, rubbing her eyes.

"I don't believe I've had such a sleep in some weeks." She looked sheepishly at the three children tucking into their breakfasts. "I'm sorry to be so late. Here you are, thinking I'm back in commission..."

"I'm happy to," Alice assured her. "I'm feeling well this morning."

Thea's eyes widened. "That's wonderful." She looked at the adults' portion of griddle cakes. "And we will all benefit from your continued good health, I think."

Alice smiled as she prepared plates for herself, Thea, and Neil.

"Is there enough for a fourth?"

She looked up to see Adam in the doorway, his eyebrows raised. "I figure I should have proper nourishment for my journey."

Adam took small bites but smiled a little after each one. Alice savored her first proper breakfast in weeks, finding and welcoming a new taste in every bite: the salt in the butter, the sugar in the syrup, the crisp outside and fluffy inside of the cakes themselves. Thea gave Alice a compliment a minute.

"They're only pancakes," Alice laughed. "They don't hold a candle to one of your pies."

"They're lovely," said Thea. "You've been a quick study, for someone who wasn't quite sure how best to crack an egg in March."

Someone tittered, and Alice looked over at Neil, who quickly wiped the smile from his face. But the emerging laughter was coming from Adam.

"Remember when you forgot to add yeast to the bread, and it yielded tiny loaves like rocks, and you tried to pretend you had meant to make unleavened bread, because it was Passover time?"

Thea badly masked a giggle behind her hand. Alice felt embarrassed, but when Neil chuckled and kissed her on the cheek, she couldn't help but join in. The ridicule grew to include a few brandy-fueled mishaps of Neil's and a time when Adam, trying to sneak a small meal in the middle of the night, managed to pull a shelf down on himself, waking the entire house. They continued until someone noticed the hour, and all went mute. It was time to take Adam to the train.

Alice wondered if this was what it must be like to send a child off to school for the first time. The temperature reminded them that summer was not over yet, however; the leaves that the warm wind rustled still clung to their branches, too green to let go that easily. She must have asked Adam several times if he had the notebook. To his credit, Adam did not once roll his eyes in response, but confirmed that he did have it tucked safely in his pack. He had even worked out a plan for the planting of the notebook: there was to be a religious service after the coffins were brought off the boat, and he would excuse himself during some New Testament reading. Of course, the actual placement would be dependent on the setup; if no crate or pile of belongings and artifacts was obvious, it would have to be placed where someone would see it and assume it fell from a pouch or a pocket.

Adam and the other pallbearers were taking the train east together, all of them from Kalamazoo except for two Grand Rapids classmates who would have already boarded the agreed-upon fourth car. Aware of their somber mission, the conductor allowed the train to sit in the station for longer than usual while their families bid them a safe and peaceful passage.

A florist had donated white rose boutonnieres for the contingent, and the wives, sisters, and mothers of the young men pinned them to black lapels, staying to fuss over ties and tuck black-edged handkerchiefs into pockets. Several of the women pulled out their own and dabbed their noses and eyes. Adam glanced at Alice when the flowers and pins were produced, but she demurred and urged Thea forward, preferring to hide in the circle of siblings and friends.

At first Alice had not realized the identity of the woman standing off to the side, assuming her to be an auxiliary relative of one of the pallbearers since she did not come forward like the other women. But then Alice saw that the teenage boy beside her was Goddy Israel.

As if she had just donned a pair of spectacles, the women around the shop clerk came into focus. Goddy and a young woman around Alice's age—who must be Edward's sister Lillie—each held one arm of the gently rounded matron, small and fair like her son. A girl of about thirteen stood behind them, looking fearful, or perhaps simply overwhelmed. Although Mrs. Israel's eyes were dry, grief contorted her face as she regarded the scene. Alice could only imagine what Edward's mother was thinking: *These boys are all alive. Why is mine not?*

Once the set of rose-pinners had stepped back, Lillie and Goddy led their mother forward, Mollie trailing behind. Alice smiled to see that Lillie had a tiny rosette of maize and blue in place of a brooch at her collar. Perhaps she wore the colors of the university in honor of her brother—but Alice remembered, as she took in Lillie's modern hairdo and confident air, that she was a college girl herself.

The eight men bowed their heads, and Mrs. Israel, in a wavering but melodic tone, began to give what Alice assumed was some sort of blessing in Yiddish or Hebrew. But however incomprehensible the actual words, the sentiment was clear. Adam's eyes were shining by the time he raised his head.

No one spoke as they walked home from the station, almost as if they had agreed upon silence in advance. Lunch occupied them for a time, but then they found themselves staring blankly at empty plates, unsure how to proceed with the day. Alice herself spent the afternoon around the house, engrossed in thoughts and meaningless activities she could not even remember an hour later. Seeing the dazed looks on Thea's and Neil's faces at dinner, she assumed that they had passed the day in much the same state.

After dinner, Alice fought off the urge to go to bed for some time before Neil suggested it. Thea's knowledge of their relationship and the lack of boarders meant they could enter Neil's bedroom simultaneously. No need to pause and listen for footsteps, no spaced-out retirings. But after twenty minutes of Neil's restless fidgeting beside her, Alice almost wished she had been given the opportunity for a head start.

"What's the matter?" she murmured, her eyes still shut in case a wave of exhaustion were to come and drown the disturbance. Alice's eyes had been trying to close for an hour, and she was grateful that she now had leave to fulfill their wish.

"Adam has hardly been out of my sight since last Christmas," said Neil. "I catch myself worrying what he's up to."

"I'm sure he'll be on his best behavior." Alice patted the forearm draped over her.

"He caught me searching his trunk for bottles before he left." Neil shifted his weight in the bed yet again. "He actually pushed me away and sat on the lid like a petulant child. I reminded him that he had only been sober for two weeks, and that was not quite enough time to make up for a year of mistrust. He let me continue then, but I found nothing."

"I would hope that being caught with a laudanum bottle among Edward's other friends would be too shameful a situation to consider," said Alice.

Edward. For all that her activity centered around him, Alice had not actually considered the possibility that he would not write her once the portraits were complete. His task was done; he had no need to continue using Alice as a conduit.

But surely he would have said goodbye?

Alice sat straight up in bed, and her tiredness fell away from her.

"I forgot to do something."

"What's that?" Neil yawned, having caught some of Alice's cast-off exhaustion. "Can't it wait until tomorrow?"

"No, no," Alice flung off the bedclothes, closing her ears against any protest from the bed as she hurried out the door and down the hall to her chamber. Her fingers quaked as they locked the door, turned the gaslamp key, searched for loose paper in her desk. What if he didn't answer her? What if the connection was broken, and he was gone for good? She was almost afraid to put the pencil to the paper. He was her friend, her confidant. She did not want to lose him.

"Edward, are you there?" Almost immediately, her hand jerked into a different grip.

Yes.

Tears of relief came to Alice's eyes. "We sent Adam today with the notebook. He'll be in New York Friday—two days from now," she added, remembering that Edward would have no sense of the calendar.

Yes, I know. The mortal world has been coming to me in flashes, sometimes before or after I talk to you. Sometimes when I am thinking about life the least. It is as if whatever electricity or force or what-have-you that connects us does not want me to become comfortable in death. It wants to remind me about all that I am missing. And that is indescribably painful. It is like dying all over again—leaving me in denial about my state, convinced that if I could just manage a deep breath, if I could reach forward and part the curtain between worlds, I could return. But I cannot ever return.

I believe, though, that I can be content here if I let go of the world my body left in May. I think there are friends, my father, waiting for me to do so before I am able to join them.

Alice sank her teeth into her bottom lip, wanting the physical pain to supersede the emotional. Could Edward see her now? Did he realize the grief he was causing her?

I am at peace, knowing I was able to do one more good deed. But now I think I have taken up enough of your time. I cannot thank you enough for your help.

"No, not at all! I have been so glad to help you with the task..."

But he did not seem to hear her; the pencil continued.

When I was dying, my addled brain came to rest upon one primary hope: that the heavens held as many auroras as we saw from below. I thought I could be happy in a world where such beauty was abundant. I confess I was disappointed to arrive here and see nothing of the kind; but then, I do not think I am in Heaven per se. It is something different than I had imagined. Occasionally I have seen flashes of color, and I think, oh, perhaps that is Heaven over that way. But I follow the flickers and they come to nothing. Just recently, however, I followed them again, and I saw a glimpse of other spirits. They looked like ordinary people, but somehow I knew they were like me, and that I should be with them.

"At least stay with me a few more days," Alice blurted. "While Adam is gone. I realize the incredible selfishness of what I ask, but..." She dropped off, unable to say anything that would justify such a request, and already feeling ashamed for voicing it.

Alice. I have enjoyed your company more than you can imagine. But I know for a fact that there are living, breathing people who deserve your time. Two in this house. One in particular.

Alice felt herself blush. She could not argue with him about spending time with the living, although her heart resisted admitting it. She tried to swallow a sob so that she could respond.

"I will always remember you, Edward. Always." The last syllable made it out before her face folded in upon itself and a sort of mewing sound made its way out of her mouth.

And I you. I hope to meet you in person—in spirit, I suppose!—one day, but not for a long time. You have a beautiful life ahead of you. Perhaps you can live it for the both of us.

There was something else Alice wanted to say, but her hand went slack before she could compose herself to speak again. Fingers shaking, she ran their tips across his last directive. She could say it once—mouth it once, and then she, too, should let go. Her lips formed three words, and that was that.

Somehow that act helped Alice take a deep breath. Edward was released, she was released. Now she felt as if she could say those words to someone else. She headed back to Neil's room, to rejoin the living.

Chapter 38

The day of the funeral, Alice felt weaker than she had in a long time. A syrupy sloth had overcome the vitality she had taken for granted for the past several months, and the sugar of immobility was crystallizing in her joints, making them stick and crack. A dull headache had settled on her head like a loose hat. The heat certainly did not help matters, bringing with it a low-hanging cloud of humidity that threatened anyone who stepped outside with suffocation.

She and Thea walked to the station together to await the train's arrival at 1:45. They had considered taking the buggy, but its black fabric only made it into a mobile oven, and at least on foot they had some chance of catching a wayward breeze. Neil had excused himself, promising to meet them at the Israels' during viewing hours later that afternoon. At first Alice couldn't imagine what could be so important as to make him miss the start of the ceremonies, but then she realized that Neil must have recognized this to be a private sorrow of hers.

As Alice overheated in the crush of people, who were waiting for the train in remarkable quiet, a little bubble of annoyance within her burst into anger. How many of these people were truly acquaintances of Edward? How many were here for the caché, hoping to tell their descendants that "yes, I met the train the day that Edward Israel was brought home." Wasn't it in everyone's best interest to attend a funeral hosted by one of the wealthiest families in town? Common sense told her that many of these people had known Edward, at least slightly, and by default longer than she had. But Alice, consciously selfish in her grief, resented waiting among the masses of people who had not spoken to him, and probably not much thought of him, in years.

And all the crêpe! Alice accepted that the household wore black skirts and shawls for Eleanor. She would have preferred gray and lavender, because she knew Eleanor liked purple, but no one in the house had made a move to the next stage of mourning. And with the July announcement, there was no cause to. But with Eleanor, there was a clearer division between life and death. Alive, Eleanor ran around the house, chatted with her doll, tugged at her mother's skirt. Dead she did none of those things. As much as Thea had wanted her residual presence, Alice had not had any sign that part of Eleanor remained on their side of the veil. Conversely, her relationship with Edward *began* when he died. It did not make *sense* to wear black for Edward.

A whistle sounded in the distance, and the train's rumble preceded it along the tracks. Some people jumped at the sudden rush of noise. Alice wondered if the murmurs that rippled through them formed a discussion of the appropriate reaction: should they cheer and clap for their hero, come home at last? Or should they maintain a solemn silence in honor of the dead?

People pushed nearer the tracks as the ground shook; Alice, who had committed to her small plot of earth long ago, found herself propelled past her stake by the onslaught of other bodies. When she tried to take a breath her lungs barely inflated; panic forced her to struggle for air polluted with the smell of sweat and crêpe. The headache was intensifying, no longer the innocent ache of this morning. The vibrations within her head competed with those from the ground. She was moving closer to the tracks, closer to the moving hunk of iron that contained another hunk of iron that contained Edward's body. All cold, hard things. But *her* Edward was alive, engaged in animated conversations, and bore no resemblance to the withered husk that they would bury today.

Suddenly, Alice realized what she had to do. Edward had said his goodbyes, but there was still the chance that she could reach him again with some effort. And the headache—the headache suggested that he had something to tell her. She must get to *her* Edward before *their* Edward, the one that the crowd awaited, was laid to rest in an earthen tomb. Once everyone knew where he was, all opportunity for communication would cease. She could not let that happen. She needed him.

Alice turned to see a blanket of people behind her, woven tightly together by common styles of hats and veils. They were all focused on one thing: the arriving train, its brakes screeching and sparking—the one thing she could not allow herself to see. She began to retreat, searching for space to wriggle through. But no one moved aside for her. Nobody sensed her urgency.

Feeling a hand on her shoulder, she shook it off. "What are you doing?" Alice heard Thea's voice.

"I have to get back to Edward," she cried, and she let Thea's reply be absorbed by the crowd as she tried to wedge herself between shoulders and past skirts, but the crêpe and suit-wool blended together until she could see no openings. Crouching a little lower in hopes it would help her, the smell of crêpe filled her mouth and nostrils and then she truly could not breathe—the stench of the mourning cloth had cast webs across her nose and lips.

Her fever dream had come back, in broad daylight, in this crowd. Alice sank to her knees, prepared to give herself up this time. While a few people tripped over her, others bent to offer assistance. A hand was offered, and Alice took it. She looked to the face of her rescuer.

Except the woman had no face.

She struggled to release her hand, but the woman held tight. Suddenly, Alice recognized that the woman want to bring her to Edward. She ceased fighting and allowed herself to fall into unconsciousness.

Alice dreamed that she was walking along Burdick Street with Edward. She knew it was Edward, although she could not turn to see him. The rhododendrons bloomed alongside the road, confusing her: wasn't it August? Hadn't the rhododendrons withered in June?

Edward took her hand, and Alice held her breath. She had never touched him before. But the next thing she knew, his hand had placed hers into another, one whose palm was scarred red.

She turned to look for Edward, but he was nowhere to be seen. Even his presence was gone. Her vision blurred. It was then that Alice truly understood it all.

She would always be grateful to Edward. She would go forward with Neil.

"Yes is my answer," she said to the scarred hand.

Alice woke to find herself in bed with Neil holding her hand, his pink and warm.

"Are you all right?" Neil's brow was wrinkled in concern, and Alice had the urge to smooth the skin there. She kissed the palm in her possession.

"Did you hear what I said? Did I say it out loud?" she murmured.

"Say what out loud?"

She repeated her answer and saw Neil's face shift from surprise to joy, an open mouth turning into a grin. He squeezed her hand.

Why does he not kiss me? thought Alice, until she heard a throat clearing on the other side of the bed. She recognized the Kollner family physician, Dr. Kirkland, her face less much less cheerful than Neil's.

"You had the good fortune to faint near where I was standing, Miss Boyden. But now that you seem to be fully with us again, there is a matter that I wish to discuss with you in private." Dr. Kirkland gave Neil a pointed look. Alice had a brief sense of panic before realizing what the doctor must mean.

"Yes, I know I am with child," said Alice. She smiled at Dr. Kirkland and squeezed Neil's hand. "My fiancé and I are very excited."

By four o'clock, once Dr. Kirkland had packed up her bag and departed, Alice said that she felt well enough to meet the funeralgoers at the graveyard. Neil was less sure about this idea.

"I do not want you fainting again," he said, his forehead creased in worry. He glanced at her stomach, and Alice realized that he was concerned not only for her, but for their child. She gave a little inward sigh of happiness.

"I need confirmation that it has ended, that it is all over," said Alice. "We can even watch from a distance so I have plenty of space. But I should go." Anticipating Neil's next question, she said, "I'll be fine to walk. It's not far."

Even across the street from the cemetery, it was difficult to see the gravesite. A significant crowd had gathered on and around the hill where the Jewish citizens of Kalamazoo were buried. Someone shifted, and Alice caught a glimpse of Mannes Israel's white marble obelisk. She thought of Edward's excitement at seeing his father, and smiled. She was glad, however, that the fresh grave in the Kollner plot, the reason Thea could not bear to attend the burial, was obscured from her view.

Soon the clop-clop of horses' hooves announced the arrival of the hearse. A pair of gleaming black stallions strained to pull the carriage up the hill, but the driver stopped them only when going forward would have meant running into other graves. Standing on her toes, Alice could see Adam and the other pallbearers slide the coffin from the carriage and bend down to bear it on their shoulders. The other men looked to be athletes, their broad shoulders making Adam appear even scrawnier by comparison. But Adam's side did not tilt, and he stood as straight as the others. The crowd parted obediently for the young men, and they disappeared into its dark ranks.

Alice thought she had milked her eyes completely of tears, but a few more escaped down her cheeks. She blew a kiss towards the coffin on the hill, and reached for Neil's hand. They bowed their heads.

"Rest in peace, Edward," Alice murmured.

They waited for Adam back at the house, but when seven o'clock came and there was still no sign of him, Thea began dinner in earnest. "He must be eating with one of the pallbearers' families," she said, and Alice and Neil agreed, although Alice hoped he would not embarrass himself by picking at his food like usual. She reached for a knife with which to slice carrots, at the very least, but Thea shooed her away.

"Someone who fainted earlier should not be lifting a finger to work," she chided. "I'm only ashamed I haven't fed you sooner—else you're liable to faint again."

"But I'm well," Alice protested. "I have plenty of energy."

"Then have your fiancé take you for a stroll." At the mention of the new title, Alice beamed.

"All right. But Thea?"

"Yes?"

"I must ask you something about this afternoon." Alice took a deep breath. "Whose hand did I grab before I fainted?"

Thea looked at her strangely. "No one's. I did see you reach up, but then you just collapsed in a heap on the ground."

"I just—I thought—" Alice shook her head to clear it. "Never mind."

Thea took the opportunity to push her gently out the kitchen door. "A walk will do you good."

The setting of the sun had eliminated the worst of the day's heat, and Alice took a deep, grateful breath of the thinner air. Distracted by the light blues and pinks of the slowly darkening sky, she did not notice anything amiss until something slid onto the ring finger of her right hand.

Alice stared at Neil, then down at her hand, where a ring with a large oblong stone glittered. The evening was still bright enough to reveal its golden color—a topaz, her birthstone.

"Where—when—how did you get this?" Alice stammered. She gaped for a few moments more, then looked up at Neil for an explanation. He smiled and gave her a deep kiss, right there on the street. Alice felt herself melting.

"My sister was born in November, too."

Somehow Alice recovered enough to thank him, and they talked animatedly during the rest of their stroll about plans for a small October wedding. As they neared the house again, Alice realized that perhaps she ought to tell her parents, who were not even aware of the dissolution of her first marriage. She would write them a letter tomorrow.

Morning came and still no sign of Adam. Thea wrung her hands at breakfast. "You'd think he would send word of where he was! I know that he's in his twenties and a man, but..." She let out a nervous laugh. "You checked the office again?" she asked Neil.

Neil nodded. "Both Alice and I have."

"And I've looked through all of the guest-rooms," added Alice. "No sign of him."

Lunch passed without an appearance, and Thea took to pacing in the parlor. "I need something to do," she told Alice, who was seated at the parlor desk and unsuccessfully trying to begin a letter to her parents. "What are you doing?"

"Writing a letter home." Alice smiled sheepishly. "I'm just having some trouble starting." She gestured at the crumpled sheets of paper crowded to one edge of the desk.

Thea snapped her fingers. "Mail! I'll fetch the mail."

"A good idea," said Alice, although the task would distract Thea for all of three minutes if there was nothing to be found in the box.

But Thea returned with two letters of equal shape and different thickness. Neither of them had an address on them—only names, written in a generic script.

"One for me, and one for 'the Whites.'" Thea said, rather breathlessly. She handed the second envelope to Alice, who grinned, feeling rather drunk with happiness at the idea of being Mrs. White. And yet, no one but Thea and Dr. Kirkland knew of their official engagement...

Alice had the envelope open in a moment. Her hands shook a little as she withdrew a single sheet of paper with nothing but a few numbers.

She squinted at the digits, trying to rearrange them into some recognizable pattern. Looking up, she saw that Thea was huddled over a sheaf of papers.

"What is it?" Alice tapped her paper. "All I have are numbers."

"The deed to the house." Thea looked up, her eyes wide. "And it's been transferred into my name." She ruffled through the pages, and held up the last one. "I've a set of numbers, too."

Alice compared the two pages. "The same numbers, save for the final digit. Neil?" She hurried to the foot of the stairs and called again. "Neil!"

"Coming," came a faint voice from upstairs. A door closed, and Neil followed soon after, peering down at the women. Seeing their faces, he took the steps two at a time. "What's wrong?"

"Adam has given me the deed to the house, if I'm not mistaken." Thea handed the pages to him. "And some numbers. You and Alice have some numbers as well."

"It's the deed, all right." Neil turned his attention to the numbers, frowning at them for a few moments until recognition cleared the wrinkles from his forehead.

"Bank accounts. These must be bank account numbers."

"But why would Adam give me the deed and both of us bank accounts, unless—" Thea suddenly covered her mouth. "You don't think he..."

"My God." Neil shook his head violently. "No, he couldn't have. Not today."

"Let us go to the bank—they should be able to tell us what is going on." Alice was surprised to hear her voice quiver and break. The other two needed no urging to follow her.

The young teller at the Kalamazoo Savings Bank looked at the numbers, then down at the agitated trio. "Yes, these are indeed accounts with us. I can consult my ledger for the balances." He turned away from his window.

"That's of little importance," said Neil. "What's important is if you saw the person who created these accounts, and could give us an idea of his state of mind when he came here."

The teller sniffed. "I'm afraid I didn't handle the account personally. And anyway, I am not at liberty to divulge any information about our clients, Mr. White."

Thea slapped her hand against the counter. "Mr. Menz—Jacob. How long have I known you?"

Jacob suddenly looked nervous. "Um, since I was small?"

"I've known you since the day you were born. And I've known your mother since she was Miss Leibovitz. Now, would you say I am a trustworthy person?"

"Why yes, of course." Jacob gave a shaky laugh.

"Then you will find whomever dealt with Mr. Weissmann recently, and you will bring him here, and he will tell us all about Mr. Weissmann's behavior at the time of his deposit. Or else I will make sure that your mother hears about your unwillingness to help an old family friend."

"Right away, Mrs. Kollner." Jacob leapt down from his stool and skittered into the back offices. Once he was out of sight, Neil snickered. Alice patted Thea on the back.

"'Not at liberty?' Hmmph. The nerve!" Thea muttered. But she was smiling through her grumbles.

A few minutes later, another banker came to the window. Jacob did not. Thea smiled pleasantly at the newcomer. "Mr. Stein. How is your mother?"

Mr. Stein cleared his throat. "Mrs. Kollner—always a pleasure. My mother is doing very well, thank you. About your concern—I handled Mr. Weissmann's transfers early this morning, when we first opened. We were closed yesterday due to the funeral, and Mr. Weissmann was waiting at the doors as if he were in a hurry. He looked tired, but he was perfectly calm and pleasant when he was here.

"The deed he signed over last week before departing for New York. It's highly unusual that the grantee not also be present, but he said that it needed to be a surprise, and so an exception was made." He smiled at Thea. "He then set aside some money for you and the children and some for the Whites." He nodded at Alice and Neil. "Yours is specifically for your education—both of your educations," he added, looking at Alice.

"So there were no overt signs of—an intention to take his life?" Neil blurted. Alice clutched his arm.

Mr. Stein looked startled. "No, I wouldn't say so. Why would he have withdrawn the rest of his money after making these transfers? You will not be disappointed in the size of these accounts, not at all, but he also took a fair amount for himself. He closed his own account at the same time."

The three stared at each other. Then Thea spoke, in a soft voice.

"When I was pinning his boutonniere last week, he said he was ready for a fresh start. I assumed he meant in Kalamazoo. But it seems he meant somewhere else entirely."

Epilogue

October–November 1885

Every day after Adam's disappearance, Alice had checked what national newspapers she could get her hands on for anything about the personal records of the expedition, any excerpts or even simple lists of what artifacts had been committed to the government collection. But few articles strayed from the subjects of Greely's incompetence and the suspicion of cannibalism by the survivors of the expedition. Soon she gave up on the papers altogether, preferring ignorance to sensationalized information, trusting that Neil would pass along anything important. But media interest in the expedition dwindled soon enough.

It wasn't until a July visit to Kalamazoo, almost a year later, that they had spotted something relevant in the *Gazette*: Mrs. Israel and Mollie had returned from New York with a single red notebook, said to detail the everyday happenings of the camp through May of 1884. But no mention of a second book of portraits.

It was then that the realization had hit Alice: maybe the successful placement of the notebook didn't matter as much as Adam's ability to make the trip. Perhaps that is what Edward had had in mind all along—and that sensing Alice's feeling of rootlessness, he wanted to give her, too, a kind of anchor, a purpose. She would likely never know Edward's true intentions, and she told herself she would have to make peace with that.

The day of their first anniversary, Neil managed to slip out of bed without waking Alice, who had been up in the middle of the night with the baby. She woke to bright sunshine and a bouquet of flowers at her bedside. Another vase awaited her at the breakfast table, as did a plate of rolls from the bakery and a large orange.

"Oh, this is lovely." Alice kissed Neil and settled the baby in his bassinet, where he initially whimpered about his abandonment but soon fell asleep.

"And, because the first anniversary is paper, I neglected yesterday's mail," Neil told her before dropping a letter near her plate and a bound journal near his.

Alice laughed. "I thought that cotton was the first anniversary?"

Neil looked uncomfortable. "Not according to the compendium that you have in your library."

"Which was a wedding present from Thea." Alice kissed him again. "I couldn't care who's right. You're clever and a dear, and I love you."

Neil beamed. "That's present enough for me."

They settled themselves at the table with their reading material, and Alice saw the postmark on her letter: Cambridge. She had been missing her hometown with some ferocity the other day, walking through the university campus after a class. Although the muted golds and oranges of October added beauty and variation to the landscape, Alice had found herself longing for the intense hues of New England maple leaves and the pink, yellow, and green of their pastel undersides littering lawns and streets. As if Nature had heard her, the very next day an unassuming tree outside their boardinghouse had burst into blazing crimson. Alice looked outside at it now, where it glimmered garnet in the sun.

She broke the familiar wax seal and extracted a single page. As was usual, her mother's letter came straight to the point.

Dear Alice,

Your father has had some health troubles as of late, and has expressed a desire for a visit from you. I know it is a long trip, but we would both like to see our grandchild before our final rest in Mount Auburn, and meet our son-in-law, and perhaps you would be glad to visit Cambridge, too, after these two years.

Two years. In comparison to the nineteen-year-old girl who left Cambridge with a snakecharmer of a man, Alice felt sage-like at almost twenty-two, in her first (legitimate) marriage, the mother of a healthy son, and a student of astronomy at the University of Michigan. She had finally written her parents a month after she became Mrs. White; they had sent a brisk congratulations, but none of the scorn that Alice expected. Perhaps they had caught wind of Thomas's disappearance from the spiritual community. Alice did not wish to ask how much they knew or explain the details; she had only noted that Thomas had abandoned her, and a kindly housekeeper had taken her in, and that she had fallen in love with one of the men in town.

A discreet nine months later she announced the birth of their first grandchild—even though it would not have been fair of her parents to throw stones, Alice again believed that omission of questionable details was the best approach—and her admission to the university. This news met with a better reaction; the reply included Alice's baptismal gown and a note from her father recommending professors at Michigan.

"What do you have there?" Neil had opened his journal and was perusing the table of contents.

"My father is ill," said Alice. "They'd like us to come out to Cambridge for a visit." But Neil didn't seem to be paying attention to her reply; he had spied an article of interest and was flipping through the pages.

"Neil?" She tried to keep the annoyance out of her voice, reminding herself that his lack of attention was always temporary; once he had gleaned the essence of the article, he would look up again.

"You should see this."

Reluctantly, Alice rose and came over to his side of the table. Sometimes Neil was excited to share a description of an incident that paralleled her experience with Edward. Alice feigned interest but preferred to put those days behind her. She had not had a single visit from a spirit since Edward's goodbye. This sometimes saddened her, but had not had a single headache, either. And how would she find time to fit in spirit-writing, with a family and a full schedule of classes?

Alice focused upon where Neil's finger had fallen. It was not a paragraph he pointed to, but the author of the article.

"Dr. Adam White, of the University of California." she said aloud, rolling the name around in her head. Did Neil have a relative in California? Then she gasped.

Neil nodded. "I think we've found where my cousin went."

"I suppose there's no better place to reinvent one's self," murmured Alice. If Michigan had once seemed very far west to her, California was on the other side of the world.

"I should write him." Neil reached for a piece of her stationery, his voice suddenly imbued with a sense of urgency. "We should visit him. We should tell Thea."

Alice placed her hand over his, pinning it and the paper to the table. "Massachusetts first. We do have a little one in tow. And if he wants to see us, he knows how to reach us. Thea won't leave that house, especially now that it's hers."

Thea had continued to take in boarders despite her inheritance, claiming that she would be lonely otherwise. She had finally hired help again, however—a girl to mind the children and assist with housekeeping and cooking—leaving her more time to be out in society. In her last letter Thea noted that she had started going to temple again.

Neil grimaced. "I suppose you're right." Alice patted his hand gently. An operation by one of the university surgeons now allowed it to lay flat; dutiful exercise was gradually making the fingers more agile. Neil had been surprised to find that teaching anatomy was quite fulfilling, and found some comfort in directing hands nimbler than his.

"We can tell Thea in person," Alice said. "She'll be asking to see the baby again. He's likely doubled in size since our last visit." Perhaps sensing he was the topic of conversation, the baby let out a little roar from his bassinet. Alice picked him up by his chubby waist, and he reached for her breast and yelled again.

"Hungry?" Alice asked him, rhetorically. To Neil she said, "I'll be back shortly."

"Wait, what's this about Massachusetts?" Neil gave her a quizzical look, aware that he had missed part of the conversation but unsure where it had gone.

Alice nodded towards the letter. "From my parents. Go ahead and read it while I take care of the little one's meal."

On a brisk but clear day in November, the little White family boarded the first of the trains that would take them east. They had several planned stops, not willing to test the baby's endurance for travel. Alice worried about the length of the trip—he had gone no further than Kalamazoo on the train, and for only short rides in the buggy. But after some initial fussing about his unfamiliar surroundings, the baby fell asleep on the sunny seat of the compartment, lulled into calm by the warmth leaking through the windowpane. Neil soon followed, his head slumping against the glass.

Alice breathed in the quiet, first tentatively, like an unfamiliar aroma. How long since she had been on a train without Neil's cheery chatter as accompaniment? Guiltily, she realized it was her trip to and from Detroit to see Thomas. She looked at her peaceful husband and baby, each absorbed in their own unknown dreams, and resisted the urge to wake them with a barrage of grateful kisses. How much happier her life was now!

The thought of returning to Cambridge sent a ripple of excitement—or was it anxiety?—through Alice's stomach. She gazed out the window at the landscape they passed. A series of fierce rainstorms had denuded the autumn trees, but their nakedness revealed crows' nests still cradled in their branches, long abandoned by their chicks and destined to devolve into a pile of sticks with the first heavy snowfall.

Alice felt another pang for the rich palette of fall colors that would likely be gone from Massachusetts now—but almost immediately chided herself. She had made her home in Michigan. Michigan had given her a husband, a child, and the beginnings of an education. With Adam's money, they had purchased a home in Ann Arbor—while most graduate students were in boardinghouses—and hired a sophomore girl to mind the baby while his mother was attending class. She could only be thankful for Michigan and the people to whom it had introduced her—Neil, Adam, Thea. Edward. She was also thankful for the calm of this compartment, the warmth of the sun, and…

The next thing she knew, the conductor was knocking on the door. They had arrived at their first stop.

To Alice's delight, the trees in her neighborhood had delayed their complete disrobing for her arrival. Brilliant gold and scarlet branches waved a hello, occasionally sending part of their costume up on the wind, where the scraps pirouetted before gliding back down for their final curtain call. Alice drank in the sight of her childhood home so framed. The precise sameness of the landscape surprised her. She had changed so much—and yet nothing here had. Walking up the front path with her husband and baby, Alice wondered if crossing the threshold would turn her back into a nineteen-year-old half-invalid, besotted with a charlatan.

Someone must have been watching for them, for Nora opened the door at the very first knock. "Miss Boy—Mrs. White."

"Hello, Nora." Alice stepped inside to see her mother standing directly behind the maid. The house might not have changed, but Mrs. Boyden's gray-streaked hair had turned to snow.

Alice braced herself for an awkward greeting. To her astonishment, her mother surged forward with a kiss for Alice's cheek and a hug that enveloped both her and the baby. She nodded her head toward Neil, a bit shyly. "Mr. White."

"Mrs. Boyden." Neil removed his hat and bowed. "It's a pleasure to meet you."

"Likewise." The flirtatious smile that Alice had seen used on many a younger man came out, but Mrs. Boyden promptly turned it to her grandson. Without asking, she plucked him from Alice's arms. "Aren't you the sweetest darling," she crooned.

Neil glanced at Alice. This was not the welcome he had been told to expect. Alice raised her eyebrows, letting him know that she, too, had been caught off-guard.

Bouncing the baby in her arms, Mrs. Boyden beckoned Neil and Alice into the parlor, where Mr. Boyden sat in an armchair, his head slumped to the side, his eyes closed. Alice's heart skipped a beat—had she arrived too late for a reunion with her father?—but her mother walked over and shook him by the shoulder.

"Your daughter is here," Mrs. Boyden yelled in her husband's ear. Mr. Boyden woke with a snort. "Always falling asleep nowadays," she told the visitors, shaking her head. Mr. Boyden blinked in confusion and fumbled for his glasses on the table. Once he had regained his vision, he focused upon Alice and Neil and stood up with a smile.

"My dear." He kissed Alice's cheek and shook Neil's hand with some vigor, then paused and frowned. "But where's your baby?"

Alice gestured to her mother, who had turned to leave the room. Mrs. Boyden looked back sheepishly. "I was about to call for some tea."

"Could I see him, Caroline?"

Mrs. Boyden hesitated, then reluctantly relinquished her prize to her husband. Alice found that she was holding her breath. Her parents were full of surprises today.

"Hello, Edward," Mr. Boyden addressed the baby, who giggled as his grandfather held him out, appraising him. Apparently finding the boy to his liking, he settled him on his knee. Edward looked up at this new person, his blue eyes wide and mouth agape with wonder. Mr. Boyden tickled him, and he let out a gleeful squeak.

"You're quite a handsome lad. Really, you ought to have been George Junior." Mr. Boyden looked up at his daughter. "Where *did* you get the name?"

Alice smiled, resting one hand on her father's shoulder and the other on her baby's downy head.

"From someone very special."

Acknowledgments

The best part about writing historical fiction is having an excuse to spend hours in archives and libraries. Many thanks to the archivists and librarians who patiently answered my questions and emails and allowed me to peruse their collections as I conducted research for this book. The staff of Lamont Research Services at Harvard University and Bert Lippincott of the Newport Historical Society assisted me with books and newspaper articles about Onset, Cambridge, and the summer fashions of 1883. Tom Dietz of the Kalamazoo Valley Museum, Cathy Serra of the Kalamazoo Public Library, and Dorthea Sartain of the Explorers Club gave me access to articles and artifacts about Edward Israel and the Greely Expedition. My brother-in-law Josh Fry gave us a place to stay (and plenty of Bell's Beer) while I conducted research in Kalamazoo.

I wrote much of this book in the fifth-floor reading room at the Boston Athenaeum, and made extensive use of their wonderful nineteenth-century collection. First-hand accounts of the Greely Expedition, journals on psychical research, and stargazing manuals were all readily available. I couldn't have asked for a more welcoming and inspiring place to create Alice's world. I will only say that I wish the books on spiritualism weren't housed in the darkest corner of the basement.

Eugene Kuo designed a beautiful cover for me. Having been in the publishing business for some time now, I know how rare it is for an author to be happy with a cover design, and I feel very fortunate.

John Underkoffler, Kwin Kramer, and the gang at Oblong Industries in Los Angeles not only flew me back and forth from LA to Boston while my husband was working with them, but they let me claim a desk in their office when I needed a change of scenery. It was while writing there that I discovered Edward Israel and made him a part of my story.

This book originated in William Martin's Fall 2007 Writing the Historical Novel class at Harvard Extension School. Although the plot has changed significantly since its first outline, I am grateful to Bill and my classmates for helping me build a strong foundation. Many friends and family members read a version of this book, offering kind encouragement and helpful criticism: Katharine Beutner, Alex Fleming, Jamie Fry, Kathy Fry, Karen Fry, Mike Gorman, Kelsey Helms, Helen Lefkowitz Horowitz, Angela Petro, Elizabeth Julia Smith, Dana Teegardin, and Eva Wisten. A special thank you to my parents, Jack and Laury Hunt, who have been reading my work since I could put crayon to paper. I am so lucky that they encouraged my writing and didn't try to turn me towards a more lucrative profession—though they may have occasionally hinted that perhaps I could find a creative outlet in advertising.

Most of all, I thank my husband, Ben Fry. It was because of his support that I was able to make the jump to freelance editing, and then to carve out more time for writing. I actually handwrote most of the first draft before he introduced me to the excellent writing program Scrivener, helping me overcome my resistance to composing on the computer and saving me a great deal of transcription time. He also oversaw the design and e-book formatting. It's easy enough to list the ways in which Ben made this book possible. It's much harder to explain the ways in which he's made my life better. I dedicate this book to him in the hopes that that will suffice until I find the right words.